I0831814

Postdiluvian

The Ancient Chronicle

Postdiluvian

The Tale of the Atsari

The Ancient Chronicle

by

J. D. Wise

Postdiluvian Books

Postdiluvian: The Ancient Chronicle

ISBN: 0-9992834-0-5
ISBN-13: 978-0-9992834-0-0
Library of Congress Control Number: 2017951401

Cover art by
Courtney Godbey
www.courtneygodbey.com

For my wife
And my cat

Contents

Postdiluvian

The Tale of the Atsari

Herein is recorded the tale of Jake Connolly and the deeds he performed among his Nanyanin cousins;

Of the finding of the Atsari and of its consequences;

Of the Itarlavon family—the keepers of the Earth, which, being overrun by water in the ancient past, was given solely to the Thalanin, and the Nanyanin dwell there no longer;

Of the descendants of the ancient Nanyanin who in their time feared that judgment would fall upon them, as it did upon those who dwelt on the Earth—save for one family—and who rejoiced when Divine Wrath was limited to the Earth and who agreed to leave the Earth to the Thalanin;

Of the Kenornin—descended from him who first murdered his brother in the early days of Man—and of the Keneraton who ever long for the Earth, admiring its beauty and fertility;

Of the automatons—made in days long past by men of greater craft than live in this present age—who now dwell among the Nanyanin;

Of certain Thalanin who, having left the Earth, now live among the Nanyanin;

Of many kingdoms on many worlds, great and small, that figure into the story of Jake Connolly, the Atsari, and the aggression of the Keneraton;

Of many deeds, both good and evil, and what became of them;

Of sin and of salvation;

Of love and of hatred;

Of life and of death;

And of the steadfast love of the Creator for His wayward creation.

Book 1

The Ancient Chronicle

Chapter 1

The Court of Itonilon

Day was dawning in Itonilon when the king and his council assembled in the Great Hall. From the fortress high upon the hill came the ringing of mighty bells, and the village below heard them sound the convocation. Many townsfolk climbed to the castle gates, for they wished to see the young stranger of whom they had heard many tales.

Within the fortress of the king, pages walked about lighting torches to dispel the night that still lingered in the corners of the room. Smoke billowed from the flames, drifting to the roof, where it hung like a storm-cloud before passing out a small hole into the early morning sky. The Great Doors of the hall stood open, and slowly the crowds entered, passing many whispers among themselves. A rumour of feet and voices filled the hall even as the first rays of morning fell upon the city.

Only one man stood silent—a dark figure in a tattered cloak and hood. He lingered in the shadow of a stone pillar, watching the councilmen enter and take their seats. The council were all grim-faced and wore cloaks of blue and silver. The table at which they sat was cloven in two at its centre, and in this gap stood a dais upon which was set a mighty stone chair overlaid with gold and precious gems.

A fanfare sounded, and the people fell silent, standing with their heads bowed. The doors behind the table opened, and a procession entered led by courtiers carrying banners of gold and crimson. Behind these walked a column of men clad in mail of black and silver hue. They carried tall pikes that glistened in the torchlight, and their helmets shone like mirrors.

In the midst of these guardians walked the king, arrayed in furs and velvets dyed red and black. Upon his head was set a crown of whitest gold, and a fiery jewel shone in the midst of it. Upon his fingers he wore many rings, and in his left hand he held a silver rod.

At his right hand walked Tharè, daughter of the king, a maiden at the turn of adulthood, young and beautiful. She was fair like the pale sun shining in winter, but this day her visage showed only sorrow. Her golden hair hung about her downturned face and fell upon her trembling shoulders. Tears fell from her bright-green eyes and stained her flowing dress of blue and white silk. A circlet of golden leaves was upon her brow, and about her neck she wore a silver pendant set with a bright-red stone. Her handmaidens followed sullenly behind her, each with a downcast face and some with eyes red with tears.

Tharè stood close to her father, and only those nearest them could hear their whispers. “Please,” the princess said, “tell me I may be dismissed from this council. I don’t wish to see him.”

“It sorrows me also, my dear,” said the king. “For my part, I would not have you attend this council, but it is law that you must. Yet I will see that you need not remain long. I would have your days be bright and sorrowless, but there are duties monarchs must endure for the good of their kingdoms.”

The princess sighed deeply, and her handmaidens led her to a chair beside the council table. There she remained, staring at the floor until the great iron doors at the far end of the hall opened, creaking on their ancient hinges. The princess turned towards the sound, and the torchlight danced on her tearstained cheeks.

Through the open doors, four guards entered two by two, and in the midst of them walked a young man. His hands were bound behind him, and his feet were shackled with a heavy chain. Ragged clothes hung in tatters upon his thin figure, and he squinted as though the dimmest light were painful to his eyes. The guards leading him tugged at the chain around his neck, and he stumbled forward. He looked towards the princess, but she had turned away from him.

The guards brought the young man before the council table and stood at his sides. The king had seated himself upon his chair, and his council sat motionless to either side of him. At length the king looked to one of his councilman, who bowed his head in answer and rose to his feet.

The crowd grew quiet as the councilman began to speak. "My name is Thorondoron, head of the king's council," he said, his voice echoing in the sudden silence of the chamber. "Jake Connolly, you have been brought before this council to face charges of high treason. Do you know why these charges have been brought against you?"

Jake stood for a moment without speaking, the silence of the chamber ringing in his ears. His thoughts swirled, and he could not readily find the will to answer. At last he spoke, and his voice was deeper and quieter than usual. "I know why," he said. He shifted his weight, and the chains clanked at his wrists and feet. "And I would just like to say…"

Thorondoron lifted his hand, and Jake fell silent. "Your defence has not yet begun," the councilman said. "You stand here guilty, having admitted your crime openly. You are here to be sentenced before this council, yet the king may show mercy if he will."

Jake chuckled to himself. *Not likely*, he thought.

"Bring forth the prisoner's effects," Thorondoron called. The iron doors opened again, and a pageboy entered carrying a black-metal box about the size of a man's head. There was a lever upon the front and two dials inscribed with many symbols. The boy placed the box upon the table before one of the lesser councilmen, who gingerly picked it up, looking it over. He pulled the lever, but the box would not open.

"It's shut tight," the councilman said, putting it down again. "How is it opened?"

"It cannot be, save by one who knows the numbers," said Thorondoron, and he looked at Jake intently. "The accused knows what they are, but he will not say."

"Then why have we not blasted the chest open?" asked another councilman.

"It is made of purest adamant," Thorondoron answered, "and it is beyond our craft to break it." He took the box in hand, turning it in all directions. "It is a curious device," he said. "And quite unlike anything I have ever seen." He looked down at Jake. "Is it perhaps dangerous?"

Jake sneered at him. "Would you believe me if I told you?"

"No," Thorondoron said dispassionately. "Nonetheless it is curious that you possess such an item. What does it contain?"

Jake made no answer.

"Very well," Thorondoron said and placed the box on the table again. "Keep your secret for now, but know this: you will open this chest before this council is through with you."

The pageboy, still standing before the table, cleared his throat. "That's not all, sir," he said, and he produced a cloth from which he removed a small silver ring. This he placed upon the table, and he withdrew himself.

Thorondoron picked up the ring and examined it. "A worthless trinket."

"Yet it is of value to me," Jake said, stepping forward hastily.

"Then you will declare it too before this council," said Thorondoron, placing the ring beside the adamantine box. "When the time comes."

He took a deep breath and stood taller. "Yet," he continued with a more formal air, "before you begin your defence, the king wishes to address you."

Thorondoron sat, and the king rose to his feet. A guard forced Jake to kneel.

The king's face was filled with sorrow, and his eyes fell upon Jake with a piercing gaze. "Jake Connolly," he said slowly, "you came to us from a far land, and having nothing of your own, you have enjoyed the hospitality of our city. Though there were others who might have helped you, I took you into my house because Jalzoron brought you to us, for he has done much for this kingdom and for this world. You ate our bread and made a home of this castle. No Thalani has ever been so honoured here in all our history.

"But you have repaid us with treachery. You have brought to nothing all the gifts we have given you, and now you stand before us in disgrace. Through your actions, Jalzoron's esteem of you is now made suspect, and though we still judge him honourable, you have brought a great stain upon him in our eyes.

"It is my duty to sentence you as the law and God may direct. You will be allowed this only: to appeal to the mercy of the king, as our laws demand." The chamber remained utterly silent as the king sat down again.

Thorondoron was rising to his feet when the silence of the chamber was split by a shout. "Your Majesty!"

As all turned to see who was shouting, the cloaked man stood forth from the shadows and removed his hood, revealing a face worn by age and grief. The king's guards leapt to his sides, wielding their pikes and swords. The councilmen stood, and the hall erupted in a murmur of voices. The cloaked man raised his hands to shoulder height, and a guard took hold of each arm.

Before the man could be carried away, the king spoke. "Release him!" he said firmly. "This is Jalzoron, of whom I spoke. He is known to this house, and despite all that has happened, he still has standing here." The guards retreated from Jalzoron's side. "Tell me, my friend," the king said, "why have you come to this hall in secret and not walked freely among the people?"

Jalzoron bowed low. "Forgive me, my king," he said. "I have come to help this boy in his defence, and I could not do so until now. I feared I might not get the chance if my presence were known, but now my name has been spoken in council. By the law of this land, I may now have voice in this chamber. I beg Your Majesty's pardon."

The king sighed. "This may be the second mark against you," he said. "It would be a grave matter to break our trust in you again."

"Grave indeed, sire," Jalzoron said. "I do not consider your trust to be a trifle, but there is reason behind what I do, and by your leave, I wish to proceed in this boy's defence."

"Very well," the king said. "Speak therefore, if the accused will allow it."

Jake stood bewildered, and all words failed him. He had not expected Jalzoron to appear. "I…suppose," he said at last.

Jalzoron gave Jake a reassuring glance and then addressed the assembly. "My nobles," he said, "it is true I took in this boy, for I found him wandering the wilderness beyond the borders of this land. I brought him to this kingdom because I believed he would be safe, and so he was—from all dangers except those he carries with him. Not in that chest"—he pointed to the box sitting on the table—"but in his own heart."

Jake cleared his throat. "You're not helping me," he whispered through clenched teeth.

Thorondoron ignored Jake's whispers and addressed Jalzoron. "Is it possible then," he said, "that you know where this Thalani acquired such an item as that?" He pointed to the adamantine chest.

"I do," said Jalzoron. "The box was mine, and I gave it to him."

A din of voices arose from the crowd, but the king raised his hands, and the commotion ceased. Thorondoron bowed to the king, and the king waved his hand, bidding him to continue.

"And where did you acquire this object?" Thorondoron asked. "Surely it is not of this planet."

"It is not," Jalzoron said. "I cannot reveal its origin nor how I came by it, but I can assure you it is not dangerous, for I know what it contains."

Another murmur arose in the hall.

"Tell us then," Thorondoron said.

"That must wait," said Jalzoron, "for it figures into the story Jake Connolly must tell this council."

Thorondoron glanced between Jake and Jalzoron. "What story?"

Jalzoron stepped forward and addressed the entire hall. "When I first met this boy, he told me the tale of how he came to this planet, and I believe his story is true. In order to make his defence, I believe he must repeat this story to the council. I will stand here as witness to be sure he tells it as it was told to me. It is a long story, but if the council will endure it, its telling may appeal to Your Majesty's clemency."

The king sat for a moment in silence, looking over the crowd. The onlookers murmured as to what these events might mean. The king stirred at last and looked to his daughter, who, gazing back at him with eyes clear and glistening, nodded and turned her face again to stare at the floor.

"Very well," the king said, turning to Jake. "You will tell the story of which Jalzoron spoke." Then, turning to Jalzoron, he said, "I trust, sir, that you will do what you can to assure us this story is true. Else this shall be your third fault in as many days, and it may take quite a long time to trust your word again."

"I promise you, sire," said Jalzoron. "I shall not trespass further."

"Then begin," the king said with a wave of his hand.

Jake rose from his knees, and the guards at his sides unbound his hands and removed the chain from his neck. Jake rubbed his left arm, for it pained him still.

Jalzoron stood beside him now in plain clothes, for he had removed his cloak and hood. He looked back at Jake and nodded, urging him to proceed.

Jake looked around at all the faces now turned towards him. Sudden fear pulsed through him, for he had not been prepared to do so much speaking. As he reached back into his memory to determine where he should begin, many thoughts came to him—some filled with happiness and others with sorrow. He closed his eyes, took a deep breath, and began.

. . . .

[1]The planet Rithonon circled a star near the edge of the Tharion Sea, as it is named in Eratzira. Jake Connolly lived in the Thalanin village of Brown Hill on the western edge of the mountains of Itelmir, which ran eastward to the ocean far away. Brown Hill lay

1 According to tradition, Nanyan narratives are never written in the first-person. Portions of dialogue may contain first-person narratives, but these are usually brief. Some stories have many levels of narration, as these books will demonstrate.

hard against the mountains in a long valley filled with many other villages, all given to mining. All these Thalanin villages were administrated by the Nanyan city of hCathad, whose towers dwarfed the many ancient ruins scattered throughout the valley. Long ago Rithonon had been an outpost for watchmen who guarded the borders of an ancient star-kingdom.[2] They had patrolled Rithonon's star and its neighbours and had safeguarded the rich mines of Rithonon. Those men had now been gone for long ages, but the mines remained.

Brown Hill lay below what had once been a tall fortress that had housed a garrison of many men and starships. The citadel now lay in ruins, but farther down the hill, a tall watchtower still stood. It was in this tower that Jake Connolly lived with his many birds, for he was a vèralamenasi.[3] His parents before him had also been vèralamenasin, but they had died many years before while on holiday, leaving Jake to care for the birds alone.

Chief among the vèralamen Jake cared for was a falcon named Faluin, offspring of the great Starlords of old. Jake alone had been able to tame him, and he had served Jake and his family for many years. When Jake's parents died, it was Faluin who brought him the news, and from those days Faluin became his friend and counsellor. Jake never hired out Faluin but used him only to carry private messages and to keep an eye on the lands all around.

Being the only vèralamenasi in the valley, Jake never wanted for patrons. Even Thalanin came to enlist the service of the vèralamen,

2 Nanyan: *Itarènaladon*, lit. "star kingdom" (sometimes translated "star realm").

3 One who cares for vèralamen—automaton birds who carry messages through space. Vèralamen often memorize and deliver their messages verbally. They are considered the most secure form of message delivery, and they are very good at finding people and places. It is unusual for a Thalani to be a vèralamenasi, for vèralamen speak only Nanyan, which few Thalanin can speak.

though they always wrote their messages upon small scrolls. Other Thalanin would hire Jake to translate Nanyan[4] or to serve as interpreter for meetings with Nanyanin officials. He made a good living and never lacked for anything.

In his tower Jake lived mainly in two rooms—the kitchen on the ground floor and his bedroom near the top. The rest of the rooms had been sealed off except for a large chamber on the topmost floor where the vèralamen roosted. Jake fed them when necessary, but the vèralamen often hunted their own food. Automaton creatures were not uncommon in the valley, though they were far outnumbered by animals of flesh and blood. The fields surrounding Jake's tower were wholly given to farming and ranching, and it was not unusual for Jake to see cattle grazing outside his window or to watch a farmer driving a cart down the neighbouring roads.

From the upper windows, Jake could see all the rooftops of Brown Hill, for it was a small village. One main road ran through the centre of town, and many shops and tradesmen were to be found there. Jake was friendly with most of the villagers, and they seemed to like him well enough.

Of all the places Jake frequented in the village, his favourite by far was the Grey Griffin—an inn that lay on a side street off the main road. It was sheltered enough to seem isolated, but it was always busy. Miners would eat there before their work began and then again after their long labour. Two old men were often seen playing draughts and talking about the other patrons as if no one else could hear them. There were other regulars besides—all good people and each a special kind of peculiar.

But by far the person Jake found most intriguing was Samantha Brown, the innkeeper's daughter. She was a bit younger than Jake was, bright-eyed and overflowing with cheerfulness. Jake had never

4 Nanyan: lit. "tongues." Nanyan is the universal language of the galaxy.

seen her unhappy, and she always greeted him with a shy smile. He had seen much of her in recent days, for she seemed to enjoy his company, and she had at times visited the tower on the hill just to say hello or to tell him some bit of news from the inn.

One particular day Jake journeyed down to the inn for breakfast, as was his custom. Though a number of the townsfolk were still asleep at that hour, the brown-stone streets were far from silent or empty. Jake passed several men driving their carts overflowing with produce towards the market. Miners trudged in small groups here and there—some boarding transports for the more distant mines, others following the road that led to the Brown Tunnel Mine just south of the village. Constable Gibbs was already up and about, and Robert Lofton, the town beggar, hid in the shadows as the constable passed.

All over town early risers were raising banners and streamers from buildings and lampposts. Women on tall stepladders hung lanterns from ropes strung between the streetlamps. Tents and stalls of wood and cloth appeared in many places, and in the town square, three men were building an enormous wooden platform. The Brown Hill Autumn Festival was to be held the following evening, and many of the townsfolk were busy with its preparation. Jake usually skipped most of the festival, coming down only briefly for a bit of food and a walk around to look at all the commotion before returning home. It was not much fun going all alone, but this year he planned on a change.

As he continued on through the town, Jake breathed deeply. The air was clear and cool, and only a few clouds floated lazily over the town. The air smelled of things baking in the shops along the street. Mrs Arlington's pastry shop stood near the centre of town, and every morning the smell of her sweet rolls drifted in and out of streets and lingered over the town until late in the afternoon. Jake's stomach made a noise, but he did not divert his course or his purpose, for there was more than breakfast on his mind.

The Grey Griffin Inn stood two storeys tall around a stone courtyard, making a wall on three sides. Its upper storey overhung the yard so there was a walkway underneath. Its wooden pillars held up white plaster walls, and red tiles covered the slanted rooftop. At the centre of the courtyard, a stone fountain stood, dry and partially overgrown with moss. Jake could not remember if the fountain had ever run at all. On the far side of the courtyard, two wooden doors stood partially open, and though the air outside was chill, wafts of warm air flowed ceaselessly out into the courtyard.

Jake entered the doors and, passing through the cloakroom, found himself standing in the common-room of the inn. The room was large and filled with many tables and chairs, some partitioned by half-walls or by differences in the height of the floor. A long bar with many stools lay on one side of the room, and off in the corner a few cushioned chairs sat ready to welcome weary guests.

At this time of morning, the common-room was not busy. Only a few patrons sat scattered amongst a handful of tables throughout the room. The inn was quiet and peaceful, and from the kitchen floated smells of bacon, sausage, and fatback cooking, mingled with the permeating smells of coffee and strong cider.

The two old men—who seemed always to be present at the inn—called out to Jake from their usual table in the corner.

"Good morning, young Connolly," the one man said. "Another day in the aviary, eh?"

"Always." Jake tried to sound polite.

"She's in the back," the other man said with a wink. "She was out here looking for you a second ago, but you just missed her. She was called into the kitchen—something about a pile of dishes. I guess you'll be lucky to see her at all."

"She'll come back," the first man said. "If she knows he's here, she'll come back."

"Ah, but will she know he's here?" the other said. "She could be in there for an hour or more, and her mother won't let her come out if she sees there's work to be done."

"Bah!" said the first man. "You're too old and shrivelled up to remember the burning fire of a young heart. I say she'll be here, mother notwithstanding, and young Mr Connolly will wait here, I'll wager, till she comes out—even if it takes until he's as old as we are."

Jake's ears turned red, and the two old men howled with laughter. Jake slipped away from them and took a seat at the bar near the kitchen. He strained his neck to look over the kitchen door, but he could see no sign of anyone, and no one came out to serve him.

Outside in the courtyard, voices grew loud, and a moment later a half-dozen miners entered wearing dirty overalls and carrying their hats in their hands. They were talking amongst themselves very loudly (Jake always suspected that miners were almost deaf), and they sat at a table not far from the kitchen. Jake could not help but overhear them as they spoke to one another.

"But he was a queer-looking man," one of the miners was saying. "He weren't like no Regulator I'd ever seen afore. New fellow he must have been, but where he came from, he wouldn't tell me. He just asked to see the foreman, so I shows him the way. I tried to make talk with him—'How do you do today, sir?' and all that—but he never says a blessed word. He only keeps looking round him at everybody we go by, like he was looking for something—or someone, but he wouldn't say who.

"Nanyan folk are a queer lot. They live so awful long that it don't do them no good! They get tired of living, I think, and they can't find nothing better to do than to poke their noses into other people's business."

The others asked him many questions, but he did not know any more than he had already said. Jake listened, not thinking very much of it. He rarely understood miners, for he knew little of their work or organization. He knew what Regulators were for sure; one visited him promptly every month[5] to be sure his business was run legally, but what this mining Regulator was up to, Jake could not guess.

At that moment the kitchen door swung open, and Samantha appeared, her face bright and her eyes sparkling. She walked up to the bar, wiping her hands on her apron.

"Good morning," she said warmly.

The sight of her and the sound of her voice drove all else from Jake's mind. "It is indeed," he said.

"I'm sorry I wasn't here when you came in," she said and then added quickly, "to serve you, I mean. I'd left the dishes in the sink from last night. I guess I'd forgot about them when you walked me back home yesterday."

"I hope I didn't get you in trouble," Jake said. "I didn't realize we had been talking so late."

"Oh, it's no trouble," Samantha said. "Besides, I would much rather be out walking with you than cooped up in this place all evening." She sighed. "I was born here, and I've lived here all my life. I reckon I'll probably die here too."

Jake shook his head. "Never," he said. "You'll leave this town someday. You'll be up on Telethoram before you know it, and from there, who knows? You might even make it to Earth." He gave her a wink.

5 Nanyan: *lamithila*—akin to English "month." *Lamithila* is an ambiguous term for an amount of time determined by one (or more) of a planet's moons. It does not by itself indicate a specific period of time.

Samantha smiled shyly. “That’s too much for me to imagine,” she said. “I’ve dreamt of Earth—walking its green fields, breathing its fragrant air, seeing all the stars in their primeval shapes. But I can’t let myself hope for things so impossible. Telethoram is good enough for me. Have you ever been up there?”

“Once,” Jake said, “but that was a long time ago.” The memory suddenly stabbed him. “My parents, they…they took me there. They wanted me to see it.” His voice died away, and he turned his head.

“Oh.” Samantha turned red and nervously wiped the counter with a cloth. “I didn’t mean to…I mean, I didn’t think about…I mean, your parents and all…”

Jake turned back to her and attempted a smile. “It’s all right,” he said, “but I do miss them terribly.”

“I didn’t mean to bring it up,” Samantha said. “I can’t imagine… Well, I…I’m just making it worse.” She turned away, and by the shaking of her shoulders Jake could tell she was crying.

He reached out and grabbed her arm gently. “Please don’t worry about it,” he said. “I don’t mind talking about them—at least not as much as I used to—and you don’t need to feel bad about anything. You’ve done nothing wrong.”

Samantha still faced away from him. “If you say so,” she said, her voice barely above a whisper. Suddenly she straightened up. She took a deep breath and turned back around, wiping her eyes with the cloth in her hand. “Well,” she said weakly, “this is embarrassing. I don’t usually cry in front of customers.”

“Then I’ll consider myself special,” Jake said with a grin. “So special I just might get to take someone to the festival tomorrow.”

A twinkle came into Samantha’s eyes. “Maybe,” she said with a shy smile. “Is she a special girl?”

“She’s dear to me, yes,” Jake said.

"Well then, why don't you ask her?" Samantha put her elbows on the bar, leaning over so that she stared straight into Jake's eyes.

The look on her face caught Jake off guard, and his mind went blank. He fumbled for a moment as he tried to speak. "Well, I…" he said. "I…just might do that. Do you think she'd say yes?"

"Most definitely."

"Well what if—"

Samantha interrupted with a giggle. "Oh, just ask me already!"

"Very well, then." Jake cleared his throat, and in a tone that jested at chivalry, he said, "Would you please permit me to accompany you to the festival?"

Samantha met the jest with a curtsy. "With pleasure, sir." She looked up, smiling broadly. The noise of the room seemed to fade away to a great distance, and Jake felt a great feeling of contentment wash over him.

Samantha suddenly glanced over to a nearby clock and frowned. "It's getting late," she said. "I must go, or I shall fall behind in my work."

"Well you've already delayed *my* breakfast," Jake teased.

Samantha scowled at him but could not suppress a giggle. "The usual then, sir?" she said with an exaggerated bow.

"Certainly, miss," Jake said, "and don't be all day about it."

"No promises," she said, and she stuck her tongue out at him before disappearing into the kitchen.

The table of miners nearby erupted in taunts and snickers, and Jake flashed them a fierce look—or as fierce as he could muster. He was much too happy to be cross, and his most threatening face was surely far from intimidating.

Breakfast came—scrambled eggs, sausages, fried potatoes, beans, and toast. Jake ate slowly as he watched Samantha go about her morning routine serving the hungry crowds. Most were miners coming off work, and soon the room was filled with noisy talk. Jake stayed until he could no longer bear the noise and crowding. He paid for the meal, bade Samantha a good morning, and left. Compared to the growing chaos inside, the courtyard was peaceful and quiet.

As Jake walked up the lane towards the main road, he heard a voice calling out his name. He turned and found to his dismay that Lawrence Appleton, the town magistrate, was walking towards him. Appleton was only a few years older than Jake—rather young for a magistrate, for he had inherited the position from his late father. His eyes and hair were dark, and the corner of his mouth seemed always upturned in a menacing smirk. He wore a bright-red suit, as was the custom for magistrates in Eratzira.

"Mr Connolly," Appleton said. "I've been looking for you, but you weren't at home."

"Well, what's the matter?"

"There's a new Regulator in town," Appleton said with an air both of pride and contempt.

Jake rolled his eyes. "Yes, I've heard," he said and kept walking. "Something about the mines, I guess."

"About the mines?" Appleton said with a chuckle. "You don't understand. He's going all over town asking about you."

"About me?" said Jake. "Whatever for?"

"He wouldn't say," Appleton replied. "He just wanted to know where you lived and worked."

"And what did you tell him?"

"Well, what could I tell him? I had to tell him the truth. I suspect he may be up later to talk with you. I can't imagine what you've done to deserve such special attention."

Jake smiled a fake smile. "I'm sure it's nothing," he said. "It won't be the first time a Regulator has darkened my door."

"Then I'm sure you have nothing to worry about," Appleton said smugly. "Good day, Mr Connolly. I hope everything goes well for you."

Jake bade Appleton farewell and walked back through town towards his home, muttering under his breath as he walked. Appleton had spoiled an otherwise good mood.

Jake quickened his pace when he reached the bottom of the hill upon which his tower stood. The sun was climbing in the sky, and it was time for him to open up shop.

Jake had an old print-out machine that was wired into the relay system that ran throughout the valley. Throughout the day the office of the High Magistrate in hCathad would send requests for the delivery of legal documents. For these dispatches, Jake would encode a key onto a metal band that he would attach to the foot of a vèralam. This key would identify the bird to the magistrate's office when picking up the document, and a further key (given by the magistrate) would identify the bird to the recipient—usually another magistrate's office on another world. This system worked flawlessly, for vèralamen are difficult to capture, and the keys prevented forgery.

This was the majority of Jake's work.

Requests of a more personal nature would be brought to the tower in person. Messages of this kind were most often reserved for special occasions—births and weddings in far off places, the milestone birthday of a great-great-grandparent, a letter to a lover far away—anything that needed something more significant than a weak transmission beamed between the stars.

Jake sometimes found himself feeling guilty in his labours, for there was little for him to do except send the birds on their way. He took care of them for his part, but the vèralamen ably cared for themselves, finding food and shelter of their own accord. But he enjoyed his work, and as he made a good living, he did not complain.

As Jake walked up the lane to his own front door, Faluin swooped down from an unseen height and perched on the fence that lined the road. In a single motion, he shook himself from head to foot, ruffling his brown and white feathers. Then he turned and addressed Jake in Nanyan. "Successful exploits, sir?" he asked. "Was she pleased with your outing yesterday?"

"She seemed to be," Jake said, smiling. "Anything to report here?"

"All is quiet," Faluin said. "Faldan and I flew around the planet this morning. All is at peace."

"You didn't happen to see a strange Nanyan man in Brown Hill, did you?" Jake asked. "An Overseer[6] perhaps?"

"I did not, sir," Faluin said. "Shall I go looking for him now?"

"No, that's not necessary."

"Is it not important?"

"Not really."

"Very well," Faluin said. "Shall we go up, then?"

Jake nodded and raised his arm, and Faluin perched upon it. Jake brought him into the house and set him on a perch near the open window. The first floor of the tower was mostly given to a garage whose outer door faced the hill behind. Inside Jake kept a flyer[7] that had belonged to his father. Jake used it occasionally, taking it out to be sure it was kept in good working order. Faluin would often fly alongside and guide Jake over the mountains and back home again.

6 Nanyan: *athèstol(on)*, "one who sees higher"—a government official charged with enforcing law in one particular field. The English word *Regulator* arose among the Thalanin as an epithet denoting a general dislike for the profession.

7 Nanyan: *sènambira*—a personal flying machine for atmospheric flight at low altitudes.

The remainder of the first floor was taken up by a small kitchen and a round table shoved in a corner with a few chairs. Opposite these stood an iron stove and a sink with a pump that drew water from an ancient well deep underground. Jake had asked the city leaders of hCathad to let him connect to the waterline in Brown Hill, but his request was never met with any sense of urgency. So he pumped water day after day, heating it on the stove for bathing and cooking, but he seldom drank it, preferring to go down to Brown Hill, where the water was cleaner.

From the window above the sink, Jake could look over the pasturelands that spread out as far as he could see. Beyond the fields, almost at the edge of sight, marched a line of trees, and behind them stood the distant towers of hCathad that rose in spires of grey and blue. Now and then Jake would observe a starship descending over the city to the far side of the valley, where there were many moorings for starships. Jake had visited the docks only once a long time ago, for his business rarely brought him there.

Turning from the window, Jake crossed the kitchen to the stairway that curved behind a stone wall up into the tower. Slowly he climbed the narrow stair, taking a torch[8] with him so he could find his footing. On the second storey, he passed a large wooden door on thick metal hinges. Cobwebs and dust filled the cracks between the door and the stones in which it was set. It had not been opened for many years, for the room beyond had belonged to his parents. After they had died, he had not had the heart to enter it, and he had never thought of moving into it himself though it was an enormous room, as he remembered it. He suspected that in the ancient days, it had belonged to whoever had commanded the tower.

8 Nanyan: *tariona*—any small device capable of emitting light without a flame. Not to be confused with *koriana*, which is a torch of fire.

Floor after floor he climbed, passing many other rooms long shut up or sealed. On the floor just below the uppermost, he stopped at a small wooden door not quite tall enough for him to walk through standing upright. He ducked inside, and as he entered, a few roaches scattered away from the light. The room was dark, for though there was a window in the far wall, it faced away from the rising sun. Beneath it lay a bed covered in rumpled sheets and blankets, and it was here that he slept. Besides the bed, the room also held a small table, an old trunk, and a wardrobe with creaky hinges. Jake had always wanted to replace it, but he could not think of how to remove it. It was much too large to fit through the door, and he sometimes wondered how it had been brought upstairs in the first place.

Jake took a black leather book from the table beside the bed and left the room again. He continued up the stairs until on the topmost floor he came to a landing that opened into a large room of plain stone. A few pillars of stone and metal held up the ceiling, and at the far end of the room stood a wooden door that opened upon a small storage space. Four windows opened in the walls of the room, evenly spaced to match the four directions of the compass. Upon the floor and along the walls were many tree branches and stone columns where two dozen birds of all kinds and colours sat—some sleeping, some preening, and some talking to one another.

A harrier sitting on a wooden perch near the stairs turned as Jake entered. “Good morning, sir,” he said. “Did you sleep well?”

“Fairly,” Jake said. “Has Dinarin returned yet?”

“No, sir,” the harrier said. “But Thesanumon is far away indeed. I don’t think even Faluin could have made the trip in so little time.”

At that moment Faluin swooped through the window and landed on a wooden beam that had fallen and now lay at an angle near one of the windows.

“Where could I not have gone?” he asked.

"Your pardon," the harrier said, bowing low. "I meant no disrespect."

"Are you speaking of Dinarin's journey to Thesanumon?"

"We are," said the harrier.

"Then I concur with you," said Faluin. "It is a long journey. We must await him a while longer."

"That's not very good news," Jake said. "The woman who sent the message did not pay enough for him to be gone this long. I must remember to raise prices in future."

Suddenly one of the eagles let out a cry, and a murmur arose from the other birds. Jake turned to the window and started, for there on the window-ledge sat a large bird unlike any Jake had ever seen. At first sight he appeared owl-like, but as Jake looked at him more closely, he appeared like a large falcon, keen and fierce, with a look of malice that unnerved Jake so that he backed away at once. Faluin jumped to a stone pillar near the window, placing himself between Jake and the newcomer.

"Hello," Jake said as cordially as he could manage.

The bird gave no answer.

"My name is Jake Connolly."

The bird remained silent and as still as a statue.

"Who is your master?" Jake said. "Do you have a message for someone?"

The bird paused a moment longer and then took in his beak a scrap of paper that had been attached to his foot. Slowly Jake reached out his hand to receive it. Faluin watched closely, ready to intervene if something went amiss. The bird dropped his message into Jake's palm, and before Jake had even begun to unroll it, the bird turned and leapt through the open window, soaring away at great speed. Jake ran to the window, but the bird had already vanished from sight.

Confused, Jake opened the paper scroll, and upon it he read these words handwritten in plain English:

Jake Connolly, you are in danger.

○

Chapter 2

A Strange Visitor

Jake stared at the note for a moment, and in the silence of the room, the breathing of the vèralamen echoed loudly in his ears.

"What does it say, sir?" Faluin asked, leaving his perch and drawing nearer. Jake read the message aloud, translating it into Nanyan, and the birds whispered words of confusion to one another.

"Shall I go after the messenger?" said Faluin, fluttering to the window and awaiting command. Jake nodded, and Faluin disappeared out the window.

He returned almost at once. "Sir, there is a strange man coming up the road from the village," he said. "He is attired as one of the Overseers, but there is something off about him. He walks as someone who doesn't wish to be seen."

Jake stepped away from the window that faced the road. *It's probably nothing*, he told himself. Then again, Faluin had a talent for reading people that exceeded that of other vèralamen. He had been the first to notice Samantha's interest in Jake and had encouraged him to pursue her. "It didn't take the eye of a vèralam to see that," Faluin had said, "but you Thalanin often can't see things even near at hand." Jake had found no argument against that.

A hawk peered down from the rafters. "What are you going to do, sir?"

Jake shook his head and crept to the open window. He could not see the man from where he stood, but he dared not lean his head out any farther. "I don't know," he said. "Any other day I wouldn't think anything of it, but now…" He looked back at the note he still held in his fingers. "Do you suppose it was he who sent the message?"

"If that were so, why would he come here now to speak with you?" Faluin said. "And why would he have written in a Thalanin tongue?"

"Then…" Jake said slowly, "do you suppose this is a warning about him?"

No one answered.

"I wonder who sent it," Jake continued. "No one I know would send me a message in this manner, and I've certainly never seen that bird before. Have you?" The others admitted that they had not, nor could they tell exactly what breed of vèralam he was.

Faluin flew cautiously to the window and peered out carefully. "He draws nearer," he said. "Will you go to meet him?"

Jake thought for a moment, looking from the window to the paper in his hand and back again. "No," he said. "I'm curious what he'll do if he thinks no one is at home. If there is nothing wrong, then all I'll have done is make a fool of myself. That certainly won't be the first time I've done that." He went to the stairs that led down into the house and sat upon the top step, and he waited. He shuddered at the eerie silence of the rooms below, and the cold darkness of the stair frightened him in a way it never had before. A surge of anger flashed through him that he should be afraid of the stillness of his own home.

A firm pounding on the door below shattered the silence and echoed through the tower. Jake jumped at the sound, startling a few of the birds who flapped their wings nervously. Only Faluin remained unshaken, standing on a nearby stone and peering into the darkness of the staircase.

The knock at the door came again, even louder this time, and a voice shouted something Jake could not make out. Then all was quiet again. In the stillness Jake could hear the creaking of the wooden beams as the tower swayed in the morning breeze.

Jake was about to go the window and see if the man had gone when there came a mighty crash from the depths. Footsteps sounded on the stone floor far below. Jake's blood ran cold; the man had forced his way inside and was now stomping around the kitchen. The air thundered with his every footfall, for they were made by the thick boots of a man great in stature and strength.

Jake retreated from the staircase, but he was careful to make no sound. Slow footsteps were coming up the stairs, and the intruder grew bolder with every stride. He seemed now to be confident no one was at home.

Louder and louder the footsteps grew. A locked door rattled, and the heavy boots continued on. Jake found himself trembling. He could not think of what to do. He looked around at the vèralamen about him, and most of them looked as nervous as he was.

Even so, they were sure to defend him, even if he protested, but he could not tell what the outcome of such a battle would be. There suddenly came unbidden to his mind a scene of a dozen birds lying upon on the floor—some crushed and others rent in pieces. He closed his eyes and shook his head to be rid of the image.

When Jake opened his eyes again, he found Faluin still standing resolute on the stone near the stairs. His wings were spread as if he were ready at any moment to dive into the dark passage. Faluin took in a deep breath and rose to his full height. There he stood for a brief moment, tall and proud like one of the great Starlords of his kind. Then with a sudden thrust of his head, he screamed into the darkness a piercing note, sharp and shrill. Jake had never heard any creature make such a sound, and he fell flat on the floor and covered his ears.

At once a clatter arose from below, as of someone running but stumbling over himself. Jake ran to the window in time to see the figure of a man dash through the shattered kitchen door and down the lane, kicking up a trail of dust behind him. Jake could not help but laugh, though his hands were still trembling.

Faluin flew down to the kitchen and made sure all was clear, and he returned with a grim countenance. "The door is hanging in splinters," he said. "Whoever that man was, he was strong. He roughed up the kitchen quite a bit, but nothing else seems damaged. It looks as though he tried to open some of the sealed doors, but he did not force them. They are still closed."

Jake cautiously made his way downstairs. Though he knew the tower was vacant, fear lingered in him still. The house was silent, but he expected any moment to hear a voice speak from the darkness.

Fear turned to anger when he saw the kitchen. The wooden door was split in two and lay on the floor, still attached by the bottom hinge. The table and chairs were overturned, and the open cupboards held an untidy scattering of cups and dishes. Jake grimaced and walked outside to look around. The world was quiet again.

Faluin flew out to get a look at the surrounding lands. After a few minutes, he returned, landing on the garden fence. "The constable is coming up the road," he said. "There is no sign of that other man, and I'm not sure where he could have gone so quickly. It is quite odd."

By the time Constable Gibbs arrived, he was quite out of breath. He had run all the way up the hill, and he now stood panting, with his hands upon his knees. "What's happened?" he said. "I saw a Regulator sprinting down the hill. He tore through town and didn't stop for anyone. He might still be running for all I know."

"Did you see where he went?" Jake asked.

"No," the constable said. "I came straight here. What's happened?"

Jake showed the constable the damage to the kitchen and described the break-in, though he left out the part about the strange bird and the message. Somehow it seemed better not to mention them.

The constable scratched his head and looked around. "I'm afraid I can't do much where Nanyans are involved," he said. "It's not in my authority. I'll have to send a message to hCathad. In the meantime I'll post my deputy here. Hopefully we can keep whoever did this from coming back."

Jake thanked him, and the constable returned to the village. Faluin flew up to patrol the skies, and Jake returned to the kitchen to start cleaning and putting things aright.

As he started to work, Jake suddenly became aware of a pair of eyes staring at him. He spun around and jumped back startled, for there sitting on the windowsill was the strange bird. He made no sound but sat with another scroll in his talons. Jake took the note from him, and the bird turned without a word and flew off.

Jake opened the scroll—a much larger one this time—and read these words written in English:

> My name is Silorè Niavè Felathè Rènaliè Itarlavon. Our two families have been well acquainted for many centuries. I am writing to you from nearby, and I have been circling your world. Those who seek your life are already upon you. I have been sent to stop them. Stay as safe as you can, and watch for me. I will come tonight.

Jake read the note several times, trying to make sense of it.

The name Itarlavon at least was familiar to him. They were the family of Earth-protectors who ruled the planet Iderat, a world a few days' journey from Rithonon. His parents had told him about the Itarlavon when he was a child—how they were guardians of the Earth and that whatever reward they earned was far less than they deserved. They grieved that no one seemed to care about the Itarlavon family anymore. Some people hated them, thinking that they should not meddle in the events of Earth or of Eratzira.

Faluin suddenly appeared in the window, looking almost frantic. "When did he arrive?"

"Who?"

"The strange vèralam," Faluin said. "I saw him depart, but I did not see his arrival. There are few things that can evade my watch. I tried to follow him, but he was too swift for me."

"That is swift indeed," said Jake. "But don't worry about it. He's done no harm."

"Another note?" Faluin said, looking at the paper in Jake's hands. "What does it say?"

Jake translated the message for Faluin, who afterwards looked puzzled. "That's odd indeed," he said. "I remember a girl named Silorè from when you were very young. In those days there were strange folk often coming and going, but no one ever told me what it was all about—least of all your parents. I wish they had. Perhaps then I would have some answers for you."

"But my parents—they seemed to trust this Silorè?" Jake asked. "She herself must be trusting to write her full name."[9]

"I'm afraid I don't remember much about her," said Faluin.

9 Nanyanin traditionally have at least three names (in addition to their family name). Though a Nanyani's name is not necessarily a secret, it is taboo to use one's full name without discretion.

"Well, I certainly can't remember anything," Jake said. "Do you think you could find this Silorè Itarlavon for me?"

"I am a good tracker, sir," said Faluin, "but even I need more than just a name. Without knowing where to look, it could take many days to find her."

"What about that bird of hers?" Jake said. "What do you make of him?"

"He's strange," Faluin said. "His face and markings are unknown to me. He is not from any house I know, nor is he of any breed I have met in my many travels. I would say he is old—very old, and the bloodline of his kind has faded to distant memory. But though he is old, he does not seem frail, and his wings seem as strong as mine. One thing is certain: he is swift and cannot be found if he wishes to hide himself. Whoever has sent these words to you must think them important indeed if they sent them by such a messenger."

Jake pondered Faluin's words for a moment. "But how can I meet with her?" he said. "I don't know what time she's coming. And where? And how shall I know her?"

"I don't think I can help you, sir," Faluin said. "Though I remember her name from years ago, I'm not sure I ever once saw her face. I am not forgetful, and I remember still the faces of many people long departed."

"But what would the Itarlavon want with my family?" Jake said. "Wouldn't they be better served by more important families—like the Misizhalon or the Keneraton?"

The Misizhalon family was quite renowned, and its members held many positions of leadership in Eratzira. The representative from Rithonon was Jariani Misizhalon, a young member of the family appointed by the ruling council of Rithonon. Many in Brown Hill were distressed at his appointment, for he was not sympathetic to the Thalanin. Jariani was the great-nephew of Kensilon, Solèdaron[10] of Eratzira and patriarch of the Misizhalon family—both titles that his father, Niljoron, had held before him.

If the Misizhalon family was well known, the Keneraton family was much feared. They were the strongest of all Kenornin[11] families, and they still ruled Ialanon, a faraway region near the centre of the galaxy. By far the most notorious member of this family was Eratizhal. Everyone in Eratzira knew that name, for all but the youngest Nanyanin had lived through the last war and the Kenornin invasion of Eratzira. It was that conflict that sparked the rebirth of Eratzira as a nation.

Faluin shook his head. "I do not know," he said. "But with the Itarlavon involved, this could be serious indeed."

"Agreed," Jake said. "What then should we do?"

"You have two choices, it seems," said Faluin. "You can either take this information to persons of authority, and they may council you further; or you can await the arrival of this lady of the Itarlavon house. Which shall it be?"

"Wait for her, I guess," Jake said thoughtfully. "I wonder what she's like. How old was she when she last visited?"

"Not very," said Faluin. "I cannot be certain, but I would guess she was no older than fifty years."

Jake laughed. "Regina Arlington is fifty," he said. "But I'll warrant Silorè looks a fair bit younger."

Faluin scowled. "I've always thought Madam Arlington a handsome woman," he replied. "Alas for the Thalanin that they are so short-lived!"

10 Nanyan: "one who gathers from above"—one of many names for the highest official of a Nanyan government.

11 A people-group said to be the descendants of Cain. Kenornin sometimes refer to themselves as "the firstborn," though this has fallen out of favour in recent days.

"I don't think I'd want to live as long as the Nanyanin," said Jake. "What would I do with all that time?"

"You may feel that way when you are young," Faluin said. "But I'll warrant you will change your mind when you grow old."

Jake shrugged. "Perhaps," he said. "But who knows? This Silorè person may be older now than I can ever hope to be. The Nanyanin may look young, but the years wear on them. When you meet them, it feels like you're talking to someone old and grey—perhaps not in body but in mind and in heart."

"I've not known that to be so," Faluin said. "To me, youth is not a measure of years but of spirit. Even the oldest man alive may still burn with the fire of his younger days. The joy of youth brings long life; perhaps you Thalanin burn through it too quickly."

Jake greeted the deputy from Brown Hill when he arrived. He was a young man, and Jake felt embarrassed to be guarded by someone near his own age. Faluin circled the tower for most of the day, and Jake worked inside, handling dispatches and sending out the messengers. There were few orders, which would otherwise have been welcome, but today Jake wished there had been more to take his mind off the day's events.

The day wore into the afternoon. Jake ate bread and a wedge of cheese for lunch and offered some to the young deputy. The constable came in the midafternoon to tell Jake he had reported the break-in to the constabulary in hCathad. A few officers would be coming out to investigate, but there was no telling when that would be. Thalanin never seemed a high priority to hCathad.

That evening Jake decided to go into town for dinner. The constable had recalled his deputy, and to Jake the tower now felt lonelier than it had in many years. Faluin descended as Jake started down the road to Brown Hill, and he reported that he had seen no sign of the strange Overseer, nor had there been anything else out of the ordinary.

The town was quiet when Jake entered it. He had missed the busiest time of day, and now many shops were closing, and lamp-lighters were kindling the streetlights. Night-shadows crept across the valley, descending from the mountains and filling the narrower streets. Jake tucked his hands into the pockets of his jacket and shivered. The air was growing cold.

"Jake Connolly!"

Jake turned and found an old woman walking towards him. She wore a soiled apron over a faded green dress, and her grey hair was tied in a tight bun. She advanced on Jake carrying a rolling pin. He hoped she did not mean to strike him with it.

"Good evening, Mrs Winston," he said. "Is something the matter? The tax office hasn't been giving you any more trouble, have they?"

"Goodness, no!" said the old woman. "But that's why I came running up just now. I wanted to thank you for your help in getting all that straightened out."

"You're welcome," Jake said, "but I didn't do much. Appleton handled all the legal matters."

"What about all your translating[12] work?" the woman asked. "I've heard that his Nanyan isn't as good as yours."

Jake could not help but smirk. "It wasn't difficult to translate."

"Nevertheless," the woman said, "I want to know how much I owe you for everything."

"You don't have to pay me."

12 Nanyan is the only officially recognized language in most parts of the galaxy, and as such all legal affairs must be conducted in Nanyan. Thalanin are often at a disadvantage in this regard.

"Oh, but I do!" The old woman drew closer. "Without you they would've taken the shop for sure. When my Carl died, I was sure I'd lose everything. My husband never did keep his paperwork organized properly. If you and the Appleton boy hadn't stepped in, well, I…I don't know what I would have done."

"It's quite all right, Mrs Winston," Jake said. "You don't owe me anything. We Thalanin have to stick together. It wasn't fair what the tax office tried to do to your shop, and I was only too happy to help set things right."

The old woman smiled. "You're very much like your father, Jake Connolly," she said. "He was quite generous and always willing to help. You're becoming a fine young man, and I hope I'll get to see you start a family before I die—maybe with a certain young lady who works at the Griffin." She winked at him and smiled a fairly toothless smile.

Jake squirmed. "Perhaps."

The old lady chuckled. "Well, I've probably stopped you on your way to dinner," she said, "so I won't keep you. A good evening to you."

"And to you too."

The old woman turned and walked towards the open door of a shop upon which was written in big red letters "Winston's Baked Goods."

The lamps of the Grey Griffin were already lit by the time Jake arrived. The windows on the ground floor glowed with a pale yellow light, and many shadows danced upon the drawn shades. Though the courtyard was quiet and empty, the sounds of loud dinner-commotion trickled out through the closed door of the inn. Jake thought it seemed especially noisy tonight.

He was about to open the door when suddenly it flew open before him. He staggered back, but a slender pair of arms caught him around the neck and embraced him so tightly he could not find his footing.

"I'm so glad you're all right," a sweet voice said in his ear. "I heard…I mean, we all heard…We were just worried."

Jake managed to stand up properly, and he pulled back, finding himself looking into Samantha's face, full of both joy and worry.

"What's going on?" Samantha asked. "Why did that man break down your door? Did you fight him? Were you hurt?"

"Can I come in first?" Jake said. "I'll tell you over dinner."

Samantha brought Jake inside, and closing the door behind her, she hurried off to the kitchen. The common-room was full of people talking all at once, but when Jake entered, the clamour subsided as every eye in the place turned towards him. He tiptoed to the counter, trying to act as normally as he could.

He was thankful there was no one else at the bar before the kitchen. As he took his seat, he felt as if a hundred eyes were drilling into his back, and he did not dare to turn around. He sat fiddling with a salt cellar as he waited for Samantha to return.

Samantha appeared a few minutes later carrying a plate of ham and roasted potatoes, which she placed before Jake. Then pulling up a chair, she sat across from him and listened as he told her all that had happened.

"It's a good thing you didn't answer the door," Samantha said when he had finished. "Why didn't you?"

Jake had again skipped over the part of the story about the strange bird and the note. He struggled now to find words to say. He did not want to lie to her.

"I mean, didn't you hear it?" she said. "Did Fawlin and the others not see him?"

Jake seized the chance to change the subject. "His name is Faluin," he said quickly.

"Oh, I'm sorry," Samantha said, putting her hand to her mouth. "Please don't tell him I got it wrong."

"I'll let you off this one time," Jake said with a wink.

"I wish I knew some Nanyan so I could talk with him," she said. "He's so fluffy and cute."

Jake nearly choked on a bite of potato. "Cute?" he coughed. "I don't know if anyone's ever called him that before. And as for 'fluffy,' well…"

"He's adorable," Samantha said indignantly. "Do you reckon you could teach me some Nanyan to say to him? I don't know very much—just *filay* and *thondry*."[13]

Jake chuckled. "If you'd like."

Samantha beamed. "I'm terribly jealous of you," she said. "As a little girl, I always wanted a pet that could talk."

Jake laughed so loudly that the room grew suddenly quiet again. He turned red and waited for the room to grow noisy again before continuing.

"I'm sorry," he said. "I just don't know what Faluin would think if he heard himself called a pet."

"What's the Nanyan word for 'pet'?"

"Well, there are several," Jake said, "but I think the one you mean is *nathorad*."

"*Nathorad*," Samantha repeated.

Jake grinned. "Are you going to try out that word on Faluin?"

Samantha giggled and lightly swiped at Jake's arm. "Of course not," she said. "He's a fine bird, and I'll not insult him."

13 Samantha probably meant to say *philè* and *athondri*—a common greeting and farewell, respectively. The transliteration used in the text is meant to convey the incorrect manner in which she pronounces the words.

"He'll appreciate it," Jake said. "He *is* a fine bird. He's been flying over the valley all day keeping a lookout."

Samantha covered her mouth with both hands. "I'm sorry," she said, looking suddenly guilty. "Here I am talking nonsense while you're in some real trouble."

"No, please continue," Jake said. "You're the best distraction I've had all day."

Samantha turned pink and smiled. Then a sudden urgency crossed her face, and she looked up at the clock on the wall. "You're pretty distracting yourself," she said, standing up and pushing her chair back against the wall. "I've got other folks to wait on. Can I come up later this evening to see you?"

Jake thought of the note and of Silorè's arrival. "Better not," he said. "I'd hate for you to get into trouble."

"But I can't just let you sit up there all alone," Samantha said.

"I'll be fine," Jake said. "One or two of the birds will keep watch tonight. I'll be ready if anything strange happens."

Jake's words did not seem to make Samantha feel any better, but she forced a smile and went back to work. Jake finished his dinner quickly and slipped out of the inn as inconspicuously as he could manage. The street outside seemed quiet and cold. Jake pulled his jacket tightly around him and set off for home.

As Jake ascended the hill, Faluin swooped down to meet him. "You won't like it," he said, "but that young magistrate is here to see you."

"Appleton?" Jake groaned. "What about?"

"I'm not sure," Faluin said. "His tongue[14] is not very good. How he became magistrate is not readily apparent."

14 When one does not speak Nanyan well, he is said to have a bad tongue.

Jake laughed and carried Faluin upon his arm up the hill. No one was waiting for them outside, and inside there was a light in the kitchen.

"I hope you'll forgive me," Appleton said as Jake walked through the open doorway. "I let myself in." He motioned towards the splintered door hanging precariously on what remained of the hinges.

Jake took a deep breath. "What is it that you want?"

"Justice," Appleton said. "Justice for you and this most unfortunate incident."

"I'm sure," Jake mumbled.

"How's that?"

"I said I'm sure that's what we both want," Jake said.

"No doubt," Appleton said. "I came to see whether or not you would be pursuing legal action against the man who did this."

"I might," Jake said, "if I knew who he was."

"What a shame," Appleton said. "I was quite looking forward to having you in my debt."

"Prosecuting crime is not a favour," Jake said, growing annoyed. "It's your job, and one, I'll warrant, you will fulfil to the best of your ability."

"Certainly," Appleton said, walking to the door. "Well, since there is little I can do here, I'd best be on my way."

"Certainly there's more," Jake said. "I can't believe you would come all the way up here just for that."

"As a matter of fact," Appleton said, "I thought you should know I looked into the identity of that supposed Regulator."

Appleton paused a long while. "And?" Jake said.

"He's not a Regulator," said Appleton. "I called the tax office in hCathad. They had no record of anyone fitting his description, and they certainly hadn't dispatched anyone to meet with someone as unimportant as you."

Jake rolled his eyes.

"I've also talked to everyone who saw him earlier today," Appleton continued. "No one could remember him ever giving out his name. Curious, isn't it?"

"Quite."

"Anyway, that's all I came up here to say," Appleton said with a sneer. "I'll…let myself out." He stepped over the shattered door and walked down the lane back to town. With a sigh and a shake of his head, Jake went upstairs, climbing to the very top of the tower.

From the rooftop Jake could see much of the valley, even to the distant mountains. The land glowed red with sunset, and the forests cast long shadows over the flat and treeless lands around them. In the distance the lights of other villages were just being lit, and the towers of hCathad twinkled like the stars. The skies were clear and free of starships and airships. Silent peace lay over all the valley.

Jake sat in a chair he brought up from below and stared at the sky. The slender sliver of Telethoram shone brightly above the setting sun, and the unfilled portion of the circle was dotted with a thousand points of light scattered across the continents. When Telethoram was full, one could easily see oceans and clouds on its surface, but tonight the moon was dark.

Jake closed his eyes for a moment and let the quiet of the evening wash over him. Just as he started to relax, he suddenly felt again as if he were being watched. He turned quickly, jumping from his chair with such force that he nearly tumbled off the roof. On a stone near the roof's edge sat the strange bird that had visited earlier, and in his claws was another message. *I'm getting tired of this*, Jake thought, his heart pounding from the sudden scare. He took the message, and the bird flew off silently, melting into the darkening sky.

Jake unrolled the paper and read:

I will arrive soon. Watch for me.

He stuffed the paper into his pocket and looked up at the sky again. The first stars were coming out, and the evening was growing colder. He shivered and went downstairs to make a cup of tea.

By the time he returned, the sky was dark indeed. A line of clouds had overtaken the distant mountains and veiled the stars in the western sky. The sun had vanished, and the last glow of red was fading away. The undersides of the clouds were stained crimson for a few minutes longer, but soon they too became dark.

Jake shivered and drank his tea. As he waited he kept looking from the sky to the road and back again, wondering if Silorè would be coming on foot or in an airship of some sort. His tea went cold before he finished it.

Even as his patience reached its end, a sudden noise like distant thunder arose from the west and echoed in the nearby mountains. Another roll of thunder sounded, accompanied by a bright flash in the distant clouds. A small point of light appeared against the black sky, and it grew steadily larger and brighter, drawing so near that Jake had to shield his eyes.

A fireball was streaking across the sky. For a moment Jake thought it would strike the mountains behind the ruins of the citadel, but instead it passed over the high peaks and disappeared. A brilliant flash burst into the sky for an instant, and the ground rumbled and shook. All at once the valley grew quiet again, and the sky was clear again save for a line of smoke quickly dispelled by the night wind.

Jake stood and stared for a few moments as he tried to understand what he had just witnessed. He had seen meteors before, but this was not like any in his experience. Suddenly he understood what it was—a ship! Not just any ship but the one he was expecting—Silorè's ship. He was not the only one in danger, it seemed.

He ran down the stairs as fast as he could, stumbling in the dark as he went. A minute later he was outside hurrying to his garage. Faluin flew to Jake's side.

"That was a near thing," said Faluin. "I had to fly away as it fell. It was burning hot, and it singed my feathers—even from a distance."

Jake reached into his pocket and withdrew a key on a thin chain. "I think it was a ship."

"I thought so as well."

"Go find it," Jake said. "I'll be following close behind."

"It shall be done, sir." Faluin flew off at once towards the mountains.

Jake turned the key in an iron lock that bolted the two giant wooden doors of the garage together. Then throwing both lock and key aside, he thrust the doors open upon a musty room made of stone. It was too dark even to see the straw upon the floor, but Jake knew every inch of the garage by heart. He ran inside and emerged pushing his flyer out into the night.

Jake's flyer was black and silver, with two bars at the front for steering and a wide black seat set between the grey wings. The machine floated a foot off the ground, and Jake pushed it with ease. Then mounting the flyer like a horse, Jake placed a small round key into in the slot in front of him. The machine roared to life and slowly rose higher into the air.

Jake turned the flyer, and with solid stomp on the foot-lever, he flew with great speed towards the mountains. His tower diminished behind him to a small speck on the hill, and the mountains loomed large ahead. He passed above the farthest reaches of the forest into an area where only rocks and boulders dwelt. The flyer rose above it all and climbed higher still. Jake pulled his jacket tightly around him. The rushing air chilled him and set his hands to shaking.

Jake passed over the first of the high peaks, entering a region of steep-sided mountains that descended into deep canyons and valleys. The moonlight and starlight occasionally peeking through the clouds suggested little of the terrain below, but a dim light in the distance guided him. He was certain it was the downed ship. He pushed hard on the throttle, and the flyer sped on.

Faluin suddenly appeared, flying along beside Jake. "I've found the ship," Faluin said. "But I don't think anyone could have survived that crash."

Jake's spirits fell. "It's hopeless, then?"

"Perhaps not," said Faluin. "I did find the trail of a survival pod to the north. It was barely visible, and I doubt that anyone with eyes less keen than mine could have found it."

"Then lead the way," Jake said.

Faluin dived, and Jake followed close behind. As they descended, a strange sound came to Jake's ears—a sound like the buzzing of many insects. He looked back, and through a break in the clouds above the mountains he saw the stars wink at him continuously. He perceived that these were other flyers coming at him, sent perhaps to find the downed ship. For a moment he considered turning round and joining them, but something about the matter gave him pause. He thought better of it and continued on.

Faluin led him down into a steep valley of tree-covered slopes. A night breeze was blowing, and as Jake slowed near the treetops he heard the leaves rustling like the ocean. Smaller hills of trees rose and fell all around, and Jake felt as if he were afloat in a rippling sea of waves, black and green.

Faluin circled one of the smaller hills, and Jake followed him downward in a wide spiral. Below them, hardly to be seen in the broken moonlight, lay a trail of broken tree limbs and upturned earth. A patch of grass crowned the hill below him, and Jake landed upon it. The flyer had scarcely reached the ground when Jake dismounted and ran down the path of the fallen trees. He had taken a torch from the flyer, and it cast eerie shadows all around him. He could not say for certain, but he thought he briefly saw several pairs of pale eyes staring at him through the tangle of trees. He shuddered and ran faster.

Following the trail, he came upon a small grey capsule barely large enough for a man to fit in. The outside was covered with dirt and fallen branches, and a shredded parachute lay behind it, twisted with the trees and rocks in its wake. The capsule had not landed gently, and Jake feared the passenger might be dead.

He wound his way around the fallen branches until he stood before the capsule. A bright symbol of gold was printed upon it, and though it was smeared with clay and mud, Jake recognized it as the symbol of the Itarlavon family.

The door of the capsule stood slightly ajar. Jake was about to open it wider when he suddenly jumped back in alarm, for at that moment a tiny creature leapt from the wreckage and stood between it and him.

"You shall not come near!" the creature cried with a voice that filled the surrounding woods. Jake had been so startled that he had dropped his light and could not see. From the tone of its voice, Jake imagined some sort of monstrous beast, full of rage and terror.

When Jake gathered his torch again, the light revealed a small creature about the size of any housecat in Brown Hill, though Jake had never seen any animal like this before, automaton or otherwise. Its coat glistened in hues of red and brown that seemed to change as the light moved around it. Two giant ears tipped with white fur towered over its small head, and two great eyes glowed with a pale yellow light. It snarled at Jake, revealing a row of tiny teeth as sharp as razors. Brambles and mud covered its body, and in its angst the creature panted heavily.

"You shall not come near!" it repeated. "Be gone with you!"

Jake was too bewildered to speak or move.

"Be gone!" the creature said, and it seemed to bark at him.

Jake held up his hands as if to shield himself from the creature. "I only want to help."

The creature replied with low snarls, and Jake thought he heard it hiss at him.

"I do," Jake insisted. "Is there someone in there?"

"My mistress does not require assistance from the likes of you," the creature said. "I shall do all in my power to protect her. You shall not come near."

At that moment a passing blow struck the creature, who though startled kept on its feet. It whipped its head around as Faluin perched on a fallen tree stump near at hand. "Do not come near me," the creature said, "for I shan't let you escape again."

"I do not doubt it," Faluin said. "But this is my master, and he means no harm to your mistress."

The creature laughed and spoke to Jake. "You are a Thalani, are you not?"

"That's right."

"I cannot trust the word of a Thalani," the creature said, "nor of his pet pigeon."

A fire Jake had not seen before was kindled in Faluin's eyes, and the bird spread his wings so that he looked large and menacing. Faluin gave a loud cry that pierced the silence of the night, and Jake heard many birds take flight from their unseen homes in the surrounding trees.

"I am Faluin, descendent of the House of Binrialanil," said the mighty vèralam. "Terthavi was my sire, and never have such words been spoken to us by any—and certainly not by lesser beasts. You would do well not to awaken my anger."

The creature hissed but only half-heartedly, for Jake perceived the creature was afraid. He was also certain this animal had not known much fear in its life and did not know now what to do.

Fearing that a fierce battle was soon to follow, Jake intervened, stretching out his hands between the two automatons. "Please," he said to the small creature, "we mean no harm. I am Jake Connolly. I received your messages, and I've been waiting for you."

The creature regarded Jake with suspicion. "Prove it to me," it said at length.

"How?"

"Tell me the full name of my mistress."

Jake was startled by the request, and a cold sweat broke upon his brow. He could remember vaguely how the names had sounded, but he could not remember them fully.

Faluin sensed his master's distress and said, "Silorè Niavè Felathè Rènaliè Itarlavon."

The creature hissed. "I didn't ask you!" it screamed.

At that moment Jake heard movement coming from the capsule, and the door opened. A voice came from inside—a young female voice, sweet and sorrowful. "Izhana? Izhana, where are you?"

Jake turned his light from the creature to the open door of the capsule. A girl was climbing out, holding her hand before her face to block out the blinding light of Jake's torch. Slowly she stepped down, stumbling a bit on her right leg. She braced herself against the capsule, and Jake hurried forward to help her. Before he could reach out to steady the girl, the small creature came between them, gnashing its teeth at him.

"Izhana!" the girl said firmly. "Leave him alone!"

The creature relented, and Jake took the girl by the arm. "Are you all right?" he said. He had let his light fall, but as he raised it again and looked into her face, he stood back astonished.

Even by the torchlight that cast long shadows in the darkness, Jake was quite certain he had never seen a girl more beautiful.

IO

Chapter 3

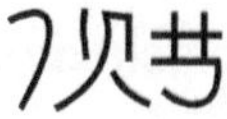

Silorè

The girl stared at Jake for a moment, scowling at him in silence. In the darkness her eyes shone with a rich violet colour. Strands of white streaked her dark-brown hair, and two long white tresses framed her face. No flaw could be seen in her, and her cheek[15] was perfect. Were she a Thalavè, Jake would have guessed her no older than twenty years.

"Are you an idiot?" she said at last, an angry timbre marring the melody of her voice. "What are you doing here?"

Jake stood dumbfounded at the sight of her, not knowing how he should answer. Her unwavering stare embarrassed him, and he could not look her in the eye for more than a moment.

"Are *you* all right?" the girl said at last.

Jake was wholly flustered. "You…" he said, "you *are* Silorè, aren't you?"

"Of course I am," the girl said curtly. "You should already know that, *Mr Connolly*. Surely you haven't forgotten…" As she took a step towards him, she stumbled, and her anger vanished.

15 Nanyan: *lorianè*—the point at which a woman's eye, cheek, and forehead meet. Nanyan tradition holds that the *lorianè* is the true measure of a woman's beauty.

Jake reached out and caught her by the hand. “You’re hurt,” he said, guiding her to sit on a tree trunk felled by the crash. He sat upon it beside her, steadying her with his arm.

“I’ll be fine,” said Silorè. “I just need to rest a few minutes.”

“I think you might have blacked out.”

“Did I?” Silorè put her hand to her head. “How long?”

“Maybe ten minutes,” Jake said. “It looked like a terrible crash.”

“I’m sure they meant it to be.”

“Who did?” Jake looked skyward but saw only the stars twinkling between the sparse tree leaves.

“That will take some time to explain,” said Silorè, rubbing her head with her fingers.

“Are you sure you’re all right?” Jake said.

Silorè nodded. “I don’t think I passed out,” she said. “I could hear you talking to Izhana, but I couldn’t move for a while. I’m sorry about her manners. She’s quite protective of me.”

Izhana had jumped into Silorè’s lap, and Silorè was rubbing her gently between the ears.

“But now isn’t the time for talk,” said Silorè. “They will be coming, and we must leave here before they do.”

“I’ve a flyer back up the hill,” Jake said. “Can you walk?”

“I think so.”

“Then come on.”

Jake helped Silorè to her feet, and together they hobbled up the hill. Halfway to the top, Silorè stumbled, and Jake took her in his arms carried her up the rest of the way. She shivered and held tightly on to his neck. The night was growing colder, and Silorè wore only a thin shirt and trousers of grey and blue.

“This is embarrassing,” she said. “I came here to help you, and now look at me.”

“You have rescued me once already,” Jake said. He was out of breath, for though Silorè was light, the hill was steep. “If you hadn’t sent that message, that man might have beaten me instead of my front door.”

Silorè chuckled. “So you know about him, do you?”

“I don’t really know much. No one in town does either. Do you?”

Silorè nodded. “I’ve much to tell you,” she said. “But I’m so tired.”

“Don’t worry,” Jake said. “We’ll soon be safe at home.”

They reached the flyer, and Jake laid Silorè gently upon the seat. The buzzing he had heard earlier was now very loud indeed, and towards the mountains he could see many points of light searching for the crashed ship.

With no time to waste, Jake climbed onto the seat in front of Silorè and started the engine as quietly as he could. Izhana jumped into Silorè’s lap and held on tightly with her claws. Silorè put her arms around Jake’s waist so she would not fall, and Izhana, pressed between the two, protested with a low growl.

At Jake’s command Faluin took off into the night sky, and the flyer followed close behind him. Jake did not turn on the lights, for he hoped to pass like a shadow over the mountains and back into the valley. However, Jake found the air filled with many flyers combing the hills for signs of the crash. A gathering of lights showed they had already located the ship, but finding it empty, they continued the search for the ejection pod.

“Friends of yours?” Jake asked Silorè as he steered the flyer into a wide arc around the searchers.

“No indeed,” Silorè said. “I’m not quite sure what they would do if they found me, but it’s better for us both if they don’t.”

“I believe you,” Jake said.

Jake heard Silorè chuckle, her head resting on his shoulder. "Be careful, Thalani," she said. "There are dangerous times ahead, and you would do well to be wary. If indeed you do not remember me, what am I to you but another stranger? Many of those searching for me are those who enforce law throughout your valley. Would you trust me over them? What if I were dangerous?"

She swooned, and Jake had to reach back his arm to steady her. "I don't think you're dangerous to anyone right now," he said, "except maybe to yourself. Be careful; it's a long way down."

Silorè shook her head and held on more tightly to Jake. "I'll be all right," she said. "I'm just tired. So tired…" She leaned against him and sighed.

"No, you must stay awake," Jake insisted. "At least until I can find a doctor to look at you. You've injured your head, and you mustn't fall asleep."

Silorè sat up and sighed again. "You're right, of course," she said. "I'm afraid I don't quite feel like myself."

"Don't worry," Jake said. "We're almost there." Even as he spoke, they passed over the last ridge of high mountains and began their descent into the valley. The night shrouded them, and only the sharpest of eyes could have detected the two small specks flying over the mountains. Jake kept the flyer close to the ground, and after a time that seemed like an eternity, he landed the flyer just in front of the open door of his garage.

Izhana jumped to the ground as soon as the flyer landed and kept near the feet of her mistress. Jake helped Silorè off her seat, and they all hurried together into the house. Faluin saw them inside and then took off again to see whether they had been followed. Jake left Silorè sitting on a chair in the kitchen while he went back outside to push the flyer into the garage.

As he started back around to the front door, Jake spied the constable's deputy running up the road. The deputy's pace slowed as he approached, and by the time he was within speaking distance, he was quite out of breath.

"I saw…that light…in the sky," he panted, "and I went to the constable. He woke me up and said I should come up here to check on you."

"I'm fine, thank you," Jake said. He turned to go inside but then stopped suddenly. "Actually, there is something you can do for me."

"What is it?"

"Go and fetch the doctor," Jake said. "Tell him to come here as quickly as he can but quietly."

The deputy looked confused, but he obeyed. With a deep breath and a weary groan, he turned and ran back to the town. Jake went into the house, stepping once more over the splinters of the shattered door. Silorè was sitting with her head in her hands, the white tresses of her hair flowing through her fingers. Izhana sat on the floor looking up at her mistress.

"I've sent for the doctor," Jake said. "He should be here soon."

"A doctor of Thalanin?" Izhana scoffed.

Jake shrugged. "It's the best I can do," he said. "A doctor from hCathad would take too long to get here, if I could get him to come to a Thalanin village at all. And there's a chance he would make known that you both are here."

"I'm sure your doctor will suffice," Silorè said, not looking up. She closed her eyes and nodded as if she would fall asleep.

Jake knew he must try to keep her awake. "You're a labnerè,[16] aren't you?" he said. "I mean, you didn't dye your hair or eyes or anything like that?"

Silorè shook her head and sat up tall in her chair, though not without effort. "No, I am a true labnerè," she said with a broad smile. "Were I not, I certainly wouldn't go making myself up pretending to be one. That would be an insult to all labnerèn. To be labnerè is a birthright, and it brings with it both blessing and curse." The corner of her mouth turned up in a sneer, and her tone changed to one of unbounded pride.

"How so?" Jake said, noting the change in her.

Silorè sighed. "I suppose it can't be helped," she said, "but it seems no one can regard labnerèn with simple kindness. We are sources of bitter jealousy to some. To others we are objects of amorous affection. You must admit there is truth in that."

Jake turned red, for even as she looked at him, he felt his heartbeat quicken. "I…uh," he said, reverting to English, as was his manner when he was nervous or embarrassed. "I don't quite know what to say."

"Don't worry; how could you?" she said, answering him in English. She spoke the language well—as well as any Thalavè in the valley. "I'm probably the only labnerè you've met." She frowned suddenly. "But I am a bit offended that you don't remember me."

"I'm sorry," Jake replied. "Faluin seemed to know your name, but I'm afraid I don't remember you at all."

16 The term *labnerè* is used to describe Nanyavèn women who possess certain physical characteristics. Labnerè women have eyes of dark blue or violet, a light complexion, and brunette hair streaked with white throughout but especially around the face. Only women are labnerè, and up to the time of this story, there have been no instances of a Thalavè possessing labnerè characteristics. Instances of labnerè women are very rare—about one in two million—and the features first appear in early childhood.

"I suppose that's understandable," she said. "After all, you were young when last I was here."

"So you *have* been here before?"

"Yes, on several occasions," said Silorè. "It was quite long ago—or at least it would seem long to you. My family was good friends with yours, and we lived all together for many years. Even after you moved to Rithonon, we visited from time to time. Things grew too dangerous though—for us and for you—and so we stayed away."

"Dangerous?" Jake said. "What do you—"

He did not finish his question, for at that moment he heard footsteps outside. He went to the door and welcomed in the constable and his deputy. Behind them followed Angus Stafford—the only doctor in Brown Hill. Tagging along at the rear and carrying a large black bag was the doctor's apprentice, a boy by the name of Blaine. Each of the four visitors froze at the sight of Silorè.

"Good evening, gentlemen," Silorè said in English. "Pardon me if I don't get up. I'm feeling a bit dizzy just now."

"She's injured her head," Jake said to the doctor, "but I'm not sure how seriously."

The doctor looked from Jake to Silorè, and it seemed to Jake that there were a hundred questions in his mind that he did not know how to ask. Instead he called to his apprentice, who brought forth the large bag, and he made everyone else go out.

When Jake and the two lawmen were outside, the constable spoke. "Who is she?" he said. "And where did she come from? Does she have something to do with that light in the sky?"

"I don't know how much I ought to say," Jake said. "And I don't know exactly what's going on, but we both—she and I—are in some kind of trouble."

"What sort of trouble?" the constable asked.

“That light you saw was the fire trail of her ship,” Jake said. “It crashed in the mountains, and even now there’s a small army out looking for her. We must make sure no one knows she’s here—especially anyone from hCathad who comes poking around.”

The constable looked worried. “I can’t do that,” he said. “If I don’t report this, the folks in hCathad won’t like it. I don’t know what they’ll do to me.”

“What they’ll do to you?” Jake cried. “Who knows what they’ll do to her! They tried to kill her just now!”

“But why?” the deputy said.

“I don’t know,” Jake said. “There’s something strange going on here, and I don’t like it.”

Jake turned to the kitchen window and watched as the doctor shone a light into Silorè’s eyes. The doctor seemed nervous for some reason, and his whole arm was shaking. Silorè, on the other hand, sat still, her hands folded before her. She did not smile, and she held herself in perfect posture. Jake thought she looked annoyed.

The constable sighed, and Jake turned back to him. “What do you want me to do?” the constable said.

“She’s got to get off Rithonon,” said Jake, “and maybe I do too. We’ve got to find some sort of transport.”

The constable looked at his deputy, who merely shrugged. “Very well,” the constable said. “But I can’t guarantee what will happen. If these folks from hCathad are looking for her, as you say, then I’m not sure what I can do to protect you both. This whole business is strange. I’ve never seen anything like it in all my days.”

At that moment the doctor’s apprentice ran out the door and down the path to the village. Jake returned to the kitchen and found Silorè sitting in her chair, with Izhana at her feet, and the doctor packing his large black bag.

"She's had a nasty knock on the head," the doctor said. "But there's no serious injury. Her ankle's a bit swollen, but nothing that shouldn't mend with a bit of rest. I've sent Blaine to fetch something for the pain and bruising, but other than that, there's not much I can do."

"Thank you, Doctor," Silorè said politely.

The doctor tipped his hat and walked out the door. As he passed by, the doctor gave Jake a dubious look but said nothing more. He joined the lawmen outside, and together the three walked back to the village. Jake stood outside and watched them go, and when he came back inside, Silorè had slumped forward in her chair again and put her hands to her head.

"How are you feeling?" Jake asked.

"Rotten," Silorè said. "But I suppose I'll be better with time. Unfortunately we have precious little of that. We cannot stay here long."

"Would you mind telling me what this is all about?" Jake said. "You're being very familiar with me, and you seem at home here. Forgive me, but I don't know what to make of you."

Silorè smiled and sat back, looking Jake up and down. "You know," she said, "you're very much like them—your parents, that is. We were friends for a long time. I knew your father his entire life. I watched him grow up, and I remember when he brought your mother into the family. She was a bit shocked at all this."

"At what?" Jake said. "See, that's just what I mean: you know more about me than I do. You're talking about things as if I should understand them, but I don't."

"I suppose not," Silorè said sadly. "Maybe they wanted it that way—to protect you, I suppose, or to keep you from worry." She sighed and brushed her white tresses away from her face. "Let me put it this way, Thalani," she said. "What is every Thalani's dream?"

"Dream?" Jake pondered a moment what she might mean. His thoughts flew to Samantha, and he suddenly understood. "Well," he said, "I suppose it would be to see Earth."

"What would you say if I told you that you *have* seen it?" said Silorè. "And that you lived there when you were very young? That you were even born there?"

Jake sat still for a moment, as if the words took time to reach him. "No," he said at last. "No, that's not possible. I've always lived here—on Rithonon."

"You mean to tell me you don't remember?"

"Remember what?"

"Summertime," Silorè said. A faraway look suddenly came into her eyes, as if she could see across many years to a time that would never come again. "Walking with you through sunlit fields in the summer season of Earth. You were very small and so curious about everything. I remember one time I took you on a picnic, and you fell on a rock and skinned your elbow. You cried very loudly and made me kiss your arm."

Silorè laughed as Jake turned pale with embarrassment.

"I remember summers from when I was a child," said Jake. "There are many images in my mind, but they always seemed to be memories of Rithonon. Forgive me, but I don't remember you in any of them."

"I understand," Silorè replied. "You were young, and your life has changed so much. It's easy to see how you could forget."

"When did we leave Earth?" Jake said.

"You were about four years old," Silorè said. "The Kenornin had become too aggressive on Earth. Somehow they kept sneaking past our scouts and watchmen. Then one terrible night"—pain flashed across her face—"they attacked without warning or provocation. That's when you left. That's when you came here."

At that moment footsteps came up the lane outside, and Blain shyly entered the kitchen carrying a small bottle. "Pardon," he said, "but the doctor asked me to bring this to you." His hands shook as he handed the bottle to Silorè. When she winked at him and smiled, he went red at the ears. "Um," he continued, "the doctor said fifteen drops twice a day. If you can't stand the taste, you can take them in a bit of water."

"Thank you," Silorè said in a saccharin voice. Blain blushed again and ran out the door as fast as he could. Silorè chuckled and placed the bottle on the table beside her. "Silly boy," she said. "It doesn't take much to make them weak at the knees. Don't you agree?" She leaned forward and grinned. Jake fidgeted, feeling he was being toyed with.

Silorè sat back, laughing and running her fingers through her hair. "You never change," she said. "Indeed nothing seems to have changed at all, and I haven't been in this house in…oh, I'd say twelve years. You were still young, but I was sure you'd remember."

"Begging your pardon," Jake said, "but how old are you exactly?"

Silorè seemed suddenly indignant. "If you must know," she said, "I've only last month passed my eighty-fourth year."

Jake must have made a face, for Silorè laughed at him again. "Too old?" she asked.

"No, not at all," Jake said quickly. "It's just that…well, wouldn't that make you older than my grandparents?"

Silorè's eyes grew cold. "Your grandfather and I were born around the same time," she said. "My family lived on Earth for quite a while, and so Vincent and I grew up together. We were great friends, and we went to the same Thalanin school. All the other children—especially the Thalavèn—used to laugh at my hair. They were always jealous of me, I suppose, and they upset me terribly.

But your grandfather stood up for me. I don't suppose we had any other friends save for each other.

"Then we grew older…and we drifted apart. I was still young, but he had to grow up fast—like all you Thalanin do. He met your grandmother at university, and they were married soon after. By that time I was living back on Iderat, and though I visited Earth on occasion, your grandfather and I were never so close again. I suppose that's for the best."

Jake marvelled at her, for though she looked young, she spoke as an old woman, recounting memories full of both joy and sorrow. She seemed to sense his wonder, for she suddenly smiled at him. "Then your father came along," she said, "and we became great friends as well. He called me 'auntie,' and I would sneak him candies from Iderat whenever we visited Earth. So much like your grandfather he was, just as you are so much like both of them. When he grew up, he would often visit Iderat for months at a time. I think he preferred Iderat to Earth, and he spoke Nanyan better than any Thalani I have met—except perhaps for you.

"Your father met your mother during a time when he was travelling all over the Earth. She came from a wealthy family, and she spoke several Thalanin languages. She was terrified when she learned about your father's family and mine. Earth-folk don't know about us, and our family tries to keep it that way.

"Anyway, your mother nearly left him when he told her about the Nanyanin, but eventually she came to accept the truth as it was. They were married, and you were born not many years later.

"You were a lively child, very loud and always at the centre of attention. On Earth you were quite spoiled, and I'm afraid I had a hand in that. Life was happier then. It doesn't seem all that long ago…" She trailed off and sighed, looking out the window at the night-covered lands all about. The ruins of the ancient citadel stood cold and grey in the dim starlight.

"What changed?" Jake asked.

"The Kenornin did," said Silorè. "They attacked so suddenly and secretly that we did not detect them until it was too late. They were relentless and thorough, and they sought out many of your distant relations—some of whom even we were not aware of. They killed them all in a matter of hours. In the end you and your parents were the only ones we got away. We brought you here to Rithonon, and here we mourned the dead and all we had lost.

"Your parents decided not to change their name, though we advised them to do so. They took great pride in that name, and they would not hide it. Thankfully Connolly is not too uncommon a name for Thalanin.

"Because your father spoke Nanyan so well, it was decided he would become a vèralamenasi, and to that end your parents started to collect birds. That's when Faluin came, and he could not be tamed by any—not even by members of my family who are expert in these matters. He seemed to listen only to you, so he became yours.

"In those early days after your family came to Rithonon, I visited in secret with members of my family, and we would talk with your parents about many things. The Kenornin had ceased searching for your family, and they began to hunt mine in earnest. Most of my family are now scattered throughout the galaxy in order to protect them. There used to be so many of us, and now the Itarlavon are diminishing."

She paused for a moment, as though she were deep in thought.

"Eventually things became too dangerous," she continued. "We had to limit our travel, and we stopped visiting altogether. I suppose that's why you don't remember us."

Jake ran his fingers through his hair. "But why?" he said. "Why would the Kenornin do this? What's my family ever done?"

"Now we come to it," said Silorè. "The story of your family goes far back into the past—indeed further back than your family name.

"In days long ago, the Kenornin had begun a widespread invasion of the Earth, and my family was desperately trying to drive them off. In the end my family succeeded, but their doings caught the attention of many kingdoms north of the Great Sea. Thousands of soldiers went out in search of my family, and they could not escape, for the skies were being watched.

"Most of my family found shelter, but Phèlimon, son of the patriarch, was travelling alone in a northern isle and was discovered by the rulers of that land. It was then that one of your ancestors—I believe his name was Wyne—sheltered Phèlimon from those who sought his life. Wyne and his kindred fought to protect my family, and from that day on the fates of our two houses have been intertwined. Many times has my family asked yours for help, and your family in turn had been protected through many generations.

"It is for this history of unity that the Kenornin hate you, but if you ask what has stirred their ire in these latter years, I will tell you. Your great-grandfather[17] Silas Connolly fought the Kenornin invasion at the end of the last war. He killed General Koroson, brother of Eratizhal, and he drove the last Kenornin from Tolitar.[18] From that time the Kenornin have pursued your family with greater resolve."

She paused a moment and took a breath. "After the war some of my family returned to Earth. We thought we would be safe there, but

17 Nanyan: *tanathi*.

18 Earth's sun. In Nanyan, the name of a star is often used to refer to its entire planetary system.

it proved difficult to protect ourselves. The Earth is changing, and remaining secret grows more difficult all the time.

"Even so, we lived happily together, and your family prospered, though their numbers were few. We hoped that at last we might have peace, but then on that terrible night, we lost all save for you and your parents. Even your grandfather, he…" She stopped suddenly, and Jake realized her eyes were wet. Izhana nuzzled her leg, and Silorè reached down and stroked her head.

"You loved my family very much," Jake said softly.

Silorè turned her face to him in an instant. "Of course I did!" she snapped. "All of them!" The change in her was so sudden that Jake nearly fell backwards in his chair. He fell silent, afraid to say anything more. Silorè turned to the window and did not speak for a while. Izhana sat by her side, rubbing her head against Silorè's hand.

"He sacrificed himself for you all," Silorè said at last, still facing the window. "Your grandfather, I mean. He led the Kenornin astray and allowed you all to escape—though not without great protest from your father. Your grandfather would not let him go with him, for he would not allow his grandson to grow up fatherless.

"He died to save you, and I wept for him more than for any other. He…was my friend, and I…I loved him dearly. I had always dreaded saying goodbye to him—as I have done with many Thalanin—but he was not yet come to old age, and I thought he would live still many years." She looked to Jake, and her cheeks glistened with tears. Her brow was furrowed, and a flame burned in her eyes. "The Kenornin are vicious."

Jake had no reply.

Silorè took a deep breath. "And that…" she continued. "That is why we tried to hide you on another world, and we thought that would be enough. For many years it was, but in the end the Kenornin learned you were living on Rithonon. By the time we discovered they were on the planet, the search for your family had already begun. My parents rushed here to help you escape, and they brought a ship they thought could make the journey."

"Wait, I remember them!" Jake said suddenly. "I do! I remember now. They were the friends my parents were going on holiday with. All this time, and I never understood!"

Silorè nodded. "Both your parents and mine must have known the danger and decided to leave you behind," she said. "It was a trap, and they did not realize it until it was too late. If they stayed, they would be found in time, and if they departed, the Kenornin were waiting above the planet to destroy their ship. There was no escape for them.

"That is why they went on holiday without you. They wanted the Kenornin to believe that all three of your family had perished. It was a clever plan—so clever indeed that until recently, even we believed you dead. We never bothered to return to this place, and the Kenornin left Rithonon having never learned where you were living."

A sudden thought struck Jake like a heavy weight. "Hold on!" he said. "Your parents…They…You don't mean to say…that they were killed too?"

Silorè bit her lower lip and nodded, and then she looked away. Tears pooled in her violet eyes and streamed down her face. The sight of her pained his heart, and he swallowed hard to rid himself of the lump growing in his throat. He wanted to say something, but he could not find the words.

When Silorè continued, her voice faltered and cracked. "I pleaded with them not to go, for I feared that something terrible would happen. My brother offered to go in their place, but my parents would not yield.

"I must admit that for some time after they were gone, I felt no love for any of your family, and I felt—no, I still feel—terrible shame over hating the dead. I thought it was so foolish—that at least if you all had died anyway, you might as well have died alone." Another tear ran down her cheek. "I have lived with this shame and guilt of hatred for so long, but my brother…he convinced me at last of what I already knew—that my parents would gladly have given their lives for your family. And so they did."

Silorè wiped the tears from her eyes and turned back to Jake. She could not look at him but stared at the floor instead. "I do love your family," she said. "That's why I volunteered to come here. When we heard you were alive, I was overjoyed, and I felt it my duty to come after you. My brother was against it, as was my great-grandfather, but they could not withstand me." The corner of her mouth turned upward proudly. "I convinced them both that I must be the one to return to Rithonon, and here I am. It seems we have each saved one another already."

A distant look suddenly came into her eyes, and she stared beyond the walls of the room. "You know," she said as if continuing a thought, "you and I are very much alike: we are both the last of our houses. Let's hope it isn't a true end and that our families may go on living long after we are gone."

Jake and Silorè sat in silence for a great while. Jake puzzled over all Silorè had said. The night grew dark, and he felt weary in mind and in heart. Outside, the last of the summer crickets chirped a farewell song, and the music of cattle-bells clinked in the surrounding hills. No sound came up from Brown Hill, and the mountains carried no noise of the search beyond them.

Silorè suddenly stretched and deeply yawned. "The day is gone," she said, rising to her feet, "and I've stayed awake much longer than I had intended."

"I'm sorry if I've kept you from sleep," Jake said.

"No, it isn't your doing," she answered. "I was worried the searchers might discover where I had gone, but I don't fear that any longer. We weren't spotted or followed, for had we been, the searchers would have tracked us here already."

"So you think it is safe to remain here?" Jake asked nervously. The danger had nearly fled from his mind while he talked with Silorè.

"At least until morning," Silorè said. "That search of theirs will keep them busy long enough. As for that fellow who was here earlier today, I wouldn't worry about him. For one, he does not yet know I have found you. For another, that crash has caused quite a stir—even in your little town. There are many eyes on the watch tonight, and the Kenornin will not risk being seen. Their hope was to get you away secretly, and that has become more difficult for them. We shall stay here tonight, but we must be off in the morning."

"Tomorrow morning?" Jake said. His mind suddenly raced to the festival. With all the goings-on, he had forgotten all about it.

"I know it's sudden," Silorè said, "but you cannot stay here any longer."

"I understand," Jake said. His life on Rithonon felt suddenly more precious to him than ever it had. He wanted nothing more in that moment than to spend the rest of his days in Brown Hill. Or at the very least, he wanted to go to the festival with Samantha. He would have to say goodbye to her now and to the town and to his tower on the hill.

"Will you be all right?" Silorè asked gently.

Jake nodded, and then he took a deep breath and pushed his thoughts aside. "If you'd like somewhere to sleep," he said, feeling somewhat embarrassed, "there's a bed upstairs. It's mine, but you may have it if you wish."

"That's…kind of you," Silorè replied hesitantly, "but there are other rooms, are there not?"

"There are," said Jake, "but they're all sealed. I haven't opened them in years."

Silorè made a face. "Is there nowhere else, then?" she said. "Where will you sleep?"

"There's plenty of straw in the room above. That's where the vèralamen roost. I'll sleep there."

Silorè looked at him with both wonder and disgust. "On a pile of straw?"

"I'll be fine."

Silorè scowled. "If you say so," she said. "And that being the case, I accept your invitation."

As Jake led Silorè up the stairs (with Izhana following close behind), he felt a bit foolish. He had never shown anyone up the tower staircase, let alone a beautiful labnerè girl. They did not speak, and the only sound to be heard was of their own footsteps on the cold stone stairs.

At length they came to the door to Jake's bedroom, and Jake led Silorè inside. He was thankful the room was fairly clean, and he had even remembered to make up the bed late that afternoon. Even so, he took all the linens from the bed and replaced them with a clean set he produced from his wardrobe. Then digging around in the old trunk, he found a spare pillow and placed it at the head of the bed.

"Here you are," he said sheepishly. "It's nothing special, but it suits me."

Silorè walked slowly about the room, frowning at everything. At length she paused beside the bed. "It's quaint," she said, "but it's bound to be better than my ship. There was no room to lie down, and I had to sleep sitting in my chair. It nearly drove me mad."

"This mattress will be more comfortable than that," said Jake, "and if you need anything else, don't hesitate to ask. I'll be right up the stairs. Feel free to make yourself at home."

"Well, thank you," Silorè said with a slight smile. "Now, if you'll excuse me, I'd like very much to get some sleep. Izhana will keep watch tonight. She's been cramped in my ship with little to do but sleep. I'm sure she will welcome the change."

"Indeed, mistress," said Izhana. "A stretch of the legs will do me better than sleep."

"I suppose that's settled," Jake said. "Good night, then."

He was about to turn up the stairs, but the look on Silorè's face made him pause. She looked suddenly worried. "What is it?" he asked.

"My ship," Silorè muttered. "The wireless in my ship transmitted my family's code signal. I destroyed it before I crashed, for I could not risk its capture. Without it we cannot contact my great-grandfather. He will be anxious to hear from me. I must let him know what has happened."

"What did you have in mind?" Jake asked.

"I think my best chance is with your vèralamen. I left mine on the other side of the planet. Tolthir will return home when no one comes for him."

"I could certainly dispatch a message for you," Jake said. "Faluin is swiftest, but I think he's more needed here to keep watch. Besides, he's been circling the valley all day, and even he can grow weary. But I could send off another tonight if you'd like."

Silorè nodded. "I would—very much so."

"Wait here," Jake said. "I know just the bird for this."

Jake went upstairs to the loft where the vèralamen roosted. Many were already asleep, but one large bird like an osprey was perching in the rafters, and he flew down when Jake called him. "What's the word, sir?" he asked. "What does all this mean?"

"I don't have the time to explain it now," Jake said. "I've a message that must be sent at once."

"I should welcome the task, sir," the bird said with a bow. "Where to?"

"I'm not sure yet," Jake said. "Come with me."

The bird was confused for a moment but obediently hopped onto Jake's outstretched arm. Though he was large, the bird was light, and Jake carried him with ease down the stairs.

"This is Isèter,"[19] said Jake when he was back in his bedroom. "He is quite fast, and though he is large, he is difficult to spot. He will deliver the message safely and swiftly." He walked to the window, and Isèter hopped onto the sill. "Go by secret ways," Jake said to him. "But do not linger."

"It shall be so, master," Isèter said with a bow. "But what is the message? And who is the recipient?"

Silorè stepped forward and spoke in a serious tone. "It is to my great-grandfather Zhialamon," she said. "He is patriarch of the house of Itarlavon. He is waiting on the circling moon in the city of Oranthedaren. There you will find a tall tower of blue and silver. Near the middle of the tower, you will see him—an old man with grey hair and beard. Can you find him?"

Isèter bowed. "With great speed, my lady," he said. "And what shall I say to him?"

"Tell him I am safe, though my ship has been destroyed," Silorè said. "Tell him I have found him whom I was seeking and that I await instruction, for I was not prepared for what has befallen. Say that the message is from Rènaliè. Do you have all that?"

"I do," said the bird.

19 Nanyan: "swift-wing."

"Then go," Jake said, "and hurry back with the reply."

"This will be done," Isèter said. Turning, he flew through the open window into the night, vanishing like a stone cast into the sea.

Once Isèter had gone, Jake turned to Silorè. "You didn't tell me you were Zhialamon's great-granddaughter," he said. "Wouldn't that make you some kind of royalty?"

Silorè laughed. "My family has never ruled in that fashion," she said, "nor do we now set up ourselves as lords of Iderat. The people there are free and always have been. My great-grandfather is merely an administrator of Iderat, and though he is the patriarch of my family, he has never used that privilege against anyone. He's a good man, old and wise. He was born in the days of Old Eratzira, and there are few alive today who remember those distant years."

"Still, you're descended from the patriarch of one of the most powerful families in Eratzira," Jake said. "Maybe even the whole galaxy. That's got to count for something."

"Less and less, it seems," Silorè said sadly. "In the high days of our house, we would not have been forced to come here in secret. We could have sent many ships, and no one—not the Kenornin nor anyone else—would dare defy us. But alas, our house has declined in size and influence. There was a time not so long ago when many people supported us in our protection of Earth. These days few see the importance of our labour. We have a duty to the Earth, Thalani, and we cannot abandon it, though everyone else oppose us."

Even as Silorè finished speaking, the tower began to quake, and the droning of the flying machines arose from over the mountains. Jake and Silorè knelt on the bed and looked out the window. The sky was overcast and dark, and they could see little. The nearby mountains stood like tears in the dark fabric of the sky.

Jake suddenly pointed up to a nearby peak. "Look there!" he said. "Do you see them?" Over the mountaintop, the lights of two large airships appeared, flying towards hCathad. A dozen flyers accompanied them, and together they descended into the valley. As the ships drew near, Jake closed the shutters and drew the curtain.

Silorè scoffed. "Hmph! I'll bet they've taken my trunk. I hate the idea of all those rough hands rummaging through my things. I wished I'd retrieved something of my stuff; I could at least do with a nightgown. I'm tired of sleeping in these clothes." She sighed. "Oh well. At least I won't have to sleep in that horrible chair."

"I hope you'll be comfortable enough here," Jake said.

Silorè nodded. "I'll certainly sleep better than I have these past few days."

"Well," Jake stammered, "good night. I hope everything will sort itself out in the morning."

"So do I," Silorè said. "Good night." She smiled at him, and her violet eyes shone with an inner fire that made Jake forget himself for a moment and stare spellbound at her. When he shook himself back to reality, he wondered with embarrassment how long he had stood there looking into her face.

"Um," he said. "Good night, then." He walked backwards out the door, stumbling over his own feet. When he made the stairs, he closed the door behind him and dashed to the next floor.

The vèralamen were all awake now, for the outside noises had roused them. Faluin had returned and stood talking to the others. They all turned to Jake as he entered, and Faluin flew over to him.

"What's the plan, sir?" Faluin said. "I saw Isèter fly off a few moments ago. I am disappointed at not being trusted with the task."

"It isn't for lack of trust," Jake said. "You've done quite enough for today—far more than I can rightly ask of you. Send someone else up to watch tonight. Get some rest."

"Thank you, sir," said Faluin. "I will watch a few more hours yet before I take a respite. I do not trust those flying machines of hCathad. None of those men searching for the girl were well-intentioned. I fear they may start searching the valley now, and if they do, I shall warn you."

Jake nodded, and Faluin flew out into the night.

Then piling straw in a corner of the room, Jake lay himself down. He did not fall asleep right away, for many thoughts filled his mind—not the least of which was the Nanyavè sleeping below in his bed.

At last, listening to the rustling of the night breeze, Jake fell into an uneasy sleep.

Chapter 4

The Town Council

When Jake awoke the next morning, he was first aware of a shooting pain in his neck and shoulder. He had rolled over many times in the night, and his bed of straw had dissipated, leaving him lying with little cushion on the cold stones. He rose slowly and rubbed his neck, and for a moment he wished he had let Silorè sleep in one of the sealed rooms.

Most of the vèralamen were gone, as was their habit in the mornings. Faluin was nowhere to be seen, and Jake groaned, realising Faluin had stayed out all night. He walked to the window and gave a sharp whistle, and in a few moments a winded Faluin landed on the windowsill.

"All's well, sir," said Faluin with effort. "No sign of any searchers in the valley all night. Either they gave up or are waiting for morning."

"Let's hope it's the former," said Jake. "In the meantime I want to know why you've not been resting."

Faluin scowled. "I could go a while longer yet," he said. "I do not tire easily."

"Yes," Jake said doubtfully as Faluin beat his wings to keep himself awake. "I see that all too well."

Jake crossed to the storage room and opened the wooden door. On the floor lay a cage made of tightly woven wire. As daylight struck it, a chorus of chirping arose, for climbing on all sides of the cage were hundreds of large crickets. They were no ordinary insects; they were automatons Jake bred to feed to the vèralamen.

Jake pulled a few crickets from the cage and tossed them to Faluin and to the few others that had remained in the tower. One cricket escaped through a window, but one of the birds was right after him and returned with the insect in his mouth.

"I'll be back soon," Jake said as he walked to the stairs. He turned to Faluin. "And I mean it: get some sleep. There are plenty of others who can carry on while you rest."

Faluin gave no answer.

Leaving the roost, Jake descended the stairs. He had intended to see if Silorè was awake, but when he reached his bedroom door, he found Izhana standing guard before it.

"You cannot enter," Izhana said firmly. "My mistress is asleep."

"Well then, I'll wake her," said Jake.

"You cannot go in," Izhana said, stepping toward him. "My mistress is not dressed."

Jake flushed. "Well then," he said, flustered, "*you* go wake her."

"She had ordered me to let her sleep," Izhana said. "She is tired, and I shan't wake her just because you wish it."

Jake shook his head. "Fine," he said, "but see that she rises soon. I'll be back in a bit."

A few minutes later, Jake was walking down the path to the village. Breakfast was the first order of the day. The morning had dawned cool and clear. The clouds of the previous night had blown away, and the sun shone bright in the valley. No haze hung in the air, and Jake could see clearly all the lands surrounding the town.

As he walked into town, he passed Tara Flanders, the cobbler's wife, who was going about tying ribbons to all the lampposts for the festival. “Good morning,” Jake said cheerfully. She did not answer but turned up her nose and continued down the street. Jake stood still a moment, puzzled by her behaviour.

Jake shook his head and walked on, but as he went, many whispers followed him, and many eyes watched him pass by. A dustman coming towards him stopped pushing his cart a moment and tipped his hat to Jake with a laugh and a sly grin. Unnerved, Jake hurried on and met the Reverend John Samuelson, who greeted Jake nervously from across the street and walked quickly on his way.

What's going on? Jake thought. He had never been treated so strangely before.

In a state of confusion, Jake arrived at the front door of the Grey Griffin. As he reached for the knob, the door suddenly flew open before him, and out stepped Samantha, looking none too happy. Her hair was dishevelled, and she glared at him with wild eyes. In her right hand she held a long kitchen knife.

“Well?” she said with a malice Jake had not seen in her before.

Jake took a step backwards. “Well what?”

“You know very well what I mean.”

“I…” Jake stuttered. “Well…”

“Who is she?”

Jake tensed. Now he understood. “She's an…old friend?”

Samantha's look did not improve, and she turned the knife in her fingers. Jake hoped she had brought out the knife by accident, though as she glowered at him, he began to worry. In her eyes there was only disbelief.

“It's the truth!” Jake insisted when she did not speak. “My family has known her for years. She's a Nanyavè, and she's rather old. She was friends with my grandfather when they were children.”

"And you felt it would be impolite to turn her out, I suppose?" said Samantha. "If you didn't want to throw her out in the cold, why didn't you bring her down to the inn? We would have been *happy* to accommodate her." The way she said "happy" chilled Jake's blood.

"You all seemed so busy down here with the festival and all," Jake said, "I just didn't want to make trouble for you."

Samantha's eyes grew large, and Jake reckoned he must have said something wrong. "Make trouble?" she said. "You *didn't want to make trouble*? Well, you've made a right nause-up of that!"

"I suppose I have done," said Jake weakly. "How did you know about her? She only arrived last night."

Samantha pointed the knife in his face. "Everyone knows about *her*," she said. "That's all anyone's been talking about this morning. Do you know how embarrassing it is? Do you know what they're saying?"

Jake stiffened. "What do you mean? What are they saying?"

Samantha's scowl deepened. "Think about it," she said. "You and a strange girl alone in that tower—what are people supposed to think?"

"Well," Jake said, reluctant to betray his comprehension, "whatever they say, I'm sure it isn't true."

"I don't care!" Samantha said quite loudly. "It was still stupid to let her stay with you. Why do you have to be so *stupid*?" She looked as if she would burst into tears, but her eyes were flaming with an unquenchable fire.

"I guess I just wasn't thinking about it that way," Jake said. "And it was late, and I didn't want to bother anybody."

"We get travellers in late at night all the time," Samantha said. "You know that! Face it—you're just being stupid!" Her voice grew raspy from shouting. "Just go," she said. "I don't really want to see you right now."

"Well, can't I at least get some breakfast?" Jake asked.

Samantha was livid. "You really expect me to let you come in?"

"Well…no," Jake said sheepishly. "Actually, I need takeaway."

Samantha shrieked with rage and stamped back inside, slamming the door in his face. A few guests on the second storey peeked out their windows to see what the commotion was about. Jake felt their eyes boring into his back as he walked away, wondering whether that would be the last time he would see Samantha or the Griffin.

As he started towards home, Jake spied the constable walking up the opposite side of the street. The moment he saw Jake, he turned around at once and hurried back the way he had come.

"Oi!" Jake called out and crossed the street. The constable tried to get away, but Jake was too quick for him. "All right then," Jake said as the constable gave up running and faced him. "What's going on?"

The constable looked pale. "I'm…not quite sure I know what you mean," he stammered.

"About the girl!" Jake said. "That's why everyone's been acting so strange to me. You've been telling everyone about her, haven't you?"

"Well, I didn't mean to," said the constable. "It just sort of happened. A man can't keep silent about someone like her, can he? I'd never seen a labnerè lady before."

"That's not the point!" said Jake. "No one's supposed to know she's here. She's in danger; we're both in danger!"

"I *am* sorry," the constable said innocently. "I didn't know things would get so far out of hand. I meant to tell only the magistrate."

Jake felt a sudden knot in his stomach. "You told Appleton?" he croaked.

"Well," the constable stammered, "I usually tell him news that affects the town—particularly if there are strange folk about. I also told him about that fellow who broke down your door. You can't fault me for that one."

"No, I suppose not."

"Now, if you'll excuse me," the constable said, trying to sound important, "I have a lot to do this morning. I'll be by to check on you later."

The constable shuffled off down the street, walking briskly in case Jake should give chase. With a heavy heart and an empty stomach, Jake trudged out of town and climbed the hill towards the tower.

Faluin met him halfway up the road. "A group of men just arrived," said Faluin. "I believe they are lawmen of hCathad. They asked for you, but I said you were out. They said they'd wait till you returned."

"I don't really care to see them," Jake said. "Is Silorè still inside?"

"She is."

"Do they know she's there?"

"I don't think so," Faluin said, "but I don't think they're looking for her."

"Even so," said Jake, "I have to find a way to get rid of them."

Jake rushed to the house but slowed as he neared the front door. He did not want to appear hasty. In the road before the tower lay a large open-air flyer with many seats. Jake could not remember ever having seen such a vehicle before, and he walked cautiously into the house, eyeing the strange vehicle.

Inside the kitchen waited five Nanyanin men dressed in the dark-grey uniform typical of security men of hCathad. They glared at Jake as he walked in. None of them was smiling.

One man stood forward as Jake entered. He was taller than the rest, and he wore a dark-blue badge upon his chest. "Good morning," he said. "Are you Dasiom Javani?"

"That is my Nanyan name," Jake said evenly.

"We received word of a break-in here yesterday."

Jake looked at the kitchen door lying on the floor in splinters. "Obviously," he said. He did not like this man's look or tone.

"A man dressed as an Overseer?"

"He did look like one, yes."

"I see," the man said, drawing closer. "It seems you have been the victim of a misunderstanding. These things do happen sometimes."

"When?" Jake scoffed. "This was no accident. Even if he was an Overseer, that shouldn't excuse him from breaking into a man's home."

"Very well," the man said. "Perhaps you would like to come back with us and file your complaint before the magistrate in hCathad."

The other men rose and formed a half-circle around Jake. Jake took a step back, looking side to side at the figures towering over him. "I can't go now," said Jake, "and I shouldn't have to. Besides, I've got work to do, and if I go to hCathad now, it'll be hours before I get back."

Jake tried to walk around them, but they barred his way.

"I must insist," said the tall man, taking Jake by the arm.

Jake froze as he looked into the man's face. "You!" he said. "It's you, isn't it? You were the one here yesterday. You're no lawman. What are you doing here?"

The man seemed not to hear. "Take him," he said to the others. "Put him on the flyer. Bind him if he won't cooperate." Two men came forward and grabbed Jake roughly by the arms. Their grip was paralyzing, and Jake could do nothing to wriggle free. He managed to kick one of the men in the shin and received a punch in the gut for his efforts. The other men stepped forward to subdue Jake, picking him up with ease and carrying him away.

A commanding voice suddenly rose over the clamour. “Stop!”

The men turned around to see Silorè standing at the foot of the stairs. A look of defiance was in her eyes, and she stood with her hands on her hips, glaring at the men with such a stare that for a moment no one moved.

Shaking himself from her gaze, the tall man stepped towards her. “So you’re here too,” he said. “I suppose I should have guessed it. A profitable morning this will be indeed!”

“Not for you, Ianjori,” Silorè said, stepping down from the stair. “Did you think this disguise could hide you from me?”

“It has worked well enough on many other fools,” Ianjori hissed. “You should have stayed on Iderat with your great-grandfather and the few filthy cowards that remain of his household. Little girls shouldn’t stray far from home.”

Silorè’s expression flinched for but an instant before growing cold again. “Let him go.”

“Don’t worry,” said Ianjori with a grin. “You’re coming with him.”

Two of his men had slipped behind her, and one of them now reached out to grab her arm. Silorè’s head whipped around to face him, and her labnerè hair flew about her. Her violet eyes seemed to pierce the man, who, being struck with sudden fear, released her. The other man did not move towards her but looked to Ianjori for instruction.

“What are you waiting for?” Ianjori said. “Grab her! Bring her out to the ship.”

As the men reached out to seize her, a streak of red and brown sprang from the top of the stairs. The two men jumped back as they were struck by a flurry of claws and teeth. Izhana landed on the floor before Silorè's feet, growling and showing her fangs.

Ianjori drew a knife and stepped towards Silorè, but Izhana sprang on him, sinking her teeth into his right arm. The two men holding Jake tried to carry him away, but they were each struck down in turn by Izhana. She had left Ianjori lying on the ground and nursing a deep wound.

As Jake got back on his feet, Silorè rushed forward and grabbed his hand. "Hurry!" she shouted, and together the two ran out the door and down the hill, with Izhana close at their heels. At that moment Faluin suddenly appeared, swooping down over their heads with two other vèralamen he had rallied, and they fought with the Nanyan men so that they could not pursue.

"Where can we go?" Silorè asked as she, Jake, and Izhana reached the outskirts of the village.

Jake could not stop and think, and the first place that came to his mind was the Grey Griffin. He led her there, weaving in and out of streets past many startled townsfolk. No one was in the courtyard of the Griffin when they arrived, and all the shutters were closed. Jake threw open the front door and hurried Silorè inside. Izhana narrowly escaped being crushed as Jake slammed the door behind them.

The common-room was nearly empty, and many chairs lay upturned on their tables. Only the two old men remained, playing a slow game of draughts. The noise of the sudden entrance broke the men's concentration, and they both looked up from their game. Startled at the sight of Silorè and her labnerè hair, they did not speak.

As Jake looked out the window for signs of pursuit, he found Silorè was looking him over. "Are you hurt?" she asked urgently.

"I don't think so," Jake said.

Silorè grabbed his arms and looked them up and down. "No cuts?" she said. "No scratches?"

"No," Jake said. "Why?"

Before Silorè could answer, Thaddeus Brown entered from the kitchen, wiping his hands on a towel. He was not a tall man, but his chest and arms were of great girth. Jake had always been frightened of him, for he was Samantha's father, and he owned the Grey Griffin. He was, as a rule, not pleased to see Jake, but this morning he seemed less amiable than usual. "What are you doing here, Jake?" he asked. "And who is this you've brought with you?"

"Good morning, sir," Jake said nervously. "Something rather… strange has just happened, and—"

Samantha suddenly burst through the kitchen door. Her eyes were wide and bloodshot, and at the sight of Jake and Silorè, the colour of her face quickly changed to bright pink. Jake almost expected her to breathe fire and consume him in a blaze of red flame, but she stood some distance behind her father and did not speak.

"Please," Jake said to Thaddeus, "could we talk somewhere else? They may be right behind us."

Thaddeus looked at both Jake and Silorè suspiciously. "Come with me," he said, and he led them away. Samantha cut in front of Jake and turned up her nose at him. Jake smiled weakly at her but said nothing.

Thaddeus brought Jake, Silorè, Izhana, and his daughter through the kitchen, past several stoves and a large sink piled high with breakfast dishes. At a long table down the centre, Mrs Brown stood kneading balls of dough. She seemed not to notice the five of them pass her by.

At the back of the kitchen stood a split-door leading to the alley behind the inn. The top half was open, and Thaddeus took a quick look outside before shutting and bolting both halves to the doorpost.

The five moved to a narrow passage beside the cellar stair, and Thaddeus turned to Jake and Silorè. "Now then," he said. "Would you mind telling me what this is about?"

Jake quickly told the tale of the strange messages and the crash landing and how he had rescued Silorè from the searchers in the valley over the mountains. He told of the return of Ianjori and how he and his followers had tried to abduct him and Silorè. Samantha listened, but her mood did not improve.

When Jake had finished, Thaddeus scratched his head and stood thinking for a moment. "Very strange indeed," he said. "I don't know what to make of it, and I'm at a loss to know what to do." He turned to Silorè. "What do you think, Miss?"

Silorè spoke calmly. "I'm afraid I'm at a loss as well," she said. "Jake and I are now trapped in this town, and our pursuers will be watching the roads and the skies. They will be more careful now, for they cannot risk any more commotion than what they have already caused. Even so, I'm afraid we may have put the whole town in jeopardy, and we will need help to escape."

"Who's 'we'?" Samantha said, arms folded across her chest.

"Both Jake and myself," said Silorè. "He is not safe here, and neither is anyone in this town so long as he remains. We must leave as soon as we can manage."

Samantha's expression changed instantly, and she looked at Jake with distress. Her anger had melted away.

Thaddeus stroked his chin. "Tonight's the festival," he said. "Maybe that will work in your favour." He turned to his daughter. "Sam, take them upstairs. They should be safe there. I'll be back in a bit, and maybe we'll be able to sort this out. Off you all go then!"

He rushed out the back door and into the alley. The sound of his footsteps diminished down the road, and Samantha bolted the door after him. When she turned around again, her wrath had returned.

"Come on," she said. "Follow me." She led them from the kitchen into the common-room, looking about first to see that there was no one waiting for them. She hurried them up the stairs and into a narrow corridor that wound away in two directions. The Grey Griffin was much bigger inside than it had looked from the outside, and the passages twisted and turned like a labyrinth. Jake had never been upstairs in the Griffin, and he soon lost all sense of direction.

At the end of a winding hallway, Samantha opened a door leading to a narrow staircase. She made them go up ahead of her, and she followed behind, securing the door after them. The stairway led up to a dimly lit room beneath a slanted roof supported by many wooden beams. A few round windows were set in the walls and ceiling, and they each had curtains closed in front of them so that they let in very little light.

Samantha had brought them to the uppermost part of the Griffin, inside the tallest gable of the roof. Jake and Silorè had stopped at the top of the stairs, but Samantha pushed past them into the room. On a nearby table, she lit a lantern that flickered to life with a steady red flame.

In the lantern light, Jake could see that the room in which they stood was furnished with several chairs and a long couch surrounding a low table and a matted rug. A lamp hung from the ceiling, but it gave no light. Three doors were set in the surrounding walls, and a short corridor opened at the far end of the room.

"This is where your family lives, isn't it?" said Jake. "I never knew this was up here."

"Yes, this is our home," Samantha said coldly. "Those Nanyanin won't look for you here. Stay until my father returns, and please make yourselves at home. I have work to do in the kitchen." As she turned to the stairs, she shot a glance at Jake that made his blood run cold. She walked slowly down the stairs, and when she had gone out, she shut the door behind her with such force that the wooden rafters shuddered and groaned.

While Jake stood alone facing the staircase, Silorè began to walk about the room, hesitating to sit on any of the furniture. "This place is rather rustic," she said. "Wouldn't you say?"

"I suppose," Jake mumbled and turned from the stairs. "Are you all right?"

Silorè seemed flustered, fidgeting with her hands. "I'm fine," she said. "I just…this room feels like my ship again—confining, like a cage." She frowned. "And stuffy." She went to the nearest window and threw it open, taking a deep breath of fresh air.

At that moment a bird came hurtling through the open window and crashed upon the floor. His entrance so startled Silorè that she jumped back with a shriek and stumbled into a nearby chair. Jake rushed to where the bird had fallen and found Isèter looking ruffled and quite exhausted.

Jake and Silorè both knelt beside Isèter. "Is he all right?" Silorè asked.

Jake looked him over. "Just a bit winded," he said. "He is swift but hasn't much endurance."

Isèter took a few moments to catch his breath before he stood to his feet. "Miss[20] Rènaliè," he said, bowing low to Silorè, "I have a message for you from Isasi."

"That will be my great-grandfather," Silorè said. "Let's have it then."

The bird cleared his throat and spoke in a voice clear and commanding. "Isasi sends that he is pleased you are safe and that you have found what you were seeking. He bids you return to him and suggests it would be safest to take the ferry to Telethoram, if you

20 Nanyan: *azhathè*—a title often used to address a young woman. It is the shorter version (*phatha*) of *azhdorathè*.

can manage it. He says he will meet you at the 'seventh place'—whatever that may mean."

"The ferry?" Jake asked.

"I had considered it," Silorè replied, "but the trouble will be getting there. The nearest port is at Thesatra, and that is a long way from here. We cannot now take your flyer, even if it could carry us all the way there. The train should be safe enough if we can board it discreetly. What do you think?"

"We can buy tickets easily enough," Jake said, "but we will need identification for the ferry—they're getting stricter about such things—and the Kenornin may be able to track us."

"Great-grandfather knows that," Silorè said. "I think it will be all right."

"But what if the Kenornin have men in Thesatra and on Telethoram?" Jake said.

"They might."

"Then how are we going to get past them?"

"One thing at a time," Silorè said. "There are many departures for Telethoram, especially at midday. We shall have to do our best to blend in. If we can slip away quietly enough, we may be safe on Telethoram before they realize we've gone."

Jake released Isèter through the window, giving him a message for Faluin. As soon as the osprey was away, Jake closed the window and drew the curtains over it. When he turned around again, he was surprised to see Silorè standing close to him and smiling. Her hands were clasped behind her back, and her head was tilted to one side. Her violet eyes looked deeply into his, and her white labnerè tresses seemed to glow. Even in the dim light, her beauty could not be obscured.

Jake felt both happy and embarrassed. "What is it?" he said.

"You remind me so much of him," Silorè said. "Your grandfather, that is. The way you looked when you turned around just now was very much like him. I can see his face with that same smile, and it reminds me of happier days."

She looked around the room and breathed a gentle sigh. "There was a large room in the attic of your great-grandfather's house," she continued. "Your grandfather and I used to hide there as children. It was our own world away from everything and everyone. We used to tell each other stories pieced together from other tales and histories we had heard. We often pretended we were commanding a starship, sailing the skies and defending Eratzira from the Kenornin and the Daseshon. As we grew older, we would still sneak up there and talk for hours—often long into the night and into the morning." She turned back to Jake. "I cherished those days, and I've often wished they would come again. Perhaps in some small way they have."

Silorè stood very near Jake now—so close he could see that her eyes were not wholly violet, but lines of dark blue radiated outward like the crown of an eclipsed star. Jake could not help but be moved by her, and the look in her eyes filled him with many feelings. He might have said something foolish but for the sudden sound of footsteps on the stairs.

Jake took a step back from Silorè as Samantha's head appeared above the floor. She scowled when she saw them both, but her voice was gentle. "Follow me," she said. "The council is downstairs, and they want to see both of you."

She did not wait for them but walked noisily down the stairs. Jake and Silorè followed close at her heels, but she seemed to be trying to leave them behind. They followed her through the labyrinthine corridors and down a narrow staircase to the ground floor.

They avoided the common-room, turning aside into a wide passage with many large doors. At one door Samantha stopped and stepped aside, motioning for them to enter. Through the door and down a few steps lay a large room with a broad hearth in the far wall. In the midst of the room stood a long grey table where a half-dozen people were seated. At one end sat Lawrence Appleton, Thaddeus Brown, and Constable Gibbs, for they were all members of the town council of Brown Hill. Thaddeus looked quite displeased, his arms folded across his massive chest.

The mayoress, a tall, slender woman with white hair and flowing robes, sat at the other end of the table with the other two members—the Reverend John Samuelson and Jonas Quincy, the tailor. The mayoress rose to greet Jake and Silorè as they entered, and the others introduced themselves in turn.

Silorè bowed to all of them. “My name is Silorè of the family Itarlavon,” she said in perfect English. “I have come to your village to help Mr Connolly escape those who seek his life, but my plans have faltered, and now we both need your help to escape this planet.” She gave a brief account of all that had happened since she had crashed beyond the mountains. No one spoke or asked any question until she had finished.

When Silorè ended her story, the mayoress looked grave. “This is unhappy news indeed,” she said. “There were rumours that strange folk were about, but I had hoped it was merely excitement because of the festival. Now a shadow seems to have fallen over the whole valley. We must proceed carefully.”

“Carefully indeed,” Appleton spoke up. “It seems Mr Connolly has put us all in peril.”

“I haven’t done anything!” Jake protested.

“Nevertheless,” said Appleton coldly, “much danger has come here because of you. The sooner you are gone, the better for all of us.”

"Do not speak in haste," Silorè said. "Danger may remain whether we stay or go."

"Why then do we not simply hand you over to the Kenornin?" Appleton said with a smirk. "They would certainly show us appreciation for our help." Jake glared at him and hoped he was merely joking.

"I've never known the Keneraton family to show favour to anyone but themselves," Silorè said.

"I only meant that it couldn't hurt us," Appleton said. "They may yet leave us in peace."

"Perhaps," Silorè said, "but there is more to lose than this village alone. The Kenornin stand ready to destroy the last of a noble house."

The other council members murmured to one another, but Appleton laughed. "Jake Connolly?" he said. "From a noble house?"

"You know nothing of the Connollys, then?" Silorè asked.

"Should I?"

"All of Eratzira should know their deeds," Silorè said. "That they are not known is a disgrace, but perhaps it is for the better. Were the name Connolly well known, news of Mr Connolly and his family might have reached the Kenornin much sooner, and all would have been lost." Her face grew stern, and Jake marvelled at the power of her voice.

The mayoress rose to her feet, and all eyes were on her. "There can be no argument about this," she said. "We cannot give up one member of our community to save all others. Doing so would leave us with little left worth saving."

"Hear, hear," the Reverend Samuelson said.

"Then are we all agreed?" said Quincy.

All eyes turned to Appleton. "Why are you all looking at me?" he said innocently.

"You stand perhaps to lose the most of all of us," the mayoress said. "Your high office could be put in jeopardy if it were known you were at this meeting."

"If you're wondering whether you can trust me or not," Appleton said in an even tone, "you may put your minds at ease. I dislike Mr Connolly, 'tis true, but I intend to go on disliking him, and I can't very well do that with him dead, now can I?" Jake fidgeted uneasily. "But I am loath to die for him," Appleton said turning to Silorè, "so how do you propose we get the two of you off this planet?"

Silorè could not suppress a smirk. "The festival will provide our means of escape," she said. "If I remember rightly, many people will be coming from all over the valley to Brown Hill tonight, is that not true?"

The mayoress nodded. "It is."

"Then with so many comings and goings, we might manage to leave undetected," Silorè said. "Our enemies will be watching for certain, but they will not cause turmoil if they can avoid it. No doubt they have paid people from hCathad to aid them, and they will send men into the festival to look for us."

"Then you must stay here," said the constable. "Stay here until the festival is over and everyone returns to his own village. We will smuggle you out then."

"We cannot stay here," said Silorè. "They will search every building in town before the night is out, and you must not hinder them. Don't worry: they will damage nothing. Indeed it will seem as though they were never here, but they must search and find us nowhere."

"Where then will you hide?" asked the constable.

"In the festival itself," said Silorè. "The streets will be crowded, and we shall hide among the people. If we are careful, we will not be found among so many." She looked at the clock that hung upon the wall. “Time is growing short,” she said. “There is work to be done before evening falls.”

Chapter 5

The Festival of Brown Hill

It was two full hours later that the council finally adjourned.

It was decided that Jake and Silorè would attend the festival together. Silorè would need help hiding her labnerè eyes and hair and procuring proper clothes. Upon hearing the plan after the meeting, Samantha reluctantly agreed to assist her. Silorè seemed to be about her size, and Samantha had clothes she could spare.

Jake, on the other hand, would have find new clothes elsewhere. It was too dangerous to return home, and the clothes he was now wearing were not suitable for the festival. Quincy agreed to bring Jake proper clothing from his shop. “I can tell your size without even measuring,” he said proudly. “It’s a gift.”

The only outstanding issue in the plan was finding a way out of the valley, but Appleton and the constable volunteered to work out that problem.

“Leave it to me,” Appleton said. “I have a few ideas on how to get you out. I think I can get you as far as Valegate; after that you are on your own.”

With the meeting over, the council members left one by one. As the Reverend Samuelson departed, he took Jake and Silorè by the hand. “I’ll be praying for your safe journey,” he said earnestly.

Jake fidgeted in his grip, but Silorè smiled and bowed. “Thank you, Reverend,” she said. “We will certainly need it.” With a bow

Samuelson departed, walking calmly through the common-room and out the front door.

The other council members left in different directions at separate times so as not to draw attention to themselves. If the Kenornin knew such a meeting had taken place, they would certainly have surrounded the building, captured Jake and Silorè, and killed Samantha and her family.

As he thought on these things, Jake felt as though his innards were braided into a giant knot. The anticipation and uncertainty were more than he could bear, and he almost wished the night were over, whatever the outcome.

Once the council members had gone and Samantha had taken Silorè upstairs, Jake had nothing else to do but wait. Sitting alone in the room where the council had met, he closed his eyes and listened to the quiet all around him. The soft crackling of the logs in the fireplace seemed to ease his nerves a bit, and he tried to put his present circumstance out of his mind.

He must have dozed, because when he sat up again he found the fire had died to a few embers, and the room felt cold. He put another log on the hearth and blew on the coals to revive the flames. With a scrap of paper and a few small twigs, he succeeded, and he returned to his chair, putting his head in his hands. The clock on the wall showed that it was now late afternoon. He had not eaten anything all day, and that only made the pit in his stomach worse.

A few minutes later, a gentle knock came at the door. Jake rose to his feet, startled by the sudden noise. "Come in," he said.

The door opened, and Samantha walked in carrying two bowls upon a tray. One was filled with vegetable soup and the other with sausages and mash. The rage Jake had expected to see in her face was gone, and she seemed shy and sad. She did not look at him but said softly, "I thought you might be hungry."

Jake did not speak as Samantha placed the bowls on the table and laid out a fork and spoon upon a napkin. When she had finished, she did not turn around but stood a while staring at the floor.

"Are you all right?" Jake said at last.

"Just tell me one thing," said Samantha. "What do you think of her?"

Jake opened his mouth to speak, but no words came out.

"That's what I thought," Samantha said. She turned and rushed to the door.

As she reached for the doorknob, Jake caught her by the hand. "Wait."

"Please let me go."

"I will," said Jake, "but first I want you to know I'm sorry. I didn't want any of this to happen, and I was looking forward to going to the festival with you more than anything."

"It's all right," Samantha said coldly. "I can't be angry; I suppose you can't help yourself."

Jake scowled. "What do you mean by that?"

"She's very beautiful," said Samantha. "A Nanyan lady born of nobility. She's strong and intelligent, and she spoke with a wisdom that rivalled the town council. What Thalavè could compete with that?"

"That's not fair," Jake said, "and besides, you didn't give me a chance to answer your question."

"It doesn't matter," Samantha said stubbornly. "You're leaving now, maybe forever—who knows? I don't care now what your answer is."

She wriggled from his grasp and left without another word. Jake stared at the door for a long while after she had gone. At length he pulled up a chair to the food she had left him, and there he sat without moving, staring blankly at the table until the food went completely cold.

Evening fell outside, but the windowless room saw no change. The fire died again, but Jake did not rebuild it. After many hours of sitting in the dark, another knock came at the door—a sturdy knock that echoed in the silence of the room. Before Jake could speak, the door flew open, and Jonas Quincy walked in carrying a large box under one arm.

"The town's gone mad," he said, hurriedly closing the door behind him. "Plenty of strange folks out tonight. It's getting rather crowded out there: everyone's waiting for the lamps to be lit so the festival can begin. Here!" He threw the box on the table. "Open it."

Jake pulled the lid off the box, and inside, wrapped in brown paper, lay a pair of brown trousers, a grey shirt, and a dark-green waistcoat with golden stitching. There were also socks and a pair of brown shoes with long laces.

"Nothing fancy," said Quincy, "but I figure you'll blend in enough with these. I've a brown overcoat to go with them. I'll fetch it while you change."

Quincy left again, and Jake hurriedly put on the trousers and shirt, leaving his old clothes on the table. The new clothes were a bit tight, but the waistcoat fit well, as did the shoes. Jake did not ordinarily wear clothes of this quality, and they made him feel tall and sophisticated.

"Splendid," Quincy said when he returned carrying a large brown coat. "You look very smart, young Jake. It's a pity you haven't been to my shop in so long."

He handed Jake the coat and collected the old clothes in the empty box and carried them out the door. Jake slipped into the overcoat and found it thick and warm. At least he would not freeze outside.

Jake waited several minutes for Quincy to return, and when he did, he wore a broad smile. “I’ve just been upstairs,” Quincy said. “They’re ready for you now. I saw your lady, and I think you won’t be disappointed.” Jake was not quite sure whom he meant.

Together Jake and Quincy walked up the back staircase and through many corridors to the sitting room at the top of the secret stairs. There they found Mrs Brown waiting for them. “It’s about time you were here,” she said to Jake. “The folks downstairs have begun to leave, and the streets are filling up. Your pursuers could be along any minute, and what will happen if you’re still here?”

Even as Mrs Brown spoke, Samantha emerged from one of the side rooms. Her hair was neatly curled, and she wore a violet dress trimmed with ribbon. In her hair was a dark flower, and her eyes were painted in deep hues of green and purple. For all her beauty, she looked completely cheerless.

Jake walked up to her and bowed. “You look very nice,” he said.

“Thank you,” she said softly. “I think you should know I bought this dress weeks ago, and I planned to wear it when you asked me to the festival. I’d almost given up hope that you would until yesterday.” She sighed. “I wasn’t going to wear it now, but I like it ever so much.”

“If you’d like,” he said, feeling rather guilty, “you could always come around the festival with us.” He regretted the words as soon as he spoke them.

Samantha turned away. “I’d rather not,” she mumbled. “Anyway, you’ll blend in better with just the two of you.”

At that moment another door opened, and out stepped Silorè in a dress of dark red with sleeves of scarlet lace. About her waist she wore a thin silver belt with a jewelled clasp. A silver ornament lay upon her neck, and her hair was drawn into a silver headband where the white tresses were braided with small flowers and beads. No one looking at her now would have guessed she was a Labnerè woman.

"What do you think?" Silorè asked, fidgeting with the folds of her dress. "Do you suppose this will do?"

Jake gaped at her. Samantha frowned. "I thought the point was not to stand out," Jake said without thinking.

Silorè smiled. "I must admit I too was surprised," she said. "I think I did quite well under the circumstances."

"And what exactly does that mean?" Samantha said, putting her hands on her hips.

Silorè bit her lip. "Not that I'm putting you down, my dear," she said. "I think your clothes are quite…nice." She looked away nervously, avoiding Samantha's gaze. "Well, it seems we're all here," she said quickly. "I think it would be wise to join the party now, don't you?"

Taking leave of the upstairs room, Jake, Silorè, and Samantha walked downstairs together. Even through the thick walls, the three could hear festival music trickling in from the streets. The common-room was deserted, but the courtyard was filled with people. As Jake opened the front door, a wave of sounds and smells rushed in. Though the night was cold, Jake hardly felt it. There was a strange warmth all around him, and the very air seemed to be alight.

In the courtyard of the Griffin, Samantha parted company and hurried off alone into the crowds. Jake watched her until she disappeared from sight, becoming just another body in the crowd.

When he turned around again, he found that Silorè was smiling at him. "Well," she said, "where shall we go first?"

The look on her face made Jake giddy. "Are you hungry?" he asked.

She nodded.

"Come on then," he said. "I know just where to go."

Jake started to walk ahead, but Silorè grabbed him by the arm. "We must look the part," she said, pulling close to him. "Lead on."

The street beside the Griffin was already filled with people who had stepped off the main road to escape the growing multitude. They were talking to one another with loud voices, and many of them held plates of food or half-drunk bottles of red liquid. Men tipped their hats and ladies nodded as Jake and Silorè passed by.

The way to the main road was barred by a wall of people lining the pavement between buildings. Jake and Silorè politely squeezed through them into the street bustling with festivalgoers all moving in different directions. Walking among them was slow work, but neither Jake nor Silorè cared, for it gave them both a chance to absorb the sights and the sounds of the autumn festival.

Throughout the town stood many booths selling a variety of goods—brightly-decorated festival hats, jewellery with an array of precious stones, ceramic trinkets in the shapes of people and animals, wreaths of woven leaves and cones, shawls and scarves to keep out the cold air (which would certainly be needed as the night wore on). There was every kind of craftsmanship on display and for sale, from basket-weaving to haberdashery to metalworking to pottery. Paintings and sculptures were to be found everywhere, exhibited by cheerful artisans who thrived on the energy of the festival and gave it back again fourfold.

The smell of food hit Jake and Silorè from every direction. They passed booths selling sweet cakes of fried dough glazed with honey and sugar. One booth sold a variety of apples—some raw and some baked into tarts and pies. A butcher and his family were grilling sausages beneath a canopy. Young men walked about selling skewered meats and vegetables. Soups and stews were sold by the bowlful, with large slices of crusty bread instead of spoons. Roasted chickens turned on giant spits between the largest hams Jake had ever seen. Many other foods there were besides these, but they did not interest Jake at the moment. He knew his destination.

As Jake led Silorè onward, they came upon an area of the street partitioned by ropes. Inside, many men and women danced in bright costumes embroidered with gold and silver. Some of the women wore large headdresses and swayed to the music as the others danced around them. To the side a band of six men played a lively tune on pipe, fiddle, and drum.

Jake and Silorè passed a group of three jugglers throwing lighted torches to one another. They were so skilled that even though they threw the torches high into the air, they never hit any lantern or banner overhanging the street. They would jump and tumble about as they kept the torches aloft, but they never faltered.

At a crossroads with a broad street, many children had gathered around a large puppet theatre. On the stage two marionettes were arguing with one another concerning their love for some unseen lady they both fancied. But as they quarrelled, an alligator sneaked up behind them and devoured them to a chorus of delighted screams.

Pushing past the crowds, Jake and Silorè at last came to the main square of the town. Thousands of lanterns lit the area as bright as day, and the column that stood at the centre hung with many banners and streamers. A wide green lawn lay about the column, and upon it were the largest tents of the festival—all of them devoted to foods of many different kinds. In one corner of the square stood a wooden platform raised ten feet off the ground.

"Where are you taking me?" Silorè chuckled, looking around at all the food they had passed up. "I thought you were hungry."

"I'm quite hungry," Jake said, "but not just anything will do. You see over there?" He pointed to the platform on the opposite side of the square.

"Is that where you're taking me?"

"It is," Jake said, "and I promise that once you taste the food there, you'll agree it was worth the walk and the wait."

With Silorè on his arm, Jake crossed the square to one of several sets of stairs that led up onto the platform. As they climbed they found many tables set with white tablecloths and golden lamps. There were many people already seated when Jake and Silorè arrived, but they managed to secure a table near the centre.

"Are you sure it's wise to be up here?" Silorè asked as Jake pulled out her chair for her.

"It shouldn't be too easy to spot us," Jake said. "There are a lot of people around, and besides, this may be my last festival. Kenornin or no, I'm not passing up this food."

"What is this place, then?" Silorè asked, warming her hands on the lamp sitting on the table. "Did they build this platform just for the festival?"

"They do every year," Jake said. "This place is sponsored by a restaurant in a village to the north. The food is delicious, and I get to eat it only at festival time. I've never been to that village, but I've often been tempted to make the trip just to eat there."

Silorè picked up the menu card from her place setting and began to read. "What is so special about it?"

"I don't really know," Jake said. "But if you try it, I think you'll agree."

At that moment a girl in a green dress embroidered with white flowers came to their table. She bowed and smiled at the two of them. "Good evening," she said. "The Snow Dragon welcomes you, and we are humbled by your patronage. Have you made a selection?"

"Stuffed chicken for me," Jake said, "and be liberal with the sauce, if you please."

"Of course, sir."

Both Jake and the waitress turned to Silorè, who looked over the menu and frowned. "Nothing for me, thank you," she said at last.

The waitress bowed again and walked away.

Jake was puzzled. "I promise you the food's good," he said. "I'll let you have some of mine, if you care to try it. You'll change your mind when you taste it, and you'll want to order the whole menu."

"It's not that," Silorè said. "I forgot to tell you I do not eat meat. Neither does most of my family. But that seems to be all that is served here."

Jake felt suddenly embarrassed. "Oh," he said, turning red. "I didn't realize you were arakasè. Would you care to leave?"

Silorè laughed. "Silly boy," she said. "I don't mean that either. We are arakasin, and that is all. I have no moral objection to eating meat; it is simply something I do not do. It may sound silly to you, but that's the way it is."

"So you've never eaten meat?" Jake said. "Not once?"

"Once," said Silorè. "On Earth long ago, when I was a child, your grandfather dared me to eat some sort of meat sandwich with a strange red-vinegar sauce. I took one bite and vomited, and I was sick all the next day. My parents were furious. Since then I have not eaten any meat. To tell the truth, I don't really want to."

Jake shook his head. "I don't believe it," he said. "None at all? What about steak? And smoked-pork? And bacon?"

Silorè wrinkled her nose. "Meat has no appeal to me," she said. "Even the smell of it makes me ill. Indeed, this whole festival reeks of it." She cast a brooding glance to the street.

"I don't have to eat anything," Jake said. Even as he said so, he felt his stomach churn, and it made a loud noise.

"No, please," Silorè said. "Do not abstain on my account. It does not offend me if you eat it. You are a Thalani, and even arakasin permit Thalanin to eat meat."

Jake said no more, and Silorè stared off into the distance. Her eyes seemed deep as a well in sunset-shadow, and her face betrayed nothing of her secret thoughts. She rested her chin upon her hand and breathed deeply, and then, closing her eyes, she remained completely still until the waitress returned with Jake's food.

Jake felt guilty as he ate with Silorè looking on. She assured him she would be fine, but Jake ate quickly all the same. The chicken he had ordered was grilled and stuffed with cheese and bacon, and the dish swam in a mustard sauce the likes of which Jake had tasted nowhere else. Only during festival was he able to eat it, and he was going to enjoy it regardless of the present danger.

When he had finished, he paid for the meal and walked with Silorè down into the square. "Come on," he said. "Your choice. Where shall we go?"

"It doesn't matter to me," Silorè said. "I've not been to many parties of this kind. I want to see everything."

So Jake and Silorè wandered about the festival, stopping at many tents and booths and sampling many foods. They looked through a multitude of stalls selling a variety of goods—paintings and engravings, baskets and bags, hats and gloves, chocolates and other dainties. They laughed together and spoke of frivolous things, and for a while they almost forgot their peril.

As the crowds thinned near the edge of town, Jake and Silorè turned back, for they dared not leave the safety of the festival. As they started back up the street, they passed a narrow side-road that turned a corner between two buildings to join a broader road that ran out of town. As he and Silorè passed by, Jake heard the distinct sound of flapping wings. He stopped a moment to listen, but he could not hear the sound again.

"What is it?" Silorè asked him.

"I thought I heard something," said Jake. "I thought it might be…"

A sound came from the shadows like the cry of a bird, but it was quiet and strange like a whisper. Jake looked at Silorè, but she had not seemed to hear it.

Suddenly a hoarse whisper came from the shadows. "Will you not come here?" it said.

"Is that…?" Silorè asked.

"Shh," Jake said, and taking her by the hand, he led her into the alley. They could not see in the darkness, and they stumbled over a few fallen trash barrels.

"Who's there?" Jake whispered.

All at once there came a rush of wind and a loud flutter that passed near their heads. Jake and Silorè put their hands before their faces as a dark form landed in front of them.

"I have tried attracting your attention many times tonight," came the voice of Faluin, "but you never heeded me once."

Jake and Silorè lowered their hands and saw the silhouette of Faluin perched on a nearby rain barrel.

"We didn't see you," said Jake. "I've been wondering where you've been. Did you see Isètcr?"

"Yes," said Faluin, "and he told me where to find you."

"You haven't seen Izhana, have you?" Silorè asked.

Izhana suddenly emerged from the shadows. "I've been around," she said, "and like Faluin, I too can remain unseen if I wish it. We both have been surveying the town, and things do not go well. I have seen Ianjori, and he is not alone. Every way out of town is watched, and many cannon have been set up throughout the valley to be used if you try to escape by air. Our enemies are determined, and they are quite thorough."

Jake took a deep breath. "How many men are there?"

“At least a hundred,” Izhana said. “Faluin may have seen more.”

“I have not been able to count them all,” said Faluin. “There may be many more, but they are careful to hide themselves. The festival is protecting you right now. When it is over, I am not certain what will happen.”

Jake felt his legs giving way beneath him, and he staggered backwards. Silorè reached out and grabbed his arm, propping him up. “You cannot despair, Thalani!” she said. “All is not yet lost!”

She kept hold of his arm until he was able to stand again. “I’m all right,” he said. “It overcame me for a moment, but I’m better now.” He turned and gazed into Silorè’s eyes. The look in his face must have been quite serious, for it startled Silorè so that she blushed. “Just let me say now,” he said solemnly, “that no matter what happens, I’m glad I got to meet you.” At the edge of his vision, Jake saw the glare of two small eyes. “And you too, Izhana.”

Izhana chuckled. “For my part,” she said, “I will fight for you both until there is no breath left in me. If we are all to die, I promise you I will be first.”

“And I second,” Faluin said.

Jake and Silorè smiled at one another, and the two automatons bowed to them. Then Faluin flew up and away, melting into the darkness; Izhana ran down the street and vanished into the shadows, leaving Jake and Silorè alone in the alley. The sounds of the festival, which seemed to have disappeared for a time, returned to their ears.

“Come,” Silorè said. “It is not wise to linger in one place too long.”

The two reentered the main street and walked down to where the crowds were larger. The festival was still as lively as when it had begun, and much food and drink fuelled the spirits of the festivalgoers to keep it so.

When Jake and Silorè returned to the town square, they found the area was now sectioned off with ropes. A band of many instruments played upon the lawn, and in the streets the people danced. Jake and Silorè stood among those who had gathered around to watch. The night was growing colder, but no one seemed to notice amidst the merrymaking.

Shapes of many colours whirled by Jake and Silorè as they watched the dance. A thousand puffs of breath turned white in the chill air so that the head of each dancer was wreathed in mist. The lanterns above the square cast swirling shadows upon the ground, and the music carried a secret fire that warmed every heart so that winter seemed to lie behind instead of ahead.

Suddenly Silorè spoke words Jake had not expected to hear. "I want to dance."

Jake flushed. "Dance?"

Silorè nodded. "Now."

"Right now?"

Silorè seized Jake's hand and stooped beneath the rope, dragging him along with her. He was caught unprepared, and his chin caught on the rope as he followed her.

Stepping into the square, Silorè put Jake's right hand on her waist and took his other hand in hers. Without waiting for him, she started into the dance, leading him until he managed to catch up. Everything happened so fast that Jake could hardly tell how he had come to dance with the most beautiful girl in the square.

The tune was lively and merry, but soon it ended, and the band began a much softer song. The dancers slowed, and the swirling dizziness Jake had been swept into subsided. Silorè drew near, dancing so close to Jake that her forehead rested upon his cheek.

It was then that Jake first breathed the aroma of Silorè's hair. It was a sweet and alluring scent that seemed to fill his entire body.

Indeed he felt quite light-headed. Her face was warm, and he felt her gentle breath upon his neck. In that moment he quite forgot himself and the crowds and even the danger that pursued him. Even the music seemed to fade away, leaving him alone with Silorè and the sound of his pounding heart.

The end of the song brought Jake back to reality, and he could not tell how long they had danced. To him it seemed just as easily a few seconds as a few hours.

The crowds applauded the musicians, and Silorè spoke over the noise. "Do you see those men over there?" she said. It was then that Jake realized they had danced to the opposite side of the square. "Back where we started. See? There!"

She pointed to two men who slowly searched the faces around them. They wore dark-blue suits and black hats that hung low upon their heads. "I see them," said Jake.

"Those are Ianjori's men."

Jake tensed. "Are you sure?"

"Quite sure," said Silorè. "They were nearly upon us when I saw them, and there was nowhere else to go."

So that was why Silorè had suddenly wanted to dance. Jake's elation fell from the crown of his head to the pit of his stomach like a heavy stone. There it lingered like a cramp that would not subside.

"What should we do?" Jake asked, lowering his voice as the applause died away.

"Carry on, I suppose," said Silorè. "The music is starting again. We must continue."

The new song was livelier than the last, and Silorè did not dance nearly so close. Jake was unsure of the new steps, and he stumbled over his own feet, much to Silorè's amusement.

"Do you not dance, Thalani?" she asked.

"Not often," Jake said. "I learned once upon a time, but I suppose I've forgotten. You, on the other hand—how is it you know all the Thalanin dances?"

"It is my business to do so," Silorè said proudly. "These are not unlike many dances I learned on Earth. Your grandfather once took me to a dance when we were young. He was quite a good dancer, but I'm afraid you haven't inherited his footwork."

"No, I suppose I haven't."

Silorè smiled. "Please don't think I'm making fun of you. I think it's quite charming."

Her words made Jake forget himself, and he must not have been watching where he was going, for he spun Silorè directly into the path of a tall man wearing a blue jacket and a black hat. They collided, and Jake turned white as he recognized him as one of the Kenornin men Silorè had pointed out.

Silorè turned and looked the man in the face, and without even stopping to think, she shouted at him in an accent the Thalanin of Rithonon call North-Plains. "'Ere!" she said. "Watch where you're goin', love! You can't be walkin' where folks is dancin'." She eyed him up and down. "What's your game, then? Fancy a dance?"

The man looked down at Silorè with contempt and walked away, running into several other dancing couples as he went. Jake and Silorè watched him until he disappeared into the crowd.

"That was a near thing, wasn't it?" Silorè said, her voice back to normal. "Startled me terribly. I guess we're not that much safer dancing, are we?"

Jake gaped at her. "That was quite impressive."

"What was? My voice?" said Silorè. "To tell the truth, it was the first Thalanin accent that entered my head. A bit excessive, wouldn't you agree?"

"It fooled him, didn't it?"

"I certainly hope so."

Jake took Silorè's hand, and the two rejoined the dance. Jake kept a better look out for Ianjori's men this time, but he did not see them again.

Just as Jake was beginning to relax once more, he felt a light tap on his shoulder, and a hoarse voice whispered in his ear. "Mr Connolly!"

Jake turned round to see Constable Gibbs dancing beside them with his wife, who was a bit taller than her husband. "Good evening," the constable said cheerily. "I trust you two are enjoying yourselves?"

The smirk he wore made Jake cringe, but Silorè answered politely. "Yes, we are," she said. "Thank you."

"Good," the constable said. "I thought you would like to know we've arranged transportation for you both."

"Where?" Jake asked.

"Old Dartford Road by Wellington's grocery. Old Man Wellington takes folks home in his cart after the festival every year. He can take you all the way to Valegate."

"When shall we go?" Jake asked.

"Soon," the constable said, "but not until the crowds begin to thin out. I won't be there to see you off, so good luck, Mr Connolly. And to you too, miss. I shan't forget either of you." He tipped his hat and danced away with his wife, who glared at Silorè with a most unpleasant expression.

Jake and Silorè danced a while longer. Then, growing tired, they stepped outside the ropes and stood catching their breath and watching the endless parade of dancers. Jake felt weary—more in mind than in body—and he closed his eyes, content to listen to the swirling music and the chatter of the crowds.

One voice suddenly rose above the others. "You may wish to know," said Silorè, "that Miss Brown is dancing with that rather unpleasant fellow."

Jake's eyes were open in an instant, and he scanned the dancers' faces wildly. He knew whom Silorè meant, and he was hoping she was wrong. But he knew Appleton without a second glance. There he was, no more than fifty feet away, turning to the music with Samantha in his arms. The knot that sat in Jake's stomach leapt into his throat, and he choked on his next breath. "What…are they doing?" he coughed.

Silorè looked sidelong at Jake. "I believe they're dancing," she said, sounding quite irritated.

Seeing Samantha with Appleton provoked feelings for which Jake was not prepared. A pain grew in his chest, and he found he could not look away from her. She moved so effortlessly, and Appleton guided her every step. Jake was not sure if the lamplight were playing tricks on him, but he thought Appleton was smiling.

Jake felt a sudden tug at his arm and found that Silorè was frowning at him. "Come on," she said lowly. "I've had enough of dancing."

For the remainder of the festival, Jake and Silorè walked together in silence, staying away from sparsely populated areas. Silorè seemed to have lost part of her glow, though her beauty had not faded. She seemed more sullen now, and Jake was certain there was nothing he could do to cheer her. They were both very tired, and the festival seemed already to be passing away into memory.

Slowly the crowds began to dissipate. In the streets the debris once hidden by masses of legs and feet now lay like so many plants trampled by wild beasts. In the town square, the dancers diminished, and the band played only placid tunes. Jake did not see Samantha anywhere.

At length Jake turned to Silorè. "I suppose we'd better get going," he said, but as he spoke these words, a great melancholy washed over him. He looked around at the buildings and the people, and for the first time he fully realized this could be the last he would ever see of Brown Hill. He felt tears sting his eyes, but he quickly blinked them away.

Silorè must have seen this change, for she gripped his arm tightly and smiled at him. "Come on," she said softly. "It's time to go."

Old Dartford Road was not far from the centre of town, and it did not take Jake and Silorè long to walk there. The side roads were deserted, and Jake worried that if he and Silorè were set upon now, they would be easily carried off.

But they arrived without incident at the grocery and found a wagon waiting in the street. It was a large wagon with a flatbed upon which stood a wooden structure like a cage. A cabin at the front housed the driver's chair and steering mechanism, and in front of all lay a rusty engine partially covered by a metal hood.

As Jake and Silorè walked up, an old man jumped from the driver's seat. His white hair lay disorderly upon his head, and his beard was long and narrow. His fingers were gnarled with age, and the veins on his hands and neck seemed as though they might burst his skin. Old Man Wellington earned well his title.

"It's about time!" he said. "I've been waiting ages for you two. I promised a bunch of folks I'd drive them home. They're going to meet us at the crossroads, but I reckon they'll be cross now on account of shivering to death in the cold."

"We're sorry," Jake said. "We didn't want to leave too early."

"Well now ain't the time for apologies," Wellington said. "Hurry inside. The innkeeper's wife has delivered some clothes for you two. Yours, Mr Connolly, are in the storeroom, and the young lady's are upstairs in the first bedroom on the left. Don't worry; there's no one at home."

Jake and Silorè hurried into the grocery, passing shelves filled with goods they could not identify in the dim light. "Make haste," Silorè said as she mounted the staircase at the back of the shop. "We must leave quickly."

She disappeared up the stairs, and Jake headed for the stockroom. He entered and found it dark and disorganized. Boxes were stacked everywhere. On a carton in the middle of the room lay a set of untidy clothes beside a dark-brown jacket and a pair of thick boots. Jake changed clothes and stuffed his festival attire in a mostly empty box, which he closed and hid among the others.

When he emerged from the storeroom, he found a dark figure standing before him. "That was fast," he said. "Are you ready to go?"

The figure stepped into the light, and to Jake's surprise, it was not Silorè but Samantha, still wearing her festival dress. "What are you doing here?" he asked.

Samantha scowled. "Are you not pleased to see me?" she said. "I can leave, you know."

"That's not what I meant," Jake said. "But it's not safe to be here. Does your father know where you are?"

"No one does," she replied, "but I had to see you off. I couldn't let you go without saying goodbye, could I?"

Jake said nothing.

"This all happened so quickly," Samantha continued. "It seems you and I have run out of time. I had hoped we might have gotten to know each other better and that this festival would have been the start of…well, I guess it doesn't matter anymore."

Jake took a deep breath. "I wish I knew what to say," he said. "I ought to, but I can't think of anything."

Samantha shook her head. “That’s your problem,” she said with a grin. “You talk too much.”

Before Jake realized what was happening, Samantha stepped forward, and putting her arms around his neck, she kissed him. The touch of her lips sent a warm tingle through his limbs, and he held her tightly, not wishing to let her go. When at last she pulled away, her face was tearstained, and her eyes sparkled.

“You’d better go,” she said. “I…I’ll remember you always, Jake Connolly.”

Jake did not move nor take his hands from Samantha’s waist.

But Silorè, who had appeared on the staircase, grabbed him by the arm and dragged him away. Jake turned back to say goodbye, but the words died in his throat ere they reached his lips.

Turning his gaze to Silorè, he saw that she now wore dark trousers beneath a brown overcoat, and upon her head she wore a cap to hide her labnerè hair. Her face was equally transformed—stern and cold. Jake wondered how long she had been standing on the stairs.

Outside, Old Man Wellington was sitting on the bed of the wagon checking his pocket watch. “It took you long enough,” he said. “We’re running late now. But never mind; climb aboard. You two will sit behind me in the cabin, and with any luck no one will even know you’re there.”

Wellington helped Silorè onto the cushioned bench behind the driver’s chair, and Jake followed after her. Then, taking his seat, Wellington turned a crank, and the engine in front of him sputtered to life. The wagon shook like a small earthquake, tossing Jake and Silorè in their seats. Silorè made miserable faces.

Old Man Wellington pulled a lever, and gears somewhere beneath him grinded loudly together. “Off we go, then!”

The wagon lurched forward, and they were all at last on their way out of town. Jake peeked his head out the window and saw that Samantha had come outside. She was shivering in the cold air but did not move from where she stood. He watched as she shrank into the distance, fading into the shadows of night around her.

Chapter 6

Escape from Rithonon

The wagon rumbled onto dirt roads as it left the cobbled streets of Brown Hill. The town behind was still brightly lit, for the festival would carry on another hour or two. After that would come the long cleanup. Jake never liked to see those days, for the town always looked like a rubbish dump, and the magic of the festival disappeared. He was glad he could remember Brown Hill as he had left it and not in its ruined state. He turned his face away and did not look back again.

The road that now lay ahead was dark, and the wagon's two lamps could see only a few feet ahead. The surrounding country was too dark to see, and Jake worried that many eyes might be watching them.

"Can we not put out the lights?" Jake asked.

"I couldn't drive without them," Old Man Wellington said. "Besides, don't you think it would be strange to see a wagon driving down the road without any lights?"

Jake had not thought of that.

"Don't worry, Thalani," Silorè said. "Sit back, and be at peace. We will soon be in Valegate and on the early train to Thesatra."

The wagon came to a crossroads where many people were huddled together, and their breath could be seen in the lamplight. The wagon stopped beside them, and Wellington stepped from his seat to help his passengers into the wagon-bed. From inside the cabin, Jake and Silorè could neither see them nor be seen. A few minutes later, Wellington mounted his seat again and drove onward into the night.

As the wagon rumbled down the road, Jake wished he had a heater to warm himself; a cold wind blew in, stinging his face and drying his eyes so that he could not keep them open. Silorè sat silently beside him, shivering in the cold.

An hour passed in which the wagon drove through several hamlets, letting off a few passengers who shouted their thanks to the driver.

Their voices made Jake nervous. "Do they have to be so loud?" he whispered to Silorè.

Silorè had been staring straight ahead, deep in thought. Now she blinked and looked at him. "What was that?" she asked.

"I was wondering why everyone is being so loud."

Silorè yawned and stretched. "Country folk seem always to make a lot of noise."

Jake made no reply.

Telethoram was climbing in the sky when the wagon turned down a road that cut across wide pasturelands. Villages were sparse here, and only a few farmhouses dotted the countryside. The night was waxing late indeed, and Jake felt it would never end. Silorè had fallen asleep with her jacket wrapped about her, and a white curl of hair lay upon her cheek. Jake envied her, for though he closed his eyes, he could find no rest.

Even as he thought on these things, a great noise suddenly rent the night, shaking the cabin and knocking Old Man Wellington from his seat. The engine faltered, and the wagon came to a stop.

Silorè awoke instantly. "What's happened?"

"I don't know," Jake said, standing up. "Is he all right?"

Wellington climbed back into his seat. “I’m not hurt,” he said. “What do you suppose…?”

A giant fireball suddenly erupted in front of them, and a blast of heat struck their faces. Jake might otherwise have thought it a pleasant relief from the cold, but as it was, his heart raced and pounded in his ears. He braced himself against the walls of the cabin and closed his eyes, waiting for the world to end.

Silorè, on the other hand, leapt from the cabin at once. She took Wellington by the hand and led him quickly away. As she ran she called out to the other passengers to follow her, and Jake heard a mad scramble and clamour from the bed behind him. He did not join them, for a mad panic had gripped him, and he could not move.

A minute later Silorè returned. “Run, you fool!” she cried.

She grabbed his hand and plucked him from the cabin as another ball of fire hit the ground nearby. They started to run but did not get far, for at that moment five men in black clothing sprang from the tall grass. Wielding their black rifles, they quickly encircled Jake and Silorè so they could not escape.

A flyer descended noiselessly from the sky, and a tall man dismounted. “Not clever enough,” he said. “I expected a much better chase. Hardly a challenge at all.”

“You took long enough to find us, all the same,” Silorè said defiantly. “It doesn’t take much to fool you, Ianjori.”

Ianjori’s face emerged from the darkness as the torch in his hand ignited. “You underestimate me, little girl,” he said. “And this time it will cost you everything. I won’t be delivering you unspoiled. Take them!”

The five men closed in, but as they did so, a shrill cry pierced every ear. Three rifles rose and fired, splitting the air with a thunderous report. A dozen dark shapes dropped from the sky in answer, knocking the armed men to the ground. Large birds clawed their flesh, and the beating of many wings drowned the screams.

A blur of brown fur sprang from the grass. Izhana had appeared, and she stood facing Ianjori. He drew a pistol, but she sidestepped his aim and leapt at him, biting him at his wrist so that he dropped his weapon. He tried to fling her off, but she held on tightly.

Silorè took the chance given her. She bounded to the flyer, and Jake followed close behind her. One of the men upon the ground tried to trip him, but Jake kicked him off.

They found Faluin perched on the flyer's steering device. "Follow me!" he said. "And quickly!"

"You get in front," Silorè shouted to Jake. "You can fly this machine better than I."

Jake jumped onto the seat, and Silorè climbed on right behind him, grabbing his waist. It took Jake a few moments to find the right controls, but after a few misfires the engine roared to life. The flyer shot upwards so quickly that both Jake and Silorè nearly fell off.

"Careful now!" Silorè cried.

"Sorry."

Faluin circled them once and flew off southward. "Come with me!" he called.

He flew as swift as the wind, and Jake could barely keep up with him. Below them Jake could see a dozen vèralamen leading Wellington and the others towards a village. They were not pursued, and Jake felt relieved to see them get away.

Faluin led Jake and Silorè high into the night sky, and the battle was soon far behind. The land beneath them now was featureless in the dark save for the scattered lights of distant villages. The stars shone bright above the dark rim of mountains all around them.

Suddenly a great fireball exploded beside the flyer, knocking Jake off course. Silorè screamed as they veered to the left and fell a great distance. Jake regained control after a moment and flew higher just as another blast of fire passed beneath them.

Silorè looked about her. “I think they’ve given up capturing us,” she shouted over the roar of the engine. “Now they’re trying to kill us!”

Even as she spoke, a third shot struck the flyer’s left wing, spewing black smoke and green fire. Jake pulled hard on the wheel, but the flyer could not stay aloft. Instead it pitched and plummeted down onto a grassy plateau. The flyer tried to spin, but Jake held it steady enough so that as it struck the ground, he and Silorè managed to jump clear. The tall grass cushioned their fall and brought them to a stop, but even so, they both found themselves covered with dirt and blood.

Jake ran to Silorè and helped her to her feet. “Are you all right?” he asked.

“Of course not,” Silorè said, filled of outrage. “I’ve had enough of crash-landings for any lifetime—Thalavè or Nanyavè.” She ran her fingers through her hair as a midnight breeze blew it in her face. Her cap had fallen off, and in her haste she had left her jacket in the wagon. She shivered. “Come on,” she said. “We must hurry.”

Faluin descended, perching on Jake’s shoulder. “They will not be far behind,” he said. “Already I can see far off a score of flying machines approaching.”

“Then lead the way,” Jake said.

Faluin flew low, and Jake and Silorè ran behind as best they could. They had both been injured more than they cared to admit, and they stumbled as they forced their way through the waist-high grass.

After a few minutes of running (if running it could be called), the grass grew shorter, and a line of trees loomed ahead. This was the beginning of a large orchard in the southern part of the valley, and Jake knew it well. He had journeyed here as a boy and had climbed many trees.

Without even a look behind them, Jake and Silorè plunged into the grove. Jake thought it fortunate that it was autumn and the limbs above them were bare, or else they may have never found their way under the shadow of the boughs. It was difficult enough to see through the crisscross of branches, and though the rows between the trees were wide, the roots tripped them up.

A distant droning came to their ears, and they fled deeper into the orchard, hoping its shadows would hide them. The smouldering ruins of their flyer could not be seen, but a plume of black smoke, lit underneath with fire, billowed high into the sky.

"Where are we going?" Silorè said. "I see nothing ahead but darkness. Where is Faluin?"

"Above us," Jake said. "I cannot see him either, but I know where we are. I'm taking us to Southanjou. It's nearby, and we should be able to stop there and rest a moment."

The trees came to an end at the edge of a small town. The roads there were broad, and the buildings were dark. The only light in the place came from a tavern halfway up the street. A ruckus of shouting and music issued from it, and from its doors half-drunken men tried to tiptoe home. Brown Hill was not the only place celebrating tonight.

"Come on," Jake said, hurrying forward. "We'll be safe in there."

Silorè hesitated. "That place?" she said. "I don't…I mean, it's so…" She made a noise and shook her head.

"There's no need to be afraid," Jake said. "The people here have no loyalty to any Nanyanin—the Kenornin least of all. Around here being in trouble with Nanyanin is a good thing."

"That's not what I'm afraid of," Silorè mumbled, shivering in the cold. "I don't like the look of that place."

"Don't worry," Jake said. "They're all perfect gentlemen."

Jake took Silorè by the hand, and together they descended the hill into the streets of the town. Their quick footsteps were loud on the pavement, but they dared not walk slower. Even so, they scarcely seemed to draw closer with each step.

The door of the tavern stood slightly ajar, and warm air issued from it, laced with a stench of smoke and drink. Loud singing arose, and a well-soused man stumbled out the door, saluting Jake and Silorè as he tripped down the steps. Jake and Silorè looked at one another doubtfully, but the promise of a warm shelter from the cold overcame their misgivings, and they hurried inside.

They stepped up into a large room with floors and walls made of old wooden boards. Some were bent and splintered, and all of them had long faded to grey. There were tables and chairs in abundance, but these did not look so old. The ceiling was high, and from it hung iron chandeliers on long chains.

The room was filled from wall to wall with many people—men for the most part—some simply talking (rather loudly) and some playing table games of various sorts. A dozen or so men were gathered along one wall, watching one another cast darts at a small round target. In the corner an aged man picked a tune on an old banjo that was missing a string.

Women in brightly coloured dresses stood throughout the room. Their eyes were thickly painted, and their hair sat upon their heads in garish shapes of many colours. Each woman held the attention of no fewer than six men, watching and listening to her with unbroken interest.

As Jake and Silorè entered, the general noise of the room subsided, and many heads turned round to look at the strange newcomers. Jake stood frozen in place, and Silorè looked around scornfully. Slowly she stepped forward as if in defiance, and Jake followed her, feeling much like a puppy tagging along after its mistress.

Silorè headed towards the far corner of the room, but a man with thick orange hair stepped suddenly into her path. He eyed Silorè up and down and whistled. "Look here," he said. "It's one of them Lanbairee girls. Say, where you going in such a hurry? I've got an empty seat that's been waiting for you."

He reached out to grab Silorè's arm, but as he did so, Silorè stuck him squarely in the face with a closed fist. He stumbled back with a cry and clapped his hands over his nose. He might have retaliated against her, but whether it was self-restraint or the look in Silorè's eyes, he merely brushed himself off and sat facing away from her at the bar. He dared not come near her again. Jake stifled a chuckle; Silorè was not to be trifled with.

The other men in the room, who had at first moved towards her like a pack of ravening dogs, stepped aside, leaving a wide path for her to pass them by. Jake followed close behind, smiling sheepishly at the many stares of anger and envy. The room was deathly quiet.

Jake and Silorè sat opposite one another at a table on the far side of the room. "Perfect gentlemen?" Silorè said in English so everyone could hear. Jake simply shrugged.

In a moment the commotion began again, and a barmaid approached Jake and Silorè. "I hope you'll pardon us," she said. "It's usually not so busy here. Festival time, you know? Things always get a bit out of hand." She paused a moment to clear her throat. "So, what are you having?"

There was silence for a moment, and Jake and Silorè looked at one other. "Oh, nothing for me, thank you," Jake said at last.

The girl scowled and turned to Silorè. "Nor for me," said Silorè.

The barmaid's cheerful mood vanished. "Look, I can't let you be in here unless you order something," she said.

"We're not thirsty just now," Jake said, "but we'll pay just to sit."

The girl leaned upon the table and looked side to side at Jake and Silorè. "All right," she said resting her weight upon her out-stretched hand, "what's going on?"

She did not have to wait long for her answer. At that moment the doors of the tavern were thrown open, and a half-dozen men entered wearing long overcoats such as no Thalanin wore.

A hush returned to the room.

"We're looking for a Nanyavè," the foremost Nanyan man said in broken English. "She's a labnerè; surely you know what that is?" His companions snickered and scoffed.

The Thalani with the thick orange hair stood up and walked up to the men at the door. "Sounds more like you're looking for trouble," he said. "Be careful, or trouble might just find you."

The Nanyani snorted. "I've no time for your childish threats," he said. "Have you seen the girl or not?"

"What business is that of yours?" A brawny miner in a thick plaid shirt rose to his feet and stood beside the other Thalani.

The Nanyan man took a step towards the Thalanin. "I've not come looking for trouble," he said, "but I did bring it with me." His companions stepped up behind him.

At least thirty Thalanin came forward and stood beside the others. At the sight the Nanyanin backed away, looking at one another and muttering in Nanyan.

The Thalani with the orange hair stepped forward until he was face to face with the Nanyan leader. "Then I guess we've both got trouble."

The Nanyan men turned to flee, but as they did, strong hands seized them by their coattails and pulled them into a circle of large Thalanin men with thick arms and stout legs. Others stood outside the circle cheering, and when any Nanyani tried to escape, they would kick him back into the ring again. The tavern girls stood on a nearby table laughing to themselves and jeering at the Nanyan men.

Jake and Silorè had hidden themselves beneath their table, but as the fighting began, they ran together out the back door and into the dark alley between the tavern and a high brick wall.

Jake turned to Silorè as they ran. “See? What’d I tell you?” he said. “Perfect gentlemen.”

The train to Thesatra hastened on through the rain. Though it was early morning, the train was not empty. Many people had come to the valley for the festivities not only of Brown Hill but of a number of other villages, and now all were returning home. Jake and Silorè had been grateful for the crowds. Even on the platform at Valegate, over a hundred people had boarded the train, many of them Nanyanin.

Jake awoke with his head against the window of the small compartment he and Silorè had secured. He sat up and rubbed the side of his face that had grown cold from leaning against the glass. Silorè lay asleep on the seat across from him, covered in a blanket. Izhana lay beside her; she had met them as they boarded, emerging from the shadows so suddenly that Jake nearly kicked her in his alarm. She had not been forgiving, and even now she eyed Jake cautiously.

Jake wiped away the fog on the window and watched the countryside passing by. The mountains were behind them, and the train now passed through a land of gently rolling hills covered with dense grass and many trees. Thick clouds roamed the sky, occasionally dampening the ground with light drizzle. Jake sat back and closed his eyes. There were still many miles to go until they reached Thesatra.

Silorè stirred and stretched, pushing Izhana to the edge of the seat. Without sitting up or opening her eyes, she spoke. "What's the time?"

"Early," Jake said, "but it's after dawn, if that's what you're asking."

"How far are we from Thesatra?"

"I'm not sure."

"No trouble yet?"

Jake smiled. "We're still alive, aren't we?"

Silorè pulled the blanket tightly over her and sighed contentedly. "When I get home," she said, "I'm going to sleep for three days straight. No, first I'm taking a bath—a very long bath."

Silence followed in which all that could be heard was the gentle hum of the train running on its track. Silorè curled up to go back to sleep, and Izhana shifted her position on the blanket. Jake leaned back and closed his eyes again, but he found his mind swimming with questions.

"Can I ask you something?" he said at last.

"Hm?"

"It's about Ianjori," Jake said. At the sound of the name, Izhana's ears perked up, and she turned towards him.

Silorè did not stir. "What of him?"

"I'd like to know more about him," said Jake. "Who he is and why he hates you so much."

Silorè sighed and sat up, wrapping her blanket tightly around her. Izhana growled as the blanket was pulled from under her, and she jumped down to the floor, glaring at both Jake and her mistress.

"Ianjori is a warrior from an ancient order," Silorè said drowsily, "one that goes back almost to the Second Epoch. He is crafty and quick, and I have never seen anyone fight as he does. He rarely uses firearms, preferring instead all manner of knives and swords. He is one of three brothers of the Utarelamon family in service to the high family of Ialanon."

"You mean the Keneraton?"

Silorè nodded.

"Who leads that family now?" Jake asked. "Not Eratizhal, surely."

Silorè shook her head. "Eratizhal is old—quite old and very weak. He disappeared after the last war and has not been seen in public since. His nephew Dinarion rules Ialanon in his stead. He is the one who has rallied the Kenornin these past decades, and with him they have grown in power and influence. They are rebuilding Ialanon, regaining much of their former strength.

"But more dangerous than Dinarion is Eratizhal's daughter. Ilavè is her name, and she is perhaps even more treacherous than her father. The people of Ialanon love her, and she performs many duties of state. To her people she is a daughter of the glory of the Kenornin, which they lost in the war. Dinarion may rule Ialanon, but Ilavè leads the Keneraton family."

"Even the Thalanin know of her," said Jake. "But I've always heard she was well loved—even in Eratzira. How then is she dangerous?"

"It is precisely for that reason," Silorè said. "Many of her words and deeds go unnoticed by those who should examine her more closely. Did you know she is a priestess in the Temple of Koreva? In that capacity she speaks out against the Thalanin and their dominion of Earth. The Earth is precious to her and to her followers, and they believe the Thalanin are poor stewards of it.

"It is an old argument—one the Kenornin have used to justify many wars. Yet now they say they do not wish to bring death—that the old hostilities are gone—that they want peace with the Thalanin. Do not believe them, Thalani. Though their words have changed, their hearts have not, and they will bring ruin upon all who will not follow them."

She paused and smiled grimly. "Not everyone in Eratzira will agree with what I'm telling you.

"Eratzira is changing. It was not that long ago that most people believed in what my family was doing: protecting the Earth from outside influence—keeping the Thalanin safe and separate so that they might thrive on their own and in their own way. But now the prevailing winds of thought have begun to blow in a different direction. Even in my lifetime, the ways of the Nanyanin of Eratzira have grown more *nildèrina*[21]—hoping that when all things are made equal, all troubles will cease. Yet troubles continue to grow, and the blame is cast upon my family. My family…"

Silorè sighed deeply and did not continue. She turned away from the window, her face filled with pain.

Jake leaned forward in his seat and spoke softly. "Your family is in trouble, isn't it?"

Silorè nodded sadly. "Always."

"You've helped me," Jake said. "Perhaps I can help you."

Silorè turned to him and shook her head with a smile. "You and I are still in the thick of our own troubles, Thalani," she said, "but I'm grateful for your offer. The problems my family faces are not readily

21 Nanyan: from *Nildèra*, "the levelling time." In the branch of Nanyan philosophy called *Falduara*, Nildèra is the idealized final state of the universe. In the ancient Nanyan Theory of Pools (or Wells), the universe is said to consist of pools of *ritholan* (life-energy) that flow into one another. The imbalance of *ritholan* is called *itonsèra* and is one of the five components of evil (*kona*). The ancient philosopher Dirzhi taught that when the *ritholan* in the universe comes into balance, all evil will disappear, and the universe will enter a state of total harmony.

evident, else they would be easy to combat. In the past my family fought warriors and weapons; now they fight more subtle battles of words and ideas, and it is not only the Kenornin that I mean. Many in Eratzira no longer think well of the Itarlavon family. Few care anymore about the protection of Earth—or if they do, they wish it to be protected from the Thalanin who live there.

"But the Earth is still in danger. Ilavè has a mind and heart like her father's. She longs for the Earth, and she leads the cause to remove the Thalanin from it so that she might care for it properly.

"So you see, Thalani, there is danger on many sides. My family is caught in the midst of a circle of troubles."

"So why did you take time to come after me?" Jake said. "Don't get me wrong: I'm very grateful, but why would you risk your life for me when you are needed elsewhere?"

Silorè's eyes twinkled as she grinned at him. "Is that not clear? You're quite important to me—and to my family. I loved your family, and I won't see it destroyed. Why else do you think I would agree to come *here* and go about for days looking like *this*?" She grabbed the ends of her hair that hung in untidy clumps around her dirty face.

A long pause followed in which neither of them spoke. The train car was quiet, and the world rushed by the window.

Suddenly Jake sprang from his seat and stared into the distance ahead of the train. "Look!" he said. "There it is! I was hoping we hadn't passed it yet."

Silorè moved next to Jake and gazed out the window. The train was riding high on a hill above the surrounding lands, and Jake and Silorè could see for a great distance. A forest fell away into the grey sky beyond, and a haze hung over all.

From the grey mist, a dark structure slowly emerged, dwarfing the surrounding trees and hills. It was massive and pyramid-shaped, though it lay at an angle, with its peak firmly planted in the earth.

Silorè gasped, and Jake smiled, for he knew she had just realized what it was—a starship. Its hull was entirely black, and it shone as though it had been newly made. Few vines or other plants grew upon it, or at least they could not be seen at this distance, for the scale of the ship was mammoth. So large indeed it was that though the train sped along beside it, it scarcely seemed to move.

"What sort of ship is that?" Silorè asked, her voice scarcely a whisper.

"I don't think anyone knows for sure," said Jake. "It's said it crashed in a battle long ago—a battle fought on this very plain before the forest grew. I don't know if I'm right, but that ship makes me think of the tower and citadel near Brown Hill. I think that ship belonged to the same people who once lived in that valley. They must have fought here long ago, before this planet was part of Eratzira."

"The Dariasin[22] once dwelt in this area of the galaxy—very long ago indeed," Silorè said. "Perhaps it is theirs. There are many tales of their wars with the Shavitorun, who tried to take their lands. The Dariasin were stargazers, and they often settled planets rich in ores and gems and precious metals. Could that be what they were fighting for when this ship crashed?"

"Who knows?" Jake said, and he looked back to the ship. "I've never seen anything quite so large in my life. How many thousands of people could it hold, I wonder?"

As the ship passed slowly by, Jake and Silorè could see a section of its left aft was missing, as if a beast of monstrous size had taken a bite from it and, finding it distasteful, had left the rest of it alone.

The train clattered on, and the ship drifted into the distance, a grey monument shrouded in mist. Silorè watched it steadfastly through the window, but Jake found his gaze often shifting to her. Though her face was dirty and bruised, her visage was not spoiled,

22 Nanyan: from *dari*, "to watch."

and her eyes shone clear and fair. Even so, she would make faces at herself whenever she caught her reflection in the window glass.

On through morning the train rolled, passing fields covered in tangled grasses or left fallow after harvest. Many roads and paths cut their way through the land, and some crossed over the train rails. Upon these roads a number of small vehicles waited for the train to pass. Some had wheels, and others hovered near the ground. A few flyers soared over the train, and the drivers of the grounders[23] looked up with envy.

Around noontime, as Jake and Silorè ate sandwiches delivered by a small silver automaton, the countryside gave way to cities and towns. The train, which had travelled almost continuously from the time it left Valegate, now made frequent stops at platforms of varying size, most too small to handle the large number of passenger cars.

Jake and Silorè would sit back from the window at each stop so they could not be seen from outside. To Jake everyone on the platform seemed suspicious, and he felt relieved each time the train resumed its journey. Yet with every passenger that came aboard, Jake grew more uneasy. What if the Kenornin were aboard, searching the cars?

Another hour passed, and the cities grew larger and more oppressive. Tall buildings stood close at hand on both sides of the tracks, blocking out the sun. Lights flickered on in the compartment as the train plunged underground. The clatter of the wheels echoed in the tunnel, and passing shafts of light flashed upon the travellers' faces.

23 Nanyan: *adamzira*—a term for any vehicle primarily used for ground transportation. *Grounder* is the Thalanin term and will be used to translate this word.

After several more minutes in the dark, the train slowed with a loud screech. "This stop will be ours," Silorè said, folding her blanket and placing it neatly on the seat. "When we get off the train, follow me closely. Don't look at anyone, and don't fall behind. Just keep walking."

The train stopped with a lurch, and Jake and Silorè hurried from their compartment with Izhana close behind them. Jake stepped wide-eyed onto the platform, which was so long it could service more than fifty cars. A cavernous place it was, cut from the bedrock through which the tunnel ran. Ornate designs were carved into the roof, though they had worn down with the passage of time. In the far wall, a number of doors led into a wide circular room with a high ceiling.

Though there were masses of people upon the platform, it was hardly crowded on account of its size, and Jake, Silorè, and Izhana crossed it with ease. Passing through the doors, they mounted a moving staircase that curved upwards in a large circle, leading to a broad concourse. There, thousands of people moved about, criss-crossing paths as they hurried to and from many other platforms. All travellers were laden with much luggage, for this was the Tasarchènon of Thesatra, where many train-paths converged.

Jake felt safer in such a crowd, though the commotion overwhelmed him. He had been to Thesatra once before, but only to dispute the revocation of his license as a vèralamenasi. The Overseers of hCathad had rejected his appeal, and he had been forced, at no small expense, to travel to Thesatra to stand before the High Magistrate. The magistrate had thought the matter too trivial for his involvement, and he dismissed the claim, renewing Jake's license. When Jake had returned to Brown Hill, there was a celebration at the Grey Griffin, and it was then that he and Samantha began taking interest in one another.

As he thought on these things, a great longing to return home overtook him, and he no longer heeded his surroundings.

"Come on! Keep up!" Jake was shaken from his trance by the shrillness of Silorè's voice. She stood several steps in front of him, having turned around when she found he was lagging behind. "Honestly!" she said as he walked up. "Weren't you listening on the train? Keep close behind me." The change in her voice caught Jake by surprise.

From that moment Jake thought of little else but staying near Silorè. She weaved through the crowds like a fish through water, but Jake found he could not navigate the currents so easily, and he often fell behind. He could no longer see Izhana, but he suspected she was somewhere underfoot.

The station entrance was gated by a marble archway filled with panels of thick glass that filtered light in many colours. Enormous doors of black adamant hung upon giant hinges and stood open to the city. Inscribed upon the outside of the arch were the words "*Atzi Minan Medan-ta Rithonon-ga*,"[24] written in a formal script, rigid and angular. The light outside was blinding compared to the darkness of the tunnel and the concourse, and Jake shielded his eyes with his hand as he stepped into the day.

As his vision cleared and adjusted to the afternoon sun, Jake beheld the skyline of Thesatra—a city void of tall towers and obelisks, but one wide and broad, encompassing many square miles.[25] Among the buildings of white stone, many parks and gardens lay lush and green, even as the season grew colder (for Thesatra was far south and west of hCathad and the mountains of Itelmir). Trees of many kinds and sizes grew there, and blossoms of Adamathèla

24 Nanyan: lit. "beyond these doors, Rithonon"

25 Nanyan: *reldèriasi*—a unit of area roughly equivalent to 0.751 square miles.

and Othamasanda still stood open-faced in the unseasonably warm air. Children played games upon the grass, chasing one another and tossing brightly coloured orbs. Overhead the sun had passed its zenith, and in the warm afternoon, Jake doffed his thick jacket.

Silorè led Jake on through city streets filled with pedestrians and the occasional grounders that herded them to the sides of the road. She navigated with ease, and Jake suspected she had been to this city before.

"We're in haste," Silorè said as Jake followed close behind her. "But I don't think it safe to take any transportation. We'll have to walk, but we haven't far to go."

They cut across a wide avenue and turned onto the side streets open only to foot-traffic. There they saw many small shops and cafés all filled with people enjoying the afternoon air. From a bookseller's shop wafted the scent of musty paper. Tables from a small café encroached upon the road so that passers-by had to walk around them. To the side a grouchy old man sold vegetables from a cart with a broken wheel.

Emerging from the side streets, Jake and Silorè found themselves in a large square surrounded by tall government buildings with many inscriptions chiselled upon them. In the middle of the square rose a column upon which stood a rotating sculpture of General Rondaron Misizhalon, citizen of Rithonon and military leader of the last war, which saw the return of sovereignty to Eratzira.

Jake and Silorè quickly crossed the square and passed into another side road. Narrow and dark, it wound its way among many deserted buildings. Jake cringed, feeling that at any moment he and Silorè would be set upon again. His breath felt stifled, and the warm afternoon air was heavy and stale. All around was silence, and even the sound of their footfalls fell dead on the air.

Just as Jake felt he could endure the place no longer, he and Silorè emerged into the open air again. "There it is!" Silorè cried. "We're here."

Jake looked up and saw that before them lay a vast stone courtyard, flat and featureless. Beyond it stood a dome of blue crystal that dwarfed all other structures of the city. A spire stood upon its peak, and from it a yellow banner blew in the afternoon breeze. Around the spire turned a circle of dark-blue stones that formed the words "*Tazèlam Thesatra*."

"Those characters[26] are new," Jake said. "The last time I was here, this place was a bit run-down, but I see they're making use of the new mining tax."

"So will you," Silorè said, "for that is where we are going. Come on. If we are fortunate, we can make the next ferry."

The two crossed the courtyard at a jogging pace, dodging pedestrians and grounders that crossed their path. Izhana ran after them and was nearly overrun several times.

The dome loomed before them, and Jake marvelled at its size. He had been here once before with his family and had travelled to Telethoram on the ferry, but he had forgotten most everything about the trip, and he saw everything now as if for the first time.

Tall steps led up to the dome, and Jake and Silorè hurried inside, finding themselves in a large concourse, cool and tinted blue by the glass that rose up behind them. The concourse wrapped around a core of white stone broad and tall. Banners of many colours hung from the ceiling, each with the name of a city—some of Rithonon, some of Telethoram, and some of other planets, near or distant.

26 Nanyan: *phathamen*—logographs. Nanyan has many writing systems, but it is most often written in *Phadathon*—a logographic writing system that, in conjunction with *Daninasè* (a syllabic writing form), makes up most modern Nanyan writing.

Before Jake and Silorè turned towards the sign for the Oranthedaren ferry, they were met by three men in red uniforms, each bearing the seal of Thesatra upon a golden triangle—the symbol of Thesatra security.

"Excuse me, miss," one of the security officers said, "but I must ask you and your companion to come with us."

The two other men flanked Jake, Silorè, and Izhana.

"What's this about?" Silorè asked.

"We are to escort you through the security checkpoint," the officer said.

Silorè scowled. "Why?"

"It's for your protection."

Silorè laughed. "From what?" she said. "Who sent you?"

The man frowned. "Please come with us," he said. "We cannot speak here, but I promise that all will be made clear to you soon."

"I'm certain," said Silorè, and a fire was kindled in her eyes. "You may go on your way. We'll be fine on our own, thank you."

"I must insist." The officer stepped forward, looking quite stern.

Silorè was unmoved. "You may drop your pretence," she said. "I know who you are, or at least I know your employer."

"I'm sure I don't know what you mean, miss," the officer said. "We only want to ask you a few questions."

Silorè glared back at him. "I very much doubt that."

The officer stepped back, and then, turning to the others, he said, "Bring them." His men stepped forward and seized Jake and Silorè. Izhana lunged forward to rescue them, but another officer grabbed her firmly around the middle, and though Izhana squirmed, she could not break free of his grip.

As the officers turned to lead Jake and Silorè away, they discovered a tall figure in a grey overcoat standing in their path. A young man he seemed, with thick brown hair and dark eyes, and his face was travel-worn. He stood firm before the gate, and in his presence the security men stood still.

“Thank you for your service, gentlemen,” he said, “but I’ll be taking them with me now.”

For a moment Jake could not move, alarmed by the newcomer, but the joy that appeared suddenly in Silorè’s face dispelled his fear. The security men, on the other hand, were terrified, but the lead officer stood forward. “Step aside,” he said, perhaps a bit timidly. “You are interfering with Thesatra security.”

“Not at all,” the tall man said. “I am answerable for them, and they shall come with me.”

The officer scoffed. “And what authority do you have in this matter?”

The tall man smiled. “The authority of the house of Itarlavon.” Then he raised his right hand, clenched in a tight fist, and displayed a bright ring set with a blue stone that shone with many facets. “I am Adjaron, Nisthèni of the Itarlavon family, and by the law of Iderat, I claim protection of these two.”

The two officers cowered, but their leader stood strong. “She may be a citizen of Iderat,” he said, “and a member of your house, but he is not.” He motioned towards Jake.

“He is Thalanin,” Adjaron said, “and so the Itarlavon are responsible for him.”

“He is a citizen of Rithonon,” the lead officer said, “and that makes him ours.”

“He is a citizen of Earth,” Adjaron said, “for that is his birthplace and heritage. You cannot withstand me in this matter, for this is law in Eratzira and has been for millennia.”

The lead officer stood silent for a moment and tried as best he could to appear menacing, but Adjaron would not be moved. The officer cringed, for he stood at least half a head lower than Adjaron.

It looked to Jake as if the officer were thinking things through—weighing just how much trouble he would be in if he let his captives go free.

At last, with a sigh, the lead officer grudgingly nodded to his men, and they released Jake and Silorè. Izhana jumped from her captor's arms with a firm kick of her claws into his flesh. The other officers turned to leave, and as he turned to join them, the lead officer scowled at Adjaron. "It may be law now," he said bitterly, "but laws can change." He turned and sulked away behind his men.

As the officers departed, Silorè turned to Adjaron, and they embraced one another.

"I'm so glad you're safe," said Adjaron. "We feared you had already been captured."

"But why are you here?" Silorè asked. "I thought you would await us on Telethoram."

"We had planned to do so," said Adjaron, "but it was after your messenger departed that Tolthir returned to us. He had scouted Oranthedaren and found that your arrival was greatly anticipated. At great risk we have brought the *Lamarenor* to Thesatra, and I'm afraid the Kenornin have discovered our arrival already. They tried to stop us, but they could not catch the *Lamarenor*, and we were able to slip by their ships. Some followed us down, but they were poor surface-flyers. They chased us all over the planet, and once they had given up, we came here. The city is filling with Kenornin, and we must go quickly."

Jake was still bewildered. "I don't understand," he said. "What just happened? Who are you?"

Silorè laughed and turned to Jake. "Jake Connolly," she said formally, "this is my brother Adjaron. He's to become patriarch after Zhialamon."

Adjaron bowed. "Mr Jake Connolly," he said in English, though his accent was not perfect. "It's a pleasure to see you again. I almost mistook you for another of your kin; the last time I saw you was long ago on Earth, and you were quite young. I'm pleased the house of Connolly still lives, but we haven't time now for long speech. If we are to preserve your house and mine, we must hurry. No doubt the Kenornin would love to get their hands on all three of us."

Thus said, he turned and led them outside the dome and across the stone courtyard. Adjaron and Izhana walked in front, and Jake and Silorè, tired as they were, struggled to keep pace.

"I still don't understand," Jake said to Silorè as they walked. "Why did they leave us alone? What was that ring?"

"It is the signet of our house," Silorè answered. "Each of the high families possesses a ring of that kind. They were created long ago as the symbol of authority for each house, and they each contain a hidden seal that cannot be duplicated. Those men could easily have verified the ring, but I think they knew its validity the moment they saw it."

"And what is the *Lamarenor*?" Jake asked. "Is it a ship?"

Silorè nodded. "She is an old ship but a good one, and she has served our family for millennia. As such she's easily identified, but it is difficult to follow her in space. On a planet, however, she's quite easy to find, and let's hope no one saw where she landed."

Adjaron led them through the city in a confusing pattern, criss-crossing the path Jake and Silorè took from the train station. As they left the city centre, the buildings of white gave way to ones of brown and grey. The paving stones were not as even here, and in places there were large cracks through which tufts of grass grew in search of sunlight. The sounds of the busy city were distant echoes now, and Jake began to feel very much alone despite the two Itarlavon with him. Indeed no one else seemed to be about—at least no one who could be seen.

Jake looked around him nervously, fearing that at any moment scores of Kenornin would jump out at them. Indeed, he felt as if he were being watched.

"I don't like it here," he whispered to Silorè.

"Neither do I," said Silorè. "Where are we going, Adjaron?"

"You'll see soon enough. We're nearly there."

As they went, the road and everything around it became larger and more ancient, splendid yet ruined from long ages of neglect. Each once-proud edifice was now a scattering of stones covered with moss and fungus, and many lay half-buried in the earth. Jake could only guess at what sorts of buildings these had been in ancient days, for they retained little indication of their purposes. Still, the ancient city must have been great, for it spread out as far as Jake could see, and the columns of many buildings, ruined as they were, towered high over the heads of the travellers.

The road descended a hill and passed through a high wall surrounding a vast courtyard. The paving stones within lay buried beneath a layer of earth from which grew many weeds and grasses. The encircling wall still stood, though many of its entrances had long ago collapsed. At the centre of this courtyard, the ancients of Thesatra had built a stadium of white stone. It towered ten storeys above the travellers, though portions of its walls lay crumbled and ruined.

Jake and the others crossed the courtyard, stepping cautiously through the tall grass. Some of the enormous pave-stones lay upturned in their path, and they carefully climbed over them. The stadium dwarfed the travellers as they approached one of its entrances—a giant arch that recalled only an eroded memory of its once-ornate splendour.

Just as Jake began to feel that he was within reach of safety, a dark shadow moved into the archway, blocking the path. Jake felt as if his heart would crumble in his chest, and he could not command his arms and legs to move.

Before him stood a giant over ten feet tall. His body was like a skeleton, with bones of brown metal, dented and stained. Wires and hoses stuck out all over his body. His limbs were long and thin, and his head was like a skull—round pits for eyes and a silver grate for a mouth. Though the giant had no eyeballs, Jake sensed he was looking directly at him.

"Silorè," Jake said, his voice squeaking, "it's a…Daseshon."

"And you are one of the Thalanin," said the giant, and his voice echoed as though he were speaking from within a metal drum. To Jake it sounded cold and menacing. "Don't tell me that you are the reason for our toil," the giant continued. "With all this fuss, I expected someone with a look of more importance."

Jake was too terrified to reply or even to feel insulted.

Silorè stepped to Jake's side. "You're scaring him, Remni," she said to the Daseshon, "and you're not half giving me the creeps too. Where's our great-grandfather?"

"He's aboard ship," the giant replied. "All is ready for our departure."

"You…" Jake choked, looking at Silorè, "you…know this…?"

Remni glared down at Jake. "Choose your words carefully, soft-skin," the giant said. "It is no wonder you speak so poorly, for I perceive you are not of the Tongue."

"Let him alone," said Silorè to Remni. "You'll have plenty of time to insult all of us later. Let's go in."

Remni turned slowly and lumbered through the archway, ducking his head to walk under it. Silorè and Izhana followed close behind, but when Jake did not follow, Silorè returned and grabbed him by the arm. Jake had not noticed until that moment that Adjaron had already gone ahead of them and could no longer be seen.

Remni led them through ruined passages of carved stone. Flecks of ancient paint still clung to the walls, recalling scenes of ancient games that had been played there. Carved statues worn away by time still stood in carved recesses atop columns of marble. Another archway took the travellers into a corridor, dark and cold, for the sunlight could not reach it. The tunnel went on for many strides before it opened into the arena.

The remnant of an ancient playing field stood before them, covered in grass grown lush and tall without any weed or plant besides. The galleries all around that had once held thousands now stood silent and empty.

At the centre of the field, a mighty starship lay, sleek and black. Two wings ran along its body, stretching forward in two sharp points that doubled the length of the ship. A dozen spidery legs held the ship off the ground, and a ramp led up into the left wing. A cloud of vapour issued from underneath, but it dissipated in the gentle breeze that crossed the arena. The ship hissed and rumbled, and it seemed to Jake as though it were breathing.

The giant turned back to Jake and Silorè. “Hurry up!” he said. “I know your legs are small, but we are in haste!” He turned and strode towards the ship, leaving them behind.

Jake turned to Silorè. “Where did that Daseshon come from?” he whispered.

“Remni has served our family for as long as I can remember,” Silorè said. “It’s best to keep your distance from him. He is loyal but not kind, and he does not think highly of ‘soft-skins.’”

“He doesn’t seem to think highly of anyone,” Izhana grumbled as she walked before them.

A loud cry suddenly split the air. Jake looked up and smiled, for he knew that sound well. From high above a hawk swooped down at great speed and perched upon Jake's waiting arm. His feathers were ruffled, and some were wet with blood.[27]

"Good morning, sir," said Faluin with a bow.

Jake looked him over and frowned. "What's happened?"

"Don't worry," Faluin replied. "I am not hurt, but I have come to warn you that you are being followed. Even now twenty men are approaching from the east. They had been following you from a distance, but they lost their way. I fought one of their scouting birds high above the ground. He struck first, catching me off my guard; but at the last, I cast him down. You must hasten away now: they have found your trail again."

"You've done well," said Jake.

"Yes, thank you," Silorè said with a smile.

Faluin bowed low to Silorè. "My lady."

"Go now," Jake said. "Tell the other vèralamen that I release them from their service. They are free to go where they will." Jake took a deep breath. "That…that goes for you too."

Faluin shook his head. "Far be it for me to abandon my master at a time such as this," he said. "I will relay your message, and then I and those willing to go with me will travel to Iderat. There we will meet you."

Jake found he could not speak, and he had to clear his throat twice before he found his voice again. "Thank you," he choked. "Now make haste. This day isn't over yet."

Faluin nodded and spread his mighty wings. With a few swift strokes, he launched himself into the air and flew out of sight.

27 Automaton blood is generally colourless.

Adjaron suddenly appeared at the top of the ship's ramp. "We must go at once," he said. "Three Kenornin ships are searching the city, and they will soon be upon us."

Jake, Silorè, and Izhana hurried into the ship, and just as Jake stepped inside, the plank behind him retracted and the door closed with a loud clang.

Chapter 7

The Lamarenor

Jake coughed, and the sound echoed through the Great Hall of Itonilon. No one had spoken during his story, which had lasted many hours. He had talked through the chimes that sounded the evening hour, and his voice was beginning to fail. He had been given no pause, and only after he had asked for a drink was he given any water. The king and his councillors had eaten a little in the middle of the day, as was their custom, and other provisions were brought in for the townsfolk who had gathered to listen.[28] Even Jalzoron had grabbed a heel of bread and bit of cheese.

The king's daughter had sat quietly in her chair while Jake spoke, and she did not move even when the king sent one of his attendants to give her his leave. She refused all food and drink offered her, and her handmaidens likewise neither ate nor drank. Jake had glanced only briefly at the princess as he spoke, but each time he looked at her, her eyes pierced him with an unwavering gaze he could not endure.

28 The days on Atralam are so short that it is customary to eat only two meals—one at sunrise and another just before sunset. At midday many persons of high station usually have a small morsel to hold them over until evening. As such it would be considered generous of the king to have provided those in attendance with food.

Jake stood silent now, and when he remained so for too long, one of the councilmen spoke. “Will you not continue with your story?” he said. “How much longer is it to go on?”

“I said it was a long story,” said Jalzoron, rising from his chair and walking to Jake’s side. “There is much more to tell; indeed, the tale has hardly begun.”

A murmur arose in the hall. Thorondoron, who had sat with his head upon his fist during Jake’s tale, rose now to his feet and held up his hand so that the people grew silent again. “The day is spent,” he said. “Could the prisoner not tell the remainder of his tale in brief?”

“There is still much to say,” Jalzoron said, “and to cut it short would render the telling worthless.”

Thorondoron grunted. “Perhaps if the accused would speak more quickly and not stumble over his words, we might finish ere the Thalani grows old.” He laughed at his own joke, but few others did. He turned to address Jake. “Are you sure, Thalani, that you are of the tongue?”

“I’ll let you judge that,” Jake said, his voice dry and crackly. “My dialect is not yours, to be sure, and I haven’t been with you long enough to learn it properly. I am a child of Eratzira, and I make no apologies for that.”

“And yet you left Eratzira,” the councilman said, leaning forward. “Why?”

“That is what my story is about,” Jake said.

“Strange how you have never told anyone before,” Thorondoron said.

Jalzoron stood between Jake and Thorondoron. “He has told me,” he said, “and it is indeed a long tale, for he told it to me over many days when I first found him. He was open to me, and I promise he will be the same to you all if you give him the chance.”

“If you know the story so well,” Thorondoron said, “then perhaps you can tell it in fewer words so that we are not needlessly held here, wasting the time of the king and his council.”

“I will not tell the story for him,” said Jalzoron. “It is his own, and he must be allowed to tell it.”

The king held up his hand to his councilmen and spoke at last. “We will hear him out,” he said, and then he turned to Jake. “But I advise you, Jake Connolly, not to prolong this trial with many words, for that will not save you. However, for today what you have said is enough. We will convene again tomorrow so that you may continue. Until then, a pleasant evening to you all!” He said these last words to the visitors filling the hall, and they bowed to their king as he stood and walked out with his courtiers. The king’s daughter and her handmaidens followed close behind him.

A pageboy came forward, escorted by two guards, and he took the adamantine box and the ring beside it and carried them away, and strong men guarded him.

Other guards advanced and bound Jake’s hands. As they did so, Jalzoron approached. “I believe that things go well for you,” he said.

“That’s doubtful,” Jake said as his hands were shackled. “Besides, they’re only humouring me—or I should say, humouring you.”

“What?”

“This was your idea.”

Jalzoron frowned. “Then would you accept your punishment outright?”

“It’s better than wasting my voice on words no one really wants to hear and won’t make any difference anyway.”

“That remains to be seen,” Jalzoron said. “You certainly held the attention of everyone in the room—even the princess.”

“She’s the last one I want listening,” Jake muttered.

The guards hauled Jake roughly away, and together they left the Great Hall, stepping out into the evening air.

The castle of the king stood upon a hill above the city of Itonilon. Beyond the city grey hills rose high towards the horizon, behind which slowly sank the bright-red sun. There were no towers or pyramids in the city below, and it would not have been called a large city by any standard of Eratzira.

A crowd of people lingered outside the doors to watch the prisoner's procession. Jake hardly cared, and he ignored them as best he could. The people were mostly silent, but here and there he caught a few words mumbled about him, none of them courteous.

Jake was led across the courtyard to a small tower standing on an arm of rock that jutted from the hill and formed sheer walls of stone descending down to the village. An iron door opened in the tower, and a hooded man came forth bearing a flaming torch. Behind him walked other hooded men carrying short swords upon their belts. One man bore a small rifle, and he stood a ways back from the others, keeping his eyes fixed upon Jake. The castle guards relinquished control of their prisoner to the guards of the tower and returned to the castle.

Jake was led inside, and the metal door closed behind him with a loud clang. The echo of it travelled far below, and faint replies rose from the depths. A narrow passage led down a spiral stair into the caverns beneath the hill. The way down was dark, and though the torch-man led the way, Jake stumbled often. At such times the guards would roughly set him on his feet again and push him forward.

After walking together down many steps, Jake and his captors crossed a narrow bridge spanning a chasm of unknowable depth. The walls and ceiling dripped cold water from jagged cave-teeth, and one drop struck Jake by his ear and trickled down his neck, sending a chill through his body. He longed to scratch the spot where it struck him, but he could not move his hands in their bindings.

After a few minutes more, the torch-man turned aside into a cavern so small that two people could hardly have sat down in it. Tall bars of black iron rose from floor to ceiling and from wall to wall, forming a web of woven metal. In one place, the metal lattice was cut and placed on hinges, making a square door only a few feet wide. The torch-man opened the door, and two guards forced Jake through it on his hands and knees. Once Jake was inside, another guard came forward and bolted the door with a giant lock.

The guards left without a word. As the torch-bearer turned the corner, Jake found himself surrounded by total darkness. His hands fumbled on the ground for a moment as they tried to find the dirty blanket that lay on the stones beneath his feet. He wrapped the tattered cloth around him, trying to warm himself, but the blanket was damp and cold.

In the silence of his cell, Jake could hear his stomach rumbling, and it was then that he realized he had not eaten that day. He thought of calling out for one of the guards, but thinking better of it, he lay himself down on the floor.

He had just begun fall away into sleep—which was no small feat given the unevenness of the stony floor—when he heard footsteps drawing near. He sighed and sat up, pulling the blanket around him. It had just begun to warm up.

A glow of firelight pierced the darkness, and to Jake it seemed positively blinding. He squinted as his eyes adjusted to the light, and when at last he could see, the princess Tharè was standing before him. Two burly guards flanked her, making her seem small and fragile. She smiled at him in a way that did not quite seem genuine, and in her hands she held before her a basket covered with a white cloth.

"Would you please let us alone a moment?" she said to her guards.

"We are instructed to protect you," one of the men said gruffly, "and we cannot leave you alone with him. The prisoner is dangerous."

"I know he is," Tharè said, looking at Jake intently, "but I know I will be all right."

"We can't—"

"I insist!"

The two guards looked at each other. "We will be standing in the passage if you need us," one of them said. "Be careful, my lady."

The two guards departed, leaving the princess alone with Jake. For a moment neither of them spoke.

"Um," Tharè said at last, rubbing her arm and looking at the floor, "I…I brought you some dinner. I had a feeling you hadn't eaten today." She held the basket before her and placed it on the ground. When she stepped back, Jake reached through the bars and managed to pull the basket inside. He lifted the cloth, and in the dim light of the torch that one of the guards had hung upon the wall, Jake rummaged through the contents. There was a loaf of fine bread with a ripe cheese, a fillet of fresh fish, a blanched potato, and an assortment of vegetables with long stalks.

"This is from the king's table," he said.

Tharè nodded. "My maidens brought me dinner," she said, "but I wasn't hungry."

Jake began to eat at once, not minding how ill his manners were. The princess stood by and watched him in silence.

"Does your father know you're here?" Jake asked between mouthfuls.

Tharè looked at the floor and shook her head. "No," she said, "no, he doesn't. I don't know what he would say if he knew I'd come down here."

“Then why are you here?” Jake asked.

Something about Jake’s tone incensed her, and she answered sternly, “I’m sorry if you don’t like to be pitied.”

“I don’t,” Jake said.

“That’s a lie!” the princess shouted, and to her surprise, her voice echoed loudly around her. The guards came running in, but she dismissed them again. “That’s a lie,” she repeated, her voice now scarcely above a whisper. “You crave the pity of others, and without it you certainly would have perished. Even the story you told today proves that true.”

“As you say,” Jake said scornfully and went back to eating.

“If you must know,” Tharè said, “I came because I do still care about you, no matter what you’ve done to me, my father, and the kingdom. I didn’t think I would until today. Your story…”

“What do you know about my story?” Jake interrupted. “And what do you know about me? You haven’t heard even a tenth of what I have to say, and I don’t think you’ll like what you’ll hear. You’re in luck, though; when I’m done, you’ll be witness to the final chapter. I fear the ending won’t be a happy one.” He made a gagging noise as he put his hand to his neck.

Tharè shuddered. “But…my father is a merciful man,” she said.

“I’ll get none of his mercy,” Jake said. “Nothing I can say will change that. Why do you care anyway?”

In the torchlight the eyes of the princess began to glisten. “I’m not sure,” she said bitterly. Thus saying, she turned but did not yet walk away. She took a deep breath and spoke in a quavering voice. “That girl,” she said. “You don’t hide very well your feelings for her.”

Jake was silent.

Tharè waited a moment, but she did not face him again. Then slowly she stepped forward, and in a few steps she was gone. A guard returned and removed the torch from the wall, plunging Jake into darkness once more.

Jake ate the rest of his meal and then lay himself down upon the blanket, and at length he fell into an uneasy sleep.

Morning dawned, but Jake did not see it. In this underground world, day and night were the same, and only the arrival of the guards told him morning had come.

"Get up!" a guard shouted. "The morning is waning, and the council is convening again. Get up!"

Jake struggled to open his eyes, for though he had been on Atralam for many months, he was still not accustomed to the short days and nights. He blinked in the torchlight that fell upon him, and when he looked up, he saw many guards standing outside his cell.

Opening the iron door, the guards brought Jake up through the tunnels to a small round room with an open drain in the middle. Forcing him into the chamber, they commanded that he should undress, and once he had done so, they poured buckets of cold water upon him from a trough high above. Once he had dripped dry, they gave him a clean set of clothes and brought him up from the dungeon into the morning sun. Jake blinked in the harsh light, and only by the guiding hand of a guard did he cross the courtyard to the king's court.

The hall was filled with so many people that it was difficult for Jake and his escorts to push through the crowds. A narrow lane at last was made, and Jake came to the front of the hall where the king and his councillors were already seated. To the side sat Tharè surrounded by her handmaidens. Her face was cold and expressionless, but she gazed at Jake steadily and did not look away. Jalzoron sat nearby on a chair that had been brought for him.

A bell sounded, and Thorondoron rose to his feet. "Jake Connolly," he said. "You are here to answer to the charges against you. Are you prepared to continue?"

"I'm ready to keep talking, if that's what you mean," Jake said. He looked over at Jalzoron, who rolled his eyes and shook his head.

"Continue, then, Thalani," the king said.

Some of the gathered townsfolk sat upon the floor, and others crowded as close to Jake as the guards would permit. Unnerved by the attention but determined nonetheless, Jake took a deep breath and continued the story.

....

Slowly the darkness dissolved, and Jake Connolly found he was standing in a narrow corridor of black metal. One by one, lights flickered to life in the dark ceiling. The ship had a musty smell—like the inside of an old wardrobe seldom opened.

Silorè took a deep breath as she leaned against the bulkhead. "We made it," she sighed, running her hand along the wall. "Back in your village, I almost doubted I would see this ship again."

Remni the giant slouched his way down the corridor, his head scraping the ceiling at times. He was mumbling something to himself, but Jake did not listen, for he was certain it was nothing pleasant.

From the darkness came an unfamiliar voice that startled Jake so that he almost jumped into the wall. "At last!"

Jake turned and saw in the shadows an old man wearing a long blue robe tied at the waist with a golden cord. The crown of his head was bald, surrounded by a ring of short white hair. A white beard hung upon his chin, and though his face was heavily wrinkled with age, his eyes shone with a spark of youth.

The old man threw his arms about Silorè and kissed the top of her head, and Silorè embraced him tightly.

"I should never have let you go alone," the old man said.

"I'm all right," Silorè said. "But I owe much to the young Thalani."

The old man released Silorè and turned to Jake. "Jake Connolly!" he said. "I must say I'm pleased to see you. We worried we were too late, but now here you are! Not all may have gone well, but it seems all has worked together for good. I am Zhialamon, patriarch of the Itarlavon family and leader of Iderat. You've already met my great-grandchildren."

Jake looked at Silorè. "Yes," he said, "I have."

The old man held Silorè in his right arm and squeezed her tightly. "They are all that remain of my house—the Lamoroson. They are dear to me, and I am grateful for your protection of Silorè."

"It seems I should be thanking you," Jake said. "If it weren't—"

Adjaron's voice suddenly echoed through the ship. "We're ready to go," said the amplified voice. "Strap yourselves in; this may be difficult."

Silorè took Jake by the arm. "Come with me."

Together, Jake, Silorè, and the old man walked down the corridor, and taking a right turn they entered a large, oval room. At the front stood a large window of many panes, and before it sat Adjaron behind a panel of dials and levers. Beside him were a number of displays and readouts with which he busied himself, and at times he would shout things to Remni through a radio. Behind him at some distance stood five rows of chairs with red cushions and black restraints. Silorè and Jake sat together in the front row, and the old man strapped himself in behind them. Izhana had followed them into the control room, and now she curled up on the floor in front of Jake and Silorè.

"Everyone in?" Adjaron asked, turning around. "Good." He turned back to the console, and touching a certain switch, he said in a commanding voice, "Are we ready, Remni?"

The giant's mechanical voice echoed from nowhere in particular. "As always."

"Then here we go."

The ship rumbled, and from somewhere far behind the passengers, a great noise erupted. A strong wind whipped the grasses about in the arena outside, and in the section of wall visible ahead, a column of stone shook and then collapsed. Slowly the *Lamarenor* lifted off the ground and hovered a few feet in the air.

Jake sat with his hands tightly clasping the arms of his chair.

"Are you all right?" asked Silorè.

"I haven't been off-world in a long time," Jake said. "I prefer to keep my feet on the ground."

Silorè's brow puckered. "But you were so skilful with your flyer."

"Well…" Jake said, "that's different…somehow. At least on the flyer there's still air around you, and I'm never too far from the ground. I'd rather leave the off-worlding to the vèralamen."

Silorè shook her head and took Jake by the hand. "Hold tight, then," she said. Jake felt heavily patronized, but feeling her hand in his, he could hardly protest. Her hands were soft and cool.

She is *a princess*. He chuckled to himself.

The *Lamarenor* rose into the air, higher and higher until the stadium outside fell away and the skyline of the city arose. In the open air, several starships flew over the city, and the horizon beyond became less defined—a blue haze beneath receding clouds.

Adjaron put his hands to the steering levers set before him, and the *Lamarenor* shot into the sky. Rolling to the right, the ship turned away from the city and sped toward open country.

The window before Adjaron changed suddenly, and it seemed that it now looked behind the *Lamarenor* at the lands diminishing into the distance. There appeared to be no change in the ship, and the window did not seem to be overlaid with any projection. It was as if the entire room had suddenly changed position, though that was not the case. Jake blinked, for the sensation was odd to him.

After a moment Jake understood why the window had looked behind them. In the distance three black shapes were quickly approaching. Jake felt his heart sink.

"Is that them?" he asked. "The Kenornin?"

"They've been waiting for us," Adjaron said as the window turned to face front again. "Hold on. I'm taking us up."

Jake felt himself pushed to the back of his seat as the world fell away below him. Clouds rushed by, and the colour of the sky slowly faded to black.

The ship suddenly lurched with great force, jostling the passengers in their seats.

"What was that?" Jake asked in a panic. "Are they firing at us?"

"Yes," Adjaron said. "Their ships have many cannon."

"Have we been hit?" asked Silorè.

"I'm not sure," Adjaron said. "It felt near, but I think we've been grazed only. Hold on tight; we're getting out of here."

The window turned again to show the three ships, now moving apart from one another.

"They're trying to surround us!" Silorè said, and she squeezed Jake's hand tightly.

Open space lay before the *Lamarenor*, and as his eyes adjusted to the darkness, Jake saw stars appearing. An explosion rocked the ship, and Jake nearly leapt from his seat despite his restraints.

"We're hit!" Adjaron said, and he threw the steering levers to the right. The star-field swung violently to the left, but Jake found he did not feel the force of the turn. The window spun round in many directions until it found the Kenornin ships spreading out in the space above Rithonon. They seemed to be unaware of the *Lamarenor*, for they flew about wildly in search of her.

"Can't they see us?" Jake asked.

"The skin of the ship blends into the stars," Adjaron said. "If they've lost us, they will not find us again."

"Well done, Adjaron," the old man said from his seat behind Jake and Silorè. "Let's go home."

Adjaron smiled, and turning back to the controls, he pushed a lever forward. A mighty roar arose from deep within the ship, and the window shifted to show Rithonon and Telethoram slowly shrinking into the field of stars. Everything Jake could remember of his life was on those two spheres, and as they drifted away into the distance, he felt suddenly small.

The sun of Rithonon diminished, and soon it appeared as any other star in the sky.

As Adjaron set the *Lamarenor* in its course, Zhialamon took Jake and Silorè to a long room near the centre of the ship. Here there was a long table surrounded by a dozen padded chairs. On the far side of the room stood a small kitchen with several large stoves and cupboards filled with all manner of cookery. In the corner of the far wall, a door led to a large storeroom of food.

The three sat together around the table, and Jake and Silorè recounted everything that had befallen them. Silorè did most of the talking, and Jake interjected only the few parts of the story she did not know. Adjaron joined them before long, and entering the storeroom, he procured a small meal of bread and cheese and various dried fruits.

"A remarkable story indeed," the old man said once all had been told. "A tale of Providence, to be sure. Do not be troubled, young Connolly; this danger has passed."

"Yet be wary," said Adjaron, "for the danger may return."

"The night may have many troubles," the old man said, "but soon comes the morning that dispels them. Night will fall again, 'tis true, but it cannot make the day shine less brightly. There is a season for everything, and now is a time of rest."

"I hardly feel like it, if you'll pardon me," Jake said. "I'm still uneasy about everything that's happened. Only a few days ago, my future—and my past, for that matter—looked quite different, and though I feel a certain bond for having endured these things with you, I still don't really know who you are. You've saved my life, it seems, and for that I'm quite grateful."

"Perhaps it is odd we treat you with such familiarity," the old man laughed, "but in a way we know you already. You're very much like your parents, and I'm glad of that. I had worried you had become unlike them, for you grew into a young man in their absence. They were fine people, Thalani, as were my grandchildren who perished with them." Jake looked between Adjaron and Silorè, who sat with bowed heads and grim faces.

"But take heart," the old man said, "for we are together, and though we cannot forget what has been lost, we cannot for the sake of what was lost neglect what yet we have." He reached out and grabbed the hands of his great-grandchildren and smiled. Jake looked over at Silorè and found tears in her eyes. Adjaron was solemn, but he was stern-faced and betrayed no other emotion.

The old man sat back and sighed. "Your presence, Thalani, has brought back memory of those days—days when our families were together. It was not so long ago that we sat around this very table and laughed and cried and spoke of many things. Sometimes I come here alone, and I feel I can hear voices from the past return to me." He closed his eyes, and for a minute he seemed far away. From beneath one of his wrinkled eyelids, a teardrop ran down his time-worn face.

At last he opened his eyes again. "Ah, enough of dwelling on such things. This is a time for merriment!"

The old man fetched a bottle that was half-filled with a fizzy liquid. He poured out three glasses of the drink and distributed them to Jake and his grandchildren. To Jake the drink smelled of cherries.

When the old man had poured his own cup, he lifted it and said, "To the reuniting of two great houses."

"Sèveran!" said both Silorè and Adjaron together.

The four drank at once. Jake was at first alarmed at the taste of the drink, for it was strongly flavoured, and the bubbles burned his tongue and throat. "What is this?" he coughed.

"It is *Jazavina*," Silorè said. "I know of no one who bottles it besides our family. As such, it is rarely seen beyond Iderat, and even then it is served mostly in Itarlavon households."

"It's rather pungent," Jake said. "What's in it?"

"That's something of a family secret," the old man said with a wink. "But it is not intoxicating—not in any reasonable amount. Your parents were never fond of it, I fear, but your grandfather relished it."

They all finished off the bottle and then sat together in silence, listening to the gentle hum of the ship. The old man sat back and closed his eyes, breathing slowly and deeply, as if drinking a deep draught. Silorè sat with her cheek resting upon her hand, looking as if she might fall asleep. Adjaron stared blankly at the wall.

At length Adjaron sat up and looked to Zhialamon. "I suddenly remembered," he said, taking the blue-stoned ring from his hand. "I return to you what is yours."

"It shall not be mine much longer," the old man said with a smile, and taking the ring, he placed it upon his finger next to a small ring of silver. The gem seemed to shine a faint blue light on the old man's face.

Across the table Silorè stretched and rose from her chair. "Well, it's getting late," she said. "If you'll excuse me, I'll be in the bath. I've grown tired of feeling dirty as of late."

The old man looked up at her, and an anxious look crossed his face. Jake thought he looked like a man watching the approach of a storm-cloud. "I'm afraid there isn't enough water, my dear," said Zhialamon.

Silorè was halfway out the door, but she stopped cold at his words. Her head whipped around, and her eyes flashed. "What?"

"We left in great haste," the old man said. "There was little time to take on provision. We have enough water to drink, it is true, but there isn't enough, I'm afraid, for such an indulgence."

Silorè returned to the table and slumped into her chair. "What times do we live in," she muttered, "when a hot bath is an indulgence?"

"I'm sorry, my dear," the old man said, "but it's only a few days more."

Silorè sighed. "I suppose it's just as well," she said. "I have none of my clothes here. They were all in my trunk. I don't want to think about where they are now or who's been rummaging through them. On top of that, my head really hurts. I wish I'd remembered that medicine." She sighed again. "I suppose I'll live," she said, "but I won't enjoy myself."

The old man smiled at her. "Yet the hour is indeed late," he said, "and Sorenon will be ahead of us six hours when we land. It would do us well to start into the proper schedule and get some sleep. I'm afraid the days on Iderat are shorter than what you're used to, young Connolly."

"After what I've been through these past few days," Jake said, "I'll learn to live with it."

"Perhaps so," the old man laughed. "Well, then, the men's cabins are on the *lama*[29] side. Remni and I have just cleaned them all. We'll put you in number six. I'll see you all in the morning. Good night."

Zhialamon rose and departed, and the others were close behind him.

"Good night, Thalani," said Silorè at the door. "I'm going *tolma*-side. I'm in number three, if you want to know. I'm loath to go to bed dirty—especially in clean sheets—but I suppose it can't be helped. When we get to Iderat, you must see the bathhouses. I'm heading straight there as soon as we land, and I may never leave. For now, good night." She bowed to Jake and to her brother and then scurried off down the corridor, disappearing around a corner.

"Come with me," said Adjaron. "I'll show you the way."

He led Jake down a narrow corridor that turned a corner into a passage with many doors standing open along both sides. The doors were closely spaced, and there were too many for Jake to count with just a glance.

Adjaron led Jake along to a door on the right. Inside was a small room just wide enough for the bed that lay beneath the window on the far wall. A lamp stood on a low table beside the bed, and a washbasin hung upon the wall to the left. There was little room besides, and Jake presumed he would not be spending much time here.

29 Nanyan: *lama* and *tolma*. According to Nanyan tradition, these terms originated on Earth. A man facing south on Earth would observe the sun setting at his right-hand (*tolma*—"towards the sun") and the moon rising upon his left (*lama*—"towards the moon").

"They're not spacious, I'm afraid," Adjaron said. "But they're comfortable enough. If you require anything, just help yourself. The pantry is always open. If you hear any noises in the night, don't worry; it's probably just Remni walking about the ship. Good night." Adjaron bowed and walked back down the corridor to the control room.

Jake stepped carefully through the doorway, ducking low so his head did not strike the sloping ceiling. As he shut the door behind him, he felt as though the walls were closing in upon him.

He had not realized how dirty he felt until he contemplated climbing into bed. He turned the knob on the washbasin, but the faucet spat only a few cold water-drops. Resigned to his fate, Jake climbed between the sheets and lay on his back, staring up through the slanted window. Outside, the stars were slowly passing by, and in the distance he thought he saw a bright gas-cloud of red and green.

His mind raced, and though he was exhausted sleep eluded him. Brown Hill filled his thoughts. Every sight and sound of his life there rushed through him, and the events of the past few days replayed themselves in an endless loop. Foremost in his thoughts were Samantha and her parting kiss, and he desperately wished himself back home. He imagined sitting in the Grey Griffin, eating a hearty dinner and talking over his day with her. He could see her bright eyes and smile with perfect clarity, and restlessness overwhelmed him.

In such a state, it was hours before he finally managed to fall asleep.

He was awakened in the middle of the night by the sound of heavy footsteps in the corridor. Half-asleep, he sat up, hardly remembering where he was. He strained to listen, but the footsteps passed and faded away. He lay down again and fell almost at once into a deep sleep.

When next he awoke, a rim of light was spilling around the edges of the closed door. He had no idea what time it was, and he fumbled around looking for a clock. Finding none, he rose and stretched. He felt stiff but rested, though still grimy from the previous day's excursions. He had slept in his travel-clothes, and he supposed he would have to do so until the *Lamarenor* arrived at Iderat. Already he could smell his own pungency, and he hoped the trip would not last much longer.

He stumbled down the corridor, trying to remember the way to the room from the night before. With a little effort, he found it and discovered Silorè sitting at the table and reading a book.

"Well, at last you're awake," she said as he entered. She was neither pleased nor irritated. "Still on your home-time, I suppose?"

"I've never travelled much," Jake said groggily. "And I've only seldom crossed the hour-lines on Rithonon."

"You'll get used to it," Silorè said, closing her book. "But it is nearly noontime. You've missed breakfast—not much of one, it's true, but satisfactory. Wait till we get to Iderat and home: there will be plenty to eat and drink. We'll have to find you some new clothes, to be sure. What I wouldn't give for a change myself!" She looked at herself disapprovingly. "Not that I mind Thalavèn clothes, you understand," she added hastily. "I'm just not particularly fond of these, but considering all we've been through, I suppose I'll tolerate them for a day or two longer. We should be arriving the day after tomorrow."

As tired as he was, Jake could not follow the speed at which Silorè spoke. He slid into a chair, resting his head in his hands, and she tilted her head at him and giggled. "You do look a mess," she said. "I suppose I don't look much better."

"What's there to eat?"

"Not much," said Silorè, "but I had a bowl of oats with some dried fruit."

"That sounds fine," Jake said.

"Would you like me to fetch you some?"

"No, I'll get it. If you'll tell me where it is."

"It's really no bother."

Before Jake could protest, Silorè disappeared into the storeroom and returned a few minutes later with a small bowl filled with rolled oats topped with red berries Jake could not identify. She placed this before him and ruffled his hair in a maternal sort of way. Jake felt quite embarrassed, and he ate quietly as Silorè returned to her reading.

When he had finished, Silorè showed him around the ship. The *Lamarenor* was so well designed that it felt much larger than it had looked from outside. Two main corridors ran along the sides of the ship, joined at the front and rear. Short passages connected this outer circle to an inner loop where the mess was located, as well as storage rooms, a study, a ladies' dressing room, a chartroom with large screens on which many maps were displayed, and a few other rooms left empty. Silorè had much to say, and she told some of the history and uses of each room.

"There is also a lower deck," she said. "It's mainly storage, but there are stables there for our horses."

"You have horses?" Jake said.

Silorè nodded. "Both automaton and otherwise."

"Are any there now?"

"No," Silorè said. "They do not often travel with us, but we have taken them on occasion to other worlds where they can run freely. Paliran is their favourite, I think. Do you ride, Thalani?"

"Not really," said Jake. "There weren't many horses in Brown Hill, and they were mostly workhorses. There was a riding stable at

Green Ridge, and though I visited a few times, I never quite got the hang of it."

Silorè chuckled. "What do you mean?"

"I don't think the horses liked me very much," Jake said. "They didn't trust me, I guess. I suppose I didn't really trust them either."

"That's a shame," Silorè said. "I love my horses, and they are the finest on Iderat. We trust one another, and they bear me without objection. I shall introduce them to you, and we shall go riding together if we get a chance."

At the rear of the ship, they passed through a thick door into a diamond-shaped room. Wires and pipes covered the walls and ceiling, crisscrossing one another in patterns exhibiting order and purpose. At the heart of the room stood a chamber of black metal surrounded by long tubes of glass that pulsed with a red light. As Jake and Silorè entered, they found Remni monitoring a cluster of gauges on the far side of the room.

"This is no place for soft-skins," he muttered when he saw them.

"I'm showing Jake around the ship," Silorè said. "I thought he'd want to see the Itarsin[30] chamber."

"You speak of her with so little respect," Remni said, striding towards them. "The *Lamarenor* has a soul, and she feels deeply. She has more spirit in her than any soft-skin I've ever known."

"I didn't know you two were lovers," Silorè quipped.

30 Nanyan: "star-stone." Itarsin is the substance cast off by certain stars as they shed outer layers of matter. Itarsin is rare, and each star generates a different kind with its own properties and uses. Certain varieties give off enormous amounts of energy that can be used to power starships (though not all starships are powered in this way). Related to Itarsin is Itartholan ("star water"), which has the same properties as its counterpart but remains liquid—even under extreme heat and pressure.

Remni stood still, staring at Silorè with his large, pale eyes, but she did not flinch. "Make your jokes," he said, "but the *Lamarenor* is a finer lady than any soft-skin could aspire to be."

Jake could not be certain, but he thought the giant was smiling—a gruesome sight indeed, for in the dim light, he had all the appearance of a skeleton.

Silorè did not smile. "We will leave you two alone, then," she said sternly. Then she turned, and grabbing Jake by the hand, she led him from the room. The giant doors closed behind them with a loud clang.

"What was that all about?" Jake asked. "I thought you two would come to blows before long."

"Oh, that's nothing," Silorè said. "You should see Remni and me when we really turn it on. We each know the softest parts of the other, and we show little mercy."

"Why do you hate him so much?"

"I? Hate him?" Silorè scoffed. "I'd just as soon let him be, but he has such contempt for everything and everybody that I can't seem to control myself. That's why we quarrel with one another. It's mostly done in jest—for my part, anyway—but it's gone on as long as I can remember. He never even liked me as a child. He once accused me…" She had been talking rapidly, but she suddenly trailed off.

Before Jake could ask any question, he found they were back at the front of the ship. Adjaron and Zhialamon stood talking in low voices to one another in the control room. They grew suddenly silent when Jake and Silorè entered, and Zhialamon walked to them.

"Is something the matter, my child?" Zhialamon said.

"No, nothing," Silorè said. "Just the usual matter with Remni."

Zhialamon chuckled. "I've told you to stay away from him," he said. "He's old and cunning. There's no one I've yet met who can match wits with him."

“He certainly does seem angry about something,” Jake said.

“Have you not known many Daseshon?” the old man asked.

“None,” Jake said. “Though Rithonon is near the border, we never traded with the Daseshon. I’d never seen one before, but I’d heard plenty of stories, and your Remni seems to live up to them.”

Silorè laughed. “This is only your first day,” she said. “Spend more time in his company, and he’ll surpass the worst of the lot.”

She and Jake walked back to the dining room, where they found Izhana lying on the table and trying to sleep.

“Get down from there,” Silorè said, shooing her from the tabletop. “Honestly, you’re as bad as any animal. You’ve got a mind, so use it.”

Izhana made no reply but lay down in a corner of the room with her back turned to them. Silorè smiled and shook her head, and sitting down in a chair, she leaned back and stared at the ceiling. “What a few days it has been!” she said. “Successful ones, at least.”

Jake nodded. “It’s strange how quickly things can change,” he said. “A few days ago, I never would have dreamed I’d be here. I didn’t even know what ‘here’ was! I didn’t know who you were—or who I was, for that matter. I suppose I’m only now realizing everything that’s happened.” He became suddenly melancholy. “I don’t suppose I’ll ever see Rithonon again, will I?”

“I’m sure you will,” Silorè said, “if that’s what you wish, but Eratzira is a big place, and there are many worlds you could visit. It’s lucky you’re with us; we can even take you to see Earth.”

“Perhaps,” Jake said, “but Earth never really had much of a pull on me. I know it’s supposed to be every Thalani’s dream, but what makes Earth so special anyway?”

“It is our origin,” Silorè said. “Life began there, and though it may seem like any other planet, none is nearly so beautiful. The star-shapes of Earth are the same ones our ancestors saw before the

Deluge—the Hunter, the Bear, the River, all of them. It is the nexus of all mankind. Doesn't that interest you at all?"

"I'm not certain," Jake answered. "I don't really think about it much."

"You may yet get to see it," Silorè said. "We go to Earth from time to time. I'm sure great-grandfather will want to bring you along. We have relatives who live there, you know. They secretly travel the world in search of Nanyanin. There are more living on Earth than you would think."

"What happens when they find someone?"

"That person is brought to Iderat," Silorè said. "It is the job of the Itarlavon to determine what to do with them. We often just send them on their way, but some are imprisoned for a time. There has been argument recently that we Itarlavon should no longer judge these Nanyanin ourselves but that they should be brought before a court of Eratzira."

"I take it you think that's a bad idea."

"Indeed I do. We Itarlavon have performed this task for thousands of years. It is not fitting that we should give up doing so now."

Jake and Silorè talked for an hour or so, and after that they played a few games of Zhonda,[31] of which Jake won none at all. The time passed slowly, but Jake was content to remain in her company. In the afternoon she went off to take a nap, and he wandered the ship, stopping for some time in the control room to watch the stars through the large window.

Jake saw Adjaron and Zhialamon only at meals, which the four ate together. At other times Adjaron was busy with the ship, and the old man sat in the study reading large books and scrolls.

31 See Appendix B.

Night came at last, but Jake hardly felt tired. He lay upon his bed trying to count the stars outside his window, but though he soon wearied of the task, he was not inclined to sleep. The change in time-schedule already troubled him, for he was used to longer days and nights. He drifted at last into troubled sleep and awoke late the next morning.

The new day proved uneventful, and Jake welcomed a rest from all his recent trouble. He and Silorè played more games of Zhonda, and he lost each time. He ate meals with the others, and they talked together of many things. When he was left to himself, Jake tried running the circuit of the corridors to try to tire himself. The day was calm and peaceful, and Jake slept better that night.

On the last day of their journey to Iderat, the *Lamarenor* encountered another ship.

It was early afternoon, and Jake was walking about the corridor. He had grown tired of losing at Zhonda, and to his dismay Zhialamon could not give him any advice. "You'll have to discover how to defeat Silorè on your own," he had said. "Mind you, she's quite a good player. I've stopped challenging her, for though I have played Zhonda for many centuries, I can scarcely defeat her."

As Jake roamed the ship trying to think through a strategy that might win against her, an alarm sounded—a high musical tone that echoed through the ship. Jake was stunned by the noise, and he stood still, not sure what he should do.

"Out of the way!" a gruff voice called from behind him. Before Jake could move, a pair of wiry arms shoved him aside, and as Jake struck the wall, he saw Remni run past him at great speed. Gathering himself, Jake followed him to the control room and found Adjaron and Zhialamon staring out the window. Silorè followed soon after, with Izhana at her heels.

"There's another ship on scope," Adjaron said. "She's right in our path. I think she's spotted us, and she's coming to meet us."

"She's a sailing ship," Remni said. "A fine one at that."

Zhialamon nodded and pointed to something outside the window. "But she's running crosswind and losing speed," he said, drawing a line in the air. "She must want to meet us very badly. We could outrun her, to be sure. What's she up to?"

Adjaron looked at his scope again and then turned to Zhialamon in surprise. "She's the *Itnanya*!"

Zhialamon stepped towards the window, which seemed to turn to a certain part of the sky. Against the field of stars, Jake observed the approach of a starship, square and flat like a stiff piece of paper. Its golden sails turned around a central housing, and a web of struts and rigging gave the ship a delicate look, though it was indeed large and sturdy.

"Are you certain?" the old man said slowly.

"Quite," Adjaron replied.

The old man stared out the window with an unwavering gaze. It seemed as though he were in a trance. "That's him, all right," he said, as if to himself. "But what's he doing in this part of the galaxy?"

Chapter 8

The Star Sailor and the Shadow

"What ship is that?" Jake asked, confused.

"She's the *Lamtu Itnanya*," the old man said. "Her captain is Thiriton Sindoron, an old friend of mine. He ferries cargo to all corners of the galaxy, but he has not been in Eratzira in many years."

"They're signalling," Adjaron said. "They wish for us to come alongside. We're running at each other at the moment, so we'll have to turn into the neighbouring star-system."

"How long will it take?"

"About an hour."

"Then begin at once," the old man said. "We must not be long delayed, but if Thiriton is as desperate to speak with us as he seems to be, then it must indeed be important."

"It's a miracle he found us at all," Silorè said.

"The *Lamarenor* and the *Itnanya* are sisters," the old man said. "They know each other well, and Thiriton is a skilled tracker."

"Then I'm glad he's on our side," Jake said. "He *is* on our side, right?"

"I'm not sure about 'sides,'" the old man said. "He lacks treachery, if that's what you mean."

The *Lamarenor* altered course, and the *Itnanya* followed, dwarfing her sister-ship with her golden sails that glistened in the light of the nearby star. As the two ships drew closer, the sails of the *Itnanya* retracted all at once, leaving visible only a skeleton of rigging. There was a jolt as the two ships attached to one another.

"Come with me, young Connolly," the old man said. "Thiriton will be pleased to meet you, I'm certain. He has met many members of your family, and he knew your great-grandfather well. He will be glad to see that you are yet living."

Jake followed Zhialamon and the others to the hatch in the tolma corridor. Jake was confused as to what was happening, and before he could protest, Adjaron pulled a nearby lever, and the doors flew open.

"What are you…?" Jake said as he grabbed hold of the bulkhead, expecting to be blown outside. But instead the door opened quietly, and all was at peace. The *Itnanya* lay about a hundred feet off, and between the two ships there was now extended a white plank with no rails. "I don't understand," Jake said, only slightly more at ease. "What's happened?"

Silorè smiled and laughed. "It's an itardèrin," she said. "With it we can walk freely between the ships. Have you really never seen one before?"

Jake shook his head. "Are you sure it's safe?" he said, peering cautiously through the open door.

Silorè scowled. "I've never heard of an itardèrin ever failing."

"There's always a first time."

No one replied to him, but the old man stepped out onto the walkway, and Adjaron and Silorè followed him.

"Come on, Thalani," Silorè said. "You may take my hand if you wish, but do not worry: you cannot fall." She stretched out her hand to him.

The offer of her hand was tempting (albeit belittling), but Jake resolved not to appear weak. Summoning his courage, he stepped through the door and onto the plank. Instinctively he held his breath, and when he could hold it no longer, he gasped and found to his surprise that he could breathe quite well.

He turned back and found Izhana standing in the open door. "I shall not follow," she said. "I will stay behind with Remni until you return."

"You'd rather stay with him than go with us?" Silorè said.

"Say what you will," Izhana said, "but I will not go out on that walk."

"Suit yourself," Silorè said, and she started across the plank.

"Maybe I'll stay behind too," Jake muttered.

"Don't be silly," Silorè said. "You are perfectly fine out here. There's nothing to fear." She walked across, and Jake followed after her as best he could. The further he walked from the *Lamarenor*, the faster his heart beat. He walked on shaky legs, expecting at any moment to fall and tumble forever through the darkness, but he found it was impossible to do so. It seemed that something kept him standing upright.

At the end of the plank, where it attached to the *Itnanya*, a door slid open, and an old man in a tattered white robe stepped forth. "Zhialamon!" he cried, raising his hands. "I've been looking for you all over Eratzira. You weren't at home, and no one would tell me where you'd gone. What secrets are you after this time?" He chuckled warmly in a booming voice.

"My old friend," Zhialamon said and embraced him. "It's good to see you again, but what brings you to Eratzira? When last I heard, you were in Seldin."

"I was," the other man said, "but I still travel a bit. And it is fortunate for you that I do, for I have heard things that I think you shall find of interest. Come inside. It is a much better place for talking." He put his arm on Zhialamon's shoulder, and together the two old men walked into the sailing ship.

Jake entered the ship behind Adjaron and Silorè and found himself in a dark, metallic corridor—one similar to the *Lamarenor*'s. Several passages diverged from where he stood, and here and there dim lights hung upon the walls.

Adjaron led Jake and Silorè through the passages. There were many forks and branches, but Adjaron knew the way. As they turned a certain corner, Jake gasped, for they suddenly ran into a dark figure, short but broad. It had a round face with two mismatched eyes—one small and glowing white and the other large, with a red point of light at its centre. Its body was wedge-shaped, with sprawling arms and legs issuing from it.

Jake stepped back from the automaton.

"Don't be afraid," said Adjaron. "He's a member of this crew."

The automaton nodded at Jake without saying a word and hurried off down an adjoining passage. His gait was awkward but swift, and the clatter of his limbs was thunderous.

"They are Tamèthleron," Adjaron said once the automaton had gone. "As of late, they are the only crew Thiriton will hire. I don't think he trusts anyone else."

Jake followed Silorè and Adjaron up a flight of stairs into a broad, circular room. Its walls were covered with charts of many star systems, and at its centre sat a large, round table of silvery metal. Zhialamon and Thiriton were already seated when Jake and the others entered. Several Tamèthleron stood about, coldly watching the newcomers.

"Welcome!" the old sailor bellowed. "Sit down! Sit down! Have some tea!"

The visitors sat, and two Tamèthleron came forward bearing tea and biscuits.

"It's a pleasure to see you all again!" the old sailor said. "Adjari, the title of Nisthèni suits you well, I think. And Silorè, are you starting to wear Thalavèn clothing?"

Silorè opened her mouth as if to speak, but only a whimper escaped her lips. Jake thought she might cry. Adjaron stifled a chuckle.

"And who is this, then?" the old sailor said, looking directly at Jake. "Silas Connolly? No, that was too long ago."

"His great-grandson, sir," Jake said. "Jake Connolly."

"Splendid!" The old sailor's voice echoed in the small room and made Jake's ears ring. "I'm Thiriton Sindoron, and I've known Zhialamon from the days before the Daseshon ruled Eratzira. That was many lifetimes of Thalanin ago. Those days are now at the edge of memory, ready to fall into the pit of time and forgetfulness. I never planned to grow old, but I have all the same. There was a time when I travelled all over the galaxy—from Thesitel to Itarpala—but now I never travel so far.

"The universe is changing. The days grow swift and perilous, and I diminish. My time is ending, and the universe belongs no longer to old men like me." He looked at Adjaron. "Younger men must replace the old, and that time is soon approaching."

"It is indeed," said Zhialamon, and he turned to Adjaron with a grin.

"But old men still have work to do," said Thiriton, "and I hope to prove that with what I have uncovered.

"I've been to Ialanon, and I have met with trustworthy persons who are near the Keneraton family. They hear many things, and they know much of what goes on in Ialanon that most do not. More happens there than you know."

"And what news do you bring from Ialanon?" Zhialamon asked.

The old sailor leaned forward and spoke in a low voice. "Ilavè seeks the seed of the Atsari,"[32] he said, "and to that end, she is after the Chronicle of Sierduon."

"Sierduon?" Jake said. "Is that a person or a place?"

"Sierduon was a man," said the old sailor. "An ancestor of the Itarlavon house who lived in the years after the Second Epoch. He travelled both the Earth and the heavens, and he performed many deeds, some of which are recorded in the Chronicle.

"In one such tale near the end of the book, it is written that Sierduon found a certain seed as he roamed the Earth. Though it seemed a small thing, it filled him with great fear, and he took it and hid it somewhere among the stars, hoping it would never be found. Though the Chronicle does not identify the seed, other writings reveal it to be the Seed of the Atsari, for by that name it has passed into story and song. There are some lore-masters who doubt the credibility of the Chronicle, but I am not one of them. Nor do I suppose are any of the Itarlavon."

"Indeed not," said Zhialamon. "But even were it not the Atsari that he found, the chance is enough to warrant attention. We certainly cannot let the Keneraton—or anyone else—obtain this thing."

"Has no one gone looking for it before?" Jake asked.

Zhialamon paused and then answered in a voice that was quiet and sad. "Many there are who pursue life unending and look for it in the wrong places," he said. "The Atsari is not where mortals should seek Eternal Life."

"I'm afraid that is exactly what Ilavè is doing," the old sailor added. "How strange that she and her family can doubt so many things and yet be certain of this."

32 Nanyan: "life-tree"—a legendary tree said to grant immortality to anyone who eats of its fruit.

"Strange indeed," said Adjaron. "But you said she yet needs the Chronicle. Are there not many copies from which she could choose?"

"'Tis true," the old sailor said. "I've heard she has obtained many of them—some nearly as old as the Chronicle itself—but they are not enough. For her purposes she requires the manuscript written in Sierduon's hand.

"The true Chronicle is on Thesalara. But Ilavè is cautious: she will not openly come after it, for she fears drawing attention to what she is trying to do. She needs only an excuse to come to Eratzira to fetch it." The old sailor sat back and sighed. "Now one has been given her."

Zhialamon frowned. "What do you mean?"

"She's been invited to the summoning of the patriarchs in Ithèlimon," the sailor said.

"A summons?" said Adjaron. "When was it called?"

"Do you not know of it?" Thiriton asked. "It has been recently announced."

Zhialamon shook his head. "We've been away for many days," he said, "and I ordered that no messages be sent to us."

"Then Kensilon will certainly be awaiting your reply," the old sailor said. "Though I'm sure he'd like nothing more than to see the Itarlavon absent from the Council of Families."

"But why has Kensilon issued a summons?" asked Adjaron.

The old sailor shrugged. "I do not know," he said. "Where the Misizhalon are involved, there is no certainty, but if Ilavè is invited to represent the Keneraton, this Council will be memorable indeed."

"That it will," Silorè said gloomily.

Adjaron sat forward. "But what of the Chronicle?" he said. "That book has been examined for millennia. What secrets does she hope it can tell her that it has told no one else?"

"She has more than a little hope," the old sailor said. "It seems Ilavè has gathered many rare and valuable writings concerning the Atsari, many of them quite ancient. Among these was a fragment of an old scroll. Though I am not sure exactly what it contained, it has led her to believe there are secret words in the Chronicle written with Teletholan."

"What is that?" Jake interrupted. "I've never heard of it."

"Telethitartholan?"[33] the sailor said. "It is a rare kind of Itartholan, mostly used as an ink. Once a star shines upon it, the ink is bound to that star and will vanish by any other light. Writings of Teletholan cannot be read except by the light of the star under which they were penned."

"But if the Chronicle indeed contains Teletholan," said Silorè, "by what star can it be read?"

"I do not know," said Thiriton, "but I believe Ilavè does. No one to whom I spoke knew any more than what I have already said. When I learned of these things, I turned at once for Eratzira, for I feared even to send a vèralam. I went to Iderat, but they told me you were away. I briefly despaired, but the *Itnanya* found you on her own, and here we all are together."

The old sailor looked at them all, and it seemed his eyes began to shimmer. "It reminds me of days long ago," he said. "There was certainly then—as indeed there is now—a storm all about us, but we sat in a calm in the midst of dangerous winds. In those days the Daseshon were strong and made themselves an ever-present threat, but we did not seem to care that they were stronger than we were. Our homes were in trouble, and we rose up to defend ourselves.

33 Teletholan is a *phatha* (shortened version) of Telethitartholan. Modern Nanyan has many such words that have arisen from their older and longer counterparts.

"Yet it *felt* rather different then. The world seemed newer—less corruptible and more trusting. Perhaps I've lived too long and know too much. I've seen many men of great privilege and leadership fall away into ruin—much of it of their own making. Indeed, when the Daseshon conquered their way across Eratzira, much that I had once admired was destroyed. That is when I began my wanderings. Men arose with promises of security and freedom, but they did not charm me. I heard many words, but they were all vain. I saw many leaders rise, but they all fell to their own devices.

"Never forget, Thalani, how quickly life can change, and never let comfort and leisure override your better sense. Trouble often springs from places unwatched and unguarded."

Jake suddenly realized the old sailor was talking directly to him and not to the others, but he could not determine why. The attention unnerved him, and he slouched in his chair, wishing for some way to escape.

"Those were days of sorrow to be sure," said Zhialamon, "but they were also mingled with joy. Despite the pain I would have those days again. It seems heartache often accompanies happiness, but perhaps the reverse also is true. Not all was lost when Eratzira was overtaken, and now it has been regained."

"Only for a season, I fear," the old sailor said, and he breathed a sigh that heaved his entire body. "But enough of such things. What brings you all here away from Iderat, and how is it that the great-grandson of Silas Connolly is with you?"

"I'm afraid we're still in the middle of that story," Zhialamon said. "I'll let those who know it best tell it to you."

Jake and Silorè looked at each other, and Jake shrugged. Then, drawing a deep breath, Silorè began the story. She told how on Iderat, word came to the Itarlavon that the Kenornin had entered Eratzira and had found where the last survivor of the Connolly family lived.

She had begged to go to Rithonon, and with much pleading she was at last permitted to go. "Although," she said in the middle of her story, "I hardly knew what I was in for."

She told how she went to Rithonon and began observing both Jake and the Kenornin. At this point she let Jake take over with his part of the story, and together they narrated the crash and how they met one another. They told of the coming of Ianjori, of how they escaped him, and of how they hid among the crowds at the Thalanin festival.

Adjaron interrupted with the tale of how he and Zhialamon had followed Silorè to Rithonon a few days after she had left, and though Silorè had objected when she learned of their coming, she was nonetheless grateful for their presence. He told of Silorè's departure to fetch Jake from the planet, of the messages delivered by the vèralamen, and of the secret landing of the *Lamarenor* in Thesatra. Together the three told how they escaped the security men and came safely at last to the *Lamarenor* and departed from Rithonon.

When the story was over, the old sailor laughed so loudly that his voice filled the chamber. "A story of disaster indeed!" He chuckled. "But then if everything went according to our own plans, we'd think ourselves too clever and credit ourselves with the success!" He wiped a tear from his eye as his fit of laughter subsided. "But that's not to say we can't try to do what we must, and it seems now that prudence dictates that we should part ways. The *Lamarenor* may be invisible, but her sister is not. Go now, and perhaps we will see each other again and talk of things of much less importance."

The old sailor bade them all farewell and escorted them back to the itardèrin. Jake walked slowly back to the *Lamarenor*, though perhaps a bit faster this time. Izhana greeted them all coldly upon their return and walked off with her nose in the air. Zhialamon and Adjaron went on to the control room, but Jake remained with Silorè as she saw to the retraction of the itardèrin and the closing of the door. There was a question that was bugging him.

"What was that about not sending a vèralam?" he asked her. "Certainly it would have been safe, and he could have saved himself this needless journey."

"Thiriton trusts very few," Silorè said. "And he has reasons to do so, which I will not go into now. Suffice it to say he has not lived a life of comfort and friendship. My great-grandfather may be the only person in the universe he trusts fully. I think that is also the reason why he recruits only Tamèthleron for his crew, for they are the most loyal of the Eshgarin."[34]

"He's an interesting man," Jake said. "He's like Zhialamon, but not quite. He's…less serious somehow and yet still very grave."

"There are no other men in all the universe like them," Silorè said, "and as such they are not quite like each other. But they are both wise, and I trust them without reservation. If either of them were leading Eratzira, things would go much better."

Jake and Silorè walked together to the control room, where they watched the *Itnanya* depart. Her great sails were unfurled, and she shone golden once more in the light of the nearby star. The window of the *Lamarenor* turned to follow the *Itnanya* in her course, and soon the ship was lost to sight.

Adjaron took his seat at the helm and set the ship on a path to Iderat. The stars swirled, and the *Lamarenor* headed for home.

Late that afternoon Zhialamon called everyone to the front of the ship.

34 Nanyan: "artificial men"—commonly translated in this book as "automatons." This is not by itself a proper translation. The Nanyan word *Atheviron* ("self-minded ones") is the source of the English translation "automaton."

Jake was sitting alone near a long window in a side corridor. The air was fresher and cooler there, and if he closed his eyes, he could almost make himself believe he were sitting somewhere on Rithonon. When Zhialamon's voice echoed through the ship, Jake opened his eyes and strolled to the control room, where he found the others already assembled. They stood all together near the window, staring straight ahead. Izhana stood atop one of the consoles, and Silorè was scratching her between the ears.

Everyone was silent.

"What's going on?" Jake asked.

Silorè looked at him but did not speak. She motioned towards the window, and Jake stepped up so that he could better see what had fixed everyone's attention.

Directly ahead lay an immense cloud of black dust and gas. No star could penetrate its darkness, and the only colour within it came from ghostly wisps of thin green smoke that swirled about its edges. Every so often, a white flash would light the cloud, revealing dark shapes spinning round one another like phantoms. The sight struck Jake's heart and filled him with fear.

"That's the Thasadres,"[35] he said. "Isn't it?"

"One of them, yes," the old man said in a low voice. His tone did not allay Jake's fear.

"Will we go around?" Jake asked.

No one answered.

Jake grew more panicked. "We will go around, won't we?"

35 Nanyan: "cloud of blood"—one of many travelling clouds of dark gasses known to swallow passing ships. Their origins are not known, and though they are rarely seen in modern-day Eratzira, they are greatly feared among star-travellers.

Adjaron turned in his chair. “If we can,” he said grimly. “But that cloud is moving at great speed, and it will soon overtake us. I fear there is no escaping it.”

Jake felt the blood rush from his head. He staggered and fell into one of the passenger seats close at hand. “So it is hopeless, then?” he said. “I may not know much about star-travel, but even I know the dangers of the Thasadres.”

“There are many dangers in the universe,” said the old man softly. “Those you cannot avoid, you must confront.” He stepped forward and placed his hand upon Adjaron’s shoulder. “Take us as much around it as you can.”

The cloud grew until it filled all the window and its edges could no longer be seen. Like a dark creature, it reached out its tendrils, and the *Lamarenor* began to shake.

Darkness filled the cabin like black slime leaking through the window. All sound fell away save for the breathing of Jake and his companions. The lights in the ceiling could do little to dispel the darkness, and soon they were lost to sight. Jake put his hand before his eyes, but he could see only a dim shadow of his fingers. Whether the cloud had entered the ship or merely played tricks on his eyes, Jake could not tell. Outside the window, swirls of blue and green rose in thin columns, twisting round each other in ghostly dances.

Then, as if echoing from a great distance, many sounds arose. A low rumble came like the thunder of a far-off storm, but as it grew, it seemed more like the wailing of many voices. Amid the chorus of moans and cries, at the very edge of hearing, laughter rose and fell in shrill notes that mingled with the other voices.

Jake felt a chill ascend his body from his toes to his crown. He looked to Silorè and found he could see only the faint shape of her, blurred by the fog that had passed between them.

The walls of the room had vanished, replaced in every direction by never-ending night. The air grew damp and cold. A breath of plague surrounded him, and Jake expected at any moment to fall from the world into death. He stumbled to the floor and clutched his chest, for his heart felt like ice within him. A hand seized his arm and tried to lift him up, but the hand slipped, and in a shroud of black mist, Silorè fell at his side.

"Thalani…" Her voice was like a whisper crossing a wide room. "Thalani…"

"Come on," Jake said in English. "We'll…get up." He heard himself speak, but it hardly felt like his own voice, for the words seemed to come from a great distance.

He reached out to Silorè and seized her arm. She leaned against him, and together they stood to their feet. As they did so, a shrill voice rose above the others and filled their ears. It spoke no words they could understand, and it echoed from all directions. Slowly it rose to a scream, and the *Lamarenor* quaked.

Another voice joined it and then another and another, each wailing a different shrill note without pause. The discord of voices struck the travellers at the heart. Silorè cried aloud and buried her face in Jake's shoulder. Jake felt the tremor of her voice but could not tell which among the many was hers.

Zhialamon rushed to their side and embraced them both, and even over the unbearable noise his voice rang clear. "Do not fear it, my children! Do not fear!"

Lightning split the darkness, and the cloud seemed to fold on itself, dredging up husks of great ships, some from times and nations long forgotten. Having been snared by the cloud long ago, they drifted like dead men in a pool. Gasses engulfed them, pulling them deep into the cloud again. Jake watched with wonder, fearing the *Lamarenor* was soon to join them.

As Jake despaired, another sight turned his gaze from the window. In the darkness, silhouetted against the flashing light, the form of Zhialamon stood tall, and his lips were moving. Though the screams filled the air, Jake could still hear the old man's voice, which, though softer than the surrounding tumult, rose strong above it. Until he heeded the words, Jake could not tell what they were, but as he bent all his thought upon the old man, the words grew clearer. "…they shall not overflow you. When you walk through the fire, you will not be burned…"

A blast shook the ship, and Jake's focus was ripped away. He fell, but the arms of the old man caught both him and Silorè. Though patriarch's strength had waned in his old age, he held both Jake and his great-granddaughter in an embrace stronger than the cloud had power to overcome. The darkness grew, and the lightning flashed. Thunder roared to a deafening height, and the chorus of fell voices grew to a terrible climax.

Jake's mind swam, and just when he thought he could endure no more, the old man's voice pierced the clamour again. "Heed not the voices, my children! Already they are passing away!"

Even as the old man spoke, Jake thought he heard the voices diminish. One by one they died to whispers, ever murmuring in the travellers' ears. The darkness fell away, and Silorè looked up at Jake with tearstained eyes. Then she looked down again and shook with great sobs, and it was some time before she was comforted and wept no longer.

Outside the window stars began to appear as the *Lamarenor* slowly emerged from the cloud. The window turned back to watch as the cloud shrank into the distance, for it no longer pursued them.

The old man walked Silorè from the room, and Izhana followed them. Remni lingered only for a moment before leaving in the opposite direction. Adjaron remained, gripping the arms of his chair so that his fingers lost all colour.

Jake collapsed into one of the passenger seats and held his head in his hands. Darkness still weighed heavily on his mind and heart and lingered there long afterward.

At length Adjaron turned around in his chair. "That was far closer than I had intended," he said, his voice weak at first.

Jake looked up. "Out of all the stories of the Thasadres," he said, "I have never heard of any experience like that."

"That is not without cause," Adjaron said gravely. "The dangers of the Thasadres overpower many ships—even those as ancient as the *Lamarenor*. The cloud is without mercy, but the *Lamarenor* is old and wise. She knows its power, and she is not reckless concerning it. Alas, I led her too far into the cloud, but she was strong enough to bring us safely out again. We're fortunate to have her, for a lesser ship surely would have perished.

"Nevertheless," he added seriously, "know that neither skill nor strength alone bore us through that cloud."

"But what is the Thasadres?" Jake said. "And where does it come from?"

"Who can say?" said Adjaron. "The Thasadres is ancient beyond reckoning. It is a body of malice travelling through the galaxy, but for what purpose, I do not know."

A great span of silence followed in which Jake felt the terror of the cloud pierce him again and again. The voices echoed still in the chambers of his mind, though they grew ever fainter.

Zhialamon returned at last and sat in a chair that stood against the wall. He clasped his hands before his face and bowed his head wearily. He seemed to have aged.

"Are you all right?" Jake asked.

"I shall be in time," the old man said. "The night shall not last forever."

"How is Silorè?" Jake asked.

"Shaken," said the old man, "but not defeated."

"May I see her?"

"If she will have you," the old man said. Jake sprang from his seat and hurried to the door, but the old man caught him by the arm. "But beware, young Connolly: my great-granddaughter is very proud, and there is a darkness upon her heart that she does not wish others to see."

"I understand."

Jake hurried to the dining room, peering slowly around the corner when he reached the door. Inside he found Silorè seated at the far end of the table. She was wrapped in a blanket, and in her hands she held a cup of steaming milk set before her. Seated upon the table, Izhana was looking at her mistress with great concern. Neither she nor Silorè looked up as Jake entered.

"I wanted to see if you were all right," Jake said softly.

Silorè turned away from him. "Please go away," she said sternly.

Her tone arrested him. "If you wish," he said. "I was just concerned about you."

"Thank you." There was no sincerity in her words. She pulled the blanket tightly around her and buried her face in it.

Jake turned slowly and walked out, and traversing the circle of corridors, he came to his own room. There he slumped upon his bed and stared out the window until the *Lamarenor* arrived at Iderat.

Chapter 9

The House at Sorenon

Iderat was the second planet in a system of five worlds. Blue ocean dominated its surface, divided by two large continents. Swirls of white cloud churned through its skies, bringing heavy rains to its lands of many hues.

Iderat had only a single moon named Calisa, and as the *Lamarenor* approached, both the planet and its companion grew out of the myriad points of light behind them. Idtolitar, the orange sun of Iderat, shone brightly from a great distance, and Jake shielded his eyes against it.

In the control room, Adjaron sat at the helm, and Jake and Zhialamon stood behind him gazing out the window. Silorè had retired to her room, and Jake had not seen her since.

"What do you think of our home?" Adjaron asked as Iderat drew close enough for Jake to see its clouds and seas.

"She looks very much like the Earth," said Jake, "or at least like the pictures I've seen."

"She does," the old man said. "Iderat is a pleasant world, to be sure, and as much like Earth as anyone could wish. They are sister-worlds, though the Earth is the fairer of them."

"Yet Iderat has defences the Earth lacks," said Adjaron. "The strong winds of Idtolitar beat upon Iderat, and though the planet repels them, they make trouble for star-travellers. Many outposts circle Iderat to guide friendly ships through the turbulence, for without such aid, a ship cannot even circle the planet in safety, to say nothing of landing there. It is for this reason that Iderat has not been invaded in over two thousand years."

Iderat soon filled all the window. Jake and the old man strapped themselves into the passenger seats. Summoned by Zhialamon, Silorè entered a few minutes later and sat silently in the back row. Izhana followed and curled up beside her. Jake looked back at Silorè, but she did not regard him at all.

The star-wind shook the *Lamarenor*, and Jake began to feel ill. He must have looked it, for the old man passed him an empty bag of brown paper. Jake held the bag before him, but though he felt awful, he did not become sick.

Between waves of illness, Jake watched the surface of Iderat passing beneath the gaze of the window. The ocean was vast and empty except for a few stray islands sitting atop shallow reefs. The shoreline of the larger continent appeared over the horizon, and slowly the azure sea was replaced with flats of brown and green. Grey rivers crossed the land, and white mists swirled over all. Between forested hills lay large cities connected by broad roads running in straight lines all over the continent. So wide were these roads that they could be seen from high above the planet.

The sky glowed crimson around the ship as it descended. The blue haze at the horizon grew brighter, and the sky lightened all around. The air grew violent, shaking the ship so that Jake felt as though he might break free of the restraints holding him in his chair. Though Adjaron guided the ship with skill, Jake found himself filled with anxiety, for the view outside the window was chaotic. When he could no longer endure the sight, he closed his eyes and gripped the arms of his chair, hoping the descent would not last much longer.

When at last Jake opened his eyes again, he found that the *Lamarenor* was flying through a heavy rainstorm. The view outside had turned dark-grey, and streaks of rainwater covered the window. Flashes of lightning split the sky, illuminating the fog all around the ship.

Then all at once, the *Lamarenor* plunged beneath the clouds, and Jake saw that the ground was near. Below the ship a wide plain lay dotted with solitary trees and large buildings of stone and brick. Mountains rose near the horizon, and a forest of dark trees ran down from the hills into a valley beyond the plain.

Directly ahead, near the edge of the valley, stood a large house made of brown stone. Five gables dominated its tiled roof, and its exterior walls were filled with large windows. Before the house lay a wide lawn bordered by a road that ran to the far end of the plain. It was for this lawn that the *Lamarenor* appeared to be heading.

Through the haze Jake discerned a number of trees and buildings that stood in a wide space behind the house. In the valley beyond, he could see with great effort the line of a brown river running in its winding course. The rain grew suddenly heavy, and a grey sheet hid the valley from sight.

The *Lamarenor* slowed as it approached the house, and the window turned towards the ground. The ship descended, and with a jolt it settled upon the grass, and then all was still. The window turned to face forward again as water-drops pooled and ran down its face.

The passengers rose from their seats and walked together into the corridor. Silorè did not speak. Indeed, she hardly seemed to take notice of anyone but walked with her head bowed and her hair hanging in her face.

The sound of the rain echoed through the ship, and when Adjaron opened the outer door, a gust of wind blew large raindrops inside. As

Jake peered into the storm, he saw that the ship had landed so that its ramp faced the house, though it was hard to see through the deluge. The house stood tall, and its chimneys rose high above its roof—a shadowy silhouette against the grey sky behind.

As he looked towards the house, Jake suddenly became aware of several figures advancing through the thickening rain. There were five of them—four men and one automaton. Though the sky-water poured down upon them, they did not hasten but walked as calmly as on a cloudless day. The automaton, who stood taller than the rest, walked a bit ahead, and in his hand he held at head's height a rod topped with a glowing orb. As the group neared the ship's ramp, Jake saw that though they had walked many strides through the downpour, they were not the least bit wet. They mounted the ramp, and when they reached the top, the rain seemed to turn aside from the door.

The men standing behind the automaton wore black tunics trimmed with silver, each with an emblem of gold across the chest. Every man was broad and strong and grim of face. Jake wondered if they ever smiled.

The automaton standing before them was arrayed in a tunic of golden metal that did not bend or move as he walked. His face was as the face of a man, though silver in colour and smooth. He had no nostrils, and his mouth was only an unmoving gap between silver lips. His eyes likewise were no more than slits beneath his brow, and though his hair was a solid piece of metal, it was shaped like golden curls. When he spoke his voice rang as if he were talking into a metal goblet. "Good evening, masters and mistress," he said. "It is a pleasure to see your safe return."

"And we are pleased to return home," said Zhialamon.

One of the men standing behind the tall automaton spoke, and his voice was low and gruff. "I wish you had let us come with you, sir," he said. "All regions have grown dangerous, and it is reckless to go wandering alone."

"No more of that now, Sondari," said Zhialamon. "I know well your arguments, for you made them to me ere I left. All is done, and all is well, and here we are returned."

"But the lady Silorè is without her ship," Sondari said. "What has become of it?"

"All things in their time," Zhialamon said, "but first let us get out of this rain."

"Certainly, sir," the tall automaton said. "This way, please."

The uniformed men stepped aside and let the travellers pass through their midst, forming a circle so that Jake and the members of the Itarlavon household were surrounded. With the automaton at their centre, they all proceeded together towards the house. No rain fell on any of them, and Jake found that for a short distance around the rod the automaton carried, the air was dry. He reached outside the circle and felt rain strike his hand in cold drops.

Jake turned back and looked at the *Lamarenor* standing black against the grey haze beyond. Remni stood at the top of the ramp, watching the travellers depart. His eyes were glowing with an eerie yellow light, and Jake turned away with a shiver.

Suddenly, from the direction of the house, there arose the sound of footsteps running and splashing in many puddles. Jake turned and saw a girl sprinting through the rain. She was no Thalavè, and as such Jake could not guess her age, though she had the appearance of one a few years younger than him. Her long black hair fluttered behind her as she ran. She wore no shoes or sandals, and her green dress was so saturated with rain that it appeared brown. The white bow in her hair lay flat against her head, beaten down by the rain.

"You're back!" she screamed. "You're back!"

She ran through the uniformed men and threw herself at Silorè with such force that she nearly knocked her to the ground. Silorè, suddenly shaken from her miserable state, steadied them both and brushed the wet hair out of the girl's face.

"You're soaked!" Silorè said as she looked her over. "Couldn't you have waited inside?"

The girl frowned. "But I wanted to come out as soon as you arrived," she said. "I didn't see the ship until just now. I had meant to come out with the Protectors,[36] but I was too late. I don't mind the rain, Silorè. Really I don't." Then she smiled broadly, and her eyes were like sunshine in the surrounding gloom.

The girl suddenly became aware of Jake, and she hastily stepped to the side so that Silorè stood between her and the stranger. The procession, which had stopped at the young girl's approach, now continued towards the house, and no one spoke again until they were all inside.

The front portico of the house stood a few feet above the ground, with tall pillars that rose to an overhang of white marble. Inside stood a double-door of black adamant trimmed with raised circles of gold. Spanning both doors was a haloed star with many points of varying lengths. Half-eclipsing this star was an orb like a planet, and a sweeping line surrounded both of these, crossing the edge of the planet and passing behind the star. This was the symbol of the Itarlavon family—an ancient sign well known throughout Eratzira.

Beneath the shelter of the portico, the tall automaton extinguished the glowing rod and pushed open one side of the great door, which swung with a deep groan. The travellers hurried inside, and as Jake crossed the threshold, he found himself stepping into an oblong room lined with paintings and mirrors all trimmed with gold. Two staircases—one at each hand—spiralled upward into the high

36 Nanyan: *jolaziren*.

ceiling. A chandelier of many lights and facets of glass illuminated the room with a brilliant light. The stone floor shone like a mirror, reflecting shadowy images of the people and furniture above. On the opposite side of the room, a broad arch led into a hall of great size and splendour. In all his life, Jake had never seen so rich a place.

Even as Jake marvelled at the house, a number of servants entered and attended to the travellers, ensuring they were dry coming out of the rain. Two lady-servants waited on Silorè only. They were dressed differently from the others, and they worked with great proficiency, wrapping a shawl around her shoulders and ensuring that her hair was dry.

"Welcome to the House of the Itarlavon, Jake Connolly," Zhialamon said, stepping forward and raising his hands. "This house has stood for over two thousand years, and many of your ancestors walked its halls. As they were welcome here, so shall you be, and you shall be as any member of my family."

The men in uniform stepped forward and stood on either side of the old man.

"And we, Jake Connolly," Sondari said quite seriously. "We also are at your service. I am Sondari Arakani, Chief Protector of the Itarlavon. It shall be my duty—and that of my men—to keep you from danger, and we swear to you, as we swear to the Itarlavon, that if our deaths may preserve your life, so shall we die for your sake. This is the wish of Zhialamon, patriarch of the Itarlavon."

"So say I," said Zhialamon.

The other protectors stood tall and answered together, "So say we all!" Then, in unison, each man raised his left fist to head-height and struck his forearm with his right hand, and the sound echoed through the room. They bowed together, and two of them turned to stand sentry at the door. Jake felt that he had just partaken in a ceremony of some sort.

Zhialamon and Adjaron took their leave, saying they would find Jake later, once he had settled into his room. Sondari and the other protectors went with them, and all the servants left except for the two young women who stood by Silorè.

When the others had gone, Silorè breathed deeply and sighed. "I feel much better now," she said. "Home heals wounds that cannot be otherwise mended." She turned to Jake. "Pardon me for my lack of hospitality, Thalani. I am the Lady of this house, and I should have been the first to welcome you." She stood before him and politely bowed. "Welcome to Sorenon, Jake Connolly. It is my hope that you find the peace here that my family and I have known."

Though Jake was still dazed by all the new sights and sounds and smells, he managed a shaky bow. "I thank you," he said.

"I want you to feel quite at home here," Silorè said. "There is much for you to see and to do, and there are many people to meet." She turned to the young girl and, taking her by the hand, brought her face to face with Jake. "Thalani, this is Sinarè of the family Faloroson. You already have something in common, for being in need of protection, she also has come to stay with us."

Sinarè looked around nervously but composed herself long enough to manage a polite curtsy, fingering the corners of her water-soaked dress. "I'm pleased to meet you, sir," she said with a nod.

Jake bowed. "And I you."

Sinarè smiled, but she would not look him in the eye for more than a moment.

"And these are the *lisarèn*[37] of Sorenon," Silorè said, waving forward the lady-servants who stood by. "This is Calandè, and this is Lithè." She motioned to each girl in turn. They were both young

37 Maidservants who serve the lady of a Nanyan household, answering only to her. Lisarèn are usually esteemed above other household servants, though they are usually not as young as Silorè's.

and fair, and they each wore a dark-blue dress with a white sash tied tightly around the waist.

Calandè was dark-haired and stood a bit taller than Silorè. Her face was grim, but her green eyes were bright. Lithè smiled shyly when Silorè said her name. She was shorter than Calandè and stood with shoulders slouched and hands clasped before her. She bowed her head as she was presented, and her fair blonde hair fell into her face.

"A pleasure," the girls said together, and they curtsied.

Silorè turned back to Jake. "Now, if you'll pardon me, Thalani," she said, "I must take my leave of you. If I do not change out of these clothes this instant, I shall probably go mad. I will see you at supper." Thus saying, she turned and walked with her attendants up the left staircase and out of sight.

Sinarè followed close behind her. "Goodbye," she said softly and was gone.

Jake suddenly realized he was standing all alone. As he wondered what he should do, a man in a blue uniform approached and bowed before him. "Good afternoon, Jake Connolly," he said. "My name is Jardir. I am chief of all the servants of this house, and I have been instructed to show you to your lodgings. Please follow me."

He led Jake up the right-hand stairs into a vast chamber supported by many tall columns. These pillars all surrounded an enormous hole in the floor that looked down into the Great Hall below. A giant window where the staircases emerged looked out onto the green before the house, and Jake glanced over his shoulder at the *Lamarenor* weathering the storm upon the lawn.

Jardir led Jake across the marble floor to a door in the far right corner that opened on a carpeted hallway. After a few turns through the corridor, Jardir stopped at a certain room and led Jake inside.

Jake found himself in a chamber that was utterly blank. Purest-white stone covered every surface, and the ceiling was carved with intricate reliefs of many patterns. On the right lay a bed topped with white linens, and upon the other wall stood a chest of drawers and a mirror. Beside these were two doors—one leading to a private bathroom and the other to a closet with many shelves and hangers.

To Jake's surprise there was no wall opposite the door. Instead a thin white curtain veiled the room, and beyond it a balcony overlooked the gardens below. Though only the curtain divided inside from outside, the room was not cold; neither did the wind blow, nor did any rain fall inside.

"I trust you will be comfortable here," Jardir said. "If there is anything you need, just ask. Another server or I should be nearby, and if not you can always find someone downstairs. There are Thalanin clothes in the closet and chest. If they do not suit you, let me know.

"If you are weary from your journey, you have your own bath, or if you prefer the bathhouses, they are down the garden path to the left. There will be someone there to guide you. If you require nothing further of me, I shall return to my duties." He bowed and departed.

Jake stood for a moment as one struck on the head, for he could not clearly hold in his mind all that had happened to him in so short a time. In this stupor he walked through the curtains onto the balcony, and there he stood looking over this new world to which he had come. He could not see the garden properly in the storm, but it appeared to contain all manner of plants and trees arranged in many tiers, with stone paths winding throughout. A summerhouse open on all sides stood at the centre, its posts covered in vines and creepers. Curiously, there was a spot nearby bare of any living thing, whether tree or flower or grass—only a patch of dirt whereon stood the remains of a shrivelled tree stump of great girth.

At the far edge of the garden ran the path of which Jardir had spoken, and Jake followed it with his eyes to the bathhouses—two buildings of red stone standing apart from the garden, separated by lines of trees. Their forms were barely visible through the storm, for they stood near the opposite end of the main house.

I suppose a bath couldn't hurt, he said to himself.

He left his room and found a staircase that led down to the covered terrace overlooking the gardens. Walking along the back of the house, he found the proper path and hurried along it down the hill, not heeding the rain, though it chilled him.

The bathhouses stood tall, with roofs of cloth strung up like sails over rooms open to the air. The walls were made of giant blocks of red stone carved in pleasant shapes and patterns. Jake hurried beneath the awning of the nearest house and stood a moment, combing his water-soaked hair with his fingers.

A sudden voice rose over the noise of the storm. "Where do you think you're going?"

Jake looked around for the voice and found Izhana standing before the door of the bathhouse. "I…I was looking for a bath," he said.

"Then look elsewhere," she said and nodded upwards. Above her was a sign upon which was written in golden characters "Ladies' Bath."

Jake blushed. "Sorry," he said. "No one told me which house was which."

Izhana glared at him. "Then you are fortunate," she said doubtfully, "that I was here to direct you."

"I think you misunderstand me," Jake said. "I wasn't—"

Izhana cut him off with a snarl. “Get going,” she said. “The men’s house is over there.” She motioned with her head in the direction of the second house, standing not far off.

Jake skirted by Izhana, who did not look away from him as he passed. From within the ladies’ house, Jake heard sounds of voices, but when he stopped to listen, Izhana growled deep in her throat.

Jake lingered no longer but plunged into the storm and sprinted to the shelter of the other house. Looking back, he saw Izhana still watching him, her unblinking eyes glowing with a pale light. He turned hastily and looked back no more.

The door of the men’s bathhouse stood open, and warm air issued from it. Cautiously Jake entered, finding himself in a small square room, empty except for a few benches and a large door in the far wall. A long window on the right opened on a storage room filled with towels and dressing gowns, soaps and shampoos, sponges and brushes. Inside stood a short automaton with bright yellow eyes and a round face.

“Good evening, sir,” the automaton said with a bow. “Jardir said a young Thalani might visit. Would that be you?”

Jake nodded.

“Splendid!” the automaton said, and though his mouth did not move, he seemed to be smiling. “You’ve had a long journey, I’ll wager. Nothing for it but a good bath.” He disappeared into the room behind him and returned with a stack of items he handed to Jake: a dressing gown, a thick towel, a bar of brown soap, and a dried sea-sponge, stiff and green. On top of it all lay a card upon which was written the Nanyan number seventeen. “Here you are, sir,” he said. “If you are unfamiliar with the baths, just follow the numbers in each room; I’ve given you number seventeen. If you require anything further—perhaps a brush or a phial of soap—just ring the bell, and I’ll be along presently. Just leave your clothes in the first room, and I'll collect them for you. A pleasant evening to you, sir." He bowed again.

Jake passed through the large door into a room filled with wooden partitions arranged into rows. He entered one of the stalls and changed out of his clothes into the dressing gown. It was soft and warm, and made of material finer than any item of clothing he had ever owned.

He left his clothes behind in the changing room and passed through a curtain into the room beyond, which was wholly dark. He hesitated to enter at first, but as his foot crossed the threshold, many lights blazed to life, illuminating a large room lined with benches draped with towels. In the centre a copper boiler ignited, and in a moment great puffs of steam issued from it, filling the room with a thick fog. Jake disrobed, and wrapping himself in a towel, he sat on a bench and let the steam envelop him.

He did not stay long, for he felt rather silly just sitting there. Gathering soap and sponge, he continued through the far door into a long corridor of grey stone. Wooden doors lined both sides, and each had a number engraved above it. Jake opened number seventeen and entered a square room of stone, with a bench near the door and a grated drain at the centre.

As he stepped inside, a waterfall came to life in the far wall, casting streams of hot water upon the floor, and Jake washed beneath the shower. After many days of dirt and cold, the water refreshed him. At length the waterfall ceased, and Jake wrapped himself in a towel and continued on.

The next room held a large pool filled so high that its green water lay even with the floor. A walkway surrounded it, and many columns lined its longer sides. From a stone spout in each column, a stream of steaming water issued, refreshing the pool. The surface lay calm, rippling gently and lapping at the surrounding stones.

Jake laid his towel and dressing gown aside and stepped down a descent of shallow steps into the pool. The water was deep and came up to his shoulders, but long benches lay beneath the surface along the sides of the pool, and he sat upon one of these. The water was hot, approaching the very threshold of his tolerance. He tried swimming around a bit, but that made the water seem hotter. As he sat down again, he began to worry that someone else might enter the room. He kept his eye upon the door, but to his relief no one came.

When he could stand the hot water no longer, he climbed out and journeyed through the far door. There he found a circular room with a high roof. All about its edge lay many tubs inset into stone slabs standing many feet off the ground. Narrow steps on their sides led up so bathers could easily reach them. Behind each slab stood a fountain fed by a channel running high above, emptying into the tubs so there was no lack of hot water. Jake found number seventeen and climbed in for a good soak. The water was not nearly as hot as the last room's, and he felt he was finally able to relax.

Just then Jake heard a loud splash from the pool room and the echoes of a low voice coughing and spluttering. Someone else was in the bath. Whatever ease Jake had begun to feel evaporated instantly. He debated whether to leave or stay, but before he could make up his mind, the doors opened, and in walked Zhialamon wearing a green dressing gown.

"Aha!" the old man said. "I wondered who it was that had come in before me. I'm usually the first here in the evening, and I start the steam and the fountains. It was a pleasure to enter with everything already begun. The steam room always starts out so cold, and it's even worse in the winter. I'm glad someone mentioned the baths to you; I had forgotten to do so. There's nothing like a good bath before supper, eh?"

He walked to number ten across the room from Jake and climbed the steps. Jake turned away and did not look again until he heard Zhialamon enter the tub. The old man's dressing gown lay folded upon a shelf nearby.

"What do you think of the Itarlavon baths?" the old man said. "They're very old, you know—perhaps as old as the manor-house itself."

"I can't say I've ever seen anything like this place," Jake said. "The best I could manage on Rithonon was a hot shower at the inn, but most of the time I boiled water at home to fill the tub in the garage. This place is so…open."

The old man laughed. "Bathing was not always a secluded custom," he said. "But that is why I have always been first to the baths in the evening: so that I may leave before the house grows crowded. I'm old, young Connolly, and I prefer to be alone with my thoughts."

"Then I shan't bother you," Jake said, and he sat forward, trying to determine how best to exit his tub.

"No," the old man said, "that's not it at all. Men of age tend to babble. I only meant I prefer to enjoy what peace I can. Not much is given me, for a planet as old and large as Iderat requires much attention, and my station does not permit me much tranquillity. But I do not resent your presence, and others will be along in a minute."

The old man closed his eyes and lay back.

A long silence followed in which neither Jake nor Zhialamon spoke. Indeed, there was little sound except for the trickling of the fountains and the drumming of rain upon the sails above. Jake sat watching the steam rise through openings in the roof. The warmth of the water and the lulling of the rain nearly put him to sleep.

Jake at last took a deep breath and sighed, and when he spoke, being near sleep, he reverted to English. "It's been quite a week."

“An ordeal, to be sure,” Zhialamon replied in English, and his accent was as plain as any Thalani. “When we heard the Kenornin had gone to Rithonon, we despaired, but now here you are! I know your parents would be pleased that you have come at last to Iderat. They had always hoped to come back someday.”

“Why didn’t they just live here?” Jake asked.

“I wanted them to,” the old man said, “but they would not have it so. I don’t know whether they did not wish to be a burden—which I assure you they would not have been—or whether they feared greater danger for both our families.”

“But is it not safe here?” Jake said. “Surely the protection of Eratzira is enough for Iderat.”

“You think so?” the old man said. “The Kenornin easily came to Rithonon, penetrating much of its security. Don’t think that you escaped because the Kenornin were not thorough; they were. No, there was more at work than skill or mere chance.”

The old man fell silent and said no more.

At length many voices arose from the pool room along with much splashing. Not keen on meeting new people—especially not in the bath—Jake stepped quickly out of the tub, and wrapping his dressing gown around himself, he hurried through the far door.

To his surprise the door at the end of the room brought him full circle to the entrance of the bathhouse. There the small automaton still stood behind the counter. Outside, the rain came down as heavy as ever it had.

As Jake entered, the automaton bowed. “Greetings once again,” he said. “I trust you had a pleasant visit. A warm bath will do you good on a day like this.” He gave Jake a larger grey dressing gown, which Jake tied around himself, and from behind the counter the automaton produced a clay tile on a chain circle. The tile was about the size of Jake’s hand, and it was warm to the touch.

“The chain goes around your neck,” the automaton instructed. “It is to warm the blood and the breath, for I don’t want you to catch cold walking back to the house. You may also take a shadow-rod,[38] if you wish.”

“No,” Jake said, “I’ll be fine.”

“In that case, farewell,” the automaton said, “and return soon.”

When the automaton had bowed low once again, Jake thanked him and walked out into the storm. He had never known any rain that fell so hard and lasted so long, and he was amazed that the grounds were not flooded.

He ran to the awning of the ladies’ bathhouse and found to his relief that Izhana had gone. He paused a moment to listen, and he now heard many more voices than before. Afraid someone might come out and find him standing there, he hurried along to the path that ran up the hill to the house. A few steps up the path, he found Silorè calling to him, with Sinarè beside her.

“Thalani!” Silorè shouted over the storm. “Hurry if you want to stay dry!”

She motioned to him, and he ran up the path into the protective circle of the shadow-rod she carried. “It won’t do you any good walking in this cold rain,” she said as she held the rod high. “Will you not take this? You’re far too tall for me to hold it up comfortably.”

Jake took the rod from her hand and held it aloft. Sinarè stood quietly by, not looking at him. Both she and Silorè wore flowing dressing gowns of white, and their hair hung wet upon their shoulders.

“Watch it!” Silorè said, and she stepped closer to Jake. “You have to hold it steady. I’m not about to get wet again.”

38 Nanyan: *tèriona.*

"I'm sorry," Jake said, but he did not quite mean it, for she now stood very close to him.

"See? Look!" Silorè said, turning and grabbing Sinarè by the arms and pulling her forward. "You got her shoulder all wet."

"Oh, I don't mind," Sinarè said as Silorè brushed off her shoulder. "It's no matter. Really."

The three of them walked up the path together, and Jake took great care to see that he kept both girls out of the rain. When they came at last to the top of the hill, Silorè led the way into the house, and turning a corner, she found a staircase.

"This is where we part ways," she said to Jake. "Your room is on the other side of the house. We'll see you at supper." Then she and Sinarè climbed the stairs and disappeared.

Jake traversed the first-floor corridors, weaving his way around their many turns. After some wandering (and indeed a lot of walking), he came to the opposite end of the house and to a staircase that was a mirror of the one where he had separated from the two girls. He debated within himself for a moment whether he might have come full circle, but thinking better of it, he climbed the stairs and found himself near to his own room.

Once he had shut himself in, he dried himself and dressed, and he combed his hair before the mirror. Though Jardir had called them Thalanin clothes, the contents of the wardrobe were foreign to Jake, and he felt terribly conspicuous as he walked down to supper.

It was then that he realized, to his surprise, that all the corridors were empty and had been empty the entire evening. He had expected many people to be going down to supper, but as he passed other rooms, he found them all vacant. *Does no one live here?* he thought.

As he wondered at the emptiness of the house, he came again to the chamber with the tall columns, and he took a moment to look around. The floors were made of stone slabs of many colours laid out in pleasing patterns, and his footfalls echoed loudly in the silence of the room. Large paintings hung upon the walls, and two giant vases stood on either side of the staircase leading down into the Great Hall.

As Jake reached the stairs and began to descend, he came across a Nanyavè girl in a black dress. Pink buttons ran down the front, and bows of pink lace were tied upon the skirt. Her blonde hair was combed in many directions, held together with pins and clips unevenly placed. Many rings pierced her ears. Jake stopped upon the top step when he saw her, and the girl looked up at him through darkly painted eyes.

"Where are you going in such a hurry?" she asked with great bitterness in her voice.

"I thought supper was to be served soon," Jake said.

"It is," said the girl. "What of it?"

"Well…I'm hungry," Jake said, "and I don't want to be late."

The girl did not respond to him but stood looking him over. "You're that Connolly boy, are you not? I guess you do look like old Vincent after all."

"Yes, I'm Jake Connolly."

"I know who you are," she said, walking around him.

Jake hardly liked being made to feel like an annoyance. "May I ask *your* name?" he said.

The girl stopped beside him on the stair but did not look at him. "If you must."

Silence followed.

"Well?" Jake was growing impatient.

The girl sighed mournfully. "My name is Andarè."[39]

39 Nanyan: "delicate flower." At the time of this story, only very old women were named Andarè, for it was a name that had fallen out of favour quite a long time ago.

Jake stifled a laugh, and the girl took a step towards him. Jake retreated down a few steps, for he could see no levity in her bright-blue eyes. “You don’t think it suits me?” she said.

Jake shook his head. “No, that’s not what I meant. I think it’s quite—”

“That was my great-grandmother’s name,” she said. “She died when the Kenornin attacked Darthola. She was a great lady, and I won’t have you speaking ill of her, understand?”

Jake quickly nodded.

“Good,” Andarè said, and she turned to walk away.

“Wait!” Jake called after her. “Aren’t you coming to supper?”

Andarè gave no reply but walked swiftly away.

Shaking his head, Jake descended the stair into the Great Hall. Though the room above had been dark, many chandeliers illuminated the hall so that its walls seemed to glow. Upon the floor lay the symbol of the Itarlavon family made from shapes of coloured stone. White columns separated the main floor from the walkway running all around. Many passages opened in the walls, and Jake at once began to doubt which way to go.

Thankfully Jardir appeared and showed him through a door to the left and down the corridor to a squarish room at the front of the house. He said it was called the “breakfast room,” for that was its usual function, though in recent years it had become the primary dining room for the small number of family who lived in the house. Its walls were covered in dark wood-panels with golden trim, and a white marble fireplace stood to one side. Over the windows hung white gossamer curtains drawn behind red draperies with golden tassels. In the middle of the room stood a large, round table covered with a white cloth upon which five places had been set with fine plates and cutlery. The centre of the table was splayed with white and violet flowers with sprigs of greenery throughout.

As Jake stood by the table, a lady-servant entered through a side door. "Good evening," she said, bowing to him. "My name is Felisè, and it is my pleasure to serve the table of the Itarlavon."

Jake bowed. "Where is everyone?"

"They will be along," said Felisè. "It will be a small supper tonight. Some of the household are on holiday in Seritolma and will not return until late tonight." She turned and walked from the room, and Jake sat at the table and waited.

In time Zhialamon and Adjaron appeared and took their seats. Felisè brought *sabagansa*[40] and *golphanan*,[41] and she filled the glasses with *Jazavina*. Zhialamon and Adjaron were continuing a conversation they had begun earlier, speaking of things pertaining to the governance of Iderat that they had missed in their absence. Jake did not pay much attention to what was said, for he understood little of it, and he found he was too tired to be curious.

Some time later Silorè arrived, wearing a green dress with a bodice laced tightly around her waist. Her hair, lightly curled, rested upon the tips of her bare shoulders. Above her left elbow, she wore an armlet of gold, studded with gems. Her eyes were bright, and she wore an irrepressible smile. Sinarè followed her in a simple dress patterned with green and white diamonds. She seemed to hide behind Silorè as they approached.

"Sorry to be late," Silorè said as she sat down across from Jake. Sinarè quietly slipped in beside her.

"You're a bit overdressed for the occasion," Adjaron said. "Wouldn't you say so, sister?"

"There is no harm in looking presentable," said Silorè with half-feigned snobbery. "Indeed, it would do you good to have a care.

40 A spicy bean-paste often served with crisp flatbread.

41 Peppers stuffed with cheese and *sitonen* (a fruit related to other edible nightshades, like peppers and tomatoes).

Besides, I have been in ratty clothes for the past few days, and I've missed my wardrobe. Alas for my trunk!" She looked off through the window at the sky as if she might see all the way to Rithonon.

Felisè entered carrying large trays laden with food, and though to Jake it seemed enough for a feast, she returned again and again until the tabletop was crowded with dishes. No one began to eat until all was brought, and Zhialamon stood up and spoke with a bowed head. "We give thanks to God for this food and for the many blessings afforded us. Let us truly be thankful. Amen."

"Amen," said the others in unison.

Then the meal began.

Jake was quite hungry, and though he ate more than his share, there was no lack. A magnificent spread it was: breads and cheeses of many flavours and kinds, steaming bowls of vegetables Jake had never seen before, noodles cooked in spicy sauces of many colours, mushrooms of odd shapes and textures, fried buns filled with rice and beans, and many other dishes that were entirely foreign to him.

By habit Jake looked first for a meat dish, but he had quite forgotten that Silorè and her kindred ate no meat. The meals on the *Lamarenor* had been ill-provisioned, and so he had not comprehended that the lack of meat was by choice and not by necessity. A moment of panic swept over him, and his memory flew back to the festival in Brown Hill and all the foods that had been there. As he thought on them, his stomach rumbled.

Zhialamon must have seen Jake's difficulty, for he said, "You'll have to excuse our customs, young Connolly. There are some foods that have not been served in this house for many lives of Thalanin. If you require more familiar dishes, there is a Thalanin village across the valley. I'm certain they will have food more to your liking."

Jake turned red. "I'm not ungrateful," he said. "I guess my stomach is as much Thalani as I am."

The old man laughed. "I would not have you change your ways for us," he said, "for we don't begrudge Thalanin to eat that from which we abstain."

"Even though it is revolting," Silorè said with a grin.

Jake greatly desired to change the conversation. "I've noticed a great many rooms in this house are empty," he said. "How many people live here?"

"All whom you see here," said the old man, "plus a few others who are away. They won't return until late tonight, so it will be best if you wait to meet them until tomorrow."

"But surely there are others," Jake said. "I passed a girl on the stairs earlier. She said her name was Andarè."

A chuckle arose from the others at the table.

"I'm sorry, Thalani," Silorè said. "We should have warned you about her."

"But who is she?" Jake asked.

"One of a handful of youths sent to live here to escape the Kenornin," said Adjaron.

"And you said they are not here this evening?" Jake asked. "Then whose were the voices I heard in the bathhouse?"

"There are other houses in Sorenon besides this one," Adjaron said. "Members of our family live all around, and they will often visit the baths. Many of them are anxious to meet you."

"Is that so?" Jake said nervously. "Where are they now?"

"I've sent them off," Adjaron said. "I told them you needed time to rest and settle in, but you will meet them by and by. They do not regularly eat with us, but we have feasts and parties on holidays, and we mark births and weddings together."

"And funerals," Silorè said grimly. "Alas, there have been too many of those of late. Perhaps that is why our family have grown apart—too much sorrow and not enough joy."

The Itarlavon all fell silent, and Jake did not ask any more questions.

After a dessert of fruit and cream, Silorè led Jake and Sinarè outside onto the back porch overlooking the gardens. The rain had paused, and the last rays of Idtolitar lit the scattered clouds with orange fire. The ground beyond the porch was too muddy for walking, so they kept to the paved stones.

At first they said nothing to one another as they looked out over the gardens, but Jake felt he should say something. "You…look very nice," he said to Silorè. "Are you feeling better?"

Silorè nodded. "I feel like spring after a long winter," she said. "I'd had about enough of those dirty clothes and of being dirty myself. Now all is remedied."

Silorè took a deep breath of the evening air, and then she turned to Jake and smiled. "What do you think of our home, Thalani?" she said. "Is this not a lovely place to live?"

"That it is," said Jake. "Even so, I feel the pull of Rithonon and home." He looked up and saw the first stars beginning to appear. "I wonder which one it is."

"You won't be able to see it from here," she said, "for it is only visible in the southern regions of Iderat. But if you wait a bit, you might see Tolitar. It is visible all year in northern Iderat in the constellation Tiromon."[42]

"I've seen Tolitar only once, on the floor of an *itarzhona*,"[43] Jake said, "but otherwise it was too distant to see."

At that moment there came a sound like the fluttering of wings. Jake looked up, and Faluin flew out of the sky, perching on the stone

42 Nanyan: "the Great Chariot."

43 A stellar observatory where phenomena are projected onto a flat surface, usually the floor.

balustrade. Both Jake and Silorè jumped back, startled, but Sinarè let out a shriek of surprise and delight.

"Good evening, sir," Faluin said to Jake. "I'm pleased to see you have arrived and are in good health."

"Have you only just now found me?" Jake asked. "Were you not following us?"

"Indeed we were," Faluin said, "but the winds of this star are strong, and besides that, it was raining here. This did not pose a problem for us, but being in no hurry, we huddled together in the shelter of a cliff until the storm passed."

Sinarè, who had been standing on the other side of Silorè, pushed her aside and stepped forward to meet Faluin. "Who is this?" she said excitedly.

"This is Faluin, my vèralam," said Jake. "Faluin, this is Sinarè."

Sinarè stroked his chest-feathers with her finger. "He's so cute!"

Faluin did not seem to know what to make of her words, and he tried suddenly to seem stern and serious. Jake, on the other hand, stared at her with a thoughtful look upon his face.

"What's the matter?" Sinarè said, suddenly withdrawing from Faluin. "Did I do something wrong?"

"No, not at all," Jake said. "It's just…you reminded me of someone just now."

"Someone pleasant, I hope," Sinarè said meekly.

Jake looked up blankly at the sky. "Yes," he said. "She was."

From the corner of his eye, Jake thought he saw Silorè scowling at him.

"I only meant he's a handsome bird," Sinarè said. "I think he's wonderful. Is he the one I've heard of? The one that helped you all escape?"

"I'm certain my part in the matter was greatly exaggerated," said Faluin.

“Nonsense,” Jake said. “Credit where it’s due. Your eyes and ears were invaluable, to say nothing of your attack on the Kenornin.”

“A desperate act,” said Faluin, “when it seemed you would be captured.”

“And so we might have been but for you,” Jake said.

Faluin bowed.

Sinarè stared at Faluin with an unwavering gaze. “Of what house are you, noble Faluin?”

“Of the House of Binrialanil,” said Faluin. “It is the greatest house of all the Starlords.”

“Indeed, I have heard of it,” Sinarè replied with wonder. “Did you know Terthavi the Star-Runner?”

“He was my sire,” Faluin said proudly.

Sinarè’s eyes grew wide, and she put her hands to her mouth. “You are truly a noble bird indeed!” she exclaimed. “Then you are descended from Isèkor the Firebird, are you not?”

“Indeed, my lady,” Faluin said with a bow. “You appear to know much about my kind.”

Sinarè nodded. “And more,” she said. “I’ve read a great deal about the Starlords and their history.”

“I would be happy to talk with you concerning these things,” Faluin said. “But it shall have to wait for a later time. Now there is much to do.” He turned back to Jake. “Sir, there are five of us that have followed you from Rithonon—”

“There are more of you?” Sinarè was delighted.

“And we’ve nowhere to live. The cave in which we waited out the storm could serve our needs, but we would prefer more comfortable lodging, if we can find it.”

“You’re welcome to stay in the aviary,” said Silorè. “Seek out Thavèlig. He leads the vèralamen in Sorenon. He is old and wise, though he wears his age and wisdom irritably. If he questions you, tell him the Lady Silorè grants this and that he may inquire of me concerning it."

Faluin bowed low. "Many thanks, my lady," he said. "We thank you for the hospitality of your house." He turned to Jake. "With your permission, sir, I will make this known to the others."

Jake nodded. "I will visit you by and by," he said. "There's a message I would like you to deliver to Rithonon, but I'm too tired now to think of what I want to say."

"Then I shall see you early tomorrow morning," Faluin said. "Until then, good night, sir." He turned and bowed to both Silorè and Sinarè. "Good night, fair ones." Then he mounted the air and flew swiftly over the garden to the valley beyond. Sinarè climbed upon the garden rail so she could watch Faluin until he disappeared from sight.

Idtolitar had vanished behind the distant mountains, and the sky, though it had remained light for some time, was fading to blackness. At length the evening bells chimed, and Silorè looked towards the house. "It's growing late," she said. "I must still be accustomed to the days on Rithonon. It hardly feels the time for night to fall."

"All the same," Jake said, "I feel tired enough."

"Then it's off to bed," said Silorè, and Jake thought she sounded suddenly maternal. "We'll see you in the morning. Breakfast is served the first hour after sunrise. Don't be late."

Jake accompanied Silorè and Sinarè into the house and parted ways with them upon the staircase in the Great Hall. When he returned to his room, he found the lamps lit and his bed covers turned down. A pair of pyjamas lay folded upon his pillow. Taking care to stay out of sight of the open window, Jake changed clothes, and after washing his face and teeth, he passed through the curtains and onto the balcony.

The world outside was dark except for a few twinkling lights across the valley. A light rain had begun to fall, and Jake felt a fine mist upon his face. The rain pattered in the garden, but there was no sound besides. The air was cold and fresh, and Jake breathed it deeply. He was not used to air so clear, for the valley in which he had lived always smelled of smoke and soot.

He remained on the balcony a few minutes more, content to listen to the music of the weather until at last sleep overcame him, and he retired to his bed. As he lay himself down, the lamps faded and went out. The sheets were cool, and his head sank deeply into his pillow. Thus almost at once he fell into a deep sleep, and he was troubled by no dream.

Chapter 10

Message from Rithonon

Sunlight streamed through the curtains at the break of day. The rain had moved off, and cheerful clouds made their slow voyage across the sky. The air that passed the curtains was clean and cool, and Jake awoke feeling more refreshed than he had in many days. His bed was far more comfortable than the one he had slept in aboard the *Lamarenor*, and he was content to lie for a while with his eyes closed.

At last he sat up and looked around, and to his surprise, something was staring at him from on top of the covers. He cried out, but he clasped his hand to his mouth when he saw it was Izhana.

"My mistress sent me to fetch you," she said. "She was wondering why you have not yet come to breakfast."

"Is it that time already?" Jake asked.

"Indeed, it has passed," said Izhana, "and if you want anything to eat, you'll be down quickly. Get dressed and hurry!" Thus saying, she jumped down and bounded through the door.

Jake sat a moment in bed, feeling suddenly tired now that it came to starting the day. The night had indeed felt short. Slowly he forced his legs out from under the covers and onto the floor. The cold tiles stung his feet as he walked to the balcony and looked out on the morning of Iderat. The house cast a shadow over the garden, for the sun rose on the other side of the house. A light mist hung in the valley beyond, lingering in the low places around the river.

Jake changed clothes and headed downstairs. He met no one in the corridor.

The breakfast room was nearly empty when Jake arrived. Felisè was busy clearing away used dishes from the table, but three settings still remained unused. Before one of these sat Sinarè, holding a grey kitten against her shoulder, and all her focus was bent upon it as she scratched its chin and hummed softly. Silorè sat beside her, arms folded, looking far less than happy. When Jake entered, her gaze fell hard upon him.

"Where have you been?" Silorè asked as Jake hurried to sit beside her. "I told you breakfast was served at sunrise. It's been more than an hour since then. Everyone's already eaten and gone. Sinarè and I have sat here all that time waiting for you."

"Oh, don't worry about me," Sinarè said looking up from her kitten. "I'm not really hungry anyway."

"You could have eaten without me," Jake said as he put his napkin in his lap. "I wouldn't have minded."

"You are our guest," Silorè said. "It's only proper for us to wait for you, and that is just what we have done. If the other members of our house had any manners, they would have done the same. Zhialamon would have stayed, but he has many things to do." She looked at the clock hanging upon the far wall. "As have I. I only hope I shan't be late."

"Well, that's why you should have eaten without me."

"If I had known you were going to be this ungrateful, then perhaps I would have done." Silorè turned away from him and did not speak further. Sinarè held her kitten tightly, and the same expression of panic was upon both their faces.

The three ate their breakfast in silence. Jake had oats with honey and fruit, a rather runny boiled egg, rice pudding, and toasted flatbread with cheese and tomato jam.

Breakfast quickly came to an end, and Jake grabbed a strawberry tart as he left with the girls. "Well," he said with his mouth full, "what's on the agenda today?"

"I don't know at present," said Silorè. "I've been gone from Iderat quite a while, and there are many things that need my attention. I had hoped to walk around with you both after breakfast, but now it is late, and I must be off. Sinarè will keep you company, if you wish."

"But where are you going?" Jake asked.

"Into the city," Silorè said. "There is a meeting about the forthcoming Games, and I mustn't be late. I shall have to hurry now."

"Games?" Jake asked. "What games?

"Sinarè will tell you about them," Silorè said as she walked away down the corridor. "Goodbye, Thalani. Take care of him, Sinarè."

"Very well," Sinarè mumbled.

Silorè turned a corner and was gone.

"What was she talking about?" Jake said.

"Oh…" Sinarè said. "It's…well, it's…the Games."

"Yes," Jake said slowly, "but what are they?"

"The Itelon Games."[44]

"Are those this year?" Jake said. "Will they be on Iderat?"

Sinarè nodded.

"I hardly remember the last ones," Jake said. "Do you?"

44 The Itelon Games and Exhibition is a two-month-long event in which participants from different planets gather to compete in sport and other games and to display examples of art and science from their worlds. There are usually many galleries and shows alongside the various sporting events. A different planet hosts the event every ten years or so.

Sinarè shook her head. "I've lived only twenty-two years," she said. "I remember something of them when I was a child, but I was in Nonzira then."

"You lived in Nonzira?" Jake asked. "Why?"

"That is where my family was."

"Silorè said your family name is Faloroson, right?" Jake said. "What family is that?"

Sinarè bit her lower lip. "It was once a large family," she said. "We are one of the ring-holding families, and my father is the patriarch. It's no wonder that you've not heard of us, for we're not many now. The Kenornin don't like us very much."

"Then you and I have something in common," said Jake with a small grin. "But why do the Kenornin hate you?"

Sinarè shrugged. "Why does anyone have to hate anyone else?"

"Fair enough."

"Actually it has something to do with the last war," she replied. "My family gave aid to the Itarlavon, and we've helped many of their family members go into hiding. I wish we were as good at hiding ourselves."

"Is that why you're here?"

Sinarè nodded sadly. "Years ago, my father asked Zhialamon to let me stay in Sorenon—to protect me, and so I came to live here. Iderat is nice, I guess, but I miss home." She sighed and held her kitten against her cheek. "It's so far from here," she said and stared blankly ahead of her.

Jake watched her silently. In that moment she looked so fragile, like a leaf tossed about by a strong wind. "I'm sorry," he said. "I guess we've both been exiled to this place, haven't we?"

Sinarè did not look up at him. "I guess." Gloom was etched in her face, and her eyes had lost their sparkle.

Jake sought quickly to change the subject, and he turned his attention to Sinarè's kitten. "Who's your little friend?"

Sinarè turned to him and smiled. "This is Korandi." she said. "He's very precious. I got him only last month. He's very small, but I like him that way."

"He's pretty cute," Jake said, rubbing the top of the kitten's head. The kitten grabbed Jake's hand with its claws and nibbled on his fingers. "He's not an automaton, is he?"

Sinarè shook her head proudly. "Not at all," she said. "He's as flesh and blood as you and I. I like automatons—don't get me wrong—and I think Faluin is wonderful, but I just adore real cats. Do you like them too?"

"I've not known too many," Jake said. "There was an old tabby that would wander up the hill where I lived and scratch at my door. He caught a mouse in my garage one night, so I rewarded him with can of fish paste. I suppose I liked him all right, but I've not seen him in over a year. I don't know what happened to him."

"If it were me, I would have adopted him straight away," Sinarè said, rubbing her cheek against her kitten's face. "I've not had a cat since I came here, but I wanted one so terribly. Then one day I found a notice someone had posted in the town about a litter of kittens, and I fell in love with this one the moment I saw him." She held the kitten up so that it stared Jake in the eyes. "Isn't he adorable?"

"Quite," Jake said, putting up his hand to shield himself, for Sinarè held the kitten very close to his face. After a few moments, she withdrew the kitten to rest on her shoulder.

"So," Jake said, "what shall we do first today?"

Sinarè grew quiet once more and shrugged. "I don't know," she mumbled.

"Well, I need to send a message, so I should find Faluin again," Jake said. "You're welcome to come along."

Sinarè's eyes lit up. "Really?"

"Of course."

"All right," said Sinarè. "I'll meet you in the garden. I just have to put Korandi in my room first."

"I'll come with you," Jake said.

Sinarè grew stiff and shook her head. "No," she said. "It's fine. I'll just…see you when I come back down. Is that all right?"

Jake chuckled. "Certainly."

"Good." Sinarè flashed a smile.

"In that case," said Jake, "could you tell me where to find paper and pen?"

"There's a writing desk in the parlour by the library," said Sinarè. "This way."

She led Jake down the hall to a dark room in the southern wing of the house. The curtains were drawn, and there were no lights lit when Jake entered. He could hardly see the furniture against the far wall, but the light slanting through the closed curtains illuminated a desk set between two windows. Upon the desk stood a neat stack of writing paper and two large quills beside an inkwell.

"Just use whatever you need," Sinarè said cheerfully. Then she turned and scampered off down the corridor.

Jake entered the room and sat at the desk, and taking pen in hand, he wrote in sloppy Latin characters:

My Dear Samantha,

It was a rough journey, but we have arrived safe at last on Iderat. I've not been here a full day yet, but I think I may starve if I don't get some real food soon. I'd give just about anything to be back at the Griffin. I hope you and your family are well and that everything is back to normal. I wish

I were there to see it. I hope you don't mind my saying so but—

A voice suddenly disturbed the silence of the room. "Do you have to be so loud?"

Jake started and spun around in his chair. In the dim light, he could just make out the form of Andarè curled up in a chair and reading a small leather book. A dark dress hung upon her thin figure, and a lopsided bow of pink ribbon was in her hair.

Jake was confused by her outburst. The only sound he had made was the light scratching of the quill-nib on the paper. "I'm sorry," he said politely. "I didn't see you there."

Andarè looked up from her book. "Just do what you need to do and leave," she said and went back to her reading.

"Is something the matter?"

"Why should anything be the matter?" Andarè said, not looking up.

Jake was stumped by the question. "I only mean, is there something bothering you?"

"Other than you, no, not at the moment." She turned a page in her book. "But that can change. It usually does."

"What does that mean?"

Andarè sighed and put down her book. "What does it matter to you?" she said. "There are a great many things in this world that vex me, but I don't go looking for them. They just find me anyway." She took up her book again.

Jake sat facing her a moment, trying to think of something to say.

"What's the matter with you?" she said angrily. "Finish whatever it is you're doing so you can run back to Silorè."

"She…she's not here," Jake said, for it was all he could think to say. "She went into town."

"Then go tag along after someone else," Andarè said, turning sideways in the chair and letting her feet dangle over the armrest. She pulled the book close to her face and would say no more.

Jake finished his letter quickly and left the room without another word.

Outside in the garden, Sinarè was already waiting for him. "Did you get lost?" she said earnestly as he walked up to her.

"No," Jake said, looking back towards the house, "but never mind that now. Stand back."

Sinarè retreated from him, and he raised his right arm in the air. Then, holding up two fingers, he waved his arm in a circle and whistled loudly through his teeth. Sinarè clapped her hands over her ears, and a gardener peered around the hedge to see what the noise had been.

Jake lowered his arm and turned to Sinarè. "It won't be long," he said. "Faluin has never failed to answer my call, even if he is far off."

In a moment there came a loud flutter of wings, and seemingly from nowhere, Faluin lighted upon Jake's right arm. "Good morning, sir," he said, and then he bowed to Sinarè. "Good morning, fair one."

"Good morning to you, noble Faluin," Sinarè said with a curtsy and a giggle.

Faluin nodded and then turned back to Jake. "What is your bidding, sir?"

"I want you to fly to Rithonon and deliver this message to Samantha," he said, and he drew the letter from his pocket. Faluin took it in his claws and spread his wings to depart.

"It shall be done," said Faluin. "I shall return before evening." So saying, he launched himself into the air and flew high into the sky and out of sight.

As she watched Faluin depart, Sinarè looked downcast.

"What's wrong?" Jake asked.

"I was just hoping to visit with him longer," Sinarè replied. "I really like him a lot."

"There are others of my vèralamen here," Jake said, "or at least Faluin has told me so. I haven't seen them yet, and I would like to know how they are faring. Would you like to come with me?"

Sinarè nodded vigorously. "Very much so."

"That's good," Jake said with a smile, "because I don't know where the aviary is."

"I'll show you the way."

Sinarè led Jake along the garden path that ran down from the main house and along the rim of the valley. The slope beside them grew steeper as they went until its side was almost sheer. The lip of the slope rose suddenly to form a small hill, and upon it stood a tower that looked over the river valley below. The tower was only two levels with a flat roof void of any embellishment. A stairway wound about it, and many windows looked out on every side. A few birds roosted upon the roof or perched in the branches of a large tree that grew nearby.

As Jake and Sinarè approached, four birds came forth and sat upon the stone wall that fenced in the small yard around the tower. Jake recognized them immediately, for they were his. Isèter was among them, as well as the twin kites Koriton and Kordir, and Faldan the eagle stood beside them.

Sinarè was trembling with excitement, but she could find no words to say. The birds regarded her pleasantly, and they bowed to her and Jake.

“Good morning, sir,” Isèter said. “And a good morning to the lady as well. We regret not having seen you sooner, but there has been quite a mix-up here.”

Even as Isèter spoke, an old owl, fat and moulting, landed with great force upon the stone wall. “No mix-up,” he said in a throaty voice. “I had not been aware that you were coming to stay here, and since no one told me about it, what else could I do but turn you away? Adjaron sorted it all out, so there’s no need to bring up the matter again.”

“Sir, this is Thavèlig the Far-Seeing,” Isèter said to Jake. “He is our host, and he commands the vèralamen here.”

“Who then is your vèralamenasi?” Jake asked.

The old owl stood tall, though with great effort. “We have none,” he said. “We need none. We are our own masters, and we serve as we choose. Presently we serve the Itarlavon family. They have given us use of this aviary, but they do not own us. We are free, and we shall remain free.

“But,” the old bird sighed, “from time to time, Jolani will come and see to it that we are well, and he will give us tasks to perform for the family.” Then he added quickly, “These things we do for the love of the Itarlavon, and not for sake of duty.”

Jake nodded. “I am grateful that you have allowed my vèralamen to stay. I trust they like it here.”

“Indeed, sir, we do,” said Kordir. “Not that we don’t miss Rithonon, you understand, but there is more open sky here, and the winds blow us all over the planet.”

“Then enjoy it, and take all the time you can,” said Jake. “There’s no more work to be done—at least none that I can see. I haven’t anything for you to do, and until I find something, consider yourselves on holiday.”

"That's kind of you, sir," Isèter said with a bow, "but Faluin already has given us many labours."

"I'm sure he has," Jake said, shaking his head with a smirk. "What has he ordered?"

"Regular flights around the planet," Isèter replied, "and around Idtolitar and even into the surrounding star-systems. He wants us to be sure nothing is out of the ordinary, but seeing as we don't know what passes for ordinary here, that may be difficult."

"Just do your best," Jake said, "and don't worry about it. Iderat is a place of safety."

"You think so, do you?" Thavèlig said with a snap of his beak. "In all my long years, the one thing I've seen little of is safety. There is no refuge in the universe that cannot be assailed—no tree so strong that it can stand any wind—no dam that can hold if the river runs too high. Those who consider themselves encompassed with safety are soonest destroyed."

As the old owl spoke, a lady falcon descended from above and perched beside him. "Your far-seeing eyes see only misery," she said. "You would seek out a shadow in the noonday sun."

"My eyes see many things," the old owl said, "and what they see behind is much like what they see before. This history of Man is but a wheel that turns and returns again to its beginning."

"I beg you to pardon him," the falcon said to Jake, and her voice was kind and warm. "He remembers too many winters. My name is Thafsèra, and I live here in the service of the Itarlavon. I welcome you, Jake Connolly, to Sorenon, and I hope you find everything to your liking."

"Thank you," Jake said with a nod. "So far I'm quite impressed, but I haven't seen a tithe of all that is here."

"Mistress Sinarè shall conduct you around, if she will," Thafsèra said, "but if not, we would be happy to lead you."

"That's all right," Sinarè said meekly. "I don't mind."

"Then we shall leave you to it," Thafsèra said and then bowed to Jake. "A pleasant stay to you, Thalani. Your birds are welcome here, as are you. Please visit us again." So saying, she departed, and the old owl followed her without another word.

Jake remained with his vèralamen for a while longer, and he recounted to them some of what had befallen him since he left Rithonon. They in turn told him of their wanderings and all they had done from the time of their attack on the Kenornin.

"They were routed," Isèter said, "and their leader could not unite them again. They were all poor shots, and none of us suffered harm in that first battle, except Èlimur. He endured an injury to his tail-feathers, but we left him in good health when we departed. He and some of the others took shelter in the high mountains, for the Kenornin sent out vèralamen of their own—horrible creatures of a kind I'd not seen before. They were large and swift but not as keen-sighted as we are, and we easily avoided them.

"When we heard that you had travelled to Thesatra, we flew there on the wind, and none too soon did we arrive, for we found the city filled with enemies searching for you. These were well organized, and they followed you to the ruins of the Old City. There we assailed them again. They fought hard, and there were too many of them for us to defeat. Faljava fell in that fight, and we others flew off, but we delayed them long enough, it seems. They could not reach you in time."

"Faljava?" said Jake, feeling a stab at his heart. "He's dead, then? I didn't want…I mean, I never asked for any of you to…" The words died in his burning throat.

"There was no need to ask, sir," Faldan said. "We would happily give our lives for the master."

Sinarè stepped forward, her eyes filled with tears. She gripped Jake's arm and wiped her wet face on his sleeve. "I'm sorry," she whimpered.

"Don't cry," Jake said. His hands hovered over her for a moment, for he was unsure how to comfort her. "Please, don't cry."

"We did not mean to upset either of you, sir," Isèter said, "but we thought we had better tell you now. Faluin would not speak of it to you, for his grief was great."

"And here I've sent him off," Jake said. "I didn't know. He and Faljava were close, were they not?"

"Quite," Faldan said, "but his death is grievous to us all, as indeed is the separation from the others who are now scattered. Perhaps we will all gather upon some future day and mourn him properly."

"What has been done with him?" Jake asked.

"We've have honoured him according to our customs,"[45] said Isèter. "Then, being in haste, we followed you here."

"I'm sorry," said Jake. "For all that has happened."

"And so are we," said Faldan. "We regret that you have been removed from your home, where all of us dwelt with the master and mistress before their departure. Take heart, good master, for those who sought your harm have failed."

Koriton hopped towards Sinarè and nuzzled her with his beak. "Dry your tears, young one," he said. "Faljava fought bravely and died in great honour. He would be touched knowing that you mourn him whom you never have met."

"She has a kind heart," Jake said, and he looked down into her tearstained face. "Thank you," he said. "It's great comfort to know that someone else shares these feelings."

45 Vèralamen are secretive about their rituals and customs. Men know little of their ways, and vèralamen do not share such things openly.

"How could I not?" Sinarè said, wiping her eyes. "You care about your birds a great deal, and they obviously care about you."

Jake took pause, for never before that moment had he realized his connection with his vèralamen so fully. He looked at the four that sat upon the wall, and they all looked back at him and seemed to smile. His vision grew blurry, and he wiped his nose with the back of his hand. "Yes," he said. "I suppose that's true."

The four birds bowed to him.

"We must now be about our morning business," Isèter said, "else Faluin will be cross when he returns. Farewell, sir."

Then the vèralamen flew straight up into the sky, each going his separate way, and they soon vanished from sight. When they had gone, Jake turned to Sinarè and discovered he was holding her hand tightly.

"Sorry," he said and released her.

"Oh, it's quite all right," Sinarè said, her eyes shining.

Jake felt himself turning red. "So," he said, "what else is there to see around here?"

Sinarè smiled shyly and walked slowly ahead. "Follow me."

Sinarè led Jake across wide lawns bordered with stone paths and well-trimmed hedges. Sprawling forest lay all about them, but there were more than a few old trees standing alone along the roads or atop shallow rises covered in grass. An orchard of fruit trees grew in the southernmost part of Sorenon, and Jake and Sinarè walked beneath branches dotted with budding flowers. Along the eastern road, they came across houses of many sizes, some inhabited and others vacant or fallen into disrepair. The ancient ruin of an especially large house stood like a monument to a once-splendid past.

Passing by a large pond, Jake and Sinarè crossed into the lands north of the main house, and it was there they happened upon fields reserved for sport. There were pitches for many kinds of football and well-trimmed greens for various lawn games. Jake knew a few of the Thalanin sports, but others were unfamiliar to him. Yet there was no mistaking the Lambati[46] pitch, for it was broad and oval, and between the two goal circles twenty or so players were kicking egg-shaped balls to one another.

Upon the hill above the field, Jake and Sinarè met a servant girl carrying a basket of sandwiches and fruit. "Felisè made this and told me to bring it to you," she said. "She was certain you would not be back to the house for lunch, and so I have been searching for you. I learned you were coming this way, so I have been waiting for you here." She spread a blanket upon the ground and set the basket upon it. Then, with a bow, she departed.

Jake and Sinarè sat upon the blanket and ate their picnic. There were many kinds of sandwiches in the basket—far more than the two of them could eat. Each contained a different filling, most with some kind of cheese and vegetables, but Jake preferred the sandwiches filled with a spicy bean-paste, which in Eratzira is called itelzikan.

As the two ate, they watched the men training on the field below.

"Do you like Lambati?" Sinarè asked.

"I haven't seen much of it," said Jake. "Ours was a Thalanin village. The only Lambati fields were in hCathad, and I saw only a passable game or two."

"I don't like it at all," Sinarè said, wrinkling her nose. "I don't see the point."

46 A Nanyanin sport played with an oval ball on a pitch with a large elliptical boundary. The pitch is divided in half, and at the centre of each half, a circle is drawn with a diameter of two Eshronen (a little over twelve and a half feet). Players score points by kicking or grounding the ball inside their opponents' circle.

"Who are those fellows down there?" Jake asked. "For whom do they play?"

"That's the Iderat team," Sinarè said. "They sometimes practise here. I suppose Sorenon is more peaceful than wherever they usually are. They're training for the Games, you know?"

"I see," Jake said. "Then I hope they do Iderat proud."

They ate quickly and said little else. When they had finished, they left everything and continued on. Someone would be along to clean up after them.

Passing the playing fields, Jake and Sinarè came to a long strip of lawn sheltered by an alcove of trees. At the far end were erected five oval targets, brightly painted, and on the near side four people stood, each holding a short bow and having a quiver of arrows slung on his back.

Three of the figures intently watched the fourth—a girl tall and slender with long dark hair that glittered in the sunshine. She stood with an arrow nocked to her bowstring, aiming at the row of targets. All at once the arrow leapt from the string, and as it flew it burst into a violet flame, singing as it cut through the air. The arrow struck its target with a thunderous noise and vanished, leaving a scorch mark near the edge of the centre circle.

"That's quite good," said one of the figures standing beside the archer. "Especially at this distance."

"Garbage," the girl with the bow mumbled. "Simply garbage."

"Come now," said another, "you're already better than any of us. Sometimes I think you bring us out here only so you can show off."

The girl shot him a fearsome look.

"Look who's here!" The first figure turned towards Jake and Sinarè. He was taller than the others, and his hair and eyes were light in colour. "It's that Connolly fellow. Thanks for bringing him here, Sinarè. We missed him at breakfast. What are you two up to?"

"I'm…um," Sinarè stammered. "I'm just showing him around."

"Indeed," said the tall figure, and then he turned to Jake. "I'm so pleased to meet you at last. My name is Jolani."

"A pleasure," Jake said, and he bowed. "I've heard your name already, for the vèralamen mentioned you."

"I'm happy for their esteem," said Jolani. "Now, please permit me to introduce my friends to you."

He gestured towards the girl who had just loosed the arrow. Her eyes were as dark as her hair, and her gaze was piercing. "This is Ianasè," he said.

She bowed. "I'm afraid I'm the reason we could not stay after breakfast to meet you," she said. "I was itching to practise at first light."

The other young man stepped up beside Ianasè, and he was shorter than she was. "We've been here all morning, and she won't let us leave," he said, his pale-green eyes twinkling with some sort of mischief.

"Jake, this is Tarandi," said Jolani, and Tarandi bowed. "And this is Azhè."

The other girl in the group stepped forward. Her fiery-brown hair fell in her face as she bowed, and she quickly brushed it back into place. Her smile was pleasant, and her blue eyes shone like a deep pool struck by moonlight.

She seemed about to say something, but Tarandi interrupted. "Her real name is Azhdarlorè," he said, winking at her. "Rather a mouthful, isn't it?"

Azhè sneered at him.

"Are you all Itarlavon?" Jake asked, looking at the four of them.

"Indeed we are," said Jolani.

"Are you siblings?"

Jolani shook his head and laughed. "No," he said, "none of us are closely related. We all were sent to live here years ago, when our families perceived the Kenornin were becoming dangerous once more. There are many other young Itarlavon all over the planet, but we are privileged enough to live here, and quite a life it is."

"Jolani is the oldest of us," Azhè said. "He brought us all together when we were left here."

"And he keeps Adjaron off our backs," said Ianasè with a grin. "As much as he can, anyway."

"Speaking of Adjaron, where is he today?" Tarandi said, looking around as though he would catch sight of him. "He left us all quite a list of work to do while he was gone, but so far he's not spoken with us."

"He and Zhialamon went off early this morning," Jolani said. "I don't think things have been going very well, and the Assembly was taken by surprise at their absence. I guess they didn't want anyone to know where they were going, and now they're having to answer for it. I don't think we'll see Adjaron for a while."

Ianasè scoffed. "Same as always," she grumbled. "We hurried to finish everything he left for us, but now he can't be bothered even to give us a little gratitude." Her fists tightened. "He's got a lot of nerve to push us around. He's not patriarch yet, and if he thinks that he and his ego can make—"

"Don't talk about Adjaron that way!"

Jake heard the voice, but it seemed unfamiliar to him. He looked round to see if someone else had joined them secretly, but he found that besides the six of them, there was no one else about. He looked to Sinarè, and to his surprise he found her glaring at Ianasè with hands clenched and lip quavering.

The others seemed surprised as well, if for but a moment.

"Don't say anything bad about Adjaron," Sinarè said firmly. "He's trying his best to be ready to lead his family someday, and I'm sure it's not easy for him—especially having no parents. The least you could do is to help out your own family a little!"

Ianasè looked away. "I didn't mean it like that," she mumbled.

Jolani stepped in, raising his hands. "We're not finding fault with Adjaron," he said.

"Yes, you are!" Sinarè said, and angry tears ran down her face. Then her mood changed, and she bowed her head. "I'm sorry," she said, crying.

Azhè stepped forward and put a hand on Sinarè's shoulder. "Come on, Sin-èsa,"[47] she said. "It's not like that. We've all been a little tense lately. I'm sure Ianasè only meant that sometimes we feel a little…undervalued. I'm not saying that's how it is, but that's how it feels."

"I know," Sinarè said, "and I am sorry."

"No harm done," Azhè said. She turned to Ianasè, who was still looking off towards the targets at the far end of the clearing. "Right, Ianasè?"

Ianasè did not look at Sinarè, but after a moment's hesitation she nodded stiffly.

"There, you see?" Azhè said. "No problem."

A tense silence followed in which no one spoke or looked at one another.

At length Jolani turned back to Jake. "Well, now that that's settled," he said, clearing his throat, "how do you like Sorenon, Jake?"

47 The suffix *-(è)sa* is an honorific used for girls and young women with whom the speaker is familiar. Such honorifics are usually combined with shortened forms of names. In this context, Azhè is probably being a bit patronizing.

"I like it very much," Jake said. "There's quite a lot to see, though I don't suppose I've seen even a quarter of what is here, and I haven't seen many people either."

"But I heard you met my sister," said Jolani. Azhè, Tarandi, and Ianasè suddenly shook off their melancholy and snickered.

"I did?" said Jake. "Who? Do you mean Andarè?"

The four friends laughed together. "How could you tell?" Tarandi said. "Was it the family resemblance?"

"Don't misjudge me," said Jolani. "I love my sister, but she's… well, she's just very…"

"Gloomy?" said Azhè.

"Rude?" Tarandi chimed in.

Sinarè glared at the others. "Well," she said defensively, "she's always been nice to me."

"She can be when she wants to," Jolani said, "and we've always gotten along—for the most part." He looked at Jake. "I just thought it was funny that of all of us, she was the first you met."

"Ahem!" A sudden voice seemed to rise from the ground. Jake looked down to see Izhana standing in the midst of the group. No one had seen her approach. "Excuse me," she said in a tone that lacked apology, "but if you all are through, I have been asked to escort the Thalani back to the house."

"What's the matter?" Jake asked.

"I'm not certain," Izhana said. "Only my mistress returned suddenly, and she sent me to fetch you at once."

The urgency in Izhana's voice compelled those who stood round, and they ran with her to the main house. Ianasè and Tarandi were swiftest and ran ahead of the others. Sinarè lagged behind, but Azhè stayed with her. Jake kept pace with Jolani but just barely, for he was not used to such a run.

When Jake reached the house, he found Silorè waiting for him in the garden. Her face was pale, and she ran to him in great haste. "Come quickly, Thalani," she said, taking him by the hand. "Something's happened."

"What?" Jake asked. "What's going on?"

She did not answer but dragged him behind her into the house and through several passages to a parlour crowded with people. Adjaron was there along with Sondari and other members of the family guard. Many of the servants were present, including Felisè and Jardir, who stood beside one another at the back of the room. Everyone was staring together at a screen that stood upon the wall, and they were all silent.

Upon the screen were moving images of flame and smoke as of a great burning, and a voice was speaking in a grim tone. Jake entered in midsentence. "…earlier today. There is still no word at this hour concerning who might have carried out these attacks. The planetary council of Rithonon have remained silent, and we do not know when we shall hear from them. The evacuation of the village…"

At the name Rithonon, Jake felt his heart jump into his throat. He tried to get a better look at the screen, but he could not for all the people who stood in front of him. "What's going on here?" he asked Silorè, though he feared the answer.

Silorè had not released his hand, and now she squeezed it tightly as she turned slowly to him. "It's Brown Hill," she said. "There's been an attack, and some people have been killed."

Jake's legs failed him, but Jolani, who was standing behind, steadied him.

"What…?" said Jake. "How…?"

"We don't know yet," Silorè said. "Zhialamon is trying to find out. It happened early this morning, but we've only just now heard about it." She grabbed Jake's arm and shouted, "Out of the way!"

Those standing nearby moved aside, and Silorè pulled Jake forward to stand before the screen. The images filled his vision, and he watched a large cloud of smoke rising over the fires that burned in all corners of the town. Much that he had once known lay in ruins.

"It's dreadful," Silorè said, aghast. "The whole town is burning."

Jake bowed his head and clenched his hands into tight fists. "The Kenornin are pitiless," he said through his teeth.

"These were, yes." Zhialamon appeared, and the crowds parted to let him through. "But they have proven foolish in this matter. There was nothing in this but rage—a rage I had not anticipated. The Kenornin are not usually so impulsive. Indeed, they tried so hard to hide their presence while they still had a chance of acquiring you secretly, but they gave up at the last. I fear this event signals more aggression in days to come."

"What then shall we do?" asked Silorè.

"I've spoken with the leader of the Rithonon council," Zhialamon said. "He's searching for those who did this, but he suspects they are already gone."

"I don't care about the council or the Kenornin!" Jake said, his voice growing louder. He had not at first felt the full weight of his pain, but now it grew steadily in his heart. He felt light-headed. "All I want to know is whether everyone is safe. What about Samantha and her family?"

"I'm not sure," said Zhialamon. "I've dispatched a few messages, but I don't know when we will hear any replies."

"I sent out Faluin this morning," said Jake. "He should be back later this evening. I gave him a note for Samantha. I hope he finds her." He put his head in his hands and loudly yelled, not caring for the crowd around him. "This is all my fault!" he said. "It's all because of me!"

Without a word Silorè took him by the arm and rushed him outside onto the porch at the front of the house. The day had grown warm, and the sunshine that had before seemed pleasant now felt oppressive. The air was clear, and without the morning haze, Jake could see all the way to the stone mountains beyond the line of forest-clad hills.

"What did you bring me out here for?" Jake asked Silorè once she had closed the door behind them. "Don't want me to make a spectacle of myself, I guess?" His voice was full of bitterness.

"No, I don't," Silorè said sternly. "But it's for your own good as well. If you wish to blame yourself for that which you cannot control, you can at least have the courtesy to do so in private."

"How do you know what I should and shouldn't do?" Jake said, feeling a surge of anger. "I put everyone in danger. They could all be dead as far as we know!"

"Yes," Silorè said coldly. "They could be."

Jake was surprised by her answer and her tone. "Don't you care at all?"

"Of course I do!" Silorè snapped. "I care about everyone who is harmed by the Kenornin. Do you not suppose, Thalani, that there have been many other people beyond Brown Hill who have suffered because of the war between the Itarlavon and the Kenornin?"

"Then what's the point?" Jake said. "What good is it to save me only to have others die instead? And how many people is too many to justify that? Two? Three? A hundred? A thousand? A million? How many?" These last words he shouted, and his voice rang in the air and echoed in his ears.

"I don't have the answer to that," Silorè said in a low voice, "but I do not need one. We cannot control what the Kenornin do. Don't forget that it is they who have done this evil—not us. To hand you over to them would only embolden them, and danger would increase for all people—not just those in Brown Hill. No, it would not be right to sacrifice you in such a manner."

"But it's right to sacrifice the lives of others to save me?"

Silorè glared at him with sudden fury, for her patience was spent. "Go off and die, then," she said. "Set your soul at peace. Waste their lives and their deaths. You obviously value them so little."

"How dare you!" Jake said, moving towards her. "What do you think I've been saying? Of course I care about them!"

"Then act like it," Silorè said. "Thalanin must grow up quickly, so be a man, Thalani! Those who helped you did so because they valued your life above their own. If you cannot accept that now, you should not have accepted it then. You should have let the Kenornin destroy you."

"Maybe I should have," Jake mumbled.

"Then do what you will," Silorè said bitterly. "Only don't make misery for others. Do you not realize that Zhialamon, Adjaron, and I risked our lives and the future of our family to help you? We are all that is left of our bloodline, and if we are gone, who then would lead the Itarlavon family? You may count yourself worthless, but do not begrudge those who still care for you, lest they change their minds."

She turned abruptly and stormed into the house, leaving Jake alone on the porch. There he remained until evening, even after the call came for supper.

Twilight had come by the time Faluin returned and found Jake standing on the lawn in front of the Itarlavon house.

"I was hoping you would hear of it before I returned," Faluin said when Jake told him what he had seen. "I was dreading to tell you."

"How is the town?" asked Jake.

"In ruins," Faluin said. "Many buildings were destroyed, but by the time I left, most of the fires had been quenched. Quite a few people have died, and many more are laid up with grievous injury."

"Did…" Jake was almost afraid to ask. "Did you find Samantha?"

Faluin nodded. "That I did," he said. "She and her mother are safe, but her father has been badly hurt. The women were not at home when the Kenornin attacked, and Samantha's father was in the cellar. Four of his patrons died, and I think when he hears of it, he will count that pain greater than his own injuries."

"So he will live?" Jake asked.

"It seems so," Faluin said. "But the Griffin is a loss. It's a wonder many more were not killed."

"Who else, then?"

"Wellington, for one," said Faluin. "His grocery was destroyed, and it grieves me to report that he perished in the explosion."

Jake clenched his fists and turned away. He felt ill.

"That's not all," Faluin said. "I'm afraid they found the mayoress murdered in her office. Lawrence Appleton has assumed leadership of the town. He is an able leader, but there is much panic in Brown Hill. He has led the townsfolk to Deep Delving, and they have set up a tent city in the surrounding fields."

"The mayoress too?" Jake said, his voice cracking. "What about the others on the town council?"

"I'm afraid I don't know," Faluin said. "I did not stay long among the town or the people, for I flew over the surrounding lands, searching for any Kenornin who might have lingered in the mountains. Yet I knew I must hurry back, for I was charged to deliver this to you."

Faluin held out his left foot. In his talons he clutched a few pieces of paper rolled up together. These he gave to Jake, and Jake unrolled them. The handwriting was certainly Samantha's. Frantically he began to read.

My dear Jake,

I'm afraid I don't know where to begin. The festival seems like a lifetime ago. So much has happened since then. Our town has been shattered, as Faluin will probably tell you.

I can't believe it happened only this morning. It was so cold outside, and my mother dragged me along to Mrs Kruger's. Seems my mother fancied new tableware for the inn, and she wanted my opinion. I can't imagine why. She'd just have picked whatever she wanted anyway.

We had just arrived when it all started. There were some loud noises and a lot of shouting. People began running up the street, but we couldn't imagine why until it was too late. Some men came in and started shouting at us in Nanyan. I never knew how ugly that language could be, if you'll pardon my saying so. They started setting bombs all over the place, and they meant to leave us inside, but Lawrence showed up with Sterling and Preston, and they got us out in time.

We all went to the Jennings' place. Lawrence and some others went back into town and left us there. We were so worried about them, but then the attacks suddenly ended, though we were all terrified they would start up again. Lawrence returned eventually and sent everyone to Deep Delving, but I had heard nothing of my father, and I wasn't going to leave until I knew he was all right. I pressed Lawrence to go with me to the Griffin, and he took me there.

It's gone, Jake. I still can hardly accept it. I certainly couldn't then. It was only a pile of rubble. Maybe that made it easier, or maybe I was too determined. I had to find my father, and together we found him in the cellar beneath some fallen beams. He seemed pretty bad to me, but Lawrence fetched the doctor and a few young men, and we got him out.

They tell me he's going to be all right. I certainly hope so. Say a prayer for him.

I hope this letter finds you well. I've thought an awful lot about you since you left, and I hope you can return to Brown Hill soon. You may return to a different Griffin, but it'll be waiting for you all the same. I promise.

Please write again soon. I hope I'll have more cheerful things to say.

With my love,
Samantha

Jake lowered the note and stared off into the distance. He hardly knew what he was feeling or thinking. He knew only that his eyes were wet and his vision blurry. Faluin stood silently by as his master wept.

Slowly Jake returned to himself. His vision cleared, and he rubbed his nose and sniffled. Then he took a deep breath and looked back down at the papers. And as his hands shook, he read the letter over and over again, with the same passion as a man might drink from a spring in the desert.

At length a call came up from the house. Jake turned and looked to the front doors, which stood far off now, for Jake had walked far out upon the lawn. A silhouette stood before the light of the doorway, and it called to him again.

With Faluin perched upon his arm, Jake walked slowly towards the house. As he approached he found that it was Adjaron who stood in the doorway. "Make haste, Jake Connolly," he said. "Zhialamon wishes to speak with you."

He led Jake through the house to a back parlour overlooking the gardens. A fire was burning in the hearth, and through the open curtains shone the fiery rays of the setting sun. Zhialamon stood looking out the window, and Sondari the Protector stood nearby. On the other side of the room, Silorè sat upon a sofa with her arms crossed. She did not turn when Jake entered but gazed steadily into the fire.

"At last," the old man said, turning from the window. "We had hoped you would return before long."

Jake said nothing.

The old man hesitated for a moment. "I'm afraid," he said, "there have been quite a few losses."

"I've heard already," Jake said greyly. "From Faluin."

"And the Kenornin who attacked the village have not been found," Zhialamon continued, "at least not up until this past hour. That is how long ago I spoke with the security minister of the Thesmira district. Because of all that has happened, he is resolved to resign his post."

"I dare say he should," Jake mumbled.

"I agree," said Sondari. "Whether he could have foreseen this catastrophe or not, the needs of his district must be considered above his own. Don't forget there were security officers conspiring with the Kenornin—perhaps even some of his own men."

"It is a grim day to be sure," the old man said, "but take heart, young Connolly, for you are safe, and the Kenornin, it appears, have departed Rithonon. Things could have gone much worse. The Kenornin chose foolishly. They destroyed their secrecy at the last, and it would have been better for them to attack while you were still upon Rithonon. And yet they did not. Curious, isn't it?"

"But what shall we do now?" Sondari asked. "If this attack is any sign, the Kenornin will surely try to collect the boy here. I have already doubled the patrols circling the planet, and I've recalled other guards to protect this estate and the nearby city. I fear it will not be enough if the Kenornin are earnest."

"But do the Kenornin know indeed he is on Iderat?" Adjaron said. "Would they not rather suppose we have taken him somewhere else—somewhere more secretive? They may be seeking him elsewhere."

"Perhaps," the old man said, "and if that is the case then no world will be safe, and many others may suffer the fate of Brown Hill. That must not happen. They must know where Jake is and halt their search."

"Pardon, sir," Sondari said, "but it would be to our advantage to make the Kenornin spread themselves thin."

"That it would," Zhialamon said, "but we cannot selfishly endanger other worlds, making of them a shield to hold against the Kenornin. And even so, they will focus their resources on Iderat, whether they know he is here or not. It is still the most likely place. Indeed it is where we have brought him!"

"Then what do you propose to do?" said Adjaron.

"Jake Connolly shall accompany us to Ithèlimon for the summons," the old man said. "Ilavè will see him there—if indeed she does attend, as Thiriton has said—and perhaps many other worlds will be spared the wrath of the Kenornin."

"And what of Ilavè and the Chronicle?" Adjaron said. "If she will use this opportunity to seize it on Thesalara, should we not warn the Thesalarin?"

"I have already sent word to Thesalara," Zhialamon said, "but I don't think they took my warning seriously." He sighed. "Send a message to Tanaron tonight. Tell him to dispatch a ship and some men to Thesalara and keep watch on the Chronicle in secret. Tell him to alert us if Ilavè or any of her house visit Thesalara."

Adjaron nodded.

"Who is Tanaron?" Jake asked.

"He is the head of all our family's efforts to protect the Earth," Adjaron said. "As such he commands many ships and men. He lives in a house at the edge of Sorenon, but he is seldom at home. Even now he is aboard the *Kanzirim*, for that is his flagship, and from there he directs the Itarlavon protection of the Earth."

The discussion turned to the details of the next day's departure, but Jake did not listen. His mind was far away indeed, and Rithonon filled his thoughts. As he had read Samantha's letter, it seemed to him that he could almost hear her voice. Even now her words echoed in his mind, and he was filled with a terrible sickness for home.

When Jake returned to the discussion, Adjaron was speaking. "I think we should bring others with us to Ianiton," he said. "It may look strange if Jake alone accompanies us to the Council. We should not draw so much attention to our pretence, and a few more companions might accomplish that."

"Perhaps you're right," the old man replied. "Whom did you have in mind?"

Adjaron grinned. “I know a few sluggards who’ve been in need of something to do,” he said. “Besides, I’m sure Jolani and Andarè would like to see their mother.”

“Who is their mother?” Jake asked. He looked at Silorè, but she turned away from him.

“Rimilèon,” Adjaron said. “She is Iderat’s representative to the Council of Worlds, and as such they see little of her.”

“Which is still more often than some,” Silorè mumbled.

“Bring along whom you will, Adjaron,” the old man said. “Just see to it that they are ready to depart early tomorrow morning. For now, good night, all.”

With that, everyone went his own way. Silorè departed swiftly, and as Jake followed into the hallway, he found that Sinarè had been waiting for her upon a chair nearby with her kitten in her arms. Without a word to one another, the two girls walked together up the back stair towards their rooms. As she left, Sinarè cast Jake a pitiful look over her shoulder, but she did not speak to him.

Jake did not want to linger lest Zhialamon or Adjaron give him further condolences. He did not wish to hear any more. Quickly he made his way through the house and upstairs to his room, where he closed the door silently behind him.

After a quick bath in the adjoining room, he donned his night-clothes and walked out onto his balcony. There he stood a while and looked out over the gardens. The night was clear, and Calisa, the Iderat moon, shone brightly upon the world, touching every leaf and blade of grass with silver fingers. Across the valley the lights of a small village dotted the hillside, and below it the river ran like a ribbon of quicksilver in the dark.

With a heavy sigh, Jake went back inside and climbed into bed, the lamps going out as he did so. He feared he might lie awake for some time, but both his mind and body were exhausted, and he fell asleep almost at once, with his hand tightly gripping Samantha's letter.

Chapter 11

Ithèlimon

It was dark when Jake arose the next morning. He had slept poorly, and his neck was stiff. Outside his window the distant hills were tipped with a bright-blue haze, signalling that morning was nigh. He stood and stretched, and he dressed quickly. He had just splashed a bit of cold water on his face when Jardir knocked at the door.

"I'm pleased you are awake, sir," Jardir said when he entered. "I've been sent to fetch you to an early breakfast and to see that you are well packed for your journey today."

"I'm afraid I haven't packed anything," Jake said sheepishly. "I didn't really think of it."

"Never mind," Jardir said. "I shall make preparations while you are at breakfast, and I shall bring your bags down to the ship by the time you are finished eating. Everyone is awaiting your arrival downstairs."

Leaving Jardir to rummage through the closet, Jake hurried down to the breakfast room, where he found the others already assembled. Jolani and his friends sat together on one side of the table, and Silorè and Sinarè sat across from them. The table was laden with many dishes, and Felisè hurried about making sure everyone was cared for.

“Good morning,” Jolani said as Jake entered. He and the others looked not quite awake.

“Are you coming along too?” Azhè asked.

“Apparently,” Jake said.

“Then you’d better eat fast,” Ianasè said. “Adjaron will make sure we all leave on time, and he won’t care whether you’ve eaten or not.”

“Come on,” said Azhè. “Sit with us.”

“If you’d like,” Jake said, and he took a seat beside Ianasè.

“We were sorry to hear about Rithonon,” Azhè said, her bright mood suddenly fading. “We all know how it feels to be far from home and—”

“I’d rather not talk about it just now,” Jake mumbled.

Azhè blinked, startled by his interruption. “As you wish,” she said softly. She and the others went back to eating in silence.

Jake hardly ate but sat staring into his plate, occasionally glancing towards Silorè, who refused to look at him at all. Sinarè was preoccupied with her kitten.

“Tell us, Jake,” Jolani said at last, “have you ever been to Ianiton?”

“I’d never been away from Rithonon until this week,” said Jake sullenly. “At least not to my memory. Silorè said my family lived on Earth years ago, but I don’t remember it at all.”

“Ianiton is great; you’ll love it,” Azhè said, trying to sound cheerful again. “Ithèlimon is huge, and there’s always something to do there.”

“If Adjaron will let us have any fun this trip,” Ianasè added. “He usually makes us run errands or clean house. Jolani usually gets out of it by claiming to visit his mother.” She winked at Jolani.

“I do visit her,” Jolani protested. “My sister and I don’t get to see her very often.”

"Is Andarè coming too?" Jake asked. "Where is she?"

"She's probably already on the *Lamarenor*," Jolani said. "She likes to get settled in early. She hates travelling."

"And everything else," Ianasè said, and took a drink of dark-red juice.

At that moment, Adjaron appeared and approached Jolani and his friends. "Come on," he said to them. "It's time to get aboard. I'm sure Remni could use a bit of help getting the ship ready."

"I'm sure he could," Ianasè said with a snort.

Adjaron was not amused, and he gave the four friends a look that spurred them to action. They hurried outside without another word, leaving Jake behind.

"Don't linger too long, you two," Adjaron said to Jake and Silorè. "We leave as soon as everything is ready." He hurried out after the others.

With only the three of them left, Sinarè suddenly spoke to Jake from across the table. "Korandi and I came down to see you all off," she said, holding up her kitten so Jake could see him.

"You're not going with us?" Jake asked.

Sinarè frowned. "No," she said. "My father insists that I remain on Iderat." She sighed. "No one will let me go anywhere or do anything. Oh well. Korandi and I will just have to be lonely together."

Silorè broke her silence. "We won't be gone too long," she said. "You'll see. It won't be like last time. We're not going far."

"I'll miss you," Sinarè said with a sniffle.

Silorè stroked Sinarè's hair. "You'll be fine," she said. "Felisè promised me she would take you shopping in the city. That'll be fun, right?"

Sinarè nodded.

"Come on," said Silorè. "We'd better hurry. Are you coming, Thalani?" She shot a glance at Jake that seemed to slice him in two.

Now that it came to it, Jake felt suddenly hungry, but he dared not tarry at breakfast any longer. "I'm right behind you," he said. "Lead the way."

Together the three of them walked outside. The air was cold and damp, and a light dew had turned the grass to grey. Upon the circle of lawn before the house stood the *Lamarenor*, with two automatons busily loading crates onto a platform lowered beneath the ship. Remni was examining one of the wings, and though the ship stood high off the ground, he had to crouch a bit so as not to hit his head. Off to the side, Sondari was giving final instructions to those of his men who would be left in charge of Sorenon in his absence. Apparently he too was coming to Ianiton.

Jake, Silorè, and Sinarè stopped on the steps of the front portico and stood looking out at the ship.

"I wish I could go with you," Sinarè said.

"So do I," said Silorè, and she put her arms around her. "Is there anything you want me to bring back to you?"

"Like a present?" Sinarè said excitedly.

"Yes," said Silorè, grinning at her. "What would you like?"

Sinarè suddenly looked panicked. "Oh, I don't know," she said. "What I really want is for you to come home quickly."

"I will," Silorè said, "but can't you think of anything you want?"

"Not really," said Sinarè. "How about something for Korandi?" She held her kitten in Silorè's face, and he sniffed her hair.

Silorè scratched Korandi's head. "If that's what you'd like," she said. "I don't know where to shop for pets in Ithèlimon. I'll have to ask Izhana."

"I'll pretend I didn't hear that," said a voice from below. They all looked down to see Izhana staring up at Silorè indignantly.

"I'm sorry," Silorè said, laughing and leaning over to rub Izhana's back. "I'll get you something nice too."

"Hmph." Izhana whipped her head around and strutted towards the *Lamarenor*, passing Silorè's maidservants as they walked up from the ship.

"Your things are all aboard, my lady," said Calandè. "Your brother is waiting for you."

"We're coming," Silorè said. She grabbed Sinarè's hand and turned to Jake. "Come on, Thalani." She and Sinarè walked together, flanked by Calandè and Lithè, and Jake followed behind.

At the bottom of the ramp, Silorè and Sinarè embraced. "I'm going to miss you so much," said Sinarè with tears in her eyes. "You just got back, and now you're leaving again."

"I'll miss you too," Silorè said, "but I'll be back soon, and I promise I'll take you to the animal park in Ralosima when I return."

"Very well," Sinarè said. "Be safe. Both of you." She turned to Jake and curtsied. "Goodbye, Jake," she said. "I'm glad to have met you. I pray for your safe return."

Jake and Silorè walked up together into the ship, and as they entered, the ramp retracted, and the door closed. In the dim corridor, they met Zhialamon talking to Sondari and another guard.

"Good morning!" Zhialamon said to them. Jake yawned, and the old man chuckled. "A bit early to be setting off, isn't it? Well, I had hoped you might have a rest after everything you have endured, and here you are setting off again."

"I'll be all right," Jake said.

"No doubt," the old man replied cheerfully, and then he brought forward the man who stood beside Sondari. He was young—at least, young as the Nanyanin reckoned youth—with bright eyes and a kind look. "Jake Connolly, I would like you to meet Rathori, a protector of the family and a student of Sondari."

Rathori bowed. "I am happy to meet you, Jake Connolly," he said, and he spoke more gently than Jake would have guessed. "I have heard much about your family and all their deeds, and it is an honour to be one of your protectors."

Jake bowed in return.

"He and Sondari shall accompany us to Ianiton," Zhialamon said, and he turned to Sondari with a look that was both grin and grimace. "Though not without protest."

Sondari stood up straight and answered in a voice respectful but firm. "It cannot be helped," he said. "I go where the family goes when there is danger, and these days have grown more perilous. Surely you don't begrudge me performing my duties?"

"Certainly not," the old man said. "Neither do I resent your presence, but I would have you accompany us as a member of the family and be at ease among us."

"I labour so that the family can enjoy that ease. That is all I require."

Adjaron suddenly appeared around the corner. "Are you all ready?" he said. "We're set to depart, if you will all take your seats."

Everyone followed Adjaron to the front of the ship. Jake and Silorè sat next to one another in the front row of seats. Even sitting side by side, Silorè ignored Jake completely, and though he wanted to talk to her, he was afraid to speak.

Instead Jake turned around in his seat as best he could and looked at the others already strapped in. Calandè and Lithè sat in the row behind, and they only smiled slightly as Jake faced them. Andarè was sitting two rows back all by herself reading a large book. Jolani and his friends were talking loudly in their chairs on the other side of the room. Zhialamon sat between the guards in the far corner, and it seemed they were arguing something amongst themselves.

Adjaron stepped to the helm and took the levers in hand. "Everyone set?" he asked, looking over his shoulder. "Good. Here we go." He flipped a few switches and brought the *Lamarenor* to life. A low rumbling arose from deep within the ship, and slowly the noise grew to a dull whine. Izhana suddenly appeared and jumped into Silorè's lap, curling up into a ball.

Slowly the ship rose into the air and hovered above the ground for a few moments. Then Adjaron threw a lever forward, and the *Lamarenor* tilted up towards the sky. With great force and a loud noise, the ship parted the clouds, and the blue sky gave way to black. The window turned backwards to watch Iderat shrinking into the distance until it was lost to the darkness.

The trip to Ianiton was generally unremarkable.

Jake did not see Silorè except at mealtimes and at the Zhonda tournament Ianasè made everyone play late that afternoon. Jake won no games except one against Azhè, who won none at all. Silorè beat Jake twice, but she said little to him as they played. Andarè, who had been reluctant to join in, won every game she played—even the final, which she played against Silorè. Until that game, Silorè had beaten each of her opponents with little effort, but Andarè bested her, to the amazement of all.

The planet Ianiton was a grey world, both land and sea. Thick white clouds swirled over much of the planet, and below them large cities spread out, grey upon grey. Roads ran like canyons between cities, and rivers flowed in straight courses of stone and metal. As the *Lamarenor* approached, a dark-green moon peeked over the edge of the world.

Watching the planet growing large in the window, Jake felt a twinge of expectation. He had seen pictures of Ithèlimon and had read much about it, but he was excited to see it at last.

Ithèlimon was ancient, and though much had changed in Eratzira, Ithèlimon remained for the most part unaltered. Even under the dominion of the Daseshon, Ithèlimon had enjoyed special privilege, and it retained much of its wealth and splendour. So large was it now that even from a great distance, it appeared as a white circle upon the northern continent.

The *Lamarenor* descended upon Ithèlimon from the southwest. The city had an overall alabaster hue, fading into a light-green haze near the horizon. The sky over Ianiton was a pale blue-green, and its flat clouds were outlined in shadows of dark violet. High above the planet, the star Korsilon shone its brilliant blue light upon the world.

The *Lamarenor* set down inside a large oval structure that stood near the wall that marked the city's outer boundary. Once the ship had landed, a glass roof closed overhead, shielding the chamber from the harsh rays of Korsilon.

"Welcome to Ithèlimon, everyone," Adjaron said. "Do try to hurry. There's a transport arriving soon to take us into the city, and we're already running a bit behind."

All the travellers went their separate ways. Jake walked to his room and gathered a bag Jardir had sent down to the *Lamarenor* before it departed. *I hope he packed more than this*, Jake thought as he slung the pack on his shoulder.

He hurried through the corridor and down the ramp into the landing bay. Zhialamon and Adjaron were already outside the ship, lowering the ramp to the cargo hold. Sondari and Rathori stood nearby, looking stern and speaking in hushed voices. Remni strolled about, checking over the pylons upon which the ship rested.

As Jake stood at the bottom of the ramp, two women in long white robes approached from an arched door on the far side of the room. Each woman wore upon her neck a silver chain and a pendant etched with a circle encompassing a pyramid, with a star shining at its peak—the emblem of Ithèlimon. At their backs no fewer than ten men followed with grim faces, each bearing a large rifle.

Sondari stood between the oncomers and Zhialamon, but the old man bade him give way to them. The women passed Sondari and bowed before Zhialamon, with hands facing palm to palm. "Greetings, Father[48] Itarlavon," they said.

Zhialamon bowed in return but said nothing.

"We welcome you to Ithèlimon," one of the women said. "We trust that your sojourn in our fair city will be one of peace and safety."

"If there is anything you require," said the other, "we are at your command."

"Did the Solèdaron send you to greet us?" Adjaron said, doing his best to conceal his sneer.

"Indeed he did, Master Adjaron," the first woman said. "We have been sent to escort you to your residence." She beckoned, and the foremost of the guards stepped forward. "This is Captain Azhkani. He and his men have been sent for your protection."

Azhkani bowed. "We welcome your family," he said. "In order to ensure your safety and that of our city, I must ask you to remove any weapons you carry and to submit your cargo for inspection."

Sondari and Rathori stepped in front of Zhialamon and stood face to face with the captain. "We are the protectors of the Itarlavon," Sondari said. "We carry arms only in defence of the family, and we are permitted do so by the laws of Eratzira and of this city."

48 Nanyan: *Tarathi*—formal title of a family patriarch.

"That may be," said Azhkani, "but I will need to see your letters of writ. If all is in order, you will be permitted to keep your sidearms only. All else must be left here, or it shall be seized."

Sondari's eyes narrowed, but there was no other hint of emotion on his face. "If that is your duty," he said in a measured voice, "then so be it. We will submit—but under protest."

Azhkani looked equally straight-faced. "My men will see to the cargo." He nodded to the others, and the armed men stepped forward towards the cargo platform. One of them stopped in front of Jake and made him surrender his bag to be searched. After thoroughly ruffling its contents, he returned the bag without a word and joined his comrades.

The security men worked swiftly to unload the containers, rummaging through each one as Zhialamon, Adjaron, and Sondari silently watched. Rathori came to Jake's side, his hand upon his pistol as though it might vanish if his watchfulness lapsed.

"A strange place," said Rathori. "Quite unlike the last time I was in Ithèlimon."

"Were there no inspections then?" Jake asked.

Rathori shook his head. "Not like this," he said. "Nor do I think all travellers to the city are so thoroughly examined."

"You think they're doing this just to the Itarlavon?" Jake asked, speaking lower.

"I do not know," Rathori said. "There is a ban on weapons within the walls of the city, 'tis true—though weapons there are aplenty, I assure you—but I've never known so many men to come so heavily armed just to inspect a bit of luggage."

He gave Jake a knowing glance and stepped away to join Sondari.

In time the other passengers disembarked and submitted themselves and their bags to inspection. Silorè seemed very put out by the whole process, and she argued at length with Captain Azhkani about the treatment of her many trunks.

It was nearly a full hour later that everything was unloaded, inspected, and brought to the transport waiting outside. (Jake was grateful to find that Jardir had indeed packed a large trunk for him, though he wondered what it contained). The emissaries of the Solèdaron kept close to the travellers at all times. Jake began to feel suffocated by them, for they walked around scrutinizing the actions of the Itarlavon. Though the guards were stone-faced, the two women went about with frozen smiles that unnerved everyone.

The women and the guards boarded the transport with the travellers, and a heavy silence hung in the air during the trip. But Jake did not mind much. The cabin in which the travellers rode had many windows in its walls and ceiling, and he busied himself with looking at this new world passing by.

The transport flew low over Ithèlimon, passing scores of towers and pyramids that grew more numerous towards the city centre. Obelisks of great girth stood as monuments to the former glory of Eratzira, though some were crumbling, and one was missing its upper half.

Flyers sparsely populated the air, but the ground was crowded with pedestrians and transports of all sizes. Elevated streets and walkways ran through the city in magnificent sweeps of stone that weaved among many buildings of varying heights. Upon one tower, the blue rays of the sun burst into a million colours that shimmered on the smaller stone structures below.

Trains ran at great speed to all corners of the city. Like a labyrinth, their rails wound their way around towers and roads, sometimes plunging into dark places between buildings—narrow lanes that no sunlight could find.

As the transport flew on, Jake became aware that as he looked to the horizon in all directions he could see only the city stretching out beneath him. He was sailing on an ocean of stone, and there was no land in sight.

A flutter caught his eye outside the window, and he turned to see Faluin flying alongside the transport. He swooped in close for a moment, and then with a wink he turned and dived out of sight. Jake searched the sky for him, but he could not find him again.

Then, as Jake turned back to the front window, he saw in the distance a great pyramid, black and immense, like a tall mountain of adamant. Stones of enormous size and weight made up its construction, fitted together without seam or crack. Its capstone was a single piece of rock hewed from a mountain-peak in years beyond remembrance, and upon its four sides it bore the Crest of Eratzira—a giant bird with wings outstretched behind a planet, and a star shining above them.

At the feet of the edifice stood many other pyramids and obelisks, each larger than any other outside the city's centre, but the Great Pyramid dwarfed them all. All around it and its lesser cousins, a wide plain of stone ran flat and smooth, surrounded by a high wall upon which many battlements stood. From each of these towers shone a faint blue light that rose high over the Great Pyramid. At the very point of the capstone, the lights from the several towers converged in a dazzling sphere shining brighter than a full moon.

"That is the Telzirim," Zhialamon said to Jake. "It is the last safeguard of the Zhènlara.[49] The city itself has a similar defence, only much larger and less visible. It is that shield—the Athèzirim—that makes Ithèlimon the City of Encompassing Safety."

49 Nanyan: "heart of law"—name given to the centre of political power in a nation. In Eratzira, the word is used as the proper name for the complex of buildings where the government business of Eratzira is conducted.

Far to the south stood a line of three large pyramids whose view of the Zhènlara was unobstructed. The transport descended upon the central pyramid and landed on one of many platforms running along its sides. A half-dozen more men met the transport and began to unload its cargo—under the close supervision of Silorè and the watchful eye of Sondari and the security men of Ithèlimon.

Jake disembarked and stood a moment looking out over the city. The Great Pyramid stood like a mountain at the horizon, and countless miles lay between it and him. The sounds of the city came to his ears, and he closed his eyes, listening to the wind and the clatter of machines and the mingling of distant voices.

When he opened his eyes again, Jake found that the men were already carrying the luggage away, and the travellers had begun to follow. "Come on," Ianasè said as she passed him by. "Don't get left."

Shouldering the bag he had carried from the *Lamarenor*, Jake followed close behind. The group passed through a narrow corridor into the main passage that ran to the centre of the pyramid. There it opened into a circular corridor lined with lift-shafts that ran through the core of the pyramid from its base to its peak. The travellers entered an empty lift-car and ascended, and the women and guards from the Solèdaron went with them. From the time they had left the landing platform, no one had spoken a word.

Jake broke the silence at last. "Where are we going?" he asked no one in particular.

"We have a residence at the top," said Adjaron. "It is one of the many Itarlavon houses in the city. Some are as old as Ithèlimon itself. The house above may not be the largest our family owns, but it is the one we most often use when we come to Iderat."

The lift opened on a foyer of dark stone that ran around the central pillar of the pyramid. They must have been near the top,

Jake reasoned, for the foyer was quite small compared to the vast chambers below.

As the travellers stepped out of the lift, the emissaries from the Solèdaron turned to them and bowed. "We are happy to convey you safely to your lodgings," one of the ladies said. "We hope your stay will be comfortable. If you require anything more of us, we are in the suite two floors below and will remain there for the duration of your stay. Summons is at the fourth hour tomorrow; we will certainly see you then." Then, bowing again, they returned to the lift.

"I have ordered transportation for you tomorrow," said Captain Azhkani, stepping forward while his men remained in the lift. "I trust my arrangements will meet with your approval. I shall see you all in the morning." Then he bowed and turned, and the lift doors closed behind him.

With the sound of the lift-car running in its shaft, Jake felt a great weight lift from him and his companions, and it seemed to him that everyone took a deep breath in unison.

As Jake turned away from the lifts, he beheld a door in the outer wall made of bronze, tall and thick, with many rivets upon its outline. In a golden circle spanning the door was the symbol of the Itarlavon family, and over all were inscribed the words "*Sèn Mezh-za Thevinil-ga*."[50]

Zhialamon passed his ring-bearing hand across the face of the door, and it opened slowly upon a staircase leading up to a landing and then turning left and right. "Everyone up, then," he said, and he led the way up the stairs.

After a few turns, Jake emerged from a floor of blue carpet into a large square room. Sunlight streamed through a giant window that made up the far wall, and through it one could see the Great Pyramid shrouded in haze at the horizon. The centre of the room was sunken

50 Nanyan: "Where there is family, there is home."

in a shallow square, and at the bottom lay a pool of rippling water casting bright reflections upon the walls and ceiling. On the near side were many cushioned chairs and couches, and upon the other three tables stood near the window. A raised walkway with a wrought-iron railing ran around the room, dividing the walls in half, with many doors upstairs and down.

Jake stood a moment, looking around while the others sat upon the chairs and floor. The luggage-men arrived with the bags and trunks, carrying them up spiral staircases onto the walkway above and through the doors to which they were directed. Silorè supervised this task closely with her maidservants, for much of the luggage was hers.

As the travellers made themselves comfortable, a chime echoed through the room, and Sondari disappeared again down the main staircase.

Sitting in an oversized chair of green fabric, Azhè put her hands behind her head and sighed. "I love it here," she said. "The chaos of the city can't reach us. It's like our little island in a raging sea. The waves break upon it but cannot disturb our peace."

"You've been here only three times, Azhè," Ianasè said. "And we've never stayed for long."

"I know," Azhè said, her mood unsullied. "All the more reason to cherish our time here." She turned to Jake and grinned. "The last time we were here was the anniversary of the *Idrineva*.[51] Though we didn't get to go out much, I loved playing *phidu*[52] in front of the window while we watched the rockets light up the sky over the

51 Nanyan: "rebirth." In Eratzira, Idrineva is the two days commemorating the independence of Eratzira from the Daseshon.

52 Nanyan: "hidden hand"—a game played by matching sets of cards according to a complex set of rules. The cards contain simple pictures divided by suit, colour, and category.

Zhènlara. It had been a warm day, but that night the air was cool and pleasant. I know it sounds silly, but it made me quite happy."

"At least someone enjoyed it," said Ianasè. "I was bored to hysterics that whole trip. The city was too crowded during Idrineva, and when we tried to go out, we ended up waiting in train queues all day. I had looked forward to that trip, but it was all a waste."

"Well," Azhè said cheerily, "now's your chance to make up for all that."

"And I shall," Ianasè said. "I've got a list of things to do, and I'm going to do them. There's no point in coming all this way just to sit around. I can stay at home on Iderat."

"I'll be happy so long as I can see a decent Lambati game," Tarandi said. "Ithèlimon is playing Derelam this week, and the points are pretty close going into the season's end. I already got Adjaron to reserve the family box for us."

Jolani looked over at Andarè, who was sitting sideways on a large chair, with her face hidden behind a book. "What do you say, sis?"[53] he called to her. "Do you want to come with the rest of us to see the Lambati match?"

Andarè looked up from her book just long enough to scowl at her brother. "I think I'd rather die," she said and went back to her reading.

Tarandi chuckled. "Then I suppose it's settled," he said with a grin.

At that moment Sondari returned, followed by a woman in a flowing blue dress. Her hair was woven into a golden circlet upon her head, and around her neck she wore a small medallion of gold engraved with the symbol of the Itarlavon.

53 Nanyan: *kisa*—a familiar term for a sister of similar age. Sometimes used among young ladies who are close friends.

"Mother!" Jolani leapt from his chair in a flash and ran to the woman, embracing her so tightly he lifted her off the floor. At that word Andarè turned so suddenly that a lock of her hair came undone and fell in her face. When she brushed it away and saw who the woman was, she sprang to her feet and ran to join Jolani, hugging both him and her mother.

The three stood embracing one another in silence for a long while, and everyone else sat by and watched them.

"They haven't seen her in at least two years," Azhè whispered to Jake. "Rimilèon usually visits Iderat twice a year, but she hasn't managed it in quite a while."

Jolani and Andarè released their mother, and they three walked hand in hand to join the others in the centre of the room. Andarè had not bothered to pin up her hair again, and it kept falling in her face.

"Why didn't you tell us you were coming today?" Jolani asked.

Rimilèon spoke with a soft voice, and its warmth seemed to fill the whole room. "I wanted to surprise you both," she said. "It has made the welcome all the better."

"We would have greeted you with no less feeling had we known you were coming," Jolani said.

"Of that I'm certain," she replied, and she squeezed her children tightly, "and I'm happier now than I have been in more days than I care to number. It fills me with joy to see you here."

"But I thought you were busy," said Andarè. "We were worried we'd get to see you only in passing at the Summons." Jake thought Andarè hardly sounded like herself, for the harsh tone in her voice had gone. *She has a nice voice*, he thought, *when she's not biting off people's heads.*

"I was," said Rimilèon, "but I was able to get away thanks to someone who managed to get me out of my committees today." She winked at Adjaron.

"But won't they miss you in your meetings?" Andarè said as she and Jolani sat on either side of their mother upon a long sofa.

"I don't expect so," said Rimilèon. "Nitani is there in my place. He will be the voice for our causes today. I'm sure he can handle my committees for one day."

"Just one day?" Andarè said. Jake thought he saw tears in her eyes.

"I'll visit more if I can," said Rimilèon, "and we'll be together tomorrow for the Council. After that, I'm not sure what will happen. No doubt there will be things said tomorrow that will cause much work for the other Councils. Don't you think so, Zhialamon?"

Zhialamon had been sitting quietly by and seemed hesitant now to interject. "I certainly hope not," he said.

"Kensilon won't tell us what the Summons is about," Rimilèon said. "He hasn't been seen much in public as of late. Rumour is he's working on something concerning the Earth and the Keneraton."

"Oh, must you talk of such things now?" Andarè protested. "Surely there will be plenty of time for that later."

Zhialamon laughed. "Of course," he said. "I don't wish to interfere with more important matters." He smiled at three of them.

"No please, Zhialamon," Jolani said. "If you have things to discuss, then speak, for we cannot sacrifice the good of the Itarlavon family for the sake of us three here."

Zhialamon smiled. "Don't worry," he said. "There is little that can trump the long-awaited reunion of a mother and her children. Besides, there is nothing new about Kensilon's plans for the Earth. It has all been said before, and it will be again."

Jake suddenly realized that the men carrying the luggage were gone. He looked around for Silorè and found her standing with her maidservants upon the walkway above and leaning on the railing. Her face was difficult to read, for many emotions played there.

Izhana sat at Silorè's feet and peered over the balcony at everyone below.

"Come, then, everyone," Rimilèon said with sudden enthusiasm. "I'm taking you all out to dinner. You are *all* my family, after all."

Zhialamon gave her a nod. "We'd be delighted."

"Splendid," said Rimilèon. Then she looked at her children and said, "Afterwards we three shall walk together by moonlight. But now, everyone get dressed. It is a fine restaurant we go to, and we don't want to sully the image of the Itarlavon family. Isn't that right, Silorè?" This last part she spoke in a loud voice towards the balcony where Silorè stood, and she gave Silorè a wink.

The question took Silorè by surprise, but she answered quickly. "I heartily agree."

"To business, then," Rimilèon said. "I have already reserved our table, and we must get there in good time to be seated. Off you go now. Everyone!"

The *Zhiniasin Itelsa* stood in the Zontolma district of Ithèlimon among some of the finest restaurants in the city. Rimilèon had procured a shuttle for the journey there, and Jake found this flight much more enjoyable than the last. To his relief neither the women from the Solèdaron nor the other security men were going with them. Only two of Rimilèon's bodyguards joined them, and these men did not seem to distress the Itarlavon like the others had.

Jake had changed into a good set of clothes Jardir had packed for him. They were not necessarily garments he would have chosen for himself, but then again, he was not really fond of any Nanyan clothing. Everyone else had dressed well, and it seemed to Jake they were suited for a party rather than a meal. Indeed, as he walked with the Itarlavon from the shuttle to the restaurant, Jake felt very conspicuous—as though he were attached to people of great importance. Upon reflection, he realized he rather was.

The *Itelsa* was a broad grey-stone building with flourishes of gold covering every window and door. The windows cast warm light into streets left dark by the setting sun, and it seemed to Jake that the building took on a magical quality, with the sounds of the city mingling with the clatter of dishes and the voices of the patrons.

Inside, the air was cool, and it smelled so strongly of so many foods that Jake supposed he could have appeased his hunger just by breathing. Underfoot, the carpets were embroidered with patterns of red and white mingled with gold. Chandeliers made of frosted glass hung from the ceiling and shone upon the white pillars that ran to the roof. Among the pillars stood many tables illumined by soft lantern-light, and the crystal vessels upon them glistened like a night sky full of stars.

The Itarlavon were taken upstairs and seated at a large round table draped with a white cloth embroidered with gold. A common menu was bound in a scroll at the centre of the table, and the group passed it around in turn. When it came to him, Jake was pleased to see many meat dishes listed, and he took his time choosing from among them.

The meal was served in short order, brought to the table by a half-dozen attendants each carrying a tray laden with platters and bowls. These they put at the centre of the table upon a large *therdanasi*,[54] and Jake was certain he had never seen so much food: dumplings floating in bowls of thick soup; skewers of blackened

54 A circular turntable found in many Nanyan cultures. In Eratzira *therdanasin* are typically found only in the finest restaurants where food is shared amongst the patrons.

vegetables standings upright in a firm *zika fènbana*,[55] a pot of *gansa*[56] beside piles of flatbread sprinkled with *rizhin* seeds; a pan of *adagorati*[57] steaming beside rice-balls with fillings both sweet and savoury.

Other dishes there were besides, but Jake's wandering gaze stopped when he found the dish he had requested—a bowl of *Rova sel Thenithoran.*[58] The smell of it overpowered the other food, and the Itarlavon looked at the dish warily. Jake thought he had never smelled anything more delicious, for he had gone without meat for several days, and he found himself craving it intensely.

So the meal began, and Jake and the Itarlavon sat at table many hours. They lacked for nothing, and they talked together far into the evening. Zhialamon, Adjaron, and Rimilèon spoke of the dominion of the Daseshon and the days leading up to the last war. Everyone asked Jake what life on Rithonon was like and what he thought of Sorenon and Ithèlimon. Jolani and his friends asked many questions about what sort of Thalanin customs Jake followed. Jake explained about his job as a vèralamenasi and how he served his fellow Thalanin as a bridge to the Nanyanin.

As the dinner progressed, Silorè would at times speak quietly with Calandè and Lithè, and though the lisarèn had seemed so stern before, with Silorè they were smiling and laughing like good friends. Even so, they would not speak to the others, and they sat quietly by when Silorè joined the rest of the Itarlavon in conversation.

55 A savoury pudding made with peppers, *kornanya* root, and crushed *idtheszin* seeds. It is very spicy and is usually served alongside bland beans and vegetables.

56 Generic term for any kind of bean-paste.

57 A stewed-vegetable dish whose primary ingredient is *adagon*—a cucumber-like gourd of many varieties and colours. Traditionally the vegetables are sautéed all together before being baked in a sauce of vinegar and herbs.

58 Stewed beef in a thick broth, flavoured with many pungent herbs and spices.

So the meal passed pleasantly, and by the time they left, they were all quite happy and full of both food and drink. On the shuttle ride back, Ianasè and Azhè argued concerning which of them had grown fatter.

"And besides," Ianasè said at the last, "I think you had a bit too much to drink."

Azhè giggled and put her hands to her temples. "I couldn't help it," she said. "They certainly have the finest wine in Eratzira. I just got carried away."

"Honestly," Andarè spoke up, "haven't you any self-control?"

"Of course I do," said Azhè, "when I care to. Anyway, who was it who kept ordering more *thilimasè*[59] after everyone else had finished eating?"

Andarè scowled and did not answer.

"Now, now," Rimilèon said, "there is nothing wrong with a little indulgence now and then, particularly on special occasions. Only do be careful, Azhdarlorè; it is possible to get too much of a good thing."

"I'm sorry, Lady Rimilèon," Azhè said, trying to sound serious. "I promise you I'm quite all right."

Tarandi snickered, and Azhè stuck out her tongue at him and put her thumb to her cheek.[60]

The travellers landed and made their way to the house at the top of the pyramid. Izhana greeted them at the door, and Silorè sat with her in a chair and scratched her behind the ears. The others sat together around the fountain, listening to the gentle music of its

59 A dessert made with fruit preserves and wafers of *labnezarè*—a shortbread-like biscuit—and topped with sweet-cream.

60 This is considered a rude (and somewhat obscene) gesture in Eratzira. The four fingers of one hand are clenched in a fist, and the thumb is brushed against one's cheek, often ending by touching the tip of one's stuck-out tongue. The origins of this gesture are not fully agreed upon.

waterfall. There was nothing else to be said, and they were content to enjoy one another's company in silence, speaking only occasionally in half-mumbled phrases that could not light any fire of conversation. Azhè fell asleep in her chair.

Rimilèon and her children had gone for a stroll on an open-air walkway several storeys below, and when they returned an hour later, Rimilèon stayed only a little while longer before departing for her own home. Jolani and Andarè would have gone with her, but she insisted they stay. "My residence is quite small," she said, "and I have no extra beds suitable for my children. Besides, I am certain you would be much happier here with your friends."

"Friends?" Andarè said under her breath, with a return of the bitterness to which Jake had grown accustomed.

Rimilèon bade everyone good night, and with a last embrace of her children, she departed. After her mother had gone, Andarè did not smile or speak any more that evening but sulked in a chair not too close to the others.

The Itarlavon and Jake remained downstairs together only a few minutes more. Night had fallen outside, and the lights of the city shone brightly into the room through the giant window. The Great Pyramid in the distance was lit up with giant spotlights whose glow rose high into the sky. The horizon beyond was a dull grey colour that faded to a dim haze above the city.

Zhialamon announced he was off to bed, and it was not long before the others followed. Yet Jake found that he himself was not sleepy. He supposed he was not yet accustomed to the shorter days, and so he sat a while longer as one by one the Itarlavon went to bed. Last of all Silorè rose with Izhana in her arms and walked with her attendants up the stairs to her rooms, closing the door behind them.

Left alone, Jake reluctantly trudged upstairs and bathed, lingering in the tub since he did not care to go to bed. When he had dried himself and dressed, he walked out again and found the lights had been dimmed and no one was about. All was quiet except for the trickling of the fountain below.

He was about to return to his room and shut himself in for the night when he noticed a door standing open in a corner of the walkway. This door was different from those of the bedrooms, and his curiosity got the better of him. He entered and found a flight of stairs that wound upward, and so he climbed.

The stairs led to a carpeted room in the capstone of the pyramid. There was no furniture or other decoration anywhere, and the walls were all made of glass, giving the room a full-circle view of the city. To his surprise and delight, he found Silorè standing before the window, staring out towards the Great Pyramid. A white dressing gown was draped about her, tied loosely at her waist with a pink sash. She was alone.

"Not tired?" Jake asked.

Silorè turned with a start, but seeing who it was, she faced the window again. "I cannot sleep," she said. "Ithèlimon is too loud."

Jake strained to listen, but the room was silent. "I can't hear anything."

"I can," said Silorè. "The noise of the restaurant and of the flight there and back still echoes in my mind."

"I know what you mean," Jake said. "I was a bit overwhelmed myself." He walked slowly to her side. She did not look in his direction, but neither did she protest his presence.

"I don't see why anyone would live here," she continued with a grimace. "It's loud, and it's crowded. You spend your life hemmed in—walking the same crowded streets, riding the same crowded trains, growing old in the same crowded rooms. I guess living in Sorenon has spoiled me—wide spaces and clean air." She sighed and shook her head. "Pay me no mind, Thalani. This happens to me whenever I come to Ithèlimon. I'll soon be over it."

Jake was not sure how he should respond. "I'm sorry you're not feeling well," he said.

"What are talking about?" Silorè said, sounding annoyed. "I didn't say I was ill. I'm just a little out of sorts." Jake caught the gleam of a tear in her eye. "But I don't think it's because of the city this time."

They stood together in silence for a few minutes.

When Silorè spoke again, her voice was shaking. "I…I want you to know that…I do care," she said. "About Rithonon and Brown Hill, I mean. Quite a lot. It's the job of my family to protect others—especially Thalanin—and I…well, I failed." She turned away and tried to hide her face from him.

Jake scowled. "Failed? At what?"

Silorè whipped her head around to face him, and the look in her eyes mingled fire with water. "Don't act stupid!" she said through angry tears. "It's the truth. If I had done my job properly, I could have gotten you off that planet before anyone knew I was there. We wouldn't have had to traipse all over Rithonon, your vèralamen would not have been endangered, and no one would have had to die."

Jake opened his mouth to speak, but Silorè put up her hand. "And don't you dare try to make me feel better about it—not after all you said to me on Iderat. I refuse to feel good about what's happened, and I can be far more stubborn than you can!"

Jake paused a moment, looking in her face so full of grief and fury. "Is that why you've been so cold recently?"

Silorè nodded, and her rage faded for a moment. "I…I was so angry. You were hysterical, and you wouldn't listen to me. I told you all the things I was telling myself—that the Thalanin were willing to help us, that nothing that happened was our fault. When you rejected all that, I suppose I started to doubt, and I blamed myself for everything."

"No one blames you," said Jake. "I certainly don't. Don't forget: you saved my life."

Silorè made no reply.

"I was angry too," Jake went on, "but you were right. I may not feel worthy of the sacrifices made for me, but what else can I do but accept them?"

Silorè nodded and stood a moment in silence, tears upon her cheeks.

At length she spoke. "Look at us," she said, wiping her eyes. "We're both a mess, aren't we?" She looked at him and tried to smile.

Jake smiled grimly in return. "I suppose we are."

Together they stood in silence for a long while. The light of the city cast a warm glow upon their faces, but the chaos of Ithèlimon could not touch them.

Suddenly, and to Jake's great surprise, Silorè drew close to him, leaning her head against his shoulder. "Still," she said softly, "the city does look beautiful, doesn't it?"

Jake nodded stiffly, unsure whether he should move away from her. "Standing here and seeing it in person," he said, "well, it feels like a dream."

She glanced up at him, her violet eyes sparkling in the dim light. "Is that so?" she said with a grin.

The look on her face stole away his words, for though her hair was unkempt and her face unpainted, she looked as beautiful as any clear night on Rithonon. At such times, a stargazer might catch a glimpse of the Falorosad—a fiery cloud of red and violet gasses swirling together beside a bright twin-star. The beauty of the Falorosad was renowned, but Jake considered how much rarer was the sight of the girl who stood before him. Her hostility had vanished, and Jake found that her smile worked in him a thousand feelings he could not sort out.

The sound of her voice suddenly shook him from his trance. "May I ask something of you, Thalani?"

"Anything," he said automatically.

"I had been wanting to ask you before," she said, "but the matter was eclipsed by so many other things. It may seem a trifle to you, but it is important to me."

"What is it?"

Silorè smiled, and then her voice grew suddenly serious and formal. She stood tall, with her shoulders and head held as though she were a queen addressing her courtiers. "If it please you," she said, "I would be most happy if you would escort me to the Council tomorrow."

"Escort you?"

"Certainly," she said. "A convening of the Council of Families is no small event. Everyone will be finely dressed, and the Itarlavon family must make a good show. I trust you have attire suitable for the occasion?"

"I suppose so," Jake said, hoping that it was the truth. "So it'll be just you and me? I thought the captain from the Solèdaron was providing transportation for us. Are we not all going over together?"

"What? With the others?" Silorè said with a frown. "I've already made plans to arrive at the council on my own, but I was hoping you would accompany me. You will, won't you?"

She leaned forward and stared into his eyes in such a manner as to make him blush.

"Of…of course I will," Jake said, his voice faltering.

"Good," said Silorè, her mood now light and cheerful. "Now, if you'll excuse me, I shall go to bed at last. I'm feeling much better now, and the city does not echo so loudly in my head." She smiled at him and then bowed. "I will see you in the morning, Thalani," she said. "A good night's rest to you." She brushed past him and hastened down the stairs and out of sight.

Jake lingered in the room a few moments after she had gone. To say he was excited by her sudden invitation would be falling well short of the mark. His heart and head were light, and he felt suddenly dizzy and had to lean upon the window to keep from falling over. He was glad he was alone, for he could not stop smiling.

With a song in his heart, he returned to his room, and there he lay wide awake upon his bed until the drowsy hours of night at last overcame his felicity, and he nodded into a contented sleep.

Chapter 12

An Unexpected Detour

Night had fallen in Itonilon when the king bade Jake end his tale for the day. Some of the assembled townsfolk had grown restless, but most had listened intently. When Jake finished speaking, a dull murmur arose as the crowds began to whisper to one another.

Jake put his hand to his throat, which felt parched and raw beyond anything he had ever before experienced. He was not accustomed to speaking so loudly for so long. Even when he had told the tale to Jalzoron, he had never said so much at one time. Then he had been weary and injured, and Jalzoron had let him sleep.

Even now it seemed to Jake that his weariness had returned, for the strain of speaking before so many people weighed heavily upon him and sapped his strength. Sitting in his cell seemed now pleasant and peaceful compared to his present agony.

Jalzoron sat nearby looking tired and reclining his head upon his hand. Jake scowled at him. *The least he could do is pay attention*, he thought. Jalzoron had been very alert earlier in the day, keeping Jake on an even pace and not permitting him to skip any detail. Apparently he remembered every part of the story Jake had told him.

As Jake turned and looked about, he found to his great surprise that the princess Tharè still sat as she had that morning when he had begun. He had not looked at her the whole day, not even when he had paused for a brief drink of water. Upon her face was the same hard look with which she had begun the day, though weariness lined her eyes and cheeks, and she shuddered as if forcing herself to sit erect.

The king and his servants retired, and the assembled crowd bowed low as he exited. Jake remained standing. The councillors dismissed the crowds and bade the guards convey Jake away to the prison. As Jake was bound again, Jalzoron rose and walked to him.

"You've done well," he whispered.

"If you say so," Jake said grimly. His legs ached from standing, and his voice was so sore it pained him to speak.

Pageboys went about extinguishing the torches in the room as Jake was taken from the hall. Jalzoron walked beside the company surrounding the prisoner, and another man of impressive girth walked behind him, as if to guard him as well.

Jalzoron went as far as the entrance to the tower, but he was not permitted to enter. The guards took Jake down the winding corridors into the darkness again, and there they left him in his cell with a stale bread loaf, a wedge of green melon, and a small water-flask. Jake felt his hunger intensely, for though he was used to the poor fare of the prison, the rich meal brought by the princess the day before had awakened his appetite, and he felt quite empty.

I'll bet she planned it that way, he thought bitterly.

As he chewed his bread crusts in the dark, many memories returned unbidden to him, and in the cold silence of his prison, the past danced before his eyes. A vast gas-cloud stood before him, shining into his dark mind. A shrill scream pierced him, and his heart recalled tears and the sound of weeping. Warm arms embraced him, and he heard a sweet voice whispering in his ear. He felt the touch of a gentle kiss upon his lips, and the memory drove him mad. From a great distance he felt a blast of fire and heard noise as of a great thunder. Pain shot through him, and then his mind raced to moments of laughter and golden sunshine. Clouds blew by him, and he stood upon the edge of a great sea watching a red sun sink beyond the horizon.

Other sounds and images came to him with growing speed. The events of many years passed in seconds and then started over again. No longer did the prison feel empty or silent, but a great cacophony filled the air all around him, and colours swirled upon the walls. He felt as though he might be smothered at any moment.

Then at last raising his hands, he drew what he was sure was his final breath and screamed at the chaos passing in front of him, "No more!"

The world faded to blackness, and every sound died away to an immeasurable distance. Jake collapsed to his hands and knees, gasping like one saved from drowning in an angry sea.

How many days will this go on? he thought as he kneeled upon the cold stones. *I haven't the courage to endure it all again. I haven't the strength!*

"I haven't the strength!" he shouted, and his voice echoed through the dungeons. Yet the sound seemed strange to him, and slowly he realized there was someone standing before him. As he looked up, he found that his eyes were wet, and when he blinked, he beheld a dark figure holding a dim torch.

"Haven't you?" the figure said. Though his face was obscured, Jake knew the voice. It was Thorondoron.

The councilman stepped forward wielding his torch as though it were a sword. "Personally I don't care what you have or lack," he said, "and now it no longer matters at all. The king will hear no more of your story, and as of this moment your life is forfeit. There shall be no more words, and you shall no longer waste the time of better men than you. You are a fool, young Thalani, and Jalzoron is the greater fool for wanting to help you."

"Help me?" Jake laughed. "You don't understand at all. How is any of this supposed to help me?"

"I don't know," Thorondoron said, growing angrier. "The story is yours. Don't you know?"

"I haven't any idea what Jalzoron is up to," Jake said. "I was ordered to tell the story, and I'm telling it. I don't care if you hate it; I don't care if *anyone* hates it. It's too long, you say? Speak to Jalzoron. He's the one forcing me to tell it this way. If you want to know what purpose any of this serves, you'll have to ask him, for it defies my understanding."

"I don't think there is a purpose," the councilman said. "You have had two days for your defence, and you have squandered that time with irrelevancies. What does it matter what the baths of Sorenon are like? Who cares what that Thalavè wrote you in a letter?"

"It's all part of the story."

"Not anymore," said Thorondoron. "Your tale is at an end. I've convinced the councillors that these proceedings are futile and serve only to buy you more time. There is little point in your continuing, for your sentence will not be changed. After what you've done, can you really expect the king to show you leniency?"

Jake did not answer.

"Jalzoron's scheming cannot save you," said Thorondoron. "All is decided, and there is nothing you can do to change it."

Jake drew a deep breath and answered in a voice devoid of feeling. "Why then, Councillor," he said, "did you come to tell me this? Take me away and kill me if that is my lot. I'm just a prisoner; I need no explanation."

"I don't have to give account of my actions to you!" Thorondoron said defiantly. "You're worthless, and whatever pity I've had for you is now dissolved." He spat upon the stones. "May your pain be great and your death not swift!"

Thorondoron turned abruptly. With a few noisy steps, he rounded a corner and was gone, and the room fell dark once more.

Jake did not move for a long time, and though the images of the past were gone, the present felt more unbearable. Every minute became years of nothingness without end or relief. All thought was gone, and the only feeling that remained was an ache in his chest as of something gnawing upon his heart.

At last, feeling quite weary, he fell upon the stones, and clutching his ragged blanket, he fell into a troubled sleep filled with strange dreams. He awoke often, and though the images faded from his mind, the horror of them did not.

All the next day—which Jake could only reckon by the two small meals brought to him—no one came to see him, and he was not summoned to the council. Though the guards would often take prisoners deep into the dungeon to dig out caverns blocked with stone, today there was no work. Jake felt relieved, for the past two days had been tiring in a way he had not before known—though he could not say whether it was fatigue of body or of heart.

So he slept on through day and night.

The following morning, he was awakened by a loud clanging above his head. Though he was still half asleep, he was sure someone was calling to him, though he could not understand the words. Everything sounded as if he were underwater. The thought of drowning sent a twinge of fear through him, and he was instantly awake.

"Get up, you idiot!" the voice shouted. It was Jalzoron, and he was striking the iron bars of Jake's cell with a metal rod.

Jake sat up and rubbed his eyes. "What?" he said. "What's going on?"

"You'll see soon enough," said Jalzoron. "You're fortunate I haven't given up as you have, or else you'd have had a much ruder awakening. Get up! I've brought you clean clothes; you're going to look the part this morning. Hurry up! Eat this, and come with me."

Through the bars a hand thrust a loaf of fresh bread sprinkled with cheese. Jake accepted the morsel and began to eat at once. Three guards appeared to unlock the cell and lead Jake up the winding passages.

As they ascended, Jalzoron walked silently beside Jake without even a glance in his direction. This morning he was arrayed in a robe of fine weave, and he held a similar garment draped over his arm. In his other hand, he tightly held something in a crumpled brown-paper bag.

The guards brought Jake to the circular room with the drain in the floor. There they made him strip, and from above, cold water was poured down upon him. Jalzoron threw the paper bag he had been carrying to Jake, who stood sopping wet and cold at the centre of the room. "Use these liberally," Jalzoron commanded.

From within the bag, Jake withdrew a cake of aromatic soap and a small phial containing a pale-blue liquid. The phial he set aside, and with the soap he washed himself many times over, for there was much grime and stench clinging to him. At intervals an icy bath fell upon him and washed away the suds. At length he took the phial and washed his hair and body with the soap it contained. The scent of it awakened his senses, and though he tended to be revolted by the smell of fragrant oils and perfumes, he thought this new scent smelled pleasant and clean—like air from the mountains after a rainstorm. There was something familiar about it too, though he did not immediately recall it.

As he picked up the phial to pour out more soap, an image flashed into his mind. He suddenly remembered where he had smelled that scent before and why he thought it so pleasant. The bottle fell from his grasp and shattered on the floor. Angry shouts poured down upon him from above.

"Hey, you!" a gruff voice said. "I'll have your hands for that! That was costly stuff!"

Jake looked up but could not see the source of the voice.

"You'll do no such thing." Jalzoron had climbed the steps and was up on high with the guards watching Jake in the pit. "What business is it of yours?"

"I'll not see a prisoner destroy treasures his overseers could never hope to possess," the gruff voice said. "Do you know how many years a man like me would have to labour for one tiny bottle such as that?"

"It's not your concern," said Jalzoron, "for the phial did not belong to you, and its loss does you no injury except in your own covetous thoughts. Cast off your greed and do your duty. If you harm him, I shall strike you down with a wrath tenfold greater than your own."

Jalzoron's voice boomed within the chamber, and Jake shrank away from it, for it seemed to him the voice grew until he was certain it could not belong to any mortal man. Yet when Jake had dried himself with a towel and put on his new clothes, Jalzoron met him in the passage outside the pit, and he was merely a man.

Guards returned and escorted both of them up towards the tower entrance.

"I'm sorry I broke the phial," Jake said. "I didn't mean to."

"Why do you apologize?" Jalzoron asked sternly.

"It was yours, wasn't it?" Jake said. "And very expensive. How did you come by it?"

Jalzoron scowled and did not look Jake in the eye. "Never you mind," he said. "It's not important. All that matters is that you no longer smell like death. But I would have liked at least to have retained the bottle, for it too was quite valuable. Why did you drop it?"

Jake hung his head. "That soap was familiar to me," he said. "It smelled like their hair—Silorè and Sinarè, I mean. They both had the same scent because Silorè shared her perfumes and soaps with her. The memory of them struck me like a hammer, and I guess the bottle just slipped from my hand."

Jalzoron was silent and said no more.

The doors to the Great Hall of the castle were open, and many people poured into the vestibule that lay before it. The guards cleared a path for Jake and Jalzoron to walk through, and together they made their way to the open area before the council table where the council members were already seated. Thorondoron sat in his place looking angry and miserable.

The guards placed Jake before the council and left him alone. The people gathered in the front of the hall now sat down upon the floor or upon simple chairs they had brought.

To the side, as always, sat Tharè surrounded by her handmaidens, who all looked quite weary and deprived of sleep. The princess appeared the worst off, for darkness encircled her eyes, and the lustre of her hair and face were diminished. Though her appearance was dishevelled, her gaze was steady and did not waver. Indeed, she did not seem even to blink as she watched him, and Jake felt a bit unnerved.

With a fanfare of trumpets, the king entered with his courtiers, and he sat upon his chair once more. Jake thought the king looked particularly displeased, and he began to wonder what exactly this assembly meant. *This could be the end*, he thought. *But why'd I get all cleaned up just to die?*

Once the throng was seated again—for they had all bowed low when the king had entered—the king rose and looked directly at

Jake. "Jake Connolly," he said in a voice warm with pity and cold with sorrow, "you are charged with a crime unspeakable. For the last two days, this council has endured your telling of a story which you have claimed is vital to your defence. There are some"—he looked sidelong at his councillors—"who believe that you should not be allowed to continue. To that end they agreed to end your trial and submit you to be sentenced, and so you might have been but for the words of Jalzoron."

Jake looked at Jalzoron. He was not looking at Jake but stood facing the king. A great weariness seemed to be upon him, and Jake wondered how long he had spent before the council, pleading his case.

"He has agreed to take charge of you," said the king. "Thus you shall come under his guardianship, and if something should happen to you—should you leave this city suddenly—then he will face judgment in your place."

Jake looked back at Jalzoron, astounded.

"Therefore," said the king, "you shall not be sentenced until your story is completed, and you shall not go forth to the dungeons again but shall be taken with Jalzoron to the house Limria, north of the castle. There you will stay under guard until such time as your tale is ended and you are justly sentenced. So say I, Tamon, King of Itonilon."

The crowd answered in unison. "It shall be done." The sound of the many voices lingered in the chamber, slowly dying away into the silence that followed.

The king sat down once more. "Now continue, Jake Connolly."

There was a stir of excitement as the crowd settled in, for they seemed eager to hear more of the story. Jake looked to Jalzoron, who had sat once more upon the chair procured for him, and he nodded.

Jake took a deep breath and picked up the tale once more.

• • • • • • • • • • • • • •

Morning dawned over Ithèlimon, and Jake awoke feeling tired and uncomfortable. He could not open his eyes all at once for the sun reflecting off the white stone buildings of the city, and he looked around the room, squinting between blinks. With effort he placed his feet upon the floor and stumbled to a small panel upon the wall. He fumbled for the proper switch, and finding it at last, he lowered a dark shade over the window, blocking all but a dim remnant of the morning light. *That's...better*, he thought. *These short nights...are going to kill me.*

He bathed in the adjoining room, and wrapping a grey dressing gown about him, he stumbled outside and down the stairs to breakfast. Jolani, Tarandi, and Azhè were sitting together at a table spread with all manner of baked goods swimming in fruit and crème. Some ways off in a large chair by the fountain, Andarè sat nibbling a buttered crumpet and reading a book.

Tarandi laughed as Jake approached. "Are you still asleep?" he said. "I've heard tell of Thalanin who walk about while still sleeping."

"Believe me," Jake said, "I would prefer to be asleep."

"And miss breakfast?" Jolani said. "I think you'll be pleasantly surprised." He picked up a small plate that had been set aside and concealed with a cloth. With a flourish he uncovered it, and Jake was instantly wide awake.

"Is that...bacon?" he said in English. It seemed quite a long time since he had seen or smelled any, and his mind flew across time and space to the Grey Griffin and his many breakfasts there.

"I wouldn't know," Jolani replied. "Adjaron ordered breakfast this morning, and it arrived but a few minutes ago. This must be for you, for I don't know anyone else who would eat it."

"Bless him!" Jake said and seized the plate.

"It smells foul," Azhè said, wrinkling her nose. "How can you eat that?"

"Quite easily," Jake said in a voice muffled by a mouthful of food. "Are you sure you don't want any?" He held out the plate to the others, but they looked at him as though he were mad. Jake happily set the plate down again and ate to the last crumb.

"Where is Zhialamon?" Jake asked between bites. "Is he already gone?"

Jolani nodded. "He left with Adjaron early this morning," he said. "Apparently Tanaron sent word that Ilavè dispatched a contingent to Thesalara, but they left yesterday before Tanaron's men arrived."

"Did they take anything?" Jake asked.

"That's the curious part," said Jolani. "Nothing appears to be missing, and the Chronicle is still in its place. Zhialamon and Adjaron have gone to contact the library on Thesalara before the Council this morning."

"I see," Jake said. Having finished his breakfast, he sat back and sighed. "So where is everyone else?"

"Ianasè is probably still in bed," said Jolani, "and Silorè is upstairs getting ready. She called in a few of our Itarlavon cousins who live in Ithèlimon, and they've been cloistered in her room for hours. I awoke when they arrived early this morning, and it was still quite dark outside. She had better not be too much longer, for we all should be leaving soon."

Azhè suddenly started. "What's the time?" she said. "I should have been dressed long before now!"

"Yes, you should have," came a voice from behind them all. They turned around to see the source, and there stood Ianasè arrayed in a fine red dress with swirls of silver running upon it like leaf-covered vines. Her hair was tightly woven, and a wooden rod held it in place. Her eyes shone brightly beneath their painted lids. The men at the table sat agape, but Azhè frowned.

"Èa!" Azhè cried in a pouty voice. "Ian-èsa, you're going to make me look bad!"

"It's your own fault," Ianasè said, sitting down at the table. "But if you go change now, you'll still probably beat Silorè." She picked up a strawberry tart and ate it in one bite.

"You may look the part," Tarandi said, "but your manners betray you at once."

"What of it?" Ianasè said, licking her fingers. "I don't see anyone mocking your lack of etiquette. Besides, I'm not going to turn prissy and proper just because I want to wear something nice now and then."

"Indeed not," Jolani said, and he elbowed Tarandi in the gut. "But she does look quite nice, doesn't she, Tarandi?"

Tarandi shrugged. "If you say so."

Ianasè made a face but said nothing.

"I certainly think you do," Azhè said to Ianasè, "and I had better get ready myself, or I'll surely be left behind." So saying, she scampered upstairs.

"What about you, Andarè?" Ianasè said. "Aren't you going to dress?"

Andarè groaned. "I already have." She stood up and revealed her black dress and black stockings.

"We're not going to a funeral." Tarandi chuckled.

Andarè scowled. "We may yet if you don't keep your tongue."

Jolani and Ianasè snickered, but Tarandi only sneered at her. "Clever, aren't we?" he said.

"Clever enough not to wait until the final hour," Andarè said. "You all had better hurry if you don't want to get left." She slumped down in her chair and held her book before her face.

"All I have to do is throw on a clean shirt and some trousers," Tarandi said, but Andarè was no longer listening.

"It's good advice nonetheless," said Jolani with a grin. "Let her be. You know you can't win a battle of words against her." He rose from the table and headed upstairs. Tarandi reluctantly followed, shooting dirty looks at Andarè.

"I'd better go too," Jake said as he stood up. "I'll see you all at the Council."

"You're not going over with us?" Ianasè said. "Adjaron has sent a transport to take the rest of us to the Zhènlara."

"No," said Jake, "I'm…going with Silorè."

Both Ianasè and Andarè stared at Jake with the same look of surprise. "Are you now?" Ianasè asked with a smirk. "How did this come about?"

Jake felt his face turning red. "She invited me."

"I see," Ianasè said. "Well, you'd better hurry, then. You'll have to look your best if you're going with her. No doubt she'll want to make a spectacle of herself."

Quite embarrassed, Jake hurried upstairs to his room and slid the door shut behind him. The room felt too dark now, and he lifted the shade on the window, revealing the busy city shining in the morning sun. Though the outside world looked hostile and full of chaos, his room was quiet and calm.

His mind wandered as he looked out over the city. Ithèlimon was vast, and no matter where he looked, there was always something new to see. He tried to imagine what someone standing on one of the rooftops might see gazing back at the pyramid, and he began to wonder what sort of life he led. *I'll bet he hasn't been uprooted*, Jake thought. *Maybe he's bored and wishes for a change. It's better for him if he doesn't get it.*

Jake did not know how long he stood there, but he suddenly remembered his purpose and quickly rummaged through the things Jardir had packed.

He found he did indeed have a fine suit of clothes. Though he was not used to formal Nanyani attire, he counted it a small price to pay for the honour of being at Silorè's side. He had difficulty putting on the clothes so they did not look a mess, and he laboured before the mirror to ensure he looked presentable. He would not have Silorè calling him sloppy.

As he was straightening his collar before the mirror, there came a scratching noise at the door. Puzzled, Jake slid the door open and found Izhana looking up at him.

"My mistress has sent me to fetch you," she said. "You have dallied up here long enough, and if you are going to the Council with her, you must come down now."

"I'm ready," Jake said. "What about you? Aren't you coming along?"

Izhana snorted. "And what would I do there?" she said. "Sit upon Silorè's lap and look like some tamed beast? That I will not do." She turned about quickly, her tail held proudly in the air. "Now come!"

Jake heeded and followed Izhana downstairs.

Jolani and the others had gone, and the room was empty except for a group of young women standing shoulder to shoulder near the far wall. Lithè and Calandè stood on one side, and three girls Jake had never seen before stood on the other. These, Jake presumed, were Silorè's cousins. They were all quite young—for Nanyavèn—and as Jake descended the stairs, they smiled at him and giggled at his confusion.

"Where is everyone?" he asked.

"They've all gone on ahead," said one of the cousins. "Zhialamon sent word that he would await you both outside the council chambers."

"Both?" Jake asked, though he already knew the answer.

Without another word the women stepped aside, and from their midst Silorè came forth. A dress of purest white and gold hung upon her shoulders with ribbons of fine lace. Ornaments of ivory and pearl adorned the bodice, which was strung with a golden cord. Accents like pale-blue and pink flowers embellished the dress, and the silken layers of the skirt flowed about her like the mist of a fountain. Her violet eyes shone brightly beneath lids painted pale shades of blue. Her hair had been combed about a circlet of silver adorned with jewels like white flowers. A white tress lay curled upon each unblemished cheek, and her lips were painted a soft pink hue. In her left hand, she carried a white fan of lace strung with golden threads.

She bowed to Jake, and stepping forward, she held out her hand. "Will you accompany me, Thalani?"

Jake stood dumbfounded for so long a time that the other girls began to giggle to one another, shaking Jake from his trance. He bowed low to Silorè, and when he stood up again, he took her hand in his and offered her his arm. His heartbeat quickened at her touch, and he nearly stumbled as he took his first step, for he could hardly keep himself from looking at her.

One of Silorè's cousins chuckled and turned to the girl beside her. "I wonder what Dirion would say," she whispered.

Jake turned his head at the name. "Who?"

Before he got a reply, Silorè whisked him away down the stairs and to the lift, and as they waited for the lift carriage, Jake turned to her. "What was that name?"

Silorè sighed. “Never mind that,” she said. “Doasè was just being stupid.” She looked into his eyes. “Don’t trouble yourself about it,” she said gently.

The sight of her and the tone of her voice drove the name from his mind.

The lift arrived, and Jake and Silorè descended the pyramid. Being alone with her in such a close space made him nervous, and he felt he should speak. “You look…” he said and found that his throat was dry. “You look wonderful.”

Silorè grinned slyly. “Did you expect otherwise?”

“No,” said Jake, “No, not at all. I just hadn’t thought…well, I mean you looked quite lovely at the festival on Rithonon, but now…” He lost his words.

“Now you can see why I much prefer my own clothes,” Silorè said. “This dress is not new, though I’ve worn it only once before. As I recall I received many looks similar to the one you’re giving me now.”

“I’m sorry,” Jake said, and he turned away from her.

“Don’t be,” said Silorè. “I don’t mind at all. You’re quite adorable. I see much of your father and grandfather in your face, and I’m reminded of happy times.” She sighed. “Alas! Those days are gone and shall not come again, but perhaps they live on in you. I hope we shall all have new days to remember in the years before us.”

“I know I won’t forget today,” Jake said shyly.

The lift doors opened, and Jake and Silorè were startled to discover Captain Azhkani and three of his men awaiting them.

“Good morning,” said Azhkani with a smile and a bow. “We were just on our way to meet you. You are running a bit behind if you want to arrive on time for the Council.”

“There is time enough,” Silorè said in an even voice, “if we are not delayed.”

“Then I will not keep you long,” said the captain, “but I must say I was concerned to learn you were going to the Council on your own. I’m afraid I do not understand your reasoning.”

“You don’t need to,” said Silorè.

“All the same,” Azhkani said, “we have met your transport and inspected every inch of it. We were going to await you there, but we worried when you tarried too long. I left one of my own men to secure your transport, and he will accompany you to the Council.”

“That isn’t necessary.”

“Perhaps not,” said Azhkani. “Ithèlimon is thankfully an easy city to secure—despite its size. But even so, there are strange people about, and I do not wish to be caught unawares.”

Silorè glared at him but made no reply.

Azhkani’s smile did not fade. “May I escort you, then?”

A voice came suddenly from behind them. “You needn’t trouble yourselves any further.” Rathori had appeared, seemingly from nowhere. “The safety of the Itarlavon family is my charge, and therefore I will perform those duties.”

“If that is what you desire,” Azhkani said, “then I shall be on my way. Only remember that as long as any of the Itarlavon are in Ithèlimon, I too am charged with their protection.” He turned back to Silorè. “If you’ll excuse me, Lady Itarlavon,” he said, “I must find my own transportation, for I too will be attending the Council. Perhaps I will see you there.” He bowed again, and he and his men went off down an adjoining corridor.

Silorè turned on Rathori once the captain was gone. “Not you as well,” she said. “I thought you were going with the others. Surely Rimilèon won’t like that her children don’t have an escort.”

"Indeed not," said Rathori. "That is why she sent two of her own men to watch over them. Sondari thought you were going with them as well, and when he discovered you were not, he ordered me to accompany you to the Council."

Silorè sighed. "Very well," she said. "Only do try to keep out of sight when we arrive."

"As you wish, my lady."

Rathori walked with them to the landing platform, where a small transport was waiting—a sleek black shuttle with silver trim. The Ithèlimon guard stood by, but he did not look in their direction. He seemed more interested in the vehicle, looking it over carefully and arguing with the pilot.

A footman stood by the cabin door and helped Silorè inside, and Jake sat next to her upon a wide seat. Rathori went to talk to the Ithèlimon guard, leaving the two of them alone. Sitting so close to Silorè made Jake nervous. He kept stealing glances at her, but she did not notice, for she was too busy looking cross and impatient.

The cabin itself was much too large for just two people. Dark leather covered every surface, and the windows let in very little light. A view-screen was set upon one side, and an ice box lay on the floor under the seats. In the far wall was an opening that faced the front, and through it Jake could see into the pilot's cabin, which was currently empty.

No noise trickled in from the outside world, and the silence soon became unbearable for Jake, so he began to babble. "This is quite a nice shuttle," he said.

Silorè's mind was far away. "Hmmm?"

"I was saying that this is a nice shuttle," he said. "Even better than the one we all took last night to the restaurant."

"Yes," she answered blandly, "it is meant to be."

Jake began to wish for silence again, but there was no returning to it now. "Where did you hire it?" he asked.

"Rimilèon chartered it for me," said Silorè. "The pilot is related to the governor of Sanbinra, and Rimilèon says he is most trustworthy. She's booked with him before on a number of special occasions." Her insipid mood cracked for a moment, and she smiled. "I thought it would be fitting to arrive at the Council in style."

Rathori returned suddenly and sat in a seat facing Jake and Silorè. "There's something off about that man," he said in a hushed voice. "I'm not sure how he came to be one of that captain's men. He was not exactly rude, but there was something about his manner that was unpleasant."

He fell silent as he heard the doors open behind him, and the pilot and the guard from Ithèlimon took their seats in the forward cabin.

"Are you ready, Lady Itarlavon?" the pilot asked, turning to his passengers.

Silorè nodded. "You may proceed."

As the pilot faced forward again, a panel rose up to hide the forward cabin from sight of the passengers. At once the transport began to rumble, and slowly it lifted off the ground, launching into the clear morning over Ithèlimon.

Silorè gazed out the windows with renewed energy. Her eyes were bright once more, and she was brimming with happiness. "Isn't this exciting?"

"I suppose," Jake answered, shifting in his seat. He still was not used to being a passenger, and he did not like the sensation. "Will there really be many people at the Council of Families?"

Silorè nodded. "Nearly all of the Great Families will be there, though some of them now dwell outside Eratzira. I imagine the Council made more sense when Eratzira was young and all the Great

Families lived here, but it is tradition nonetheless. That is the only reason why the Keneraton have been invited. The Solèdaron must have something important to discuss, for the Council of Families hasn't met in over ten years. As you can imagine, it takes quite a bit of effort to bring all these families together for what is likely to be a short meeting. Even so, there will be many thousands of people who will watch from the galleries."

Jake nodded and sat silent for a moment before asking a question that had been on his mind. "All those people," he said, "will they be watching us?"

"I certainly hope so," said Silorè.

Jake tensed and felt anxiety squeeze his heart. "But we're not participating in the Council, are we?"

"Certainly not."

"Then why would they care about us?"

"The arrival of the family members is no small ceremony," Silorè said. "Being so closely related to our patriarch, I will certainly be watched, and I must make sure to present our family well." Seeing the troubled look on Jake's face, she laughed. "Don't worry," she said. "After we're seated in the council chamber, attention will shift to the meeting."

"Can we not slip in quietly?" Jake asked.

Silorè frowned. "And be shown up by all the other families?" she said. "Never! The Itarlavon may not have as many members attending the Council, but I hope to make up for that at our entrance. When we arrive, just smile and hold on to my arm."

Jake swallowed hard. "Maybe I should have gone with the others," he muttered.

"How then would this have been special?" Silorè said, leaning towards him and flashing a smile. "Besides, the point of your coming to Ithèlimon was to show everyone that you are in my family's keeping, was it not? I assure you if you arrive with me, you are certain to be noticed."

Jake turned nervously back to the window, and it was then that he first sensed something was wrong. The shuttle had veered away from the Great Pyramid, which now was diminishing into the distance. At the puzzlement on his face, Silorè leaned over him to get a better look at the city, and Rathori also seemed not to have noticed until that moment. "This isn't right," he said.

Silorè sat back again. "Pilot," she called, "where are…" Before she could finish, the shuttle shot forward at incredible speed, pinning Jake and Silorè to their seats and flinging Rathori into their laps.

Jake tried to speak, but the sudden acceleration had taken his breath. "What's going on?" he said at last with much effort.

Silorè could not answer, for another sudden turn had thrown her onto the floor.

"Don't worry, my lady!" Rathori said as he tried to sit up again. "I will set things right!" He started to pound his fist upon the partition dividing the helm from the cabin, but the divider would not budge.

The shuttle flew on, and the world outside passed by in a blur. Jake felt he was going to be sick.

When at last the transport slowed and Jake looked out the window, he found they were at the edge of the city. The Great Pyramid could not be seen, and the buildings in this section were old and dishevelled. Every metal surface was crusted with patches of dark-red rust. The chimneys of old furnaces rose high into the air, but no smoke issued from them, and the furnaces were silent.

Slowly the shuttle descended into a narrow street between two brick buildings, and all sunlight disappeared. Silorè finally regained her seat, and she looked about in the darkness. Jake could see only the dim outline of her profile, but by her movements he could sense her panic. Indeed, Jake felt the same, and already his heart pounded within his chest. Every vein in his body throbbed, and the sound of his blood pulsed loudly in his ears.

"What's going on?" he whispered. "Where are we?"

"I don't know," Silorè replied. "I have never been here before, but I do not like the looks of this place."

"Do not fear, Lady Silorè," Rathori said, though his own voice was quavering. "I will protect you."

They passed through two giant doors into an empty storehouse with a high ceiling. The shuttle's forward lamps blinked on, dimly lighting the vast chamber before them. The ship landed with a jolt, and Jake and Silorè clung to each other in the swaying cabin.

Silence followed, and no one dared to move. The shuttle doors opened, but the three passengers remained in their seats.

A harsh voice suddenly rang in their ears. "Get out!" it said over the speakerphone. "Come out where I can see you!"

"Stay inside," Rathori ordered. He drew his pistol from his belt and slowly stepped out into the darkness. Jake and Silorè watched him with ever growing dread. He looked about in all directions, but he could see no one. "Show yourself!" he shouted.

The next moment there came a sickening sound like metal splitting sinew.

Silorè screamed. Through the window, she and Jake watched as Rathori stumbled and fell upon his knees. A silver dagger was deeply planted in his right shoulder, almost to the hilt.

"Get out of the ship!" the gruff voice commanded again.

Afraid of what would happen if they refused, Jake and Silorè stepped outside. In the halo of light surrounding the shuttle, they found Rathori on his hands and knees. Silorè knelt beside him, examining his wound and the blood issuing from it.

"Get away from him!" came the voice again.

Silorè did not move away. Jake stood frozen in fear beside her.

Then from the shadows came the figure of a man. He wore a security officer's uniform, and in his right hand he held a small knife by the blade. His face became clearer as he drew close, and both Jake and Silorè gasped when they saw who it was.

Ianjori stood before them, and he was smiling wickedly.

"Get away from him," he said to Silorè, "or you'll die beside him."

"Go, my lady," Rathori said weakly. "I will deal with this man."

He pushed Silorè away and tried to stand, but he was in a terrible state. His right arm hung limp at his side, and his pistol lay useless in his dead fingers. Each breath was agony to him, and he could not keep his eyes open. He shifted his weight, but the effort was too much, and he fell on his face.

Silorè whimpered and would have rushed to his side had Jake not prevented her, for he was afraid that Ianjori would kill her at once. Rathori tried to raise himself up but fell again to the floor.

Jake was horrified at the sight. "What's wrong with him?" he asked Silorè.

"It's the poison," she answered, her voice cracking. "The blade was drugged. Even the slightest scratch—" Her voice failed her, and she looked away, burying her face in Jake's shoulder.

"Even a scratch is deadly, yes," said Ianjori. "The poison is of my own making. Aren't you impressed? It robs the body of strength, and its victim falls quickly into a sleep from which there is no waking. One scratch, and I can make anyone completely harmless." He looked down on Rathori. "Go on," he taunted. "Pick up your weapon. Kill me if you can."

Rathori raised himself up slightly and tried to lift his right arm, but it did not move. He reached across his body to grab his pistol in his other hand, but his strength was gone. Exhausted, he sank to the floor, and Ianjori sneered at him.

With his last effort, he turned his head to Silorè. “I’m sorry, my lady,” he said. “I could not protect you.”

Silorè tried to answer him, but the words died in her throat.

Rathori fell flat upon the floor and went utterly still.

Ianjori scoffed. “Pitiful,” he mumbled. “I expected him to last longer.” He roughly pulled the knife from Rathori’s shoulder and began to clean the blade with a cloth. Then he turned and said in a loud voice, “Your family should hire better protectors in the future, Silorè. This one wasn’t worth his wages.”

Silorè found her voice at last, and it was filled with hatred. “There is no wealth,” she said lowly, “that could repay even a drop of his blood.”

Ianjori laughed loudly. “How terribly sentimental!” he said. “You weren’t that way at our last meeting—but that’s not all that’s changed.” He walked around her in a wide circle, looking her up and down. “It’s an improvement, I must say. You’re quite a pretty thing when you’re cleaned up and dressed.”

The look in Silorè’s eyes did not waver. “My family will come looking for us,” she said. “You will never get us off Ianiton. All Kenornin ships will be searched before they leave this system.”

“You’re sure of that?” Ianjori said. “Will your Solèdaron risk insulting a long-estranged people with whom he is trying to make peace? Would he accuse us of a crime for which, I assure you, there is no evidence?”

Silorè choked back hot tears. “Nevertheless,” she said deliberately, “they will come for us. They will be looking for our transport.”

Ianjori grinned. “And they shall find it.”

He clapped, and from the shadows a man and a woman appeared, dressed in fine clothes that imitated those Jake and Silorè wore. Their faces were sullen and their eyes downcast. They did not speak at all but seemed rather to be in their own world, as if in a trance.

Behind them walked a tall woman. Her hair was jet black, and her eyes were red like a sunset in a stormy sky. She wore black trousers and a short robe belted tightly at her waist. On her back she bore a curved sword in a silver scabbard.

As they drew near, the well-dressed man and woman bowed to Ianjori, and he beckoned them to step forward. "These are your doubles," he said to Jake and Silorè. "They will see to it that no one seeks your bodies elsewhere." He gestured to the corpse on the floor. "He will go too, for they must count five among the wreckage."

"You're off in your reckoning," Silorè jeered. "You were the security man we saw on the platform, were you not? Are you going to death as well? If not, you're going to be one short."

Ianjori chuckled and shook his head. "No," he said, "you'll find my accounting is correct. Little girls ought to learn their maths." This last statement got a rise out of Silorè, and Ianjori laughed all the more.

"You see, I'd always planned on seizing your transport," he continued. "I disguised myself and waited near the platform, ready to sneak aboard or perhaps subdue the pilot. When those security men arrived to inspect the ship, I will admit I was concerned. To kill so many of them would certainly draw attention to myself, but I promise you I could have destroyed them all.

"For good or bad, they left, and only one of their number remained behind. It seemed the perfect opportunity, and I took it. He was a poor fighter, on par with your unable defender." He kicked Rathori's leg so that it took an unnatural bent. "His uniform was a bit snug, but I swapped clothes with him and stuffed his body in the luggage box. No one saw me, I promise you, and the pilot did not suspect me at all until I gutted him in flight. You should have seen his face, Silorè! I have never seen so startled a man!"

He laughed heartily and motioned to the man and woman again. Silently they stepped forward and bent over Rathori.

Silorè barred their way. "Leave him!" she shouted, but the man and woman did not heed her. Pushing past her, they lifted Rathori up and carried his body into the passengers' compartment, and Jake and Silorè saw him no more.

As the man and woman made ready to depart, the dark-haired woman, who had stood silently by, stepped up and looked over Jake and Silorè with a sneer. "So these are the ones for whom we suffer so much?" she said. "They're hardly worth the trouble. What danger could Ilavèon face from nothings like these?"

Silorè stepped towards her, but the woman drew her sword in a flash and pointed it in her face.

"Mind your manners," the woman mocked. "Such temper is not ladylike." She swung her sword so that it grazed Silorè's hair but did not harm her. Silorè stood defiantly before her, and they stared into one another's eyes as if striving in some battle that could not be seen.

Ianjori intervened, standing between the two women. "You've not met Zanirè, have you, Silorè?" he said. "She is a granddaughter of the late General, and she carries in her much of Koroson's former spirit. I've learned not to cross her."

"A rare bit of wisdom," said Zanirè, sheathing her blade. "And very fitting for present company." Her gaze fell upon Jake, and he squirmed, for it seemed she was trying to bore a hole through him with her eyes.

Just then the man and woman approached from the shuttle. "All is prepared," the man said in a soft voice. "We are ready."

"Go, then," Ianjori said. "Die well, and you will be long honoured in Ialanon."

The man and woman bowed again, and together they boarded the shuttle and made ready to depart.

Ianjori and Zanirè led Jake and Silorè away from the ship and across the wide room. Behind them the shuttle roared to life and flew away through the large doors, which closed behind it, plunging the room into darkness.

A torch blazed suddenly in the hand of Zanirè, casting a white light upon the floor. She walked ahead of the prisoners, and Ianjori walked behind, driving them forward in a straight line. No walls could be seen past the reach of the torchlight, and Jake could not determine how Zanirè knew where she was going. He thought of escaping, but as he looked from side to side, he saw many pits and fissures in the floor. In the dark he was sure to stumble into one unawares.

After a few minutes of walking in the dark, the group reached the far wall. Its smooth surface rose high above the torchlight and stretched beyond sight on either hand. Following the wall to the left, Zanirè led the group through a door and down a plunging staircase that opened into a wide corridor. Down this path they went until they came to a certain door that opened into a small room where two men of great stature stood guard. Ianjori forced Jake and Silorè inside, and, following them, he shut the door while Zanirè waited outside.

The room was utterly dark. Ianjori lit a small lamp in the middle of the floor, and it cast eerie shadows upon the cracked walls. There was no window in the room, and Jake suspected they were now many storeys underground. Though the city above was warm, the air in this room was cold, and Jake could see his breath hang in the air before his face.

"Now, then," Ianjori said, "there's nothing for you to do but wait. We will take you to Ilavèon soon, and she will decide what is to be done with you."

"This isn't the end, Ianjori," Silorè said. "If you think Zhialamon will just accept this foolish deception of yours, then you've learned nothing from all these years of hunting my family."

"I've learned enough about you," Ianjori said. "I knew that you couldn't pass up the chance to exhibit yourself, and I was certain you would want to make a show of your entrance at the Council."

A low rumble suddenly shook the ground, and Jake and Silorè looked to each other, for they knew what that sound was.

Ianjori bowed his head and spoke in a muffled whisper, almost like a prayer. "May they flow swiftly to Oblivion."[61]

"You are vile," Silorè muttered.

"It is only vile to fear death," Ianjori said, raising his voice. "Life and death are not so different. One flows into the other. Life comes to death, yet from death springs life."

"Then off yourself," Silorè said, "and the rest of us will live better."

Ianjori smiled a wicked smile and stepped towards her. Steadfast though she was, the gleam in his eyes made her step backwards. "No, Lady Itarlavon," he said. "There is yet much life in me." With surprising speed, he lunged at her and grabbed her roughly by the shoulders. She cried out and tried to free herself, but he spun her around so that she faced away from him. Holding her so she could not struggle, he buried his face in her flowing hair.

Fixed in horror for but a moment, Jake felt rage boil over within him, and he sprang at Ianjori. The Kenorni was ready for the attack, and he sent Jake flying with a mighty kick. Jake fell backwards, and his head struck the far wall. His vision blurred, and he heard many cries and curses in Silorè's voice.

61 Nanyan: *Ianarim*. In Koreva, Ianarim is the Nothingness from which the universe was made.

The door suddenly flew open, and in his delirium Jake heard the scuffling of a brief struggle. Silorè's voice was silenced, and Ianjori grunted as if struck with a heavy blow. When Jake could see again, he found Zanirè standing over Ianjori with her boot upon his throat.

"You maggot!" she shouted in his face. "Trouble the dead and the dust, but touch no woman, or I shall throw your flesh to the carrion birds, and the hell-worms[62] can gnaw on whatever is left of you." With surprising strength, she hauled Ianjori to his feet and hurled him through the open door. If the guards outside had any thought of aiding him, they thought better of it and did not move. Like a wounded animal, Ianjori turned and fled.

Casting a disgusted look at Silorè, Zanirè turned and stormed from the room, slamming the door behind her.

Jake staggered to his feet. He was dizzy and nauseated, and his head pounded as though he were beating it against the wall. Silorè was kneeling in the far corner, clutching her bare shoulders and shuddering with short, broken breaths.

Jake hobbled towards her. "Are you all right?"

Silorè turned her face to him, and her eyes blazed in the darkness. "That bastard," she said. "He tore my dress."

62 Nanyan: *mirmiken*. In Ziron folklore the mirmiken are worms of the underworld that continually torment the dead.

Chapter 13

Ilavè

A sudden light pierced the darkness, rudely rousing Jake and Silorè from sleep. The lantern at the centre of the room had long since gone out, and in the darkness they had lost all sense of day or night. Deep underground, time no longer mattered, and they had fallen asleep huddled in one corner of the room.

Zanirè now stood in the doorway, outlined by a blinding light that shone at her back. "On your feet, both of you," she barked. The two guards stood behind her, but Ianjori was nowhere to be seen.

As he stood to his feet, Jake found himself stiff and sore, for he had certainly not slept comfortably on the stone floor in his fine clothes. He could only imagine how Silorè felt in her layered dress.

Jake stretched and asked, still half asleep, "Where are you taking us?"

"You will not ask foolish questions," Zanirè said sternly. "Your lives are over. It does not matter where you are going or what we choose to do with you, for now you belong to Ilavèon and the Keneraton." She turned to the two men behind her. "Bind them."

Jake and Silorè did not resist as their hands were tied roughly behind their backs. It was then that Jake first felt the truth of his captivity, and dread filled him. He looked to Silorè, and though she tried to hide her feelings, her eyes gave her away, for they were wide and full of fear.

Zanirè drove Jake and Silorè down the corridor, and the two guards followed behind. After a few turns and a climb up many stairs, they all passed through a door and into the giant storehouse. The room seemed far darker and colder than it had before. *It must be the middle of the night*, Jake thought.

By the light of a torch, Zanirè led the company through the darkness. With his hands bound, Jake felt as though he might stumble into one of the many pits that opened up in the shadows before them, but the guards made sure he and Silorè kept their footing.

After a few minutes of walking through a void, the dim outline of a small star-craft appeared, and Ianjori stood beside it. "What took you so long?" he snarled, but his voice had lost some of its menace.

At Zanirè's command the guards loaded the prisoners into the ship.

The interior was quite dark, and the carpeted walls and floor smelled musty and old. The windows were darkened, so it was difficult to see in or out. Jake and Silorè were made to kneel on the floor in the middle of a ring of seats. The two guards sat beside them while Zanirè joined Ianjori in the front cabin.

The ship roared to life and took off through the warehouse doors, climbing high into the night sky over Ithèlimon. Jake had not realized how long he and Silorè had slept underground, but now the day was gone. He wondered where the other Itarlavon were and what they were doing this very moment. Were they searching for him and Silorè? Or did they think them dead?

The ship rose higher and higher until night became absolute and the planet fell away beneath it. Through the shaded windows, Jake saw the approach of a giant ship with two great wings spread like a vulture gliding on the wind. Jake marvelled at it, for he had never seen so large a vessel in flight, and it reminded him very much of the crashed ship he and Silorè had spotted from the train on Rithonon.

Slowly the craft bearing him and Silorè neared the mammoth ship and landed inside a hangar above one of its wings. Jake was eager to see where they were, but when he rose to get a look, a guard forced him down to the floor again.

There was a long and deafening hiss as the small starship opened its hatch, and Jake felt a great pressure in his ears. The air rushing in was cold and musty, and it left a bad taste in his mouth. The guards forced Jake and Silorè to stand, which they did not find easy with their hands bound as they were.

Zanirè and Ianjori were waiting outside to receive their prisoners, and they had been joined by four men wearing dark-grey robes girt with red sashes. Each man had a sword upon his back in a sheath secured by a grey strap across his chest. Jake could hardly see their faces, for dark hoods covered their heads. These were the Imarin,[63] personal soldiers of the Keneraton family.

"Bind their eyes," Zanirè ordered, and the Imarin came forward with strips of cloth and blindfolded the captives.

Jake felt strong hands seize him, and he was dragged off so quickly that he tripped over his own feet. The chamber around him echoed with many loud metallic sounds and hisses like fire and steam. As he crossed the floor, the sounds were suddenly swallowed up, and he knew he had entered a corridor.

Down many twisted passages the guards led their prisoners, handling them roughly when they did not turn the correct corners. All the while, Jake heard a growing number of footsteps clacking behind him, and he supposed they had been joined by many more guards.

63 Phatha (short version) of *Imarenarin*—"grey ones."

With much difficulty Jake and Silorè descended a winding staircase, and when they had turned another sharp corner, the Imarin halted them. At last their eyes were uncovered, and they found themselves in a room dimly lit by a small red orb set upon a table of polished stone.

"Where are we?" Jake mumbled half to himself. In answer something struck him on the backs of his legs, and with a cry he fell to his knees.

"I told you not to ask questions," Zanirè said.

From the shadows came a sudden voice. "Manners, Zanirè. We mustn't neglect hospitality." The voice was that of a woman, and it was neither menacing nor pleasant.

Jake rose to his feet, and as he turned towards the voice, a young woman stepped into the light. She was not tall, but she was slender and graceful. Her eyes shone blue and bright, and her hair was white as snow in sunshine. She wore a dress of silver and fire-red that flowed down her frail form all the way to the floor so that she had to hold the skirt when she walked. She was flanked by a dozen men and women, all heavily armed.

"At last!" she said. "Welcome to the *Bèndinar*. It was quite a task bringing you here, but I'm pleased to see that you have arrived without much injury. I trust you have been treated well? Other than this sudden slip in protocol, of course."

When Jake and Silorè remained silent, the young woman frowned. "Come now, Silorè," she said. "I know it's been a long time since we've seen each other, but surely I deserve a reply. Is there to be no levity at the reunion of old friends?"

"I'm not your friend, Ilavè," Silorè said firmly, "and you certainly are no friend of mine."

"Oh, but I am," Ilavè said with feigned indignation, "and I'm hurt to hear you say otherwise. You will be well treated aboard my ship—at least for as long as you wish. I cannot help what happens to ill-mannered guests. Your family seems to be an ungrateful lot."

"It is dangerous to be your guest, Ilavè," said Silorè. "Too many members of my family have suffered your hospitality through the years. No guest could be considered discourteous when he is abused by his hostess."

"That is not by my choice," Ilavè snapped. "For my part I do not seek harm to you or your family."

"If that is true," said Silorè, "then leave us in peace."

Ilavè sighed, and her face filled with pain. "I cannot do that," she said quietly. "You and your family are a danger, Silorè—both to yourselves and to the rest of the galaxy. How many wars has your family started in the interest of protecting the Earth? And protect it from what? The Thalanin do not well manage their world, and they fight in endless conflict with one another, squandering the wealth and beauty of the Earth that others might have enjoyed. You cannot deny that truth."

"It has only a shadow of truth," said Silorè, "for it ignores many things. Not all dealings on Earth are evil, but the Earth belongs to the Thalanin, and they will do with it as they will."

Ilavè sneered. "Did Zhialamon teach you to say that?" she said. "He has long outlasted his useful days as patriarch of your family. He has grown too rigid in his ways and cannot conform to the ever-changing universe. To follow him is to follow the way of death, and it will soon come upon you and all who stand with you."

"Is that a promise?" Silorè quipped.

"It is not from the Keneraton that judgment falls upon you," Ilavè said, "Eratzira is turning against you. The Earth will be opened in time, and then at last there will be order upon that unruly world."

"You speak praise of both order and chaos," said Silorè. "Do they have equal virtue in your eyes?"

"Each has its purpose," Ilavè said coldly. "Both fire and ice are useful servants, but wisdom is required to manage them." She took a step forward, and it seemed to Jake that she grew in stature. "Life and death are good servants too."

"And which will you call upon for us?" Silorè said.

Ilavè glared at Silorè with contempt. "That is not up to me," she said. "I do not care what becomes of you. We are going to Thedarlamon, and there my father will decide what is to be done with you."

She took a deep breath. "Now then," she said, "if there is anything you desire, don't hesitate to ask. I will leave you to get settled, and this evening you will join me for dinner. I'll send someone for you when it is time. Until then."

With a nod she departed, and all the guards went with her. Ianjori followed close behind, but Zanirè lingered for a moment, giving Jake and Silorè a final glower before following the others.

Even as Zanirè disappeared, the room flooded with small automatons. They each stood less than three feet high, and their bodies were emaciated except for their swollen joints. Their grey-green skin only partially covered their metal bones, and over all they wore pale blue robes that ran to their knees. Together they bore articles of furniture and platters of food they began to place around the room.

"They are Nathèglasin," Silorè whispered to Jake. "The Kenornin use them as servants on their starships, for they work well in space."

In short order the automatons set up a table and a long futon, and they hung a view-screen upon the far wall. Close at hand they placed a large bed with white coverings and two giant wardrobes filled with clothes. To the side they positioned a black folding-screen upon which a mountain scene was carved and overlaid with gold. Moreover, the automatons mounted paintings on the walls and draped colourful banners from the ceiling, and upon the table they set trays laden with food.

When they had finished, the tallest of the Nathèglasin stood before Jake and Silorè. “We hope you will be comfortable here,” he said. “If you lack anything, we will acquire it for you—if it pleases Mistress Ilavèon, of course.” He bowed, and with a voice that sounded like the grind of metal upon metal, he commanded the others to leave.

When the automatons had gone, Jake and Silorè were left alone, and they wandered the room, examining the furnishings. Jake lingered by the platters of food, which included small sandwiches stuffed with cured meats. “Don’t eat anything,” Silorè cautioned him. “I don’t trust her, no matter what she says.”

Jake, having taken a sandwich in each hand, returned them to the trays and wiped his hands on his shirt. “Sound advice,” he said, making a face, “but I’m still famished.”

“So am I,” Silorè said, putting a hand to her stomach, “but I’m not yet so desperate as to accept her food.”

“I suppose not,” Jake said, looking longingly at the sandwiches, “but if she’s going to kill us anyway…”

“Don’t say that!” Silorè snapped. “I’ve not lived thus far only to be killed by the Kenornin now.”

“Then what do you suggest we do?”

“I don’t know,” said Silorè with a sigh. “I only hope Zhialamon can get to us before we leave Ianiton.”

Suddenly she put her hands to her head and drew a sharp breath through her teeth.

“What’s the matter?” Jake asked.

“My head still hurts,” she said. “It has ever since Rithonon. I thought it was getting better, but our circumstances have aggravated it. I think I'll lie down for a while." She went over to the bed and lay down with her dress splayed around her.

Jake looked at her and frowned. "Are you not uncomfortable?"

"Quite," Silorè said, her hand upon her head.

"They've brought us clothes," Jake said. "If you want to change, there's a screen over here—"

"I'm not changing from this dress," Silorè said curtly. "It is mine, and it is precious to me. I won't risk the Kenornin taking it away, and I'm quite content to die in it, if need be." She rolled over and closed her eyes.

Jake stood by and watched her for a moment, admiring her ability to sleep so readily even in such peril. She looked so peaceful, it seemed nothing could trouble her slumber.

But it was a lie, for she sat up with great suddenness. "All right," she said as if in response to an ongoing argument, "I shall relent in this one matter."

Jake was startled by her awakening and her tone. "What do you mean?"

"There is but the one bed," she said, "and I am not rude enough to make you sleep elsewhere—not after what we've been through." She took a deep breath. "I shall permit you," she continued, "to sleep upon the bed if you will lie on top of the blankets with your head at my feet. Is that not fair?"

Jake felt himself turning red. "Quite fair," he said.

"Good." So saying, she lay down again and fell fast asleep.

Too embarrassed to stay near her, Jake wandered about for a bit before sitting upon the couch on the far side of the room and closing his eyes. Shapes both light and dark danced on his eyelids, and his head swam with thought incited by the rumblings of his empty stomach.

His turmoil was interrupted by a pounding knock at the door. He sat upright in an instant, wondering what the time was and whether he had fallen asleep. Silorè awoke and sat up in the bed with a sigh, straightening her dress where it had wrinkled.

The knock came again, and the door opened. One of the Imarin entered, his grey hood hiding most of his face. "The lady Ilavèon requests your presence at dinner," he said.

Silorè did not stir upon the bed but sat with her hands in her lap. "You may tell her," she said in as polite a voice as she could muster, "that we won't be attending. Please express to her our regrets."

"You cannot refuse," the Imari said, and he turned back his cloak to reveal a *kanoram*[64] in a jewelled scabbard at his waist. He placed his hand upon the hilt and glared at the two prisoners.

Jake and Silorè looked to one another, and with reluctance they agreed to attend.

"I shall return in one hour," the Imari said. "I was instructed to give you that time to make yourselves ready."

Silorè smirked. "How?"

"That is up to you," said the Imari with a snort. "I care not." Through the door came four Nathèglasin, and they stood around the Imari. "They will tend to your needs. See that you are ready when I return." And he departed.

The Nathèglasin crowded around Jake and Silorè and looked at them eagerly. "Command us, and we will obey," said one of them, "for we are instructed to serve you. What is your will?"

Silorè sighed. "If I am to go to dinner with Ilavè," she said, "I will first need a sewing-box, for I must mend my dress."

64 A light and durable curved sword, ancient in origin. Though the kanoram is chiefly ceremonial in the present day, there are still some who are skilled in its use, and the Imarin are among them.

"Please let us mend your dress for you," cried another of the automatons.

"No," Silorè said sternly, "I must do it myself."

The Nathèglasin muttered to one another in their grinding, metallic language. After a few moments, they turned back to Silorè, and one of them stood forth. "Very well," he said. "Will you require anything else?"

"Yes, as a matter of fact," Silorè said with sudden purpose, and she named a long list of cosmetics and toiletries.

When Silorè had finished, the lead Nathèglasi bowed low to her. "Consider it done," he said. "Only give us a moment, for finding all those things will take time."

"Fine," Silorè said. "Bring the box first, and I will repair the dress while you fetch the others."

The Nathèglasin bowed and departed. After a few minutes, one of them returned carrying a large black box with a lid secured by a silver buckle. Silorè took the box from him, and he went out again.

"What are you planning?" Jake asked as Silorè opened the box and rummaged through it.

"To look good," Silorè said. "If Ilavè wants us to be guests, then I will look the part."

"But what about me?" Jake said.

"What about you?"

"Well…how do I look? They never asked me if I needed anything."

Silorè looked him over. "You will be fine," she said. "On the other hand, I have work to do."

She disappeared behind the dressing-screen, and when she emerged a few minutes later, she had changed into a yellow shirt and brown trousers. In her arms she carried her dress. With great care she laid it out on the bed, frowning as she examined the tears in the fabric.

"Thankfully it's only come apart at the seams," she said. From the black box she withdrew several instruments of strange make along with two spools of thread and a pincushion full of needles. "I'd prefer to have my own things from home," she said, "but I suppose I can make do until I can truly repair my dress." She looked up at Jake, and a fire of defiance was in her eyes. "For I *shall* repair it fully when I am safe at home again."

Jake nodded and smiled, for her determination stirred hope within him. The faces of those he had met in Sorenon flashed into his mind, and he suddenly wished to see them again.

On the bed Silorè spread out the things she needed and began with a seam in the right side of the bodice. Jake watched intently as she worked. Her fingers moved in and out with great precision, and in short order the dress began to look as it had when Jake had first seen her in it.

"You're very skilled," he said at last. "Do you do this often?"

Silorè glared at him. "What do you mean?" she said. "Of course I do. I've made some of my own clothes, you know."

"No, I didn't know."

"Well, I can't be going around looking just like everyone else, can I?" she said with a grin. "I learned the art from my mother when I was young, and I've had many years to practise it."

"And did you make that dress?"

Silorè stopped working for a moment. "Partially," she said softly. "That was long ago, in days when I could never have made anything so fine on my own. My mother helped me. You see, Thalani, this was the dress I wore to my *Ansathènè*."[65]

Jake suddenly understood why she had been loath to part with the dress.

Silorè ran her hand gingerly over the fabric, and her eyes began to shine. "That was quite a day," she said with a far-off look. "The party was perhaps the grandest I have ever attended. I have seen other *Ansathènèn*, but I've not known any that were like the one given for me. My family did not spare any expense. The grounds of Sorenon were completely transformed, and thousands of people attended. The food and drink were superb, and there was music and dancing such as I have not experienced since. The air was full of life and merriment, and it was all for me.

"I was so nervous when I was presented. Every eye was upon me. I felt as though my heart would escape my chest, but your grandfather took my hand—for he was my escort—and his touch gave me strength. I danced until my feet ached, and I received many people—popular figures, far-off family members, and dignitaries from other worlds. They all loved me, if I may say so, and I loved everything about that day."

She smiled. "This dress has remained in my wardrobe these many years, and I have kept it well-preserved, taking it out occasionally to admire it."

"And you decided to wear it to the council?" Jake asked.

Silorè blushed. "Perhaps I was looking for a reason to wear it again," she said. "It is my favourite, and the occasion seemed special

65 A ceremonial party given for a young lady entering womanhood. Though specific traditions vary, Ansathènèn are universal among all Nanyavèn. Even some Thalavèn have taken up the practise, as it is similar to the customs of some Earth cultures.

enough." She suddenly blanched as if she had misspoken, and she quickly returned to her work.

Jake only smiled. "Then I am honoured," he said with a bow of his head.

Silorè flashed him a fierce look. "I didn't wear it for you!" she shouted, and her cheeks flushed crimson. She turned away and continued with her sewing.

Jake was taken seriously aback. He froze and did not dare to speak.

At length Silorè sighed. "It was a special occasion," she said, "and I do include you in that, but that's not why I wore this dress. You see, I've never been to the Council of Families before. The last one was over ten years ago, and at that time the composition of my family was very different. My parents were living, and my father was in the position Adjaron now holds. I had no responsibilities then, and I never dreamed of attending the council. That was work reserved for others, but all that's changed now." She made an end to her sewing and looked off as if to a great distance. "I wanted to take my place in the family," she said gently, "and to show off the splendour of the Itarlavon. It felt like another coming of age, and so I wore this dress."

She put down her needle and thread and picked up the dress, holding it before her and looking at it cautiously. "That will have to do," she said. "I shall have to wait to fix it properly."

At that moment a great number of Nathèglasin returned bearing all manner of items, some in boxes and others held loosely in their hands. Behind them four automatons carried a vanity with a large mirror, and another held a stool that went with it. They set up the vanity in the middle of the room and began to lay out all the things they had brought. Silorè laid her dress upon the bed again and motioned to Jake. "Guard it with your life," she said through her teeth.

Silorè sat upon the stool before the mirror, and the automatons gathered around her. Jake reclined upon the bed and watched as the Nathèglasin tended to Silorè, styling her hair and making up her eyes and face. Jake soon lost sight of her, for the automatons stood on chairs and stools they had pulled up around her, and she was obscured by a tangle of arms and bodies.

Jake turned his attention to the dress, keeping a hand upon it. As he looked it over, he decided it was not nearly as beautiful lying flat and formless.

The Nathèglasin finished their work and scurried from the room, taking everything with them. In the commotion Silorè rushed over to the bed, and taking up her dress, she disappeared behind the screen before Jake could get a look at her.

When she had changed again, she emerged from the screen and gazed expectantly at Jake. Her dress looked nearly as it had before they had left for the Council of Families—perhaps a bit wrinkled and missing a few of its embellishments but lovely nonetheless. A soft-blue colour shadowed her eyes so that they seemed to sparkle in the dim light, and her hair was woven in a braid that crowned her head according to the customs of the Kenornin.

Jake gaped at her.

"What is it?" she asked, sounding dismayed. "Do I look bad?"

"No," Jake said quickly, "not at all. You look wonderful. You nearly made me forget all the terrible things that have happened."

Silorè smiled. "I would that they hadn't," she said, and then her face fell again. "I wonder what transpired at the council yesterday. Ilavè sat in that chamber, knowing very well that Ianjori had abducted us. She must be confident indeed."

Before Jake could ask what she meant, the Imari messenger returned with two of his fellows. They stepped forward to bind the eyes of the prisoners, but Silorè would not let them near her. "I'll not have you smudging my face," she said and resisted them as they drew close. The foremost Imari reached for his sword, intending to draw it against her, but Silorè relented as long as she was allowed to tie the cloth herself. This the guards permitted, and with great care Silorè bound her own eyes. At the same time, an Imari roughly blindfolded Jake, tying the knot all the more tightly.

Without much care the guards shoved Jake and Silorè through the doors and led them in many twists and turns through the ship, and though Jake tried to remember the way, he soon became disoriented.

When at last they came to a stop and the guards uncovered their eyes, Jake and Silorè found themselves standing in a narrow room with a long table running down the centre. A white cloth was laid upon it, and many lighted candles stood in their trident candlesticks. Empty chairs of violet fabric were set about the table, and in the left-hand wall long panes of glass looked out to the stars.

In a chair at the far end of the table sat Ilavè in a lavender dress trimmed with white lace and tied with a golden sash. Part of her hair was braided around her head—as Silorè's now was—and her eyes and lips were painted white. Two women stood beside her wearing purple robes with large hoods that covered their eyes. Two Imarin flanked them.

At Ilavè's right hand stood a pole about the height of a man, and upon it sat a blackbird like a large raven. Malice was behind his eyes, cold as the void outside the window.

"I'm pleased you are here," said Ilavè, and she rose to greet her guests. "I was so worried you might resist. Silorè, you are looking lovely this evening. Your dress suits you quite well, though I should have liked to have seen you in one of my own. All those I sent to your room belong to me, after all. Never mind that now! Let's eat; I'm famished."

The Imarin that had escorted the prisoners took their places throughout the room, and more women in long robes directed Jake and Silorè to chairs near Ilavè.

As Jake and Silorè situated themselves, Ilavè motioned towards the blackbird over her shoulder. "I would like to introduce you to someone," she said to her guests. "This is Fèrdin, the most beloved of my servants. He has been my companion since childhood. Greet our visitors, Fèrdin."

The blackbird stretched out his wings and stood tall on his perch. "Good evening," he said, and his voice was cold and menacing. "I hope you realize what an honour it is to dine with my mistress this evening." And he glared at them.

The women in purple robes stepped forward, placing bowls of steaming liquid upon the table. Ilavè laved her hands in one of them and bade Jake and Silorè do the same. Silorè sat stubbornly still, but Jake, being curious, dipped his finger into the bowl before him. To his surprise he discovered it did not contain water but a strong concoction that burned like fire where it touched him. When he removed his finger again, it felt ice-cold, and he gave a shout of surprise.

Ilavè laughed at him. "That is *korintholan*," she said. "I suppose one does not see it in Thalanin lands. It is used in the ceremonial cleansing of my people before meals." She looked over at Silorè and huffed, for Silorè sat rigidly with her hands in her lap. "I don't suppose the Itarlavon would approve of our traditions, but be that as it may. Eat with foul hands for all I care." She clapped twice, and the bowls were removed.

"I do hope you enjoy the meal," Ilavè continued. "I had a stock of *nathilasin*[66] put aboard before we departed. I know you don't eat meat, Silorè, but perhaps the Thalani has more of a stomach for good food."

The purple-robed women returned bearing food of a kind Jake had never seen before, and he stared a long while at the plate they placed before him. Upon it was a large portion of grilled nathilasi set upon a field of red grain garnished with strange vegetables of many hues. A helping of noodles swam in a thick green sauce sprinkled with roasted seeds, black with char. Beside these were mounds of starchy vegetables baked into orange cakes and fried dumplings stuffed with spiced cabbage. Each diner was also given a large crust of bread drizzled with a runny creamlike spread.

Ilavè looked out the window for a moment, and closing her eyes, she nodded her head slowly three times. Then she began to eat, but Jake and Silorè sat stolidly by, neither moving nor speaking.

After a moment Ilavè looked to her guests, and it seemed she was offended. "What are you waiting for?" she said. "Eat up!"

"I'm not hungry," Silorè said obstinately.

Ilavè frowned and turned to Jake. "Neither am I," he said.

"Oh, come now!" Ilavè said, thoroughly frustrated. "You really do trust no one, do you?" She clapped her hands, and the women in attendance took up the prisoners' plates and brought them to her, and she sampled everything in turn. When she had finished, the ladies replaced the plates in front of Jake and Silorè.

"Satisfied?" Ilavè said with her mouth full. "You may not be keen on eating after me, but if you can't get over that, then I can't help you. You'll just have to starve." She continued on with her meal in silence.

66 A small sheeplike animal whose meat (also called *nathilasi*) is considered a delicacy in certain parts of the galaxy.

Both Jake and Silorè found that having Ilavè eat off their plates was not a deterrent, but though they were hungry, they ate slowly, for Ilavè's eyes were ever on them. Silorè did not eat the meat, but Jake found that it was strange and delicious. The other foods were tasty enough, and the bread was dense and chewy.

Even as the three continued eating, servers returned bringing plates of *thigala*[67] in a spicy sauce and bowls of broth filled with squares of *numirva*.[68] The meal concluded with sweet biscuits and dishes of fruit covered in sugar and cream. There was plenty to eat, and Jake soon felt quite full.

Ilavè did not speak again until the end of the meal. "I hope you are satisfied," she said cheerily. "Come walk with me a bit. There's something I wish to show you."

Ilavè stood at the window looking out at the stars, her white hair flowing over her shoulders in loose curls. Fèrdin had perched on the railing beside her, and she was stroking his head-feathers. Jake and Silorè stood behind her, and two Imarin lingered nearby, their hands ever at their sword-hilts. They had all walked together onto the promenade that ran along the front of the ship. Long panes of glass enclosed the deck above a waist-high wall with a bronze railing. The glass was so clear, it appeared to Jake at times that nothing separated him from the stars.

At length two women in purple robes appeared carrying a white pillar upon which was set a dusty book in a brown-leather cover. When they had placed this pedestal near Ilavè, they silently stepped aside, waiting with bowed heads for further commands. Ilavè

67 A certain species of domesticated land-fowl known to the Nanyanin.

68 The edible root of the *tistana* plant. When cooked, it becomes tender and savoury.

remained still for a moment, and then she turned and lifted the book from its place, holding it so Jake and Silorè could see it plainly.

"Do you know what this is?" she asked, looking intently at Jake and Silorè. "I can see by your faces that you do." She opened the book and began to leaf gingerly through it. "This is indeed the Chronicle of Sierduon, which he penned in time long past. It has remained for countless years in the Library of Thesalara, but despite being so old and valuable, it was not well guarded.

"Several of my ladies went to Thesalara pretending to search for old manuscripts that had once belonged to the Kenornin, and I sent a few Imarin with them. They spent two days there, and the night before they left, the Imarin were able to sneak in and obtain the Chronicle." She laughed and spread her hand over the open pages. "I could not have done it without the invitation to the Council of Families. Sending anyone from Ialanon to Thesalara would have drawn too much attention. That's quite a long journey just to look at some dusty old books."

"They'll find you out," Silorè said. "When the keepers on Thesalara discover the Chronicle is missing, they'll know who has taken it. My family knows what you're planning, and you won't get away with it."

Ilavè smirked. "I don't think anyone will miss it," she said. "The Imarin replaced this book with a very clever copy, exact in every detail except one—one which no one will suspect, for it cannot be put to the test, at least not on Thesalara."

She turned to a certain place and held up the book. The right page was covered in archaic symbols scrawled in a messy hand, but its facing page was blank. "This is what I mean," she said. "The Chronicle's blank page is something of a mystery. Many have thought that Sierduon passed it over by mistake or perhaps left it empty for some ritualistic purpose. If you indeed know my plans, then you must also know what I think of it, and though I'm curious how you found me out, I won't ask you.

"Indeed, I believe there is Telethitartholan upon this page. Others have thought so as well, but none of them have dared to guess which star might reveal the writing. But where they have failed, I have succeeded, for I have found another text that speaks to this."

She reached into the sash of her dress and withdrew a small scroll bound by a gold ribbon. "This," she said, "is the last writing of Sierduon, which he gave to his heirs. They could not have known its importance, else they would have sought the seed of the Atsari as well. Indeed, that is what I seek, but you do not seem surprised to hear me say so.

"Upon this scroll is a poem in riddle-form. It tells of a star—large and green, bright and wild—and no planets circle it. It is a part of the star-cluster in the *Nisa Kithèn* constellation of the planet Zhinlam. It may be difficult to find, for it lies within a vast gas-cloud, but in the light of this star, the writing on the blank page shall be revealed. At last we shall know the location of the final seed of the Atsari, and with it the gift of Life Eternal." She replaced the scroll and set down the book upon its pedestal.

"And what do you know of eternal life, Ilavè?" Silorè asked.

Ilavè turned to her and huffed. "I know that it isn't found in any Thalani," she said mockingly. "You and your family hold to many archaic ideas, and with them you have committed many horrors. How many have you killed to protect yourselves and that Thalanin planet you fuss over? How many millions live in poverty while you profit from your self-imposed duties? Look to Iderat first before wasting so much toil on the Earth, whose inhabitants crawl like maggots upon its surface, devouring both it and one another. In their brief lives, they know nothing but enmity and hatred, and like children they destroy that for which they will not give thanks.

"They breed like flies, infesting every corner of that world, leaving less for their offspring than was given them. Their greatest empires are like the towers that children make in the sand: the waves wash over them, and they are remembered no more. Their strength is as a mist upon the wind—a vapour that appears for but an instant and, coming to no consequence, is borne away. In their frailty they gnaw at their world, spoiling their own land and sea and air until it vomits out its judgments of flood and famine; heat and cold; fire, storm, and death.

"Yet all they might learn from us is denied by the miserable members of your diseased family. Diseased, I say, for it is illness beyond measure to love these people. There is no hope for them except what fools accept as wisdom. Mercy there is in life but also oft-times in death. A man sick beyond what he can bear must be allowed release, for sorrows must end at last.

"Then we shall bring forth worlds filled with joy boundless as the universe itself, which gave life to all. All shall live well and die well, full of years free of pain and filled with pleasure. Illness will be defeated. No desire shall go unfulfilled. Nevermore shall there be need for fighting and war among any peoples. The universe will be at peace, and when at last all things are made equal—for is this not the nature of the universe?—and we are but stardust once again, then shall that Everlasting Peace endure forevermore!"

As she spoke she lifted her hands upward and outward, turning to the stars as if she could embrace the infinity before her. Her head was upturned, and tears ran down her face in great rivers. Her voice was strong, yet it shook with great feeling, raw and wild. Mad with it she seemed, and Jake feared her. He looked to Silorè, and in her eyes was a terror and an anger he had not seen in her before. Her hands trembled in tight fists, and she bit her lower lip to keep from speaking or crying.

Ilavè turned back to them, wiping her eyes, and when she saw the expressions of their faces, she laughed loudly. "You needn't fear death, Silorè," she said, and she sounded almost cheerful. "It is the nature of all things to die. The fire burns out, and all things grow cold as the universe resolves itself into oneness. No ripple will disturb the serenity of that everlasting sea that shall be its end."

Silorè pressed her fingernails into her palms as if to steel herself to speak. "Then why…do you seek the seed of the Atsari?" she said, and Jake was surprised at the coldness in her voice. "If death is your duty, then go forth and die."

Ilavè looked at Silorè with sudden fury. "There is work yet to be done in this universe," she said. "Our span within Eternity is alas too short to achieve what we would. My father is old and frail, and all he could have accomplished in his life remains undone, for his enemies have opposed him unto death.

"But with the Atsari he will outlive them all. Indeed, he will witness that glorious and everlasting Unity at the end of the universe, and then, with his task complete, he will join with Eternity of his own free will. He will be the Last of All to Die."

Jake shuddered, for it seemed a sudden fire was kindled in Ilavè's eyes. She looked out to the stars as one with great authority, and it seemed that with only a word of command she could subdue all things. Queenly she was, and her beauty lit the darkness around her like the rays of a silver moon. Both Jake and Silorè shrank away from her, and they could not speak.

"Now take them away," Ilavè commanded her guards. "There are a few days yet before the search begins. Our guests must be well rested by then, for I want them present for it all. When we find that star, I wish them to see it and despair." As she said these last words, she turned towards them again, and her face was wholly changed, terrible to behold. Neither Jake nor Silorè could endure the intensity of her eyes.

One of the Imarin stood forth. “It shall be done, my lady.”

Jake and Silorè were blindfolded again and led down many paths with many turns. When their eyes were again uncovered, they found themselves back in their room. The Imarin left without speaking, plunging the prisoners into darkness as the door closed behind them.

Jake and Silorè found nothing to say to one another, for they were deep in their own thoughts. The words of Ilavè still rang in their ears.

Lying on their bed head to foot, they fell into fitful throes of restless sleep.

Chapter 14

The Stone and the Star-Cloud

Two days passed. During that time Jake and Silorè did not leave their room, and no one came to see them save for the Nathèglasin that brought them their meals. They slept often, but not always at the same time, and even in their waking hours they said little to one another.

Jake spent most of his time in front of the view-screen scanning for transmissions, and as he did he discovered a smattering of broadcasts—Lambati matches, travelogues, news summaries from nearby worlds, a commentary on a poet whose name Jake did not recognize, a concert for the anniversary of a nearby planet's settlement, a musical slideshow of mountain-scapes, and a performance of the opera *Natharè ez Eshgari*. Jake watched them alone, for Silorè spent her time upon the bed, far off in her own contemplations.

On the third day, the *Bèndinar* passed a planet in an isolated star-system not claimed by Eratzira but still within its borders. The planet was not heavily populated, and as such it was not likely to appear on many star-maps. Nirdarason was its name, and Adamèliga was its star.

When an Imari appeared suddenly to announce the approach to Nirdarason, Jake and Silorè were shaken from their malaise.

“What is Ilavè doing?” Silorè said once the Imari had gone. “She said she wanted to bring us before Eratizhal. Could she have changed her mind, and now she means to maroon us on this planet?”

“What planet is it?” Jake said. “I’ve never heard of it.”

“Nor I.”

“Could it be a Kenornin planet?” Jake asked. “Perhaps we’re taking on supplies or replacing crew.”

Silorè shook her head. “No, there’s something strange in this,” she said. “It must be quite important to risk detection while still in Eratzira, for I’m certain we haven’t crossed the border yet. Pharzira is the last star-system we would pass before the border—if we are indeed heading in that direction—and it is at least a five-day journey from Ianiton.”

“Then we have many more days of travel to endure,” Jake groaned. “I wish we could reach our journey’s end, whatever may come. I’m tired of sitting in this room with nothing to do but await our doom.”

“Perhaps it awaits us on Nirdarason,” Silorè said. “I don’t trust Ilavè to keep her word to us.”

The ship set down with a lurch, and two Imarin came to fetch Jake and Silorè, saying that Ilavè wished to see them. The men bound the eyes of the prisoners and led them once again through the twisting corridors. At length Jake felt a cold breeze upon his face, and he realized he had been walked off the ship. *So she does intend to maroon us*, he thought.

When his eyes were uncovered, Jake beheld a barren land of red-hued mountains that rose to many peaks and pinnacles like a city made of stone. The horizon was rimmed with a rosy glow, but the sky overhead was black. There was no sun, but many stars could be seen in the dark sky. The air was cold like a winter’s day, and even in his suit, Jake shivered as he walked down the gangplank.

As he turned his eyes from the landscape, he saw that Zanirè and Ianjori now walked with the Imarin. Their faces were cold and hard, and they did not speak to anyone. Ianjori was dressed as one of the Imarin, though he was more decorated, and Zanirè wore a black hood over her normal black garb. Together they and the Imarin led the prisoners from the ship and onto the plateau.

Near the ship upon the edge of a cliff, Ilavè stood alone, staring up at the stars. "Good evening," she said to the prisoners. "This is quite a detour, but I could not come all this way and not visit this planet."

She looked at the puzzled expressions on the prisoners' faces and laughed. "You don't know what this planet is?" she said. "This is one of the Foundation Worlds—the only one in this part of the galaxy. It is sacred to me and to all who hold to Koreva. This is one of the oldest planets in existence, formed in ages long ago from ancient stardust. Its star is old—far older than Tolitar—and it has shone upon this world through years without number. Now we are come to seek guidance from these ancient stones that they may bless our journey. Come!"

It was then that Jake looked towards the slope and saw that a tall stairway had been cut in its side. It rose many thousands of steps to the summit of a nearby mountain. As he looked upon it, he despaired, for it was a long walk. He turned to Silorè, who stood rubbing her bare shoulders with her hands, and she too was frowning at the stair.

Ilavè started up the steps ahead of the others, and the Imarin forced Jake and Silorè to follow some distance behind her. Jake kept count of the steps at first, but he gave up after a few hundred. His feet and legs quickly grew weary and stiff, but the guards pressed him on. Silorè seemed tireless, and she walked tall and proud, with an air of defiance.

After a steep climb, the path levelled off and passed through a village of small houses, some made of clay and others carved from the living rock. In the street children had drawn two circles and were playing Lambati. They paused as the visitors passed by, staring at the strangers with curiosity. It was likely that none of them had seen a Thalani or a labnerè girl before. They jeered at both of them, though one little girl seemed awed by Silorè. From the windows and doorways, many other eyes watched the visitors pass, and Jake heard many hushed voices speaking words he could not discern, but they did not sound friendly. Even after he had left the village, Jake felt many eyes watching him, and he shivered.

The summit of the mountain approached, and upon it stood a shrine with a tall spire that rose above the surrounding peaks. Many pillars lined the path, each inscribed with many names, though none were familiar to Jake. Atop each pillar was a brazen bowl filled with fire. Ilavè walked slowly now up the steps, her arms outstretched and her head held high.

The shrine itself was little more than a canopied space open on three sides with the mountain-peak at its back. White pillars held up the red roof, and intricate reliefs of gold covered all. Inside upon a low pedestal stood a slab of black rock about the size of a man. It was jagged and deformed, and light reflected off it in a peculiar manner so that its facets seemed to move about and alter their shape.

Upon either side of the stone stood two women dressed in golden robes with hoods that covered their faces so that only their mouths were showing. They were as still as statues, and cauldrons of fire burned by their sides, casting flickering lights upon their glistering robes. On the stairs before the shrine waited a dozen men wearing dark uniforms and carrying spears. They withstood Ilavè and her escorts and would not permit them to pass.

The two women suddenly stood forth and cried together with loud voices, “Who comes to the High Place of Adamèdar?”

Ilavè bowed low. “Ilavè, daughter of Eratizhal, of the house Keneraton,” she said. “These with me are members of my personal guard, and they escort these two nonbelievers whom I have brought that they might see the Stone.”

“Then approach,” the women said. “Let the nonbelievers behold and believe.”

The shrine guards relented, and Ilavè climbed the stairs flanked by Ianjori and Zanirè. Jake and Silorè followed close behind, pushed onward by the Imarin.

“Who are those women?” Jake whispered to Silorè.

“They are priestesses of Koreva,” Silorè said. “Apparently they are the keepers of this shrine.”

“And that rock?”

“Ilavè called it the Stone,” said Silorè. “I assume she means it is one of the Itarenevan. The Korevanin believe such stones were the first material formed at the beginning of the universe.”

“You are correct, Silorè,” Ilavè said, for in the stillness of the mountain air she had heard their whispers. “In the depths of time, this stone was forged at the heart of an ancient star, and through countless ages it drifted in the dark places of the universe until it was found and brought here. It is sacred to us, as indeed it should be sacred to all who live, for it is the substance of life.”

At the top of the stair, Ilavè paused and stood before the stone, bowing in reverence before it. From behind the priestesses, young girls came forth wearing robes that faded from blue at their shoulders to green at their feet. One girl held in her hands a golden bowl ornamented with fiery gems set in a rim of adamant. She approached Ilavè and knelt before her, raising the bowl, with bowed head.

Ilavè bathed her hands in the golden basin, and when she had finished, she reached forth a hesitant hand, still wet with sacred water, and touched the stone with her fingertips. Her body trembled, and tears fell down her face.

"Pardon me," she said, her voice failing, "for this is the first time I have stood in this place, and I feel connected to the Universe in a way I never thought I could. This moment marks the beginning of a new life for my family and indeed for all peoples in the Universe, for I feel such clarity of mind and heart as I have never felt before. I declare here before you all that I will lead my family to do great things, and no one shall withstand our strength of will and purpose."

"The Universe empowers you, star-daughter,"[69] one of the priestesses said. "The Fire burns within you. It strengthens your heart and gives it wisdom. Listen to it, and you shall not fail."

Ilavè remained for a minute, silently touching the stone. Then, with great reluctance, she withdrew her hand, and bowing low to the priestesses, she turned and walked down the steps with Ianjori and Zanirè at her heels. When she passed Jake and Silorè, she gave them both a wicked smile and turned up her nose.

The priestesses and the attending girls turned their backs to the nonbelievers, and the temple guards formed a line between the prisoners and the shrine. In the still silence of that moment, though surrounded by many people, Jake felt very much alone, and he shivered though the air was not cold.

The Imarin prodded Jake and Silorè to follow Ilavè, and together they all walked back down the mountain in silence.

Two more days passed in which Jake and Silorè remained confined to their room.

69 Nanyan: *Itarvè*. Followers of Koreva refer to themselves and others as star-children.

In the middle of the night on the second day, Jake was awakened by a piercing scream and a firm kick to his head. He bolted upright at once and reached for the light, and when it blazed to life he beheld Silorè sitting up in bed, breathing heavily and sweating. Her eyes were wide with terror, and she was shaking.

"It's all my fault!" she shrieked, half delirious. "It's all my fault! My hands…it wouldn't come off! Where did he go? What's happened?"

Jake grabbed her arm, and she started as if coming out of a trance. "Thalani!" she cried, and then she buried her face in her hands and wept bitterly.

Jake was unsure what he should do, so he sat with her in silence, listening to her muffled sobs.

"Was it a dream?" he asked when her tears subsided.

Silorè nodded. "The images—they affected me so terribly," she said. "I have never had a dream like that before in all my life. But why did it come to me now and not days ago?"

She took a deep breath. "I saw Rathori lying in a pool of blood. Death was on his face, and his body was contorted in a grotesque pose. I reeled at the sight, but even as I turned away, I saw to my horror that, though I had not touched him, my hands and dress were wet with blood. I tried to wash it away, but it would not come off.

"Suddenly the pool of blood began to grow, and it swelled until it became an ocean. I tried to find refuge from the flood by climbing to the top of a rock, but I could not escape. The sea of blood engulfed me, and I sank into the depths, hearing Rathori's voice echoing all around me. 'Why?' it wailed. 'Why?' I tried to answer, but my voice made no sound."

She fell silent and turned away.

"It was just a dream," Jake said. "Terrifying to be sure, but just a dream."

Silorè shook her head. "You don't understand," she said tearfully. "I did this to him. If I had just gone to the Council with the others, none of this would have happened. Rathori would be alive, and we would not be on this terrible ship."

"You didn't do anything reckless," Jake said firmly, "and no one knew this would happen. You can't blame yourself on account of a dream."

"It's not just the dream," Silorè said. "These thoughts have plagued me constantly, and all this time alone isn't helping. I've tried so hard not to think about him, as horrible as that sounds. I can't feel that grief right now. I know what it will do to me. I've felt it too often before."

Jake took her hand. "He must have been dear to you. How long had you known him?"

"He had been with us only about a year," Silorè said. "He was training under Sondari to be a protector of the Itarlavon. I did not know him well, but I knew his family. His parents were servants of our house in the days when I was young, but as more people left Sorenon, we needed fewer workers, so we let some of them go. It was a shame, for his family had served ours for many generations. But his parents must have told him of his heritage, and I suppose he wanted to continue the tradition."

She closed her eyes and sighed, her face etched with pain. "I'm tired of death," she muttered. "I've seen too much of it, and it never gets easier to take. Each new grief opens the old ones again. Each time, it touches you deeper. Each time, it carves out a bit more of your soul. I can't bear that sorrow again—not here and now. So I cannot think of Rathori, though his sacrifice was great. Isn't that terrible of me?" Her eyes flooded again, and her cheeks glistened.

"I don't know," Jake said sullenly. "But I've done the same with Brown Hill—trying to block the pain and fill it with distraction. I don't want to lose myself again like I did the day of the attack. I felt like I was going mad. It was a dreadful feeling—one I wanted to lock away forever.

"It was the same when my parents died. My emotions overwhelmed me until I feared I had lost my mind. Some nights, I would sit downstairs in my kitchen, feeling that at any moment my parents would just walk through the door as if nothing had happened. They wouldn't need to give any explanation because there would be nothing wrong.

"Those nights were the loneliest of all.

"So I tried to hide my feelings away. I sealed their bedroom, leaving it exactly as they had. I packed all the old dishes and cutlery and put them in the garage. I shunned their old friends, and I kept to myself, cloistered in that old tower. But for all my effort, I could not shut out the pain.

"And yet as the years have gone by, I have learned somewhat to manage. That's why I hated losing control that day of the attack: all the grief I had worked to supress came back to me, and I hated myself for it. But I suppose loss isn't something to conquer. My parents and the people of Brown Hill are a part of me, and so their loss is a part of me too. I may not always want to remember, but I certainly never want to forget."

He had not been looking at Silorè as he spoke, but as he turned to her now, he found she was gently smiling at him despite her tears. "When did you become so wise?" she said softly.

He smiled grimly back at her. "I've had some good teachers," he said, "including a certain girl who talked some sense into me one day when I really needed it. She has a lot of wisdom herself." He put his hand to his neck. "Though she did kick me in the head in the middle of the night."

Silorè laughed, though it sounded more like a sniffle. "It wasn't on purpose, I assure you." Then she yawned and sighed. The anguish had drained away from her face, and she seemed suddenly tired. "Thank you, Thalani," she said. "I'm sorry to have awakened you."

"It's no trouble," said Jake. "Are you sure you're all right now?"

"No," said Silorè. "I'll never feel good about it—how could I?—but I do feel a bit better after talking to you. I'm very grateful." She smiled at him again, and her eyes were full of warmth and affection. "Don't forget," she said, "you're all I've got now."

Jake blushed under her intent gaze. He was afraid to move, but he suddenly desired to embrace her. Indeed, she seemed to move towards him, and he might have reached out to her if she had not suddenly looked away. "Good night, Thalani," she said, and she lay down and turned her back to him.

"Good night," Jake said quietly. He lay down at her feet, but when he closed his eyes, he found he could still clearly see her face, and the look she had given him would not permit him to sleep. The gentle sound of her breathing awakened many feelings in him, and he longed to sleep at her head with his arms around her. This urge he resisted, and after more than an hour of staring at the ceiling, he fell asleep again.

The next morning, two Imarin came for Jake and Silorè. They bound their eyes once more and ushered them through the ship up many stairs and ramps.

When their eyes were uncovered again, Jake and Silorè were standing in a room with a vast dome. A window in the far wall stretched around half the chamber, but a shade was covering it, and it was dark. A half-circle of chairs faced it, and in the midst of them sat Ilavè, with Fèrdin perched beside her and the Chronicle in her lap. Behind her upon a raised platform stood the helmsman, his hands upon a giant wheel that guided the ship through the heavens. At his side many other men of important and imposing appearance stood, and they regarded the entrance of Jake and Silorè with contempt. Many Imarin stood all around the room, and Zanirè and Ianjori were among them.

Ilavè rose to greet the prisoners as they entered. “I’m pleased you’re here!” she said. “We’ve reached our destination at last. I can’t wait for you to see it. Look!” She motioned towards the window, and the shade covering it split down the middle and pulled apart.

Beyond the glass the sky was filled with a vast cloud. Wisps of orange and gold formed shapes strange and immense, and many thousands of stars shone from deep within. Patches of dark dust hung like cobwebs strung between columns of fiery gasses. Here and there streaks of green smoke ran in rough lines, and around a particularly bright star there swirled a pink mist.

Ilavè smiled. “Isn’t it glorious?” she said. “Long before the human race came into being, this cloud was here, lighting the darkness and birthing new suns and planets. It is no wonder Sierduon chose one of these stars for his Telethitartholan, for this gas-cloud is large and perilous and far away from the common star-paths. We shall not be troubled by any other vessel, for this part of the sky is ours.”

She held out her hand, and a tall, bearded man stepped to her side. He wore a white uniform with red trim, and his waist was girt with a black belt fitted with a large silver buckle. Across his chest hung three golden medals with ribbons of many colours attached above and below. Though he stood straight and stiff, with a face empty of expression, his hands fidgeted nervously behind his back.

“This is Captain Èrmon” said Ilavè. “He commands the *Bèndinar* and her crew, and he has served my family for many years.”

"It is my honour to do so," said the captain, "and there is no greater pleasure."

"You've trained him well," said Silorè with a sneer. "Does he sit and heel on command as well?"

The captain betrayed no emotion except for a brief flare of his nostrils. Ilavè, on the other hand, glared at Silorè and scoffed. "Don't be rude," she chided. "After all, he has done you no harm. I always thought that in your family you were the most concerned with courtesy. I suppose I was wrong."

"I ask no pardon," said Silorè. "For whatever you say of the Thalani and me, we are not your guests—nor do we wish to be. And we certainly have no desire to see your menagerie perform for your amusement."

The captain frowned, but Ilavè shook her head and pulled her lips into a fake smile. "It isn't going to work," she said. "Try as you might, you cannot upset me today. Nothing can."

She motioned to two empty chairs nearby. "Come and sit," she said. "I want you by my side when we find the star. Then you shall read the writing in the book, and it shall be token to you of the new age that is upon us all—the return of the Keneraton." The Imarin forced Jake and Silorè to sit where Ilavè had indicated. The chairs were quite comfortable, and they were perfectly placed to give the best view out the window.

Ilavè took her seat again, leaning forward with anticipation. "Take us inside, Captain," she said.

Captain Èrmon bowed to Ilavè and shouted orders at those standing by him. The helmsman threw a lever forward, and the cloud grew in the window until with a jolt it engulfed them.

At once the ship lurched to the left, and Jake had to grip the arms of his chair to keep from falling. Those who were standing stumbled on their feet and muttered worriedly to one another. Ilavè did not flinch but sat tall and steady as a mountain. She stared fixedly through the window, scanning the sky for any star that might match her riddle.

The *Bèndinar* passed through a thick cloud, and the room went very dark, with only a dim ring of light around the ceiling. Jake shivered, for though his fear in this moment was different, still the cloud reminded him of his journey through the Thasadres. Silorè must have felt the same, for she reached out and took his hand, squeezing it tightly.

The ship emerged again, and the cloud before them was beautifully golden, with fountains of white smoke cascading down pillars of bright-red gasses. Five stars clustered together nearby, each shining with a different colour. Jake gaped, for though it seemed that the cloud closed in all around them, he hardly felt confined by it. The space before the ship was vast beyond his imagination. He lost himself in the moment, and his fear ebbed away.

Yet it returned quickly at the sound of Ilavè's voice.

"Have you plotted a course through the cloud?" she asked her officers. "I want to start as soon as possible."

"We have, my lady," said the captain. "The watchers have already mapped three stars to consider. We merely await your command."

Ilavè smiled. "Then let us begin."

And so they did.

Traversing the cloud was treacherous—more so, Jake sensed, than any of the crew had expected. The ship shook frequently, rattling everyone onboard until they grew irritable and restless. Strings of charged gas struck the ship at whiles, making its metal bones creak and rumble with unsettling dissonance. Flashes like lighting lit up certain parts of the cloud, and Jake hoped the ship would not have to pass through them.

Hour after hour the *Bèndinar*—though it seemed adrift in the gas-cloud—travelled great distances within it, circling many stars along the way. At each stop Ilavè would stand forth with the Chronicle in her hands and turn the blank page to the window. Each time, the page remained empty, and Ilavè would return dismayed to her chair.

The lack of success and the difficulty of the journey began to weigh upon Ilavè, and she mostly sat with her fingers drumming the arm of her chair as she stared blankly out the window. The cheer she had first exhibited waned to impatience, and she refused all food and drink offered her. The thrill of the hunt was gone.

Zanirè came to sit by Ilavè's side and whispered to her from time to time to raise her spirits. Ianjori remained slouched in a chair near the far wall, fiddling with one or another of his many knives. Jake secretly hoped he would scratch himself with one of the poisoned blades.

Time passed, and the day at last was spent. The *Bèndinar* halted for the night, for Ilavè would not permit the search to continue without her. She went off to bed, and Jake and Silorè were led blindfolded back to their room.

When they were left alone, Silorè laughed loudly. "Did you see the look on her face?" she said cheerfully. "Things are not going well. I'm certain Ilavè expected to find her star within the first hour. Either it is better hidden than she supposed or the Chronicle was not written with Teletholan from any star in this cloud."

"I hope that's so," Jake said, "but I don't suppose that helps us any. Other than delaying our trip to Ialanon, this search serves only to put Ilavè in a sour mood. It's not helping my disposition either."

"You may be right," Silorè said, "but what can we do? There's nothing for it but to endure Ilavè and her ire until…well, until the end of the journey."

"Whenever that may be," Jake mumbled.

Silence followed, and at length Silorè yawned and stretched. "We'd better get some sleep, Thalani," she said. "We can't be nodding off beside Ilavè tomorrow, or we might just see what happens in absence of her *hospitality*." She bade him good night, and casting herself upon the bed, she fell almost at once into a deep sleep.

Jake lay at her feet, and many thoughts entered his mind—thoughts of Rithonon and of Iderat and all the people he had come to know there, thoughts that kept sleep away for many hours.

Morning came, and Jake and Silorè were summoned back to the command room.

Ilavè was sitting in her chair looking quite miserable, and Ianjori and Zanirè sat by her side. The rest of the guards and the crew stood all around, and there was no joy in any of their faces.

The search resumed. For many hours the *Bèndinar* travelled from star to star, and though expectation grew, the hunt remained ever fruitless. As the ship progressed, the cloud changed to swirls of blue and green like the colour of the sea near the shore. One bright-red star held in its circle a small brown planet—a desert world with pink clouds swirling in massive storms upon its surface.

It was as the *Bèndinar* passed near this world that Captain Èrmon came forward and spoke hastily to Ilavè. "My lady," he said, his voice weak and shaking, "I do not wish to alarm you, but I have been watching the scopes for the past hour, and I must report that we have detected an incoming ship."

Jake and Silorè looked at each other, and a spark of hope was kindled in their eyes. Ilavè observed them but ignored their reactions. "What sort of ship?" she asked.

“We don’t know, my lady,” the captain said. “It is at the very edge of our range.”

“What do you suggest we do?”

“The cloud will hide us from them for a little while,” said Èrmon. “Indeed, it makes it difficult for us to track them as well, but I am certain they are coming this way.”

Ilavè slumped in her chair and gripped its arms so tightly her knuckles lost all colour. “How long until they discover us?” she asked in a low tone.

“Less than an hour,” said the captain, “and we shall need that time to navigate the cloud and emerge on the other side.”

Ilavè’s face grew red as her brow furrowed. “Very well,” she muttered. “Set our course. We will find a safe place to stay until they are gone, and then we will return.”

The *Bèndinar* set out at once, and the cloud slowly dissipated as the ship neared the boundary. One by one distant stars winked into view, and the sky grew black again.

“We’re on course for Kinalam, my lady,” Èrmon said. “It is a deserted world. We can remain unseen there for as long as we need.”

“Very well, Captain,” Ilavè said. “Ianjori, take these two away.” She motioned at Jake and Silorè but did not look at them. “I wish to be alone now.”

“Certainly.” Ianjori rose to his feet and towered over the prisoners. “Get up!”

Jake and Silorè stood slowly, and the Imarin came to their side. Jake turned to the window, taking one last look at the stars before he was to be locked away again. He tried to find something familiar in the sky, but the stars were all strange to him.

Suddenly a flash of brown streaked past the window. Everyone in the room turned, for they had all seen it but could not tell what it had been. Ilavè rose from her seat and stepped slowly to the window, but though she looked all around, she could see nothing but the stars.

As she turned back, a sudden movement caught her eye. She spun around again, and there before her flew a falcon, his eyes set upon her and his wings outstretched. He dived straight at her but stopped before he hit the glass. There he hovered a moment, and then he flew off again at great speed.

The brief glimpse was enough for Jake. "Faluin!"

Ilavè's rage ignited. "Get them out of here!" she shouted to the Imarin as she stormed back to her chair.

Before Jake and Silorè could be led away, a sudden blast knocked everyone off their feet.

"What was that?" Ilavè screamed, pulling herself into her chair.

Captain Èrmon staggered to the nearest console and glared at the flickering screens. "It's that ship, my lady!" he said. "They've circled the cloud, and they now come at us from the front."

"How?"

"They must have already known we were here," the captain said as another explosion rocked the ship. "I had expected to evade them while they searched for us. Instead they skirted the cloud as we toiled through it, and they caught up with us. They have few cannon, but they are quite powerful."

"Then return their fire!" Ilavè slumped and put her hand to her head. "It must have been that cursed vèralam," she muttered. "He must be a scout for their captain."

"Leave him to me, my lady," said Fèrdin on his perch.

Ilavè turned to him. "Destroy him," she said coldly.

The great blackbird spread his wings, and with effortless power he shot up to the ceiling. There a giant iris opened to the sky, and as the servant of Ilavè passed through it, the opening flashed and hummed where an invisible force kept out the cold void beyond.

"No!" Jake rushed forward. Sudden fear had taken hold of him, but he could only watch as the iris closed again.

He did not realize it, but he had just stepped right in front of Ilavè. "I said get them out of here!" she cried, shoving Jake out of the way as she rose from her chair again.

The Imarin quickly marched Jake and Silorè from the chamber, blindfolding them hastily as they led them back through the ship. Jake felt the floor tremble under his feet, and he stumbled more than once in his darkness.

Once the prisoners were back in their room, the Imarin were off again in an instant.

"What's going on?" Jake asked as he uncovered his own eyes. "Where did Faluin come from? And who's firing at us? Could it be your family?"

Silorè shook her head. "If they had followed us from Ianiton, they would have overtaken us long ago. Whoever it is must have been stalking us."

The ship rumbled and shook again, and the furniture around the room quivered. The folding screen fell flat on the floor with a loud noise, and then all was still again. They waited for minutes that seemed like hours, and Jake felt his blood pulsing in his ears as they strained for the slightest sound. Silorè stood beside him, her eyes wide and searching, and Jake remarked to himself—even in the current chaos—that her violet eyes were truly beautiful.

In the next moment, Jake heard a terrific noise and suddenly found himself sprawled on his back looking up at the ceiling. A whining alarm pierced the air, and as Jake picked himself up off the floor, he found that the furniture had shifted to one side of the room. Silorè had gotten herself wedged between the bed and the wall, but she managed to free herself without much struggle.

"What was that?" Jake asked, rushing over to her. "It felt like the ship was being blown apart."

"It was quite a jolt," said Silorè. "But if that had been an explosion, surely we'd all be dead."

"So what was it, then?"

Before Silorè could answer, many heavy feet sounded in the corridor, and three Imarin burst into the room and bolted the door behind them. They ordered the prisoners against the far wall, and Jake and Silorè complied.

An Imari propped up the screen in front of them. "Keep quiet," he said, "and stay out of sight."

Jake and Silorè huddled together, their hands intertwined. "What now?" Jake whispered.

The Imari's head appeared around the screen. "I said to keep quiet!" he hissed and withdrew again.

From outside the room came a scuffle and a volley of gunfire. The Imarin crowded around the door, and Jake thought they looked full of fear—an emotion he had not seen in their faces before.

Someone in the corridor lit off a bomb, and the door shattered in a blast of fire. The force threw the Imarin back, and a shard struck the screen so that it fell on top of Jake and Silorè. Gunfire filled the room, and Jake lay flat beside Silorè and wrapped his arm around her.

The battle was brief and intense. When it was over and the screen was lifted up, Jake looked into the face of four automatons. He recognized them at once as Tamèthleron. "Do not be afraid," said one of them. "We have been sent by Thiriton the Star-Sailor to rescue you. Follow us! Hurry!"

But at that moment, there came another clamour of footsteps, and the automatons threw Jake and Silorè to the ground. "Stay down!" they cried as a dozen men burst into the room, armed with pistols and long knives.

They fell upon the automatons, shooting those that stood away from the door and grappling with those close at hand. The automatons killed two men, but they could not withstand them all, and soon the men had overcome them, cutting them apart and scattering their limbs about the room. Silorè screamed, and Jake felt ill. Automaton bodies were everywhere, spilling light-blue blood onto the floor amongst shreds of metal and wire.

When the fighting was over, Ianjori appeared in the doorway. "Get them up!" He ran to the prisoners and yanked them to their feet. "I will take them with me. The rest of you must go to our lady. See to it that she is kept safe. Hurry now!"

The men bowed and hurried off.

Ianjori turned to the prisoners, pulling a knife from his belt. "All right, you two," he said, "get moving."

Jake and Silorè soon found themselves marching ahead of Ianjori down the corridor. He had not bothered to bind their eyes, and they beheld the interior of the ship for the first time. Jake felt a bit disappointed, for the ship was unremarkable. The corridors were narrow and dimly lit, and they wound in strange patterns that frustrated his sense of direction.

The three walked on for several minutes in silence. Whenever the path branched off, Ianjori would order his captives where to turn. Jake considered slipping around a corner and running away with Silorè as fast as he could, but he was certain Ianjori could kill them before they took two strides.

Ianjori was leading them up a flight of stairs when from behind there came a sudden noise. Jake and Silorè turned to listen, but Ianjori shoved them forward. "Keep walking!" he said, but even as they stepped into the corridor above, footsteps sounded on the stairs. Ianjori wheeled around in time to confront a lone automaton running up behind him. They clashed together with noise and fury, and stumbling over one another, they fell to the ground.

As Ianjori struggled with his foe, Jake and Silorè took their chance and ran, but before they could go far a horrific sound made them stop and turn back. Ianjori was standing hunched over the fallen body of the automaton, severing its limbs to an accompaniment of ghastly metallic noises. With a dreadful cry, he thrust his hands into the automaton's chest and rent him in two. Sparks danced briefly between the two halves before Ianjori cast them aside like scrap metal. The veins in his arms bulged, and he was drenched in sweat. Pain was in his face, and his eyes now burned with an evil fire.

"That was the end," he said, breathing heavily. "From this moment I follow no command but my own." He wielded two knives in his hands, ready to hurl them in an instant at Jake and Silorè, who now returned to him like cattle.

"You're coming with me, little girl," Ianjori said, pointing a knife at Silorè. "The worm can go where he pleases, though I doubt he'll get very far. I don't want him anymore. He's not worth the trouble."

"I'm not leaving her," said Jake.

"You haven't a choice," Ianjori said, turning to him. "I'm taking her, and you would only get in my way. There is but one purpose you can serve: save yourself if you can, and take word back to Zhialamon. Tell him his great-granddaughter met an end worthy of her beauty."

Enraged, Jake lunged at him, but Ianjori grabbed him by the arm and held him so that they stood face to face. The force of his grip nearly brought Jake to his knees.

“Jake, stop before you get hurt!” Silorè said, held fast by Ianjori’s other hand.

Jake tried to speak, but Ianjori twisted his arm so that he kept silent.

“Don’t you understand?” said Ianjori. “I don’t care about you anymore. You can run off to wherever you want, but I’m taking her.” Then he grinned a wicked grin. “Don’t worry, Thalani,” he said. “She won’t die right away.” Saying this, he cast Jake backwards down the stairs.

Jake arrived at the bottom step with many bruises, and he was slow getting up on his feet. The floor seemed to spin beneath him, and he staggered. When he at last regained his senses, he bolted up the stairs, but when he reached the top, there was no sign of Silorè or Ianjori. Frantically he chose a direction and ran with all the speed he could muster.

After only a short run, the corridor split before him. He paused a moment to listen, but all he could hear was the muffled sound of battle far away. He chose a path and ran on, hoping to find some sign of Silorè, but as he ran he found nothing but a few bodies—of both humans and automatons.

Each minute seemed to stretch longer and longer, and still he ran on, looking around every corner and inside every open doorway. The *Bèndinar* was vast beyond his reckoning. Soon he was completely lost, and he began to despair. He rested against the wall for a moment, looking around as if he might recognize something and find his way. When he found he could not, he started off again.

But as he turned the next corner, he came to a sudden stop. His despair became absolute, and his heart seemed to die in his chest.

Zanirè was standing in the corridor before him, and she looked none too happy.

Chapter 15

Final Confrontation

"So here you are," Zanirè said. "I thought I saw you running through these halls. I've been following you for a while. Just what do you think you're trying to do?"

Jake said nothing.

"If you're looking to be rescued," Zanirè continued, "you're going to be disappointed. There are no more Tamèthleron on this side of the ship. I've just hunted down the last of them myself. If any escaped me, then they have fled back to the others."

"Please let me go," Jake said hastily. "I need to—"

Zanirè held up her hand, and Jake fell silent. "Save your pleas for someone else," she said. "I haven't time to listen. I'm returning to my lady, and you are coming with me."

She reached out to take his arm, and when he pulled away, she drew her sword in a flash and held it to his neck.

"Don't resist me," she said. "I won't hesitate to kill you."

"You don't understand," Jake said, so frantic he hardly noticed the blade at his throat. "He's got her! He's got her, and we've got to find them."

Zanirè's brow furrowed. "The Itarlavon girl?"

Jake nodded. "Ianjori separated us, and he took her alone. I don't know where he's gone or what he's planning, but I'm sure it can't be good."

Zanirè sheathed her sword. "No doubt it isn't," she said, "but that's not my concern now."

"But you won't let him go through with it, will you?" said Jake. "You saved her from him before. Will you not do so again? I know you care about what happens to her."

Zanirè snorted. "You really think so?" she said. "I am willing to deliver you both over to torture and death all at the say-so of my mistress. What do I care what becomes of you?"

"You do," Jake insisted. "I don't know why you do, but you do care. You must realize that, don't you?"

Zanirè looked flustered. "I don't have time to go after her," she said. "I must return to my lady. I've been gone too long as it is. Your so-called *rescuers* are nothing of the kind: they seek only the destruction of my lady. They have found where she is secured, and they are fighting furiously to get at her. I must defend her, and you must come with me."

"Then we leave Silorè at his mercy?" Jake asked, growing angry.

"Yes," said Zanirè curtly. "There is nothing else to be done."

"There is," said Jake. "Let me go—only tell me where to find them."

Zanirè laughed. "Why should I do that?" she said. "For all I know, this is an ill-conceived lie."

"It's no lie," Jake said. "I would not lie about this, no matter how badly I wished to escape."

"Maybe not," Zanirè said, "but what could you do? Even if I told you where I think they've gone and they happen to be there, Ianjori would kill you for sure. He is not wholly without skill, and you would be easy prey for him. He would kill you like a man kills an insect and thinks nothing of it."

"Even so," Jake insisted, "I have to try."

Zanirè looked away for a moment, and when she turned to him again, a bemused look was upon her face. "So then," she said, "you would die for this girl? Think carefully before you answer, for death is what awaits you if you seek out Ianjori."

"I would," Jake said quickly, "but neither of us has any time to argue anymore. Will you let me go or not?"

Zanirè pondered the problem for the briefest of moments. "Very well," she said. "You must be a fool to wish this death upon yourself, but I cannot hate you for it. If you truly wish to find them, then you will need this." She walked a few paces ahead of Jake to a dark panel on the wall. Pressing the ring on her left hand to it, she tapped a sequence of characters, and a low tone sounded. Suddenly a nearby door—which had been firmly sealed—opened into a separate corridor, dark and narrow.

"There," she said. "I have opened all the tunnels for you. This is the way Ianjori will have taken." She frowned at Jake. "Don't look so surprised," she said, noting the look on his face. "I do not do this only for your sake. If your automaton friends find these tunnels, it will give them more to do, and perhaps they will leave my lady in peace.

"Now go! Take the left path all the way astern. There you will find many empty servant quarters. If I know Ianjori as I think I do, then that is where he will have taken her."

She smirked at him and bowed her head slightly. "Good luck, young one," she said. Then she turned and sprinted down the corridor.

"Wait!" Jake cried after her. "Can't you at least give me a weapon? A gun? A sword?"

Zanirè turned back to him and laughed. "So you can attack my lady as well?" she said. "You must indeed be a fool!" Saying this, she turned a corner and was out of sight.

Jake looked around. The corridor was deserted and silent. The battle was far away, and there was no hope of finding help. Unwilling to waste another moment, he plunged into the tunnels, repeating in his mind the directions Zanirè had given him.

Hurry, he thought as he sprinted through the dark. *Hurry, or it'll be too late*. Every other care and thought was gone. He did not know how he could help Silorè, but he was determined to do something. As Ianjori's prisoner, Jake felt only fear and despair in his heart, but having been freed, his will returned and surged with new strength.

I've got to find a weapon, he thought as he pressed on. *I can't very well fight him off with my bare hands.* Even as these thoughts went through his mind, he tripped and fell flat upon his face. He groaned in pain and looked back at what he had fallen over. To his horror he discovered it was a Kenorni lying dead upon the floor, barely visible in the dim light.

The man had a grievous injury to his head, and his face was crusted with drying blood. His eyes were cold and lifeless, and his features were frozen in agony. It seemed he had fled to the tunnels to avoid the fighting but had at last fallen to his injuries in that very place.

Jake rose to flee, but as he did he caught sight of the man's outstretched hand still gripping a small pistol. Quickly Jake knelt beside him and pried the gun loose from the dead man's stiffened joints. *This will do*, he said to himself, and as he started to run again he tucked the pistol behind him into his belt.

The tunnels went on for a great distance, and though the walls and ceiling were close around him, the way was straight. Many paths crossed, some leading back to the main corridors, but Jake did not follow them—not until he came to the junction of which Zanirè had spoken. He took the left tunnel and bounded up a flight of stairs into a long corridor that ran along the outer hull of the ship.

Windows lined the exterior wall, looking out on the stars. There was no sign of the *Itnanya*, for she had attached herself to the other side of the *Bèndinar*.

Not far off down the corridor, Ianjori was dragging Silorè with some difficulty to the rear of the ship. Jake sprinted towards them, hoping that in their struggle Ianjori did not see him.

But Ianjori would not be taken by surprise. He stopped at once and grabbed Silorè by the throat, turning her so she could see Jake approaching. Jake stopped twenty feet away from them.

"Jake, what are you doing?" Silorè shrieked. Her hair was dishevelled, and she had wearied herself struggling against her captor.

"I think he's here to save you," Ianjori said, putting his lips close to her ear. She squirmed at the touch of his breath, but she could not pry herself away from him.

"Let her go!" Jake said. "If you do, we'll leave at once, and you needn't be troubled by us anymore."

Ianjori threw back his head and laughed. "Are you offering me a deal?" he said. "I've been killing Itarlavon for six lives of Thalanin." He seized Silorè by her hair and held her at arm's length before him. "She will certainly be the greatest kill I have ever made, and I intend to enjoy myself thoroughly."

"Jake, get out of here!" Silorè screamed. "You idiot! He'll kill you!" She tried to wriggle from his grasp, but he just held her tighter, and she winced in pain.

"Listen to your elders, Thalani," Ianjori said, pulling Silorè back to himself. "Maybe you can escape this ship and maybe you can't, but I promise if you stay, I'll destroy you."

Jake looked into Silorè's face. "I'm not leaving."

Ianjori frowned. "You should have taken the chances I've given you," he said. "Taking the two of you together would be a nuisance, so I'll have to kill one of you. I think you'll agree, Thalani, that she is much more valuable to me alive." He buried his face in her hair, and she squirmed.

Jake took a step forward. "I won't let you hurt her!"

Ianjori drew a long knife from his boot and pointed it at Jake. As he did so, he pushed Silorè to the side but still held her arm in his crushing grip. "Last chance, worm," he said. "Turn around now or die."

Jake took his chance. Reaching behind his back, he pulled the pistol from his belt, but before he could bring it to bear, a streak of silver flashed briefly in his vision, and he felt cold steel pass through his arm. A burning pain shot through his whole body, and his left hand fell at once to his side, limp as wet cloth. His vision blurred, and he became instantly dizzy.

In the fog that covered his eyes, Jake saw a dark figure looming before him and felt the blow of a firm kick upon his chest. He stumbled and fell flat on his back, striking his head upon the floor with a great noise. For a moment all sight left him, and he heard as if far away shrill cries made in Silorè's voice.

Slowly his sight returned, and he found himself staring up at the ceiling. His left arm was cold and void of feeling.

Ianjori's face emerged from the darkness all around. "You fool," he said. "Did you think I couldn't tell you were hiding a pistol? Better men than you have tried to kill me. Did you think you would succeed where they failed?" He pulled Silorè in front of him, holding her head in his hands. "This is the last you'll see of him, Silorè," he said, and he forced her to stare into Jake's face. "I don't think he'll be bothering us any longer."

Silorè shook with loud sobs. She tried to kneel beside Jake, but Ianjori hauled her to her feet. He retrieved the knife he had thrown, and he hurled it again into Jake's shoulder. Jake winced. He felt the pressure of the blade but not its sting, for his arm was lifeless.

Silorè screamed and struggled against Ianjori, but he was too strong for her. "Come along," he said. "You and I have a lot to do."

Silorè wailed as she was dragged away.

For Jake the world grew dark and silent, and he felt as though he lay in a void where he could sense nothing but his own thoughts. There he lingered for some time, though he could not tell how long. He was not asleep, for he was fully aware of the nothingness around him. *Not yet, Jake!* His thoughts seemed to echo around him. *You can't go yet. He'll kill her...and worse...*

From the darkness came a shrill scream, and Jake saw a point of light open before him. Desperately he reached for it with all his will, and the light moved towards him at great speed.

With a jolt Jake Connolly returned to the living world. The nothingness was replaced by a blinding light and a voice screaming, "You killed him! You bastard! You killed him!"

Jake tried to move, but pain overcame him. With effort he turned his head, and the bright glow around him gave way to shapes and colours. He saw his left arm lying cold and lifeless in a growing pool of blood. It took him a moment to realize the blood was his own.

He lifted his head a bit and saw Silorè struggling against her captor some distance down the corridor. She hit his arm and managed to pry herself free, but even as she turned to run, Ianjori struck her on the shoulder, and she fell to the floor.

Jake looked about frantically and found that the pistol he had dropped was lying near his left hand. He commanded his arm to move, but it lay dead at his side. Desperately he rolled over, reaching for the pistol with his other hand. Pain racked him, and when he tried to roll back, his strength failed, and he fell onto his dead arm.

He looked towards Ianjori and found him standing over Silorè with his hand raised above his head, and in his fist there was a long knife. Silorè looked up at him like a trapped animal and waited for the killing stroke to fall.

Summoning whatever strength remained in him, Jake pushed off the floor with his good arm. As he fell back, he crudely took aim and pulled the trigger. There was a dreadful noise, and the pistol kicked back with such force that it leapt from his hand.

Ianjori cried aloud, and his knife fell harmlessly to the floor. He reeled back, and in his right shoulder was a gaping hole, charred and bloodied. He stared at Jake with eyes wide with surprise and terror, for of all the men he had cut with his blades, why should the least of them have cheated death so much longer than the rest?

Ianjori took one step forward, and he collapsed to the floor in a heap and did not move again.

Jake went utterly limp. The pain in his shoulder grew sharp for an instant before it died away again to nothingness. He closed his eyes and felt sleep overwhelming him. His breath grew slow and long. *This is the end*, he said. *At least I got Ianjori before*...His thoughts strayed incoherently.

From the night that surrounded him, there came a voice, sweet and musical, and it called his name. "Jake! Jake!" But it was no voice from beyond: the voicc was calling him back. With effort he opened his eyes and found Silorè bending over him, her face quite close to his.

"Thank goodness!" she cried and threw her arms around his neck. "I thought you were already gone."

"So did I," Jake said, and his voice was little more than a whisper. He tried to sit up but found he could not. "It's no use," he said. "I...I'm going."

"You can't leave me now!" she said. "I won't let you!" She squeezed his hand tightly, but he could not feel it.

So tired. His eyes closed, and the world grew silent around him.

From the very brink he was called back again by the sound of rending fabric, and a flash of pain in his shoulder forced his return to the conscious world. It seemed Silorè was tying something around his arm, her fingers working furiously to secure the knot. She put her face up to his, and finding him breathing, she vigorously rubbed his good hand.

He opened his eyes again, and Silorè took his head in her hands. "I won't let you go!" she said. "You've saved me. I have to save you!" Then she bent down and kissed him, her lips lingering upon his as her tears fell gently upon his face.

But even the touch of Silorè's lips could not anchor Jake to the living world, and he felt his thoughts drift away into dark places between life and death. Even as he passed into night again, he heard the clamour of many feet and felt himself being lifted into the air.

The first sense that returned to Jake was a feeling of warmth in his left hand. His fingertips were resting on something soft and smooth, and when he managed to wiggle his fingers a little, something squeezed his hand, fully waking him. He opened his eyes, and the world slowly resolved itself into a small white room with soft lights shining from the ceiling. With difficulty he turned his head and found he was lying on a bed covered in white linens.

By his side upon a chair sat Silorè, fast asleep, with her head upon the blankets, holding his left hand in hers. Her labnerè hair lay over her face and shoulders, and without thinking he reached out with his right hand and gently stroked the top of her head. She stirred and gripped his hand, sitting up slowly and stretching.

Taking a deep breath, she awoke and started. "Èa!" she cried. "You're awake!"

"And so are you, it seems," Jake said with a grin. He tried to sit up, but pain shot through his left arm.

"Don't!" Silorè put her hands gently upon his shoulders to restrain him. "You must try to be still. Thiriton has treated your wound, but you must rest to mend properly. He removed the poison from your veins, but the fibre of your arm was so badly cut it may never be fully whole again."

"Don't worry," Jake said, seeing the sorrow in her face. "I'm actually feeling quite all right, though my mind is swimming. What happened?"

"You passed out, and we brought you here to the *Itnanya*," said Silorè. "The Tamèthleron found the tunnels and secured a path to where the *Itnanya* had latched onto Ilavè's ship. They carried you here with great care but also with great speed. There were sounds of battle all around us, but the Tamèthleron held firm, fighting off the Kenornin who tried to follow. Once we were safe, the *Itnanya* pulled away, leaving the *Bèndinar* crippled in space.

"The Tamèthleron brought you to this room, and Thiriton tended you for many hours, closing your wound and bringing you back from the brink of death. You had lost much blood, and I spared you some of mine." She showed him the mark on her arm where her veins had been tapped. "Even so, it seemed you would die, and you have slept for nearly three days now. I…I feared you would never wake again."

"Three days?" Jake said. "Have you been sitting here all that time?"

Silorè flushed. "We've endured much together," she said. "I couldn't leave you. It wouldn't be right."

Jake's mind flew back suddenly to the corridor on the *Bèndinar*. "What happened to Ianjori?" he asked. "All my memories are like a fleeting dream."

"He's dead," said Silorè, "and I'm certainly not sorry to see him go. He killed so many of my family, and I also would be counted among them if not for you."

Jake turned pale at this news and stared straight ahead, unmoving. Silorè looked at him earnestly. "Are you all right?" she asked. "Is your arm hurting?"

"I'm fine," Jake said, unsure what sort of feeling was growing within him.

They both fell silent for a while.

Then Jake spoke again in a quiet voice. "How…?"

"Hm?" Silorè had been lost in her own thoughts.

"How did Thiriton find us?" Jake asked. "No one knew Ilavè was going to that cloud. How did he know to look for us there after we went missing?"

"I think I can answer that, sir." A voice came from above them, and when Jake looked up he saw Faluin perched on a high shelf. He fluttered down and landed on the bedpost. His feathers were matted and ruffled, and he moved his right wing gingerly.

Jake sat up, alarmed. "What happened to you?" he asked. He had forgotten his arm for a moment, and as he moved it a sharp pain shot through him.

"Don't strain yourself, sir," Faluin said, "and don't concern yourself about me. I am all right, though I may not look it.

"You asked how Thiriton knew where you were?" he continued. "He did not. He had only determined to follow Ilavè from Ianiton to see what sort of mischief she would make. Little did he know what she had already done.

"It was I who alerted him of your capture. When you were declared dead in the shuttle crash on Ithèlimon, the Itarlavon were distraught, but Zhialamon did not believe that you had perished. He and Adjaron searched for you throughout the city, and I went with them. In time we found the place where you had been held. I knew for certain you had been there—a vèralam can tell such things—but you were already gone.

"It was as we returned from our search that we learned Ilavè had left the planet in haste, and what's more, Kensilon had helped conceal her departure. When Zhialamon asked an explanation of him, he said he would not detain the Kenornin for what was surely a simple but tragic accident. I think he feared to anger Ilavè, so he helped her leave without incident.

"I went after you at once, but I flew straight for Ialanon, believing that the Kenornin would leave Eratzira by the shortest route. I was dismayed when I reached the border, for I knew I should have overtaken the ship. I searched urgently, but when I could find no trace of you, I began to despair.

"That's when I discovered the *Itnanya* hiding near the edge of a vast cloud. I met with Thiriton and disclosed all that had befallen, and he told me how he had followed Ilavè from Ianiton to Nirdarason and from there to the cloud. We drew up a plan for your rescue and prepared for battle, but I first had to confirm you were truly onboard Ilavè's ship, and by that time the Kenornin were starting to run off. Thc *Itnanya* pursued at once, and I caught up with the *Bèndinar* as it emerged from the cloud.

"I came to the main window, and I was greatly surprised to find you there with the Kenornin and not hidden away in some other part of the ship. I flew off again at once, but Fèrdin, servant of Ilavè, was close behind me. Though he was swift, he could not overtake me, and I reached the *Itnanya* in time to give Thiriton the signal we had arranged.

"The *Itnanya* flew off, and Fèrdin attacked me so that I could not aid in the invasion of the *Bèndinar*. He is a powerful bird for his size, and his talons are sharp. We fought long, but he mistook me for someone of lesser birth. I honoured my sires that day, for I threw off my foe and cast him away into space. Seeing his mistress's ship in peril, he returned to her as quickly as he could, though his wing was broken. I might have pursued him, but by that time the *Itnanya* had withdrawn, and I went with her, sweeping the surrounding skies until I was sure we were not followed."

"And what about the invasion?" Jake asked. "The crew. What happened to them? How many were lost?"

The countenance of Faluin fell. "Thirty-three automatons died," he said. "Even more returned gravely wounded."

Jake slumped in his bed. "A waste," he muttered. "It's happened again. What good does it do to lose so many lives to save just a few?"

Neither Silorè nor Faluin answered him.

Jake remained in bed for the rest of the day. He and Faluin finally convinced Silorè to get some proper sleep, and she followed members of the crew to a room they had prepared for her. At length Faluin too departed, leaving Jake alone with his thoughts, which were many and various. They wearied him so, he soon fell asleep.

When he awoke again, the room was dark except for a dim orange light coming from the farthest corner. There sat the outline of a dark figure, and at the sight Jake sprang up in his bed and gasped as if to cry out.

The figure stirred and spoke. "Don't be afraid, Thalani. It is I." The voice was Thiriton's. "I've been sitting here a while waiting for you. Faluin told me you had awakened, and I wanted to be sure I got to talk to you. Silorè has already revealed to me what happened on the *Bèndinar*, so I need no recounting of the story. I only want to be sure all is well with you."

"As well as things can be," Jake said, trying to sound cheery. "My arm is still bothering me a little, but I suppose I'll mend in time."

"Time can heal many hurts," the old sailor said. "But there are some wounds that cannot be seen. Though the body heal, other scars may remain."

"I don't know what you mean," Jake said, fidgeting. "Our time on the *Bèndinar* was not particularly horrible. There was the threat of what would happen once we reached Ialanon, of course, but we were not deprived of food or water, and we were not tortured or any such thing. We were actually fairly comfortable. It was a strange experience."

"I'm more concerned about what happened after all that," the sailor said. "Silorè told me what came to pass when she was taken by that brute of a man—how you rescued her at great peril and injury to yourself. It can't have been easy to do what you did."

"Do you mean killing Ianjori?" said Jake. "On the contrary, it seemed an easy choice, for he would certainly have killed her—and worse. Why should I feel bad about it?"

"The head may know things the heart doubts," the sailor said. "Is that really how you feel?"

Jake paused a moment as he searched his own feelings. "No," he mumbled.

The old sailor rose from his seat in the corner and passed his hand over a wall-panel, making the room brighter. "There's nothing I can say to ease your soul," he said, sitting again. "You know all there is to be said, for you have just rehearsed it to me. Indeed, he would certainly have destroyed her, and you acted with great courage. Even so, you bear a scar few can understand, and however just the cause, it will follow you all the days of your life."

"You don't make me feel any better," Jake said grimly.

"I don't mean to," the sailor said. "These are things with which a man must wrestle within himself. Indeed, I have fought with them too; does that surprise you? The universe is a dangerous place, and many who live in it seek more to harm than to heal. I have been forced at times to deal severely with such people, but not without much sorrow of heart. Even the decision to rescue you weighs heavy on me, for on account of that choice many have died."

"I wrestle with that most of all," Jake said. "Many of your crew were lost in our rescue, and there were others who died to save me on Rithonon. I guess I don't see the point in it. What does it matter to save a few lives if you must sacrifice so many others?"

The old sailor frowned and nodded. "I see your reasoning," he said, "and there is some truth in it. What is the measure of one man's life when compared to another?

"Yet there are things greater than our lives, Thalani—greater than yours or mine. One would readily give up that which is of lesser value for that which is greater. That's why we risked all and lost much to save you and Silorè: not because your lives were somehow of greater worth—dear as they are to me and to all those who care for you both—but because the events that entangle you are so important.

"Ilavè and her family must not be allowed to succeed. The Keneraton have been held back for many years, and we must ensure that their plans continue to fail, for in their success lies our destruction. If Ilavè seeks your harm, then we must ensure your safety."

"Even at the cost of others?" said Jake.

Thiriton sat back and sighed. "I'm an old man," he said, "and in my many years, I have seen unspeakable sorrow. The Curse affects all, and sometimes the ends of all choices seem bad. In those moments we can only pursue what is right and have faith that all will work together for good.

"But take heart, Thalani. Though the paths we tread seem cruel and perilous, we do not walk them alone, and life and death are not in men's hands. You know that now more than most, for your life has been preserved through many perils. Even now, though you were narrowly saved from the brink of death, it was ordained that you should endure in this world a while longer. That is a good gift, Thalani—a gift from above. See that you don't waste it."

Jake fell silent as he pondered the old sailor's words. Many thoughts passed through his mind, and he stared unblinking at the foot of his bed.

At length Silorè entered, and Jake turned his attention upon her.

"How are you feeling?" he asked. "Did you sleep well?"

"Fairly," she replied, sitting in a chair beside his bed. "Though I'm not concerned for myself, but for you."

"I'll mend in time," Jake said with a grin. "But I'm afraid your dress won't."

Silorè smiled slightly as she looked down at her dress. The bodice was stained with blood, and a large strip had been ripped from the hemline. The stitching had torn on many seams, and the fabric in some places was threadbare. "It is a pity," she said, "but at least it had a good end."

"I'm certain we can find you other clothes to wear," the old sailor said. "Perhaps not up to your standards, but they would be clean and comfortable."

"That's kind of you," said Silorè. "But I am quite attached to this dress. Though it is in ruins, I should like to wear it a while longer, for I shan't get another chance to do so. Besides that, you have already done enough for us, and I fear we have become too great a burden upon you."

"You are no burden," said the sailor. "I am pleased I was at hand to help you."

"That also troubles me," Silorè said. "I'm afraid that in order to be rescued, we have caused you to fail in your mission."

The old sailor tilted his head in amusement. "To fail?"

Silorè nodded. "You were following Ilavè with a purpose, were you not? To rescue us, you abandoned whatever plans you had made regarding her."

"I had no plans," said the old sailor. "I only hoped to see her safely out of Eratzira—even to the borders of Ialanon. I was distressed when she diverted from the straightest course, and I feared she had found her star. So I followed her, but I had no plans for her or her ship. What could I do? I risked the raid on the *Bèndinar* in order to save you two, but I would not have commanded it for any other reason—not even to retrieve the Chronicle. Yes, I already knew she had acquired it.

"But put your minds at ease," the old sailor continued. "For you did not divert me from my mission. Indeed, you helped me to fulfil it. I can now let Ilavè leave in peace."

"But aren't you worried she'll return to that cloud?" Jake said. "True, she did not find that star at the first, but given time enough, perhaps she would."

The old sailor sat back and smiled. "No," he said. "After Silorè told me of the riddle and of the star Ilavè sought, I no longer fear what she may find in that cloud."

"What do you mean?" Jake asked. "Is the star she seeks not there?"

A glimmer came to the old sailor's eye. "In a manner of speaking," he said. "You see, that cloud *is* Ilavè's star—or, rather, what is left of it."

Jake and Silorè looked at one another in a moment of confusion. "But how can you be sure?" Silorè asked, looking back to Thiriton.

"Because I remember that star—the one spoken of in Ilavè's riddle. I saw it many years ago before it was destroyed—before it became that cloud."

"Before the cloud?" said Jake. "But Ilavè said it was ancient—older even than the human race."

The old sailor threw his head back and laughed loud and long, and the sound of his voice lifted Jake's spirits. "No, young Connolly," he said, still laughing, "that cloud did not exist even in Sierduon's day. Ilavè is off in her reckoning. Indeed, I remember that cloud well, and I know when it was made. I was a young man then—a young captain on an old ship.

"In those days, I would bring supplies on occasion to a colony in that region, and nearby was a giant star, green and fiery, just like that which Ilavè was seeking. It was a violent star, ever issuing long trails of fire and filling the night sky with flashes of white and green and red. One night the people of that colony awoke to find the horizon sparkling with a halo of light and fire, and in the daytime they saw a bright light in the sky that rivalled their sun. I saw that light too, for I was there when it appeared. The green star had destroyed itself, and in its place were the beginnings of the star-cloud.

"Years passed, and the cloud grew large, engulfing many of the surrounding stars. Eventually the colony was abandoned as the cloud approached, for the star-wind of their sun was not enough to hold off the approaching storm of stardust. Many years later I returned and found that world again. It was dark and cold and unfit for living things.

"So you see, Thalani, the cloud itself is what Ilavè was looking for, though she did not know it. I suspect Sierduon chose that star knowing it would destroy itself. It probably outlived even his guesses."

Jake sat amazed, his mouth gaping. "Then…can the page in the Chronicle never be read?" he asked. "The light of the cloud could not reveal any writing, so is that the end of it?"

The sailor shrugged. "Who can say?" he said. "There are many places in the universe where the light of dead stars still shine. In some ancient library, there may yet be a remnant of that starlight trapped in a prism or kept in a phial of itartholan. At my age the task of finding such a light daunts me, but perhaps younger minds and hearts could manage it.

"But do not trouble yourselves with such thoughts now. Rest, for you have endured great peril and have come safe through, if only by a breath."

Then he looked at Jake and Silorè with great affection and smiled, his eyes twinkling. "Enjoy your youth—both of you. Live so that when you are old, you can look back with joy upon these days, and"—he paused, looking from one to the other—"do not neglect the opportunities that are given you, for they may never come again."

Saying this, the old sailor rose from his chair, and bowing to Jake and Silorè, he departed, grinning as he walked out the door.

Jake stirred restlessly and looked to Silorè. "I don't feel like resting," he said. "I've slept for days, and I feel as though I'll never sleep again."

Silorè took his hand. "Would you care to go for a walk then?"

Jake nodded, and she helped him out of bed onto his feet. He was dressed in thin bed-attire, so Silorè helped him on with a dressing gown that lay folded nearby. There was also a pair of shoes upon the floor, and putting on all these things, Jake went forth with Silorè through the ship. She held on to his right arm while his left lay in a sling hung around his neck. Though his arm no longer hurt him, it itched and prickled in a peculiar manner whenever it moved about.

As he walked through the corridors, Jake felt as though the automaton crew regarded him and Silorè a bit coldly, saying no words but staring blankly at them as they passed. Jake imagined he saw anger and resentment in their faces, and he was afraid.

"Is there anywhere we can go that's less crowded?" Jake whispered to Silorè in English.

Silorè had seemed lost in her own thoughts, but his question brought her back to herself. Looking up at him, she nodded vaguely and took him to a flight of stairs that led up many steps to a glass dome beneath the mainsail. From there they could see the stars in all directions. The patterns were unfamiliar, and they seemed to be moving slowly to form new shapes as the ship sped past them.

Jake had exhausted himself climbing the stairs, and he admitted that perhaps he had overestimated his recovery. Together he and Silorè sat upon a bench that lay at the centre of the room, and he tried to catch his breath.

Silorè laid a hand gently on his arm. "Don't push yourself," she said softly. "You haven't been up and about in days."

"I'll be all right," Jake said, though he still felt a bit dizzy. "I just need to rest a moment."

"How's your arm?"

"Not bad," he said, moving his left shoulder in circles. "I can't really feel it unless I move."

Silorè was silent for a moment, and when she spoke again, her voice cracked. "I'm glad." She turned to him and tried to smile, but her lip quivered, and her eyes were wet.

"I'll be fine," said Jake. "Honest."

"It's not that," she said and turned away from him again.

"What's wrong, then?" he asked. "Everything's all right now. We're safe, and that wretched Ianjori is gone for good."

"Yes," Silorè answered bitterly. "We're safe for now, but what does it matter? Everything's changed, and nothing can be as it was before. The Keneraton have passed a point from which there is no returning, and they will no longer be content to watch us from afar. They'll come for us—all of us—and they won't be careful how they go about it. From now on we're living in their shadow."

She faced him again with a look of both sorrow and rage. "There will be no freedom for us anymore. We'll be escorted by guards wherever we go, and our every move will be carefully planned for us. To keep us safe, our protectors will become our taskmasters, and we will do whatever they tell us to do—go wherever they say to go. We may have escaped the Kenornin, but we'll still be living in a prison! What good is it to be alive when you live in a cage?" She swallowed hard to choke back her tears, and she hid her face from him.

"Surely it won't be as bad as all that," Jake said. "We don't know yet what will happen." He tried to sound encouraging, but Silorè would not look at him.

He took a deep breath. "The future is a funny thing," he went on. "One minute you think you've got it all figured out, and the next everything you've planned is gone, replaced by something you couldn't even have imagined. You never know how things will work out—or who you'll meet along the way.

"But"—Jake felt suddenly bold—"whatever the future holds, you won't be alone. Whatever happens—no matter the danger, no matter the pain, no matter the grief—we'll face it together. I'd say that's something worth living for, wouldn't you?"

Silorè looked at him, her wet eyes full of sudden bewilderment. Jake could not tell from her expression what she had thought of his words. She stared at him for only a moment, and then her countenance changed as she laughed lightly. "Èa!" she said, wiping away her tears, "you *are* an idiot. What put those words into your head? Did you read them in a *korinita*?"[70]

"Pretty terrible, wasn't it?" Jake said, chuckling though her words stabbed his heart.

Silorè said no more but took his hand in hers. Her hands were soft and cool to the touch, and Jake grasped her fingers tightly. She laid her head upon his shoulder and closed her eyes, breathing a deep sigh so long and musical it stirred his blood. He squeezed her hand and leaned his head upon hers, smelling the sweet scent of her hair.

Thus they remained until Iderat and Calisa grew large in the window.

70 Nanyan: "burning heart"—a term (usually derogatory) for writings that feature strong sentimentalism and flowery prose. The term originates in the works of the playwright Zhènoroson some seven hundred years ago. His most infamous work, *Jirna Korinita-ra* ("Wish of Heart-Fire"), is often cited for its saccharine dialogue.

Appendix A

Nanyan Transliteration and Pronunciation

Nanyan is truly a universal language, spoken throughout the galaxy by all except the Thalanin. Less than one percent of Thalanin speak Nanyan, and of that number only a handful live on Earth. Thankfully there are enough Nanyanin who speak Thalanin languages so the Thalanin living off-world can communicate fairly easily.

Dialects

Over the course of time, many different dialects of Nanyan have developed, all very similar to one another. Most of the Nanyanin in this book speak with the dialect of Eratzira (called Azhasèna), which is considered the standard.

The Gonkora dialect used by the Kenornin of Ialanon contains much harsher fricatives and more distinct aspirations. Vowels are generally more rounded and tend to drift towards the midcentre.

The dialect of the people in Itonilon (a widely spoken dialect called Panimora) lends itself to slower speech, with elongated vowels (which they tend to round and front) and more distinct long-consonant sounds. Panimora is perhaps the strictest dialect when it comes to morphology, and it is doubtless that Jake had to make many adjustments to his speech when he arrived on Itonilon.

There are many more dialects that could be listed, but this guide will (for the most part) describe the standard pronunciation of Azhasèna.

Writing Systems

Traditional Nanyan is written in a logographic system known as Phadathon. Alone it is insufficient for modern Nanyan, and so it is combined with Daninasè—a syllabic system containing symbols for each consonant-vowel combination, plus symbols for single vowels and terminal consonants.

Dathtera is a phonetic alphabet that shares some symbols with Daninasè. It is not often used in Nanyan writing except as an aid to young students in learning to read and write the language.

The Kenornin have their own syllabic system, but in recent years they have adopted Phadathon as their preferred writing method, though they retain their own for reasons of ceremony and tradition.

Vowels

There are six written vowels in Modern Nanyan. In this book they are transliterated thus:

E	e	Similar to the e in the *bed*
I	i	Similar to the ee in *need*
È	è	Similar to the ay in *way*
A	a	Similar to the a in *father* (sometimes like the a in *apple*)
U	u	Similar to the oo in *loose*
O	o	Similar to the o in *wrote* (sometimes like the o in *dog*)

The vowel transliterated *O* was once two separate vowels. The modern *O* is descended from the longer vowel sound and merged sometime in Late-Middle Nanyan with the short *O* (sometimes transliterated Ò). Because Modern Nanyan does not distinguish the two sounds in its writing, this book transliterates them the same. However, the distinction in pronunciation remains. The most common occurrence of the short Ò is the honorific *-ON* and is pronounced accordingly. *Zhialamon* would be pronounced ZHYA-la-maw[n], not ZHYA-la-moh[n].

Diphthongs

Vowels in most Nanyan dialects are monophthongs, and as a rule consecutive vowels are pronounced separately. However, there are two main exceptions. Consecutive vowel sounds beginning with *I* or *U* are generally pronounced as a diphthong. *Zhialamon* is pronounced ZHYA-la-maw[n] and Faluin is pronounced FA[L]-wee[n].

For these diphthongs the letter *Y* is used to transliterate *I* vowels that are not paired with a consonant. The word *Nanyan* is pronounced NA[N]-ya[n], not NA-nee-a[n]. Therefore, the letter *Y* has been used to avoid confusion. (Note: This rule is not usually followed for the beginnings of words, such as in the name *Ianjori.*)

Similarly, the letter *W* is used in some cases for diphthongs beginning with a lone *U* vowel. Some translators would render *Faluin* as *Falwin,* but this convention is not followed in this book.

Rhotic Vowels

Most Nanyan dialects have rhotic vowels. In Nanyan syllabic writing systems, these are usually indicated by the addition of diacritic marks to the appropriate syllables. In this book rhotic vowels are indicated by the letter *R* following a vowel.

Note that *R*-coloured vowels should not carry over a consonant-*R* sound onto the next syllable (though this may sometimes occur colloquially in modern dialects). There are occasions when a rhotic vowel will be followed by a syllable beginning with a consonant *R*. Such words are sometimes transliterated with a double *R*, but in this book only a single *R* is used (except in cases where a suffix is transliterated with a hyphen).

Consonants

In transliterating Nanyan words and names into English, the following conventions have been used for consonants:

H	Like the h in *hat*.
S*	Like the s in *sort*.
Z*	Like the z in *zap*.
TS	In most dialects, the stop is softer than *T* but not quite as soft as *TH*.
TZ	Same as *TS* but voiced.
X	Some transliterations write this as *KS*, though in Nanyan it is a single consonant.
SH*	Like the sh in *shall*.
ZH*	Like the si in *vision*.
CH	Like the ch in *change*.
J	Like the j in *jar*.
C	Archaic. In ancient Nanyan it was a soft, frontal *K*, but it is now pronounced the same as *K*.
K	Similar to German *K* (like the k in *cook*)
hC	An aspirated version of *K*.
G	Always hard, like the g in *goat*.

P Like the p in *pass*.
B Like the b in *bake*.

T Like the t in *top*.
D Like the d in *done*.

L* Like the l in *life*.
R Varies. Most often pronounced like a soft t or d (as some English speakers do with the t in *water*).

F* Like the f in *first*.
V* Like the v in *valley*.

TH* Unvoiced in all dialects, like the th in *think*.

PH A plosive consonant (unlike *F*). It is pronounced by placing one's lips close together and exhaling briefly.

M* Like the m in *mast*.
N* Like the n in *not*. The long *N* is often more nasal than the short *N*.

* Indicates consonants with distinct long-consonant graphemes.

Consonant Length

A consonant that is paired with a vowel is pronounced at the beginning of its syllable. However, many words have consonants that are unpaired. These become long consonants (where applicable) and are pronounced as reduced syllables. In this pronunciation guide, these special syllables are indicated by [square brackets].

For example, *Azhdarlorè* is pronounced a[zh]-dar-LOR-è. The first syllable is slightly elongated with the pronunciation of the long *ZH.*

When appending a suffix (such as an honorific title), long-consonants are retained and do not change to become part of the next syllable, even if that syllable begins with a vowel.

In ancient Nanyan long-consonants were often pronounced in their own syllables.

Syllable Stress

Thalanin generally consider Nanyan a difficult language to pronounce. Pronunciation can vary widely among dialects, and syllable stress is not always consistent—even among words with similar syllables. Though the only real way to learn the language is to memorize pronunciation for each word, there are a few general rules.

In most Nanyan dialects, the stress of a word often depends on the number of syllables and the terminal phoneme. Words ending in vowels usually have later stress than words ending in consonants. For words ending in vowels, stress is often placed on the penultimate syllable. (*Silorè* is pronounced si-LOR-è.) For words ending in consonants, stress is placed one syllable earlier. (*Vèralamen* is pronounced vèr-A-la-me[n].)

Plurals

Plurals in Nanyan are formed by adding the short syllable [*N*] if the word ends in a vowel or the full syllable *E*[*N*] if the word ends in a consonant. Plurals in Nanyan don't always indicate number: they can also indicate status. For example, the honorific -*ON* is considered to be plural as a sign of respect and reverence. It is therefore inappropriate to say things like "Itarlavonen." "Itarlavon" is correct for both singular and plural uses. (The concept of the double plural does exist in Nanyan, but to explain its complexity is beyond the scope of this guide. Suffice it to say that double plurals are almost never used in reference to people or people groups.)

Appendix B

Rules of Zhonda

Zhonda is a strategy game in which two players place and move game pieces on a grid. It is played throughout the galaxy, and its origins go far back into antiquity. There are a number of variations, but this guide will deal with the rules most common in Eratzira.

Equipment

Zhonda is played on a board marked with gridlines. Sizes of boards vary, but the standard size is 9x9.

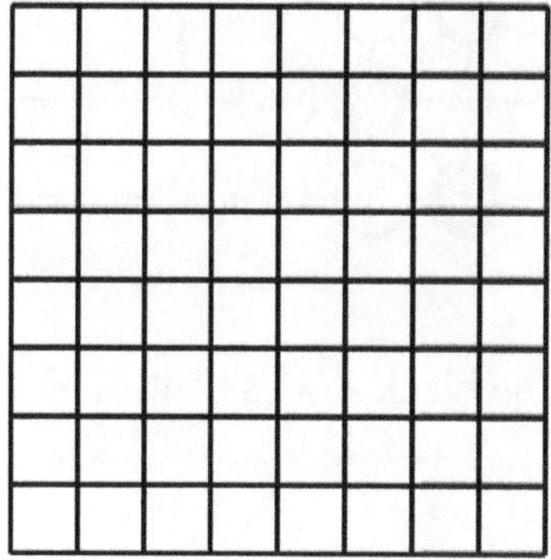

Stones are placed at the intersections of the lines—not in between them. These stones are flat and round and come in two colours, usually black and white. Each player controls one of these colours, and there is no restriction on the total number of stones that can be played in a game. Players also have "pools" of stones they have captured from their opponents. These captured stones are used in gameplay known as "Treachery" (see below).

Goal

The goal of Zhonda is to control more of the board than your opponent does. A player controls a position if he has one of his stones on it or his stones surround it such that his opponent cannot move or place a stone into that area (without using Treachery).

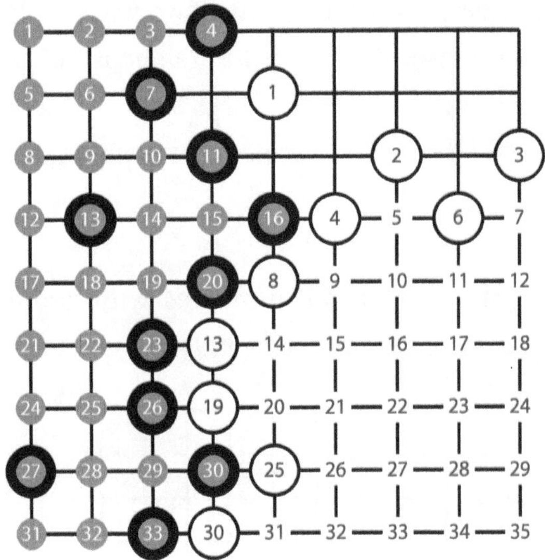

In this example the black stones control 33 spaces, and the white stones control 35.

Bidding

Before the game begins, players take turns bidding on the order of play and the starting sizes of the pools. One player (usually the more experienced one) opens the bidding by offering the other player a choice of going first or second (known in Zhonda as "First" and "Following"), with a certain number of stones in each pool. This is usually given in the form "Following and First."

For example, a bid of "Three and One" would give whichever player goes First one stone to start in his pool, and the player who Follows would get three stones. Bids almost always give the Following player more stones because of the advantage of going First.

The receiving player can opt to take the bid and choose who will go first, or he can counter his opponent with another bid. Bidding continues until one player accepts a bid, at which time players exchange stones for the pools.

Setup

Before play can begin, players must set up the board in its starting configuration. This can vary among players' preferences (sometimes even being part of the bidding process), but a standard game begins in this configuration:

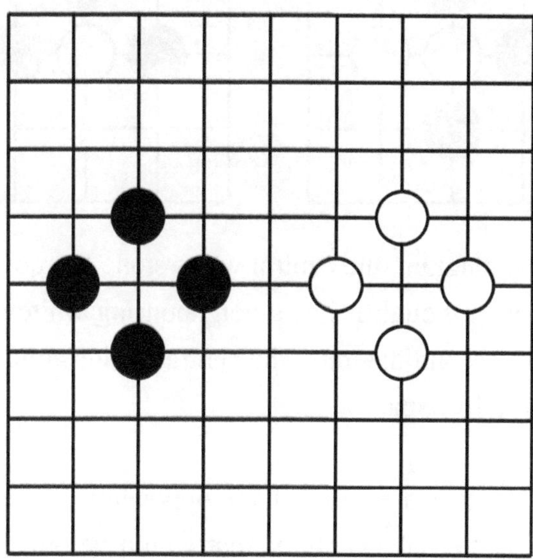

The First player always controls black stones, and the Following player controls white.

Rules

Stones in play are considered "alive" and allowed to remain on the board when they have at least one empty space ("liberty") adjacent to them. Unlike similar Thalanin games, stones do not share their liberties with others to form chains. Each stone must be calculated separately.

Stones that are totally surrounded (i.e., that have no liberties) are removed from the board. If this occurred without Treachery (see below), the stones are added to the capturing player's pool. If the stones were captured while ANY Traitorous stones were in play (even if the Traitors were not involved in the capture), the stones are simply discarded.

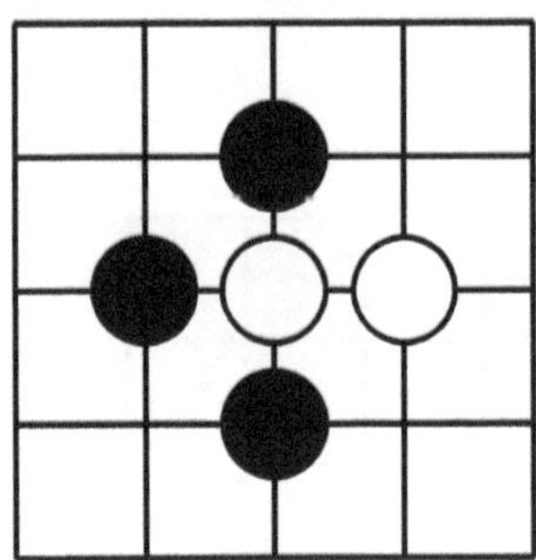

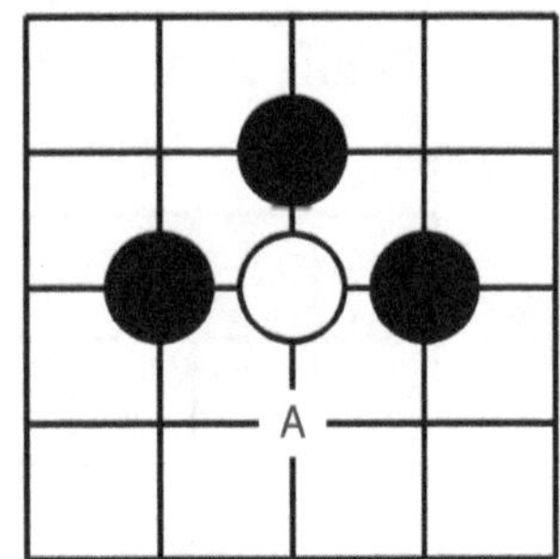

In the first diagram, the central white stone has no liberties and is captured, even though it has a neighbouring white stone that is "alive." In the second diagram, the central white stone is still alive because it has a free space at A.

Capture is always evaluated for opponents' stones first. This allows a player to make captures that would be otherwise impossible.

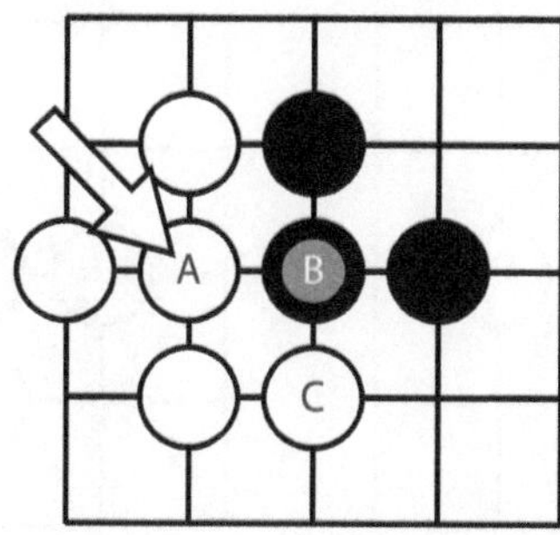

The play of the white stone at A is permitted because it leads to the immediate capture of the black stone at B, freeing up a space to keep A "alive." If there were no stone at C, placement at A would not be permitted, because B would not be captured after the placement. (Though in that scenario, the white-stone player could use Treachery at C before legally placing at A.)

Gameplay

On his turn a player must choose to do ONE of the following:

1) PLACE a new stone adjacent to another of his stones;
2) MOVE his stones a total of three spaces;
3) PASS his turn.

Placing

To place a stone, a player adds a new stone of his colour to the board in a free space next to one of his stones already in play. The placement of this stone must not cause any of his own stones to be captured (but can lead to the capture of his opponent's stones). If a player cannot legally place a stone, he must choose another gameplay option.

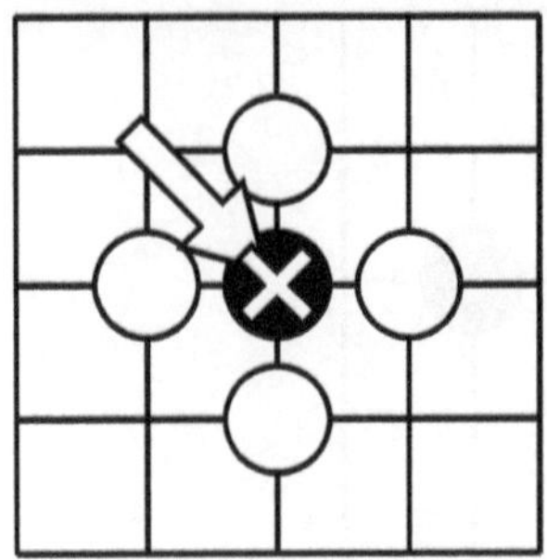

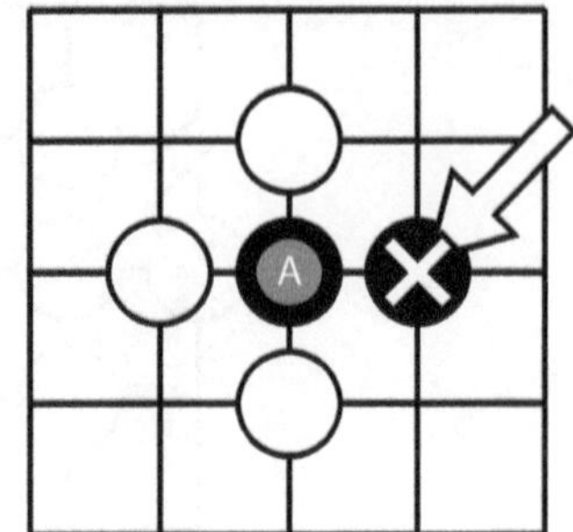

In the first diagram, placement of the black stone is not permitted because there are no empty spaces adjacent to it. In the second diagram, placement of the black stone is not allowed because it would take up the last free space of the black stone at A.

Moving

In choosing this option, a player must move up to three of his stones a sum of exactly three spaces. In other words he can move one stone three spaces, one stone one space and another two spaces, or three separate stones one space each. The player must move three spaces total and cannot move fewer (though this rule can vary among rule-sets).

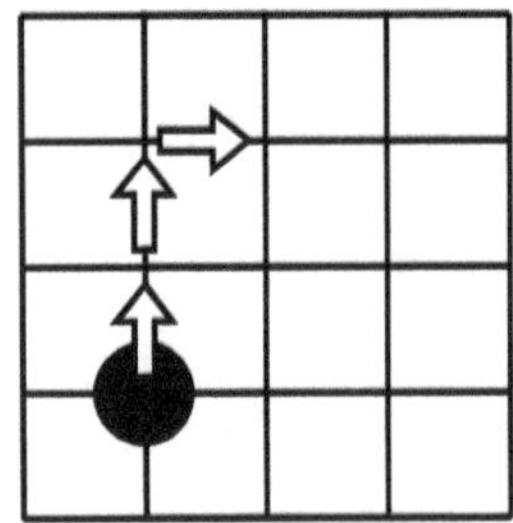

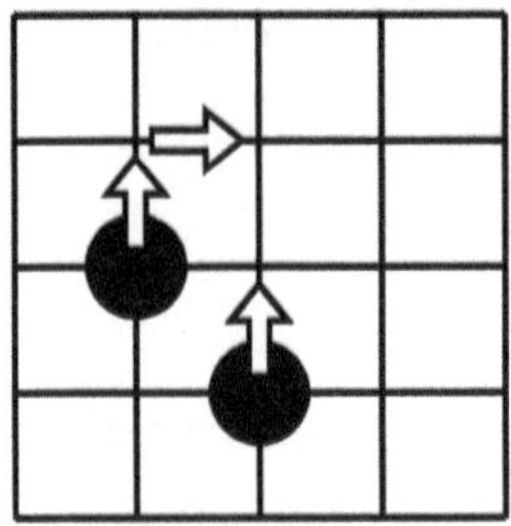

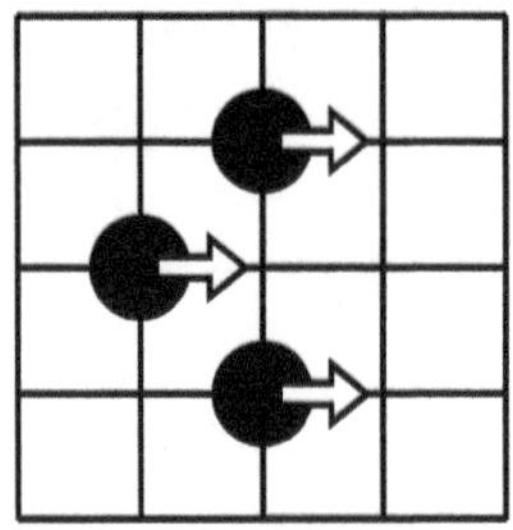

Stone-capture is evaluated after each individual move. Because of this a player cannot at any time move into a position that would lead to the capture of any of his own stones, even if those stones would be free after a subsequent move action.

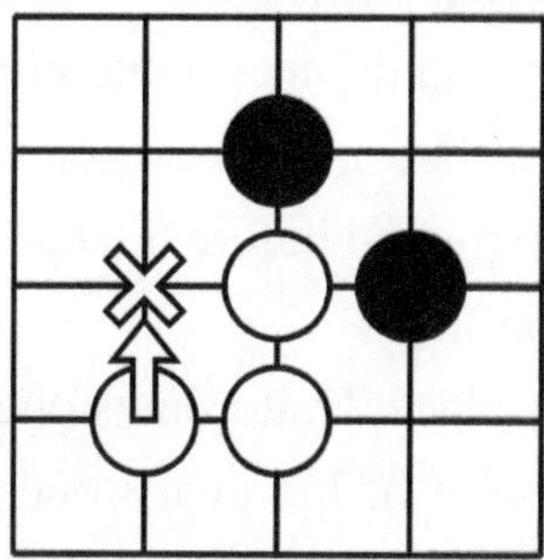

The white stone cannot be moved to A because it would cause the white centre stone to be captured.

Passing

When passing, a player performs no action. A player who passes cannot play any Traitorous stones.

Treachery

At any time during his own Placement or Move action, a player can play any number of stones out of his pool. (Remember: stones in a player's pool will be of his opponent's colour.) These stones can be played on any unoccupied space, and they do not need any liberties in order to remain in play. The current player controls how long they stay on the board, though all remaining Traitorous stones must be removed at the end of his turn. Traitorous stones cannot be moved once placed, and when they are removed from play, they do not return to the player's pool but are discarded.

Stone-capture is reevaluated after the placement (and removal) of each Traitorous stone. It may be advantageous to leave these stones on the board through the entire turn, or it may be better to remove them immediately after adding them (so as not to interfere with a Move or Placement).

While ANY Traitorous stones are on the board, captured stones are removed from play and do not go into either player's pool. This applies even to stones that are not adjacent to Traitorous stones. (All Traitors must be removed before the current player can capture more stones for his pool).

A player may not place Traitorous stones in any position that would lead to the capture of his own stones UNLESS the Traitor causes the immediate removal of an opponent's stone, leaving all of his own stones still "alive."

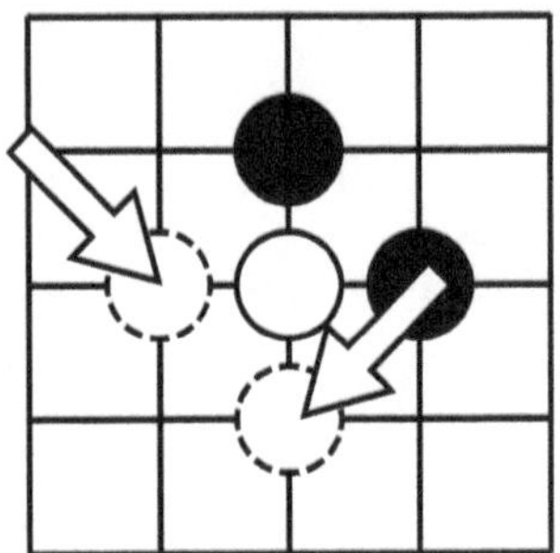

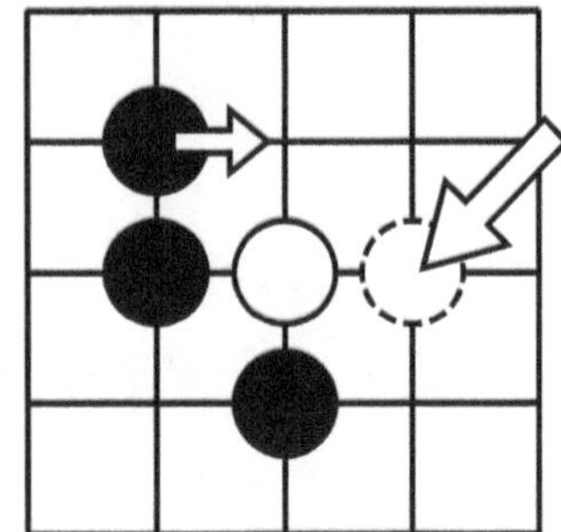

In the first diagram, the two white stones placed by the black-stone player cause the white centre stone to be captured. The centre stone is discarded immediately, and the Traitors are discarded at the discretion of the current player or when the current turn is over. In the second diagram, the black stone moves into place before the treachery of the white stone, causing the white centre stone to be captured. Again, the captured stone is discarded at once, and the others are discarded by end of turn.

Endgame

The game ends when both players pass in succession (or generally agree that the game is over). Controlled spaces are tallied, and the player controlling the greater number of spaces wins. In case of a tie, the Following player wins.

www.ingramcontent.com/pod-product-compliance
Lightning Source LLC
Chambersburg PA
CBHW030822310726
48980CB00006B/590/J

* 9 7 8 0 9 9 9 2 8 3 4 0 0 *